PAT CONTE KNEW THE LAW OF THE JUNGLE

He learned it as an orphan, early in life: to get where you want to go, you need powerful friends. For Pat, first it was the Church . . . then, the Family.

And on the way up, Pat learned about one thing the Family couldn't teach him, and these are the women he learned it from—

KATIE—She was an actress . . . and she was available. She showed Pat the ABC's of love—and nearly got him killed for it.

CONNIE—She was virginal, breathtakingly beautiful . . . and very, very, proper. Pat wanted her badly—and she made him pay her price.

ELLIE—A beautiful young radical, she knew every trick in the "marriage manual"—except how to love.

PAT CONTE WAS A MAN TO EACH OF THESE WOMEN . . . BUT TO THE MOB, HE WAS A PROPERTY, BOUGHT IN BLOOD AND PAID FOR IN COLD, HARD CASH.

THE FAMILY MAN

BY THE AUTHOR OF THE GIANT BESTSELLER
THE FRENCH CONNECTION

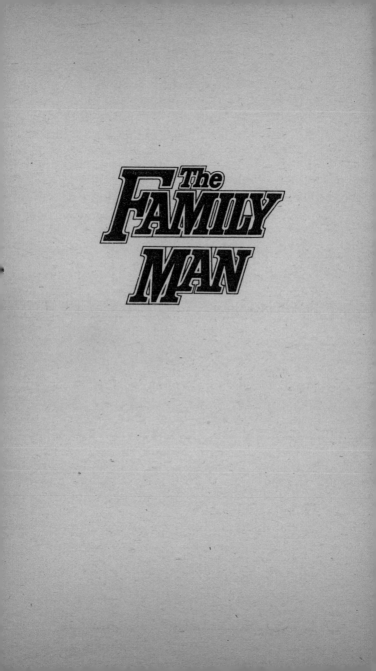

The FAMILY MAN

The FAMILY MAN

ROBIN MOORE
with
MILT MACHLIN

Manufactured in the United States of America

Bill Kane served for fifteen years with the Federal Bureau of Investigation. For ten of those years, he was head of the Mafia Squad in the New York office. He was also chief consultant and directed research for *Life Magazine's* Mafia series.

The authors wish to thank Mr. Kane for his invaluable assistance in preparing material on organized crime and the FBI for this book.

TABLE OF CONTENTS

BOOK I

CHAPTER 1

All day, Patrolman Pat Conte thought about the throwaway piece. He couldn't get it from one of the other men in the precinct. The timing would be bad. Somebody might notice that he'd acquired the gun on the day of his big collar. An untraceable piece wasn't that easy to come by. Most of the men who had one had picked it up from a suspect, or on the scene of a crime and failed to turn it in.

Buying one on such short notice would be risky, too. He certainly didn't want anyone who'd come forward and testify that he'd bought a pistol on the same day that he'd killed a burglar.

Finally, he went to West 42nd Street and bought a switchblade with seven inches of steel on the business end. As he looked at the array of serious weapons in the novelty shop, he wondered who was getting paid off to allow this place to operate. It was an arsenal of brass knuckles, gravity knives, switchblade, even handcuffs and phony cops' badges. There was no way that anybody could conceive these were being used for legitimate purposes and yet here they were brazenly displayed in a store window.

It angered him to think that someday those weapons would be turned against him or some other cop. The only thing missing from the display were actual guns. While the blades and knuckles were also in violation of the New York Sullivan Law against concealed weapons, somehow that aspect of the law was never enforced. Actually, any blade longer than two and a half inches was considered illegal. Yet, every boogie and spic on that street was probably carrying enough sharp steel to reach your kidney from the front side.

Pat was certain that enough of these stickers were sold so that no one would remember the sale on that particular day. Besides, it was hard to trace a mass-produced knife like that. In any event, the weapon would probably not get any vivid description at the time of the hearing.

That afternoon, in civvies, he walked past Napoli E Notte. A fat, gray-haired, old "Moustache Pete" was sitting out front on a folding wooden chair, drinking Yoo-Hoo. A few yards away, a younger man, in his early forties, sat reading *Il Progresso Italiano*. He guessed that the old man was the owner. The front of the shop was plastered with signs advertising hero sandwiches, pizzas, and 7-Up.

The two men seemed to take no notice as he passed, but Pat knew that they were registering him as a stranger. In his own neighborhood, in Little Italy, there were always spotters like that—sentries who made mental notes on every outsider on the block.

He kept walking up to MacDougal, where he dawdled in Rienzi's over a series of *cappucinos*, savoring the warm, spicy taste, and watching the odd mix of local Italians and weirdly rigged beatniks from the outer reaches of Bayside, Bensonhurst, and Mosholu Parkway. Twice he thought he got the eye from girls loitering over various espresso mixtures. One girl, a Nordic-looking blonde in a rough-textured Peruvian poncho, stared at him fixedly for a good solid minute, a half smile on her lips. Pat felt like a moron not being able to move in on a sure piece like that. But it was the wrong time to let any distractions jar his concentration.

At 12:45 he paid his bill and strolled back to Sullivan

Street. The shop was closed and dark now, the sentries gone to their tenement flats, or maybe to the local club for a game of *ziganette*.

The door was just a wood frame with glass. There was a steel roll-up shutter that went across the windows but not across the doorway. It was strange that the barrier had not been lowered across the main entrance, but this was no concern of Pat's. He peered through the glass door to the rear of the luncheonette. There was no sign of movement or life. From his wallet, he extracted a heavy plastic credit card and cautiously inserted it in the crack of the door opposite the lock, sliding it down toward the place where he thought the spring latch might be. Much to his surprise, the edge of the card caught the spring lock and shoved it back easily on a well-greased channel, unusual in a neighborhood where storekeepers knew as much about burglary as kids knew about playing potsy.

Though the lock itself had been recently oiled, the hinges squeaked alarmingly as Pat opened the door. He paused for a moment in the narrow corridor opposite the food counter and listened for the creak of a board or the sound of breathing. But there was nothing. Using a small pen-flash to light his path, Pat worked his way cautiously to the place in the back of the store where the room widened into a small dining room. To the left were a number of booths layered with ancient paint and set with paper napkins, salt and pepper, A-1, and catsup bottles. Straight ahead were two pinball games and a cigarette machine. On the left wall were travel posters, boasting the delights of Genoa, Palermo and Rome. The wall at the right was covered with a giant mural, executed in brilliant sign paint, of the harbor at Naples with Castel Sant'Elmo and Vesuvius miraculously uniting in the background. Moonlight through the barred rear windows shed a soft glow on the machines. But the corner with the booths was in shadow. Pat pulled out one of the bentwood chairs and moved it back deep into the darkest angle. Reaching inside his plaid sports jacket, he unfastened the clasp holding his pistol in place and loosened the .38 in its holster. With the pen-light, he checked to make sure that there was a cartridge in the chamber opposite the hammer. The grip felt warm and familiar and comfortable. He was strangely calm. His fingertips were cold. He wondered how it would be to point the gun at living flesh instead of cardboard targets.

The restaurant seemed totally quiet, but then he became aware of the organic breathing sounds of the building, the whirring of the refrigerator motors, the on-and-off rhythm of the thermostatic controls of the hot-air blower.

He made his mind blank, open to every fleeting impression. It was probably ten minutes before he heard the noise which he knew was his cue, the scraping of a key in the lock of the front door. Key?

He could hear the door being cautiously inched open on its loud hinges. Christ! They made more noise than a burglar alarm! Footsteps squeaked cautiously across the linoleum of the luncheonette. He could hear them stop for a moment opposite the cash register, which was open and empty, and then continue toward the rear of the store. Pat tried to will his pulse to be slow and his breath shallow, to make no noise which could interrupt the rhythm of the burglar. He pressed as far back into the shadow as possible as the beam of the intruder's flashlight flickered briefly over the room. Pat held the pistol ready to fire if the beam should strike him.

Then the steps moved quickly, more confidently toward the machines in the rear.

The man was his, he knew, but Pat was waiting for just the right moment. There was a grating scrape, then the sound of tearing wood and iron as the shadowy figure, silhouetted against the window, went to work on the first pinball machine, "Thunderball 10,000." Pat waited until he heard the slide of metal as the cash box was extracted, then the clinking of coins. He knew his bullets had to enter the man from the front to make it look right. He couldn't see the man's face, but the silhouette was a perfect target. He felt better that he couldn't see the face. This was just a shape, like the ones on the range.

"Okay, buddy, turn around." There was a gasp of intake in breath as the figure whirled.

"What the fuck?"

Pat aimed at the middle of the bulky shadow and fired three shots. The room was lit briefly by the flash of the pistol, and in that split second, Pat saw a surprised, middle-aged gray face, topped by a fringe of close-cropped white hair.

The man still stood after the first two shots—slammed back into the machine by the impact of the bullets. The third shot glanced off the corner of his skull, sending a saucer-shaped piece of bone against the painting of Naples. The man slid with a grunt to the floor, tearing his blue pinstriped jacket on the coin plunger as he fell.

Pat waited with his gun ready for any more sounds or any signs of a weapon. There was only the splattering sound of blood dripping to the linoleum. Cautiously lighting his way with the pen-light, he moved close to the body and pumped the rest of the bullets into the still form.

He listened for a full minute for any signs of breathing or moaning, then lifted the dead man's gray eyelid, carefully avoiding the shattered right side of his head. The face was strange to him. But it was like many he'd seen in the clubs of Little Italy, a tough, defeated face. A loser. Pat was excited, but he felt nothing for the man.

There was a pay phone on the wall next to the restroom entrance. Pat dialed SPring 7-3100—Central Switchboard.

"This is Patrolman Pat Conte of the Elizabeth Street

precinct. I got a DOA here. Sullivan, just north of Houston. Get a car over here right away."

The desk man was crisp, impersonal and sharp. He took the information without comment except, "Okay Need any help?"

"No, this guy is dead all right."

"Okay, we'll get a car right over."

Pat sat down on the bentwood chair to wait for the patrol car. As he settled onto the polished seat, he felt an unfamiliar pressure on his thigh. It was the switch-blade knife, still in his pants pocket!

Quickly he pulled the weapon from his pocket, and holding it in his handkerchief, wiped it clean. Then he pressed the chrome button releasing the long elegant shape of the blade.

Moving fast, he crossed to where the burglar's still form lay in a widening dark pool of blood. He picked up the dead man's limp arm by a corner of the worn blue jacket sleeve. Carefully, he pressed the handle of the knife into the flaccid fingers. The hand was still warm and flexible. When he dropped the arm again, the knife fell naturally away from the fingers, its blade gleaming dully in the filtered light of the back room.

From the north, Pat could hear the whine of approaching sirens.

Slipping his badge in its leather case from his pocket, he went to the door of the luncheonette to wait.

This was the first down payment for rookie Patrolman Pat Conte. The first down payment on a debt to "the family" which could never be completely paid off, a debt on which he'd be paying interest at loan-shark rates in blood and sweat for the rest of his life.

CHAPTER 2

Three Sixth Precinct cars arrived almost simultaneously, their lights flashing. Pat waited in the light of the doorway, holding his badge in its leather case for them to see. A tall, sunny-faced sergeant who didn't look over thirty was first out of the cars.

"You the guy who called in?" he asked Pat.

"Right. Patrolman Pat Conte, Fifth Precinct."

"What happened?"

"I shot a guy inside there. He was busting into the pinball machines. I think I killed him. He pulled a knife on me."

The sergeant turned to the tall young driver who'd come up beside him. "Send for the lab and detectives," he said. "Let's see what's happening inside here." Two more patrolmen followed them as they entered the store. They quickly found the switches and turned on the flickering, fluorescent lights. The dead man's face looked blue in the brilliant glare, and the blood on the floor suddenly turned black.

"Boy!" the sergeant said. "You didn't take any chances, did you?"

"The guy pulled a shiv on me. It was the first time anybody'd ever done that. I couldn't take a chance."

"You did right, kid. It doesn't pay to fool around with these motherfuckers. How'd you happen to be here?"

"I was walking home," Pat said. "I'd had some coffee at one of the joints up the street. I thought I saw some movement and a light shining in the back of the store, so I tried the door. It was open. I found this guy in the back jimmying the machine there. I told him to freeze, but he turned on me with the knife open. I had my gun out so I shot him. That was all."

The sergeant smiled sardonically. "Made sure you killed him, didn't yah?"

Pat looked him in the eye. "Wouldn't you?"

The sergeant shrugged. "Okay. Let's leave this for the detectives, go back to the station house and fill out the arrest records and all that crap. You can ride in my car."

They drove north and then west, over near the river, past a row of shabby warehouses to the old brownstone building which housed the Sixth Precinct. Pat headed for the detectives' room on the second floor to give information for the U49—Unusual Occurrences Report.

"You got to file an arrest card on this guy, too," the sergeant said. "You gotta book him for breaking and entering and attempted murder or something like that. Otherwise you'll be in a big jam."

Pat told his story to the one-two-four man who handled the clerical work downstairs, and watched as he typed up the arrest forms and the form 61 for the detectives and the lieutenant, and finally the buff copy of the arrest report, with full details of the incident.

These would be the basis of the manslaughter investigation which would follow automatically. Pat also had to help file the arrest reports on the dead man, who was charged with resisting arrest, illegal entry, assault with a deadly weapon, and possession of an illegal switchblade.

About an hour later, a bouncy young kid in horn-rimmed glasses arrived from the DA's office to pick up the details from the detective squad. He asked Pat a few more questions to fill out the story, listening intently and making salient notes on a long, yellow, legal pad.

"Sounds good," he said, as Pat finished his story. "You ought to get a commendation on this one. Be at the morgue sometime tomorrow to identify the stiff.

Meanwhile, you better go down to ballistics and have them shoot off a few rounds on your pistol for comparison."

As Pat turned away from the high desk in the entrance hall of the precinct house, a dark young man with long, wavy hair in a corduroy jacket and an open-collared sports shirt approached him.

"You Patrolman Conte?"

"Yeah."

"I'm Arnie Fein, *Daily News*. I understand you had a beef over on Sullivan Street."

"Yeah, but I don't know if I can talk about it yet."

"Well, we got most of the details from the blotter. Just wanted to get a little description from you what happened."

"Do you mind if I get a cup of coffee?" Pat said. The kid said he didn't mind. They sat in the ready room and Pat told the story again as the reporter took notes. Altogether, they talked about fifteen minutes. Pat had a lot more to say, but the reporter seemed to have enough.

"This will be okay. I'll call it in. Might make the later editions. Otherwise, maybe it will be in tomorrow."

"You gonna want a picture?" Pat asked.

"No. The story broke too late. You wanna really be a big hero? See if you can get your job done by about ten, eleven o'clock, or better yet in the afternoon, just after the *Post* and *Journal* close, say three o'clock in the afternoon."

"I was just wondering," Pat said, embarrassed that he had asked the question.

"See you around," the reporter said, shoving his wad of grayish copy paper into his side pocket.

Pat finished his lukewarm coffee and headed for the door. It seemed as if his nerves were hanging off his skeleton in shredded fibers. He had felt nothing through the whole performance, but now he was completely drained. There was a seamen's bar still open on

Christopher Street, near the river. He stopped in and
had three quick drinks. He wondered for a moment
whether he should call Arthur about the job, but
decided it was a bad idea. Besides, the body wasn't
going anywhere. There'd be plenty of time for that in the
morning.

The next day, he showed up at the morgue at Bellevue
to view the results of his night's work. The body was not
even covered with a sheet. A UF90 tag hung from the
toe. The piece of bone shot out of the skull had been recovered and fitted loosely into place with a few stitches. The man was fat, his skin purple. He had flabby
breasts like a woman and a tiny, shriveled, purple penis.
A line of stitches ran from his groin to his neck, like a
giant zipper. There were five black, ragged holes in a
neat cluster near the sternum.

"That's the guy all right," Pat said and left.

At the newsstand on Second Avenue, he picked up
the *Times* and the *News*. There was a one-column story
on page eleven of the *News*. The headline said,
"ROOKIE COP TILTS BURGLAR," and there were
three or four paragraphs. The story read:

> An off-duty rookie cop, strolling in the
> Village, shot and killed a burglary suspect
> at the Napoli E Notte Luncheonette on Sul-
> livan Street. Patrolman Pasquale Conte in-
> vestigated suspicious movements last night
> inside the Village luncheonette and inter-
> rupted an armed burglar, Giovanni Mag-
> giore, otherwise known as Johnny Majors,
> in the act of burglarizing a pinball machine.
> According to Patrolman Conte, Maggiore
> pulled a switchblade knife on him and he
> was forced to shoot the alleged burglar in
> self-defense. Maggiore has a long arrest
> record with several convictions and is a
> reputed associate of mobster "Trigger
> Mike" Coppola.

By the time he checked in that afternoon at Elizabeth Street, where he was on the four-to-twelve, everybody in the station house had heard about his collar. Even Moriarty, the sour-faced desk sergeant, congratulated him.

"Good job, kid," he said. "You'll get a commendation out of this."

From the station, Pat called Police Lieutenant Arthur Marseri and arranged to meet him during his lunch break. They met at Luna's and Pat sketched in the story in several brief sentences. Arthur Marseri asked only a few questions. He seemed to be most interested in checking on the identity of the corpse.

They had pulled the DD24—yellow sheet—on Maggiore, and Pat had had a good look at it: dates of arrest, names and addresses, borough and city in which he was arrested, the charge, the arresting officer and the disposition, date, judge and the court.

It was a long one.

Maggiore had a record of twenty-three arrests for various offenses from running numbers, breaking and entering, assault with a dangerous weapon, rape, to possession of burglar tools. But only one conviction. He had served two years at Dannemora for grand larceny, auto. Lieutenant Marseri nodded affirmatively as he looked over the list of details that Pat had drawn up on the case.

"You gotta put yourself in on this one for a commendation. You can ask for the Combat Cross on this. I don't think they'll give it to you because there wasn't enough of a hassle, but you'll probably get the commendation anyway. Then we'll see if we can get you a seat. You're probably tired of wearing out shoe leather. Try riding around for a little while. I'll put a call in for you. There shouldn't be any problem."

"Thanks."

"How's my niece, Constanza?" Marseri said as Pat got up to go. Pat was surprised at his constant interest in the still-budding romance.

"She's great, I guess. I got a date with her next week."

"Okay, kid. Keep your nose clean. You're going great."

Pat was told to report for the routine grand jury hearing at 100 Centre Street the following week. The jury would hear the evidence in the case and decide whether there was cause for an indictment for manslaughter or murder or else dismiss the charges.

"Don't worry about it," Marseri assured him. "It's all a formality."

The assistant DA handling the case before the grand jury was the same bouncy, young ADA that had interviewed him at the station. His name was Joe Domalewski. The switchblade, Pat's gun, bullets from the dead man, the autopsy report, comparison bullets from Pat's gun, ballistic photos, the coroner's report and other evidence was paraded before the tired-looking, twenty-man panel. The bullets, with rotting flesh still clinging to them, gave off a powerful stench. Lined up on the ADA's table with the tagged exhibits, were the contents of Giovanni Maggiore's pockets. A sharp-eyed juror looked over the array on the table and asked permission to question Pat.

"I was just wondering, Officer Conte, why the deceased found it necessary to attack you with a switchblade when he was already carrying that other weapon there on the table."

The juror, a tall, thin man with brush-cut gray hair and steel-rimmed glasses, looked like a retired Con Ed executive, the kind that cut off your gas and electricity with a ten-day notice. For the first time, Pat noticed among the effects of the dead man a worn but efficient-looking gravity blade with a black bone handle, obviously a much more expensive piece than the one Pat had gotten on 42nd Street, and one that had seen some use. Pat looked at the knife which the ADA brought to him to examine.

"I would have no way of knowing that, sir," Pat said. "I did not know the deceased. Maybe he was trying out a new weapon. Maybe it was a present. I just wouldn't know."

"That's all," the juror said.

Domalewski moved for a verdict of justifiable homicide, and the jury saw no problem in going along with him. When Pat got to the station that night, he got a good-natured ribbing from the other men on the squad.

"If you guineas had shot that good during the war, Mussolini would be the PC by now," Moriarty said.

"Listen," Pat said, "you fucking Irish weren't even *in* the war."

"Okay, kid. Take it easy," Moriarty said.

The next morning, before he left for work, he had a phone call from Constanza. "My father wants to know if you can come to dinner on your day off. It's Tuesday, isn't it?"

"Yeah, I can come. What's it about?"

"I don't know," Connie said. "He wants to talk to you."

"To find out my intentions?"

Connie giggled, "We *know* what *they* are."

"Did he seem angry or anything?"

"No, he just said he wanted to talk to you. I think some other people will be here too."

Pat wondered what the call from Sam Massey—ne Marseri—was all about. In some way, he felt sure it was connected with the killing on Sullivan Street.

CHAPTER 3

Pasquale "Pat" Conte's father had been a pioneer, not in the old across-the-plains-in-a-covered-wagon sense of the early settlers, but he was one of the first Italians to buck the long-term Irish dominance of the New York City Police Department.

The Irish had gotten a terrific start on the other immigrants in the early part of the century since they were the only ones who spoke English. But during the Depression, many first-generation Italians, Poles, Jews and Germans began to be attracted to the department. Being a policeman was steady, secure work protected by Civil Service and offering a substantial pension at the end of a reasonable amount of service and the fringe benefits were rumored to be enormous.

In the Prohibition years, it would have to be a half-witted flatfoot who couldn't earn a good living. Dominic Conte was not half-witted by any means. Through his family connection in Castellamare del Golfo in Sicily, Dominic Conte in his first five years on the force was able to bank fifteen thousand dollars in cash, more than double his salary. But this rosy picture was soon darkened by the outbreak of war—not World War II, but the conflict between Sicilian mob leaders, later known as the Castellammarese War. More than five hundred men died in that war before young Pat Conte had left his mother's breast. It all ended when Charles

26

"Lucky" Luciano accepted a contract from Salvatore Maranzano, one of the two rival mob leaders, to rub out "Joe the Boss" Masseria after a big feed at Scarpato's Seafood Restaurant in Coney Island.

As a result, Lucky Luciano became a very big number in the New York mob—so big that he soon found it convenient to rub out his own mentor, Maranzano, and with it to end the reign of the old "Moustache Petes" who had dominated Italian mobsters since the turn of the century. Now Lucky Luciano was in total control, and with him came his right- and left-hand powers, Vito Genovese and Frank Costello.

As Franklin Roosevelt brought a new deal to American politics, so Lucky Luciano brought a new deal to organized crime. Under Lucky's rule, there was to be less clannishness, more cooperation with other gangs, liaisons with non-Italians, particularly the Jewish mob, the clearing of all killings through a central council and the equitable division of authority and territories throughout the country.

Dominic Conte, as a native Castellammarese with the finest family connections and solid ties with the new leadership, was in an excellent position to profit from the new arrangement. Unfortunately, one night Patrolman Conte accidentally stumbled into a group of fur hijackers looting a warehouse under the Williamsburg Bridge and he became famous, if not rich, for a day. The story in the *Daily News* read:

HERO COP KILLED
BREAKING UP FUR HIJACK!

Sergeant Dominic Conte gave his life yesterday when he broke up the hijacking of a load of stolen furs from Manfredi Brothers Warehouse under the Williamsburg Bridge.

Police, who arrived on the scene shortly after what appeared to be a major gun battle, said that the gang Sergeant Conte had interrupted were apparently planning to hijack some ten thousand dollars in stolen furs from a delivery truck.

There followed details of the police reconstruction of the gunfight, but no witnesses had been found to the job itself. Dominic Conte got an inspector's funeral—a ceremony reserved for heroes only. Pasquale "Pat" Conte's mother, who had lived to see three of her family and two of Dominic's cousins cut down in the Castellammarese War, had enough of violence. She took her police widow's pension and fled to New Jersey, taking her only son and her younger sister, Maria.

Unfortunately, Dominic Conte had never taken his young bride into his confidence, so the safe deposit boxes full of twenties, fifties and hundred-dollar bills were never recovered, and hero-cop Dominic Conte's fringe benefits remained crumbling away, sealed in a steel vault in lower Manhattan.

The two sisters, Theresa, dark, dramatic and volatile, and Maria, tall, languid with chestnut-colored hair, flecked with blonde tinges, cut off all ties with their family in Little Italy. In those early years, Theresa also cut herself off from the company of men. She took a job in the Hackensack Courthouse and spent every other spare moment bringing up young Pat.

Maria, on the other hand, freed from the stifling, close supervision of her family in Manhattan, enjoyed her newfound freedom to the fullest. During the day she stayed home with young Pat and came to love him almost as if he were her own child. But in the evenings, Theresa took over and Maria was off to the bright lights of Newark, Jersey City, or sometimes even Manhattan.

Theresa worried about her sister's uninhibited behavior, but hesitated to assume the role of chaperon.

She was, after all, only three years older than her fun-loving blonde sister. Maria was interested in a free life. The minute one of her boyfriends began to bring up the subject of marriage, a glazed look would come into her eyes. She'd seen too many fat, tired, overworked, prematurely aged women caught in that trap. There would be time to settle down later. But at least one of Maria's suitors wouldn't take no for an answer.

Frank Doyle had served with Dominic Conte in the Fifth Precinct. He had even been one of the honorary pallbearers at Dominic's funeral, and it was on the afternoon of that funeral that Patrolman Frank Doyle first took Maria Conte to bed in a borrowed railroad flat on Avenue C. It was the first time for Maria, and despite the initial spasm of pain, she bled very little. By the end of that afternoon, the lusty chestnut blonde was convinced that everything she'd been told about sex by the sisters at school had been badly distorted. God would not have made anything feel that good if it were a sin.

Maria could not believe that any action so delightful and fulfilling could be reserved only for the procreation of children. On the other hand, nobody at St. Ann's Parochial School ever discussed any way to make love and *not* make babies. In fact, Maria was three and a half months pregnant before she even realized that a baby was on the way and that nobody but Frank Doyle could be the father.

Even then, Maria was convinced that she could have her child and raise it along with the infant Pat without getting married. It was not until she began to feel the movements of the child, twitching and tumbling in its amniotic sac, that Maria agreed reluctantly to couple herself legally to Patrolman Frank Doyle. They were finally married by an Italian priest just before Maria went into labor at the local hospital. So Regan Doyle missed being born a bastard by some three hours, because his mother died quietly an hour after his birth. Frank Doyle hid his agonizing grief and took his small son to be raised in the loving Irish aura of the Doyle clan.

The incident made for very bad blood between the Doyle and the Conte families. The Contes of Lower Manhattan represented everything that was anathema to the Doyles—crime in the streets, Mafia and social disgrace.

Theresa Rosario Conte wanted no part of any of them. She was bitter about her sister's death, so she stayed where she was. She made an adequate living for her son, Pat, and herself until a fondness for the bottle and a joyriding teenager in a stolen Lincoln Phaeton combined to make an orphan of Pat Conte at the age of ten.

The next six years Pat spent at the Holy Name Home for Boys in Hoboken.

CHAPTER 4

At sixteen, Pat graduated himself from Holy Name without a good-bye. Nobody came to look for him.

He arrived back in Little Italy with twenty-five dollars he had won at crap games he ran in the manual arts training room of Holy Name.

The war was on, and Pat tried several times to enlist, but couldn't produce papers giving proof of age. Work, however, was easy to get, and no questions asked. Pat quickly got a job in a machine lathe shop turning out shell casings, and soon was making two to three hundred dollars a week on the side, selling the brass turnings to a scrap yard on Sullivan Street in the Village.

On August 14, 1945, Pat Conte was returning from a profitable visit to the S. and G. Junkyard to the room he had taken on Broome Street, when he was nearly bowled over by a mob of drunken soldiers and civilians weaving in a snake dance up West Third Street.

"The war's over! The war's over! The fucking war is over!"

The Japanese had surrendered aboard the battleship *Missouri*. It was like one big New Year's Eve party in the city.

But Pat wasn't happy. He knew that the end of the war would mean that the servicemen would be coming back, reclaiming their jobs, and that there wouldn't be any more work around at big pay for sixteen-year-old refugees from Holy Name.

At the corner of Thompson Street, a group of curious bystanders were listening to a political speech. The platform was hung with bunting boosting the candidacy of William O'Dwyer for mayor and Vincent J. Impellitteri for president of the City Council. On the platform were two marines in dress blues, one of them in a wheelchair. Addressing the crowd was a fat priest, standing between an American and an Italian flag.

Pat stopped to listen, though he had no real interest in politics.

The priest, Father Raimundo Marseri, was a powerful speaker, his voice, high-pitched, but forceful and authoritative, with an accent that had to come from someplace no more than two miles from the corner where he was speaking.

"Bill O'Dwyer has been our friend and a friend of all the people of this city for many years. His fantastic racket-busting career in Brooklyn, you all know, was given up only to answer his country's call. His eventual service in Italy did much to restore peace and prosperity to that troubled nation, homeland of the ancestors of many of us.

"Vincent Impellitteri needs no introduction to the people of this district. His fine record of public service and loyalty—loyalty to his city and to his people—speak for themselves."

Pat listened, intrigued by the theatrical style of the priest.

He had seen O'Dwyer's name on election posters. Impellitteri's was new to him. Underneath the election banners, he noticed, there were some more signs: "Honor our own heroes—SANTO GANCI and FRANK ZERILLI!!!"

Pat wondered which was the one in the wheelchair and what he had done to get there.

Now he noticed that the priest was having trouble talking over the shouts of several hecklers who had pushed their way to the front of the sparse crowd.

"Go back to Sicily, you guinea fucks! Fuck Mussolini!"

The shouts were coming from four tough-looking young hecklers in sleeveless T-shirts. All carried beer cans—one of them had a can in each hand, and had apparently been overcelebrating the war's end.

"Look, the sonsabitches got a dago flag right up there with *our* flag!"

The youth with the two beer cans seemed furious over this diplomatic faux pas. Winding up as well as he could without spilling the contents of the full can, he heaved the other with its remaining few ounces of beer at the offending red, white and green symbol.

The marine who wasn't in the wheelchair leaped over the railing of two-by-fours surrounding the platform and charged head-down into the belly of the can-thrower, his fists pumping. The three other hecklers cheered and threw their beer cans in the air. As the marine and the heckler grappled on the cobblestoned pavement, the other three leaped to the platform and began tearing down the wooden structure. One of them grabbed the Italian flag and sailed it like a javelin into the crowd, shouting: "Fuck all guinea creeps!"

The marine in the wheelchair was shoved careening wildly off the platform. The priest, who tried to intervene, was jostled off the platform. Half the audience had dispersed. The rest stood watching, mesmerized by the violence.

Pat had watched for only a few seconds when a set of reflexes rising from an unknown source seemed to take over. He snatched a two-by-four from the street where it had fallen, still studded with the nails that had held it to the platform railing.

Using it as a prop, he leaped onto the crowded struc-

ture. Waving the scantling above him like an avenger's
sword, Pat caught the red-haired gang leader in the side
of the head with a glancing blow. It was strong enough,
however, to knock his opponent from the platform with
one bloody eyelid hanging like a bizarre bit of piratical
makeup, apparently torn on one of the nails protruding
from the two-by-four. A scattered cheer went up from
the crowd, and the uncrippled marine, who had apparently managed to dispose of the heckler in the street,
leaped grinning to the side of the raging Pat.

"Thanks, kid. We needed some help!"

"We ain't won yet," Pat said, rushing with his stick at
the two remaining hoods.

But the fight was over.

One of the remaining hecklers took a look at the wild-
eyed, stick-swinging Conte and leaped sprawling from
the platform.

"Let's get out of here, Marty! This guy is a fucking
maniac!"

The second youth jumped, too, but he left a six-inch
swatch of cotton T-shirt on the end of Pat's stick, and
suffered a deep red gouge across his back before he
managed to spring clear. Pat, still raging, leaped after
the fleeing pair, but was stopped by a commanding
shout from the priest, who was sprawled awkwardly in
the dusty gutter, apparently unable to get to his feet.

"Stop! Enough fighting! Come back and help."

Reluctantly, Pat stopped his pursuit and bent to look
after the stricken priest.

"Can you stand, father?" he asked, slipping his arm
under the black-clad chubby shoulders.

The priest roared in pain.

"Mother of God!"

It seemed apparent that his ankle was either broken
or severely sprained. The marine had gone over to help
his friend back into the wheelchair.

Pat got behind the massive cleric, and lifted from the shoulders.

"Lean on the good foot, father," he said, grunting at the surprising weight of the man.

After some struggle, the priest was on his feet, clinging weakly to the side of the destroyed speaker's platform.

"You are a good kid," the priest said. "God will remember you."

Pat looked annoyed.

"Listen, I don't mind giving you a hand, but don't give me any of that Holy Joe crap! Forgive me, father, but I've had a bellyful of that bull in my life already."

He offered a muscular, dirty arm to the distressed cleric, and reached as far as he could around the rotund priest's back to provide further support.

They struggled that way, like teammates in a three-legged race, down Thompson Street toward Houston, across that broad street and still further south toward Grand Street.

"You don't belong to a church?" Father Raimundo asked, his hand now damp and hot where it was attached to Pat's muscular forearm.

"I don't belong to nuthin' and nobody. I take care of myself."

"I was asking." Father Raimundo lapsed into momentary silence.

When they reached the rectory, a neat brownstone with white-painted woodwork on a side street behind the Gothic brown brick church, the fat priest was sweating with pain and puffing with exhaustion.

"Please help me into the house."

Pat half lifted, half pushed the agonized father up the steep flight of steps leading to the rectory door.

Inside, a large, pale woman, also in black, came anxiously to the front vestibule after Father Raimundo had let himself in the unlocked front door.

"Don't you lock the doors around here?"

Father Raimundo ventured a weak smile.

"We have no need to. The people know us, and then
. . . we have friends."

"What happened, father? You look terrible. You're
all stained! You'll never be ready for mass!"

"Sophia, tell young Carlo to make the mass. Send for
Dr. Giannini, and get this young man's name and address."

Pat backed away.

"I ain't giving no name and address. I don't want
nothing from you, father. I take care of myself."

"Don't be a fool," the priest said, his voice turning
steely. "Give her the information!"

Intimidated for some reason, Pat told her he lived at
184 Broome Street.

"Good!" Father Raimundo said. "We have friends
there. We will help you."

"I told you, father. I don't *need* no help," Pat said.

"*We will help you*," Father Raimundo said—and it
sounded almost like a threat.

CHAPTER 5

Pat Conte wanted no favors from the fat priest. But he was worried about his job. With the war over, he wondered how long production of shell cases would go on. He decided he'd better have some money put away against any possible personal recession.

He arranged with his scrap-metal dealer to have a dump truck pull up to the loading platform of Continental Screw and Hinge and pick up an even ton of brass turnings. He could make two or three hundred bucks on a load like that. Even if he only managed one load a week, he could be a thousand or more ahead in a couple of months when business started slowing down.

The truck was the regular scrap pickup truck. The gimmick was that Pat had arranged to tip off the driver when certain loads were taken on—loads in which a half dozen extra drums of metal waste were loaded without being recorded in the company books.

Toward the end of the shift, everybody was anxious to go home and Pat, running the drive-on Fairbanks scale, was able to slip a few extra barrels aboard the outgoing truck.

Pat picked a Friday. He knew everybody would be concentrating on getting out for the weekend.

But Manny Alpert, owner of Continental, had been doing some figuring himself. His revenue from scrap turnings had shown a dip for several months now. This was doubly irritating since many of the scrap payments, by arrangement with the scrap-yard manager, who was a *landsman*, were made in cash, no receipt.

Manny was a good contributor to the local precinct house, so it was no problem to have the captain send a plainclothesman to watch the scales that week and find out where all the shiny curls of brass were disappearing to.

Days were growing short toward the end of September, and it was almost dark when Pat felt the unmistakable hand of the law on his arm.

"Just a minute, son." It was Tony Vergaro, a new helper the boss had put on only a few weeks before. Pat had been sure he was too green to understand what was going on.

But Pat was wrong about Tony, whose carefully cultivated look of innocence and stupidity was his greatest asset to the plainclothes division.

"What's the matter, Tony?" Pat asked, his heart sinking.

Tony put two fingers to his mouth and blew a shrill whistle, which produced the perspiring figure of Manny Alpert from the storeroom behind the scales.

"You want to check these figures, Mr. Alpert?" Tony asked.

Alpert cast an apologetic glance at Pat.

"I'm sorry, Conte. I have to do this."

A few jottings with the stub-end pencil used to record the scrap traffic showed that the vouchers accounted for 1,200 pounds less brass than was on the truck.

"Okay, kid. You better come with me and get this cleared up," Tony said gently.

Pat thought about making a break for it, but decided he'd be better off to follow along and see what happened.

"Put on your jacket, kid," Tony said. "I got to talk to Mr. Alpert."

As Pat took his corduroy car coat from the locker behind the scales, he watched the conversation between Tony and the boss. He saw Alpert smile, reach into his pocket, and peel a bill off from a thick folded wad of cash.

"I'll see the others later," Pat heard Alpert mutter as Tony turned happily back to his prisoner.

Somebody had called the precinct, and a squad car was waiting to take Pat and Tony to Elizabeth Street for booking.

In the car Pat was frightened, but a part of his brain remained cool. He knew they couldn't pin anything on him except this last shortage. Since he was only sixteen and had no family, he wondered if they wouldn't try to send him to some juvenile shelter.

What worked for Alpert should work for him. He took the packet of eighty dollars he had been able to save from that month's paycheck out of his oil-stained work pants, and was deciding whether to offer a ten or a twenty when Tony caught sight of the thin roll. Casually he reached over and removed it from Pat's sweating fist.

"You shouldn't be carrying all that dough, kid. Somebody might roll you for it. I'll take care of it till later."

"Gimme that back, you sonovabitch!"

Without even turning his head, Tony backhanded him across the mouth. His Police Academy ring left a small, bloody imprint on Pat's upper lip.

"Hey, Ralph!" Tony yelled to the driver who had been dutifully watching the traffic ahead. "Did you see what the kid tried to do? Tried to open the door and jump out of the car?"

"Maybe we ought to book him for resisting arrest, if he ain't in enough trouble already. You think these punks would learn."

"He's learning," Tony said. "Ain't ya, kid?"

Pat didn't say anything.

At the dingy brownstone station on Elizabeth Street, the desk sergeant greeted Tony with an evil grin.

"Well, if it ain't Dick Tracy, boy detective! Did you buy any racehorses since you been in civvies?"

Tony grinned.

"Too bad you haven't got the right hook downtown, sarge. But I hear you got a few things going for you over on Mott Street, and I happen to know you're looking forward to a beautiful Christmas. You got to leave a little of the tit for us rookies, right?"

"Go fuck yourself, you guinea creep," the sergeant said without anger. "Whaddaya got here? A Woolworth booster?"

"No sir. This here is a genuine war profiteer. Pilfering brass from a good friend of this precinct, Continental."

"You wanna book him?"

"I better talk to him first. Anybody in the sitting room?"

"It's clear. Harry's The Broom this week. You know where he puts his time in."

The sitting room was a long, high-ceilinged room off the main entrance hall of the precinct. It was where cops sometimes sat waiting for assignments. Furniture was municipal varnished mahogany and yellow oak. A long table occupied the center of the room with cut-down beer cans on it serving as ash trays. There were sheets of typewritten information on police procedure tacked to the wall, along with wanted posters and mugshots of known gamblers and criminals in the area. Pat was sure he recognized a couple of the faces from his neighborhood in Broome Street.

Tony gestured for Pat to take one of the oak armchairs and pulled up another one alongside him. He pulled a pack of Luckies from his jacket pocket and offered one to Pat. Pat refused sullenly.

"Suit yourself," Tony said, putting the pack away.

"But you ain't gonna do yourself no good acting hard-ass."

He assessed Pat through squinted eyes as he lit the butt.

"How old are you, kid? Seventeen?"

Pat said nothing.

"You got a record?"

No answer.

"You live with your folks?"

Pat spit on the floor. Tony rapped him across the mouth again, opening the cut on the upper lip which had begun to congeal. He handed Pat a rumpled, used Kleenex.

"It'll dry. Don't worry. I told you not to act like a bad-ass. You don't seem to get the picture. The picture is this. You are gonna be busted on a grand larceny rap. That is a serious felony. Class A. We got the goods on you cold. The worse we make it look for you, the happier Mr. Alpert is going to be that we apprehended you.

"Now the way I see it, you are really a good kid, just a wee bit sticky-fingered. Somewhere you probably got a nice old-fashioned ma, and a pa that will beat the shit out of you for getting caught. But that's better than getting a record and putting in time on Rikers Island, or maybe even up the river, if you get a mean judge.

"Now, if we call your mama and papa, they will come down, and they will tell me how you are really a good kid and all that shit, right? Just a little wild like all boys, right?"

Pat sank into his chair and dabbed sullenly at the bleeding lip with the snot-stiffened Kleenex.

"You don't have to say nothing, kid. Because I know this scenario by heart. Listen, I got busted a couple of times myself, when I was a kid. Who hasn't?

"Now, all you got to do is call Mama and Papa, or Uncle Angelo or Rocco or whoever the fuck, and get

him to haul his ass down here and see me. I got nothing
against you, kid. Maybe they talk to me a while, I can
see the light, let you go, say I made a mistake, fix it so
the charge don't stick."

"You fuck. You already got my money!"

The plainclothesman started to swing his fist again,
but thought better of it in view of the relatively exposed
circumstances in the sitting room, or for whatever
reason.

"You are mixed up about that, kid. You didn't *have*
any money, and there is nobody in the world who can
say you did. You start talking like that, and you'll just
get in a lot more trouble.

"Why don't you think of that as an initiation fee?
Like you was joining some kind of club.

"Now here's my plan. You call up Uncle Angelo or
whoever, he comes to see me, in maybe an hour or so,
because I ain't got all day, and maybe we can work
something out."

Pat sank lower in the chair. He cursed his father for
getting shot and his mother for running out of the family
and then getting killed, and his father's brothers for getting shot, and his mother's family for never leaving
Italy.

He had never realized before how completely alone
he was. He didn't even have a friend who might come
down and pay off for him. Since he had left the orphanage, he had been careful to make no connections
that might give him away. Besides, he had decided he
would make it alone or not at all. But now he was beginning to wonder about that theory. Obviously, the opposite was true. The guy that tried to make it alone was
fucked. The guy with the *connections* was the guy who
had it made. Even the cops all had connections to
smooth the way for them.

Connections . . . family, church, friends. Church! Suddenly he remembered the fat priest from Thompson

Street. The old guy had practically begged to do him a favor. What the fuck was his name?

For the first time since he'd entered the station house, a flicker of expression crossed Pat's grease-stained face. He sat up in the heavy oak chair.

"Okay! You wanna call somebody? You call Father . . . Raimundo Marseri down at Our Lady of the Sacred Heart!"

A fucking priest! That ought to shut the fink bastard cop up! But would the priest put up money? This guy didn't look like he was ready to settle for four candles in his name and a couple of Hail Marys.

But Pat was surprised to see that the name had registered with the cop.

"He a relative of yours?"

"You'll find out, cop! You'll wind up checking doorknobs in Staten Island!"

The plainclothesman barely restrained himself from slugging the teen-ager again.

"I'll find out, all right, and he better be a pretty *good* connection or your name is gonna be shit!"

There was a pay phone on the wall. Hanging next to it was a dog-eared Manhattan phone book. There were about fifteen "Our Lady" churches listed. Our Lady of Esperanza, Our Lady of Lourdes, Our Lady of Perpetual Help . . . Under the listing for Our Lady of the Sacred Heart was a number for the church itself, the parish school and the rectory.

"You got a nickel, kid?" the cop asked.

"No thanks to you," Pat said, fishing the coin from his work pants.

After about ten rings, the priest's high, musical and slightly accented voice was on the line.

Pat wished that the cop weren't there to hear how tenuous his connection really was with the priest. He decided to play it as if he were an old friend.

"Father? This is Pat Conte," he consciously kept him-

self from adding, "You remember me, don't you?"
There was barely a pause before the priest answered, as
though he had been expecting the call.

"Yes, son. I remember you. What can I do?"

"I'm in some kind of trouble, nothing serious, at the
Elizabeth Street station. The detective said he would
like to speak to you."

"Put him on the line."

Pat turned to the plainclothesman.

"He wants to talk to you."

From the look on the cop's face, he knew that he had
made the right phone call.

CHAPTER 6

Pat returned to the oak chair while Tony got on the line. The plainclothesman huddled close over the receiver, purposely muffling his end of the conversation. Pat, straining to hear, could only catch a few of the words: "Not too serious. He . . . I think we can arrange something . . . I understand . . ."

But the tone was one of respect—and to Pat, it sounded like more respect than a cop would necessarily give to a parish priest. After a couple of minutes, the cop hung up and came over to Pat's chair.

"Come on, kid. We're going over to see your rabbi."

They drove over in Tony's own car, a '42 Plymouth coupe.

On the way, the policeman asked some questions about Pat's connection with Father Raimundo, but Pat felt that the wisest thing to do would be to leave all the talking to the fat priest.

Kids were playing stoop ball against the rectory steps when Tony pulled the car to the curb in front of the play zone stanchion. A couple of them didn't look much younger than Pat.

Subtly the relationship between Pat and the plainclothesman had changed since the phone call. Already Pat sensed that he was not a prisoner. If they were going to charge him, they would have booked him at the station house.

Father Raimundo was waiting for them in his office in the rear of the rectory. A couple of teen-age girl

45

volunteers were lettering signs for the upcoming bazaar. Father Raimundo gestured for them to leave the room. On the wall was a large sketch for a slum housing project apparently planned for the neighborhood. On the walls, the usual assemblage of saints' pictures familiar to Pat from his orphanage days. Behind the priest's desk was a bronze plaque of gratitude from the Italian American League. In the bookcase behind the desk were an assortment of bowling trophies and other awards apparently won by Our Lady teams. On the wall alongside was the diagram of an upcoming ping-pong tournament.

Tony Vergaro, who had donned a tweed carcoat and a gray fedora for the trip, removed his hat politely.

"Hello, father," he said. "I ain't seen you since San Gennaro."

"Hello, Tony. What's the trouble?"

"Well, it really isn't anything. I think we can straighten it out. The kid got something mixed up about the scrap brass turnings over at Continental, and Mr. Alpert thinks maybe some of the stuff is missing, but nothing is definite yet. We haven't booked the kid."

Father Raimundo doodled five-point stars on the green blotter of his desk.

"Nothing more serious?"

"That's about it. Mind you, we ain't even positive if the kid did it."

Pat was so impressed by the change in tone of the detective's voice that he considered putting in a claim for the money that had been taken from him.

"Well, why don't you tell Mr. Alpert that we are taking care of young Pasquale here? If Alpert gives you any problems, have him call me."

"He won't give no problems, father. He'll probably work up some new system so he can keep better track of that brass."

"Is that all? No other business?"

"No, father."

"You can go then. Leave young Pasquale here."

The plainclothesman replaced his fedora, turned and left, closing the door gently behind him.

The priest turned to Pat, who was standing near the wall examining the ping-pong seedings.

"Your father was Dominic Conte?" he asked.

Pat was astonished. He thought that nobody knew about his father. How had the priest learned?

He nodded his head in affirmation.

"He was a good man," the priest said. "He died a hero. You should be proud to remember him."

"I never knew him, father. He died when I was a kid. Mom didn't talk much about him. How did you find out?"

"Your name rang a bell. Your godfather, Pasquale Gagliano, was a *paisano* of mine. He came from my village, Castellamare del Golfo. It would seem that God was watching over you and put you into the right hands."

"Seems like it, father."

"Your mother died a couple of years ago?"

"Six years ago, father."

"And where have you been since then? You had relatives?"

Pat decided that he might as well tell the truth. It seemed as though this old priest could find out whatever he wanted to anyway.

"I was in the Holy Name over in Jersey. But I didn't like it, so I came over here to work. I guess I remembered that my family used to live around here and I came to this neighborhood. You gonna send me back?"

"I doubt that Holy Name is interested in what happens to you. You're almost old enough to be on your own anyway. Did you finish school there?"

"I got about two and a half years, father."

"That's no good. Nowadays you need schooling. Our people need educated youngsters. Too many Italians have the idea that it isn't manly to go to school, to be educated. That is wrong. That is why the Jews have gone further ahead than us in this country. They care about schooling."

The priest assessed him coolly. Pat was just under six feet in height. His skin was ruddy, but fair. His hair had turned a chestnut brown, and would have clustered on his head in ringlets if he let it grow longer. His teeth were strong and prominent, and his wary eyes, the blackish-brown of a cup of espresso. The lashes were dark and long. A good-looking kid, and he held himself, even in the stained work clothes, like someone who knew it.

"You have too much potential to waste it on the crazy kind of life you have been living. That life could lead you nowhere except to jail. What can I do with you?"

"You don't have to do *nothing*, father. I appreciate what you done for me and all that, but you don't owe me nothing now. We're square."

"Shut up and sit down. You are one of my people. We don't neglect one another. We take care of our own. It is a crime and a shame that nobody kept track of you after your mother went to New Jersey, but she chose to shut us out. She had a sad life, and she thought she could escape trouble that way. But that is not the way. We must all help one another. You saw what happened to-day. You know what would have happened if you were on your own, without me to help you?"

Pat nodded miserably.

"You would have ended in the shelter. They don't treat you too good up there, and don't let anybody tell you that because you're a juvenile you wouldn't have a record. It's just that there is no record to be used against you in court. But the record of your arrests and juvenile activities will always be on file with the authorities."

Was the priest trying to scare him? What was he giving him all this crapola for?

Father Raimundo remained silent, thinking for a few moments, then he slapped his hand down decisively on the desk, jeweled rings making a sharp, knocking noise on the wooden surface.

"I need someone to help me here. You will stay here in the rectory. You will help out with the young people, maybe something in the athletics program, and you will finish school. After that, we will see."

Pat started to raise his voice in protest. Who in Christ did this fat priest think he was? But Father Raimundo raised a pudgy hand, palm outward. A gesture of authority and decision that would countenance no opposition.

"Get your clothes and whatever from Broome Street, and bring it all over here this afternoon. Sophia will show you your room."

All Pat said was: "Thank you, father. I'll be back."

In fact, Pat had no intention of returning to Our Lady, but walking back to his shabby room on Broome Street, he began to reconsider. He no longer had a job at Continental, and with the war over, getting another one might be difficult, especially without a reference. He had no money, since Vergaro had liberated his tiny cash reserve. He didn't even know how he would pay the next month's rent.

There was no harm in letting the old priest look after food and lodging for him, until he could square things away. After all, Pat thought, it was only temporary.

CHAPTER 7

The transition from a free street life in Little Italy to the ordered existence at the Our Lady rectory was dramatic. Instead of wandering the streets until two and three in the morning drinking beer, shooting craps, hunting broads and running billiard strings, Pat found himself in his room by ten at the latest, sometimes even earlier, often saddled with several hours of homework in plane geometry, English or history (Catholic style).

Though he would have expected to hate the new routine, it gave him a certain satisfaction.

Having someone to worry about what, when and where he ate and slept seemed relaxing after such a long time of making those decisions for himself. But more important, it had been at least six years since *anyone* actually cared what happened to him from one day to the next. And Father Ray seemed actually to enjoy his role as a "father" in the more familial sense.

As to school itself, it presented no problem to Pat Conte, who had a quick and curious mind, seasoned by years of street-savvy.

He had missed only six months of school, and the discipline of life at the rectory under the watchful eyes of Father Raimundo helped him to focus on his studies.

Father Raimundo had a brother in the Bronx who owned a big construction company, and that summer he arranged for Pat to work there in the steel fabrication section.

Pat didn't meet his boss, Sam Massey, until some time well into July, when he was working with the acetylene torch, burning bolt holes for a fabricated door lintel.

When he pushed up his burning goggles to wipe the sweat from his forehead, he noticed that a man in a camel's hair coat had been standing there watching him, apparently for some time.

"You want something?" Pat asked.

"No. I'm watching how you work. You burn a nice clean hole—not too many beads on it. That's good."

Pat looked at the man with steady cool eyes. He was stocky, medium height, with a good suntan and white hair over a young-looking face. He stood there smiling.

Pat turned the flame off the burner which emitted its characteristic pop of protest. He laid the torch down on one of the I beams and walked over to the other end of the pile of steel to Jim King, the big, buck-toothed black man who was boss of the gang.

"That guy over there, in the coat. Who is he?" he asked King.

"Hoo, boy! You don't know who *that* is? You better learn fast! He the big boss! Sam Massey!"

Pat was glad for the soot which blackened his face. He felt his cheeks flush with embarrassment. Returning to his station, he approached Massey who was still standing there, apparently examining the steel.

"I'm sorry I didn't answer you, Mr. Massey. I didn't know who you were."

Massey made a deprecating gesture with his ringed finger.

"You did the right thing, kid. Never give any information unless you know who is asking. That's the right way. You like the work?"

"It's the best pay I ever got," Pat admitted, "and I like this . . . burning with the torch."

Massey lit a cigarette, watching him over the flame.

"I hear you are a good worker. But try to pick beams that are closer to the size specs."

He pointed with his shoe toward an eighteen-inch-long piece of waste I-beam which Pat had cut off earlier in fabricating the lintel.

"This steel is secondhand stuff, see?" Massey said. "It's all different sizes, so look around in the pile and try to find a piece pretty close to the blueprint spec. We pay for this stuff by the pound, you know."

"I know," Pat said, "but some of these pieces are pretty corroded. This was the best one I could find."

Massey spit into the rust-red dust of the yard.

"Kid, we look over all the stuff that comes into this yard. If it's in the pile, you can put the torch to it. Let *us* worry about the condition. It all gets covered with bricks and concrete in the end anyway, right? It ain't like it's part of the decorations."

Pat shrugged.

"So, you get the picture, right?" Massey said.

Pat noticed that his voice was softer and more cultured than that of his older brother, the priest.

"I get the picture, Mr. Massey," Pat said, replacing his goggles and igniting his torch.

Massey waved good-bye to him over the roaring noise of the torch and sauntered down to the other end of the steel pile where he engaged Jim King in a conversation. Pat had a feeling from the way the black man glanced in his direction that the talk was about him.

The work was hard, but Pat enjoyed it, and he also like the idea of having money in his pocket again without having to steal for it.

Nights, after a long shower to scrub the grime of the yards from his skin, he would slip into a pair of sharp summer slacks and a sport shirt and hang around with the other guys outside the Amalfi Coffee Shop on Mulberry Street. Sometimes, he would get in a game of eight-ball or snooker, or they'd set up a crap game in back of one of the social clubs on the block.

Some nights, Father Raimundo would stroll down the block stopping for an occasional chat with friends, a cup of coffee, a glass of wine.

When he saw Pat, he would only nod, giving him no more recognition than he did to any of the other kids, most of whom he knew.

Just before the school year, some of the older boys got the idea of forming their own club, the Mulberry SAC.

"Why should we hang around all the time in those other joints? If we get our *own* joint, we can play cards and shoot crap and all that, and we can have broads come in if we want."

It was Paul Ganci who had the idea. Ganci was into all sorts of social activities, always organizing dances at the church or selling raffle tickets. Like most of the other boys, Ganci was a couple of years older than Pat. But because of Pat's size and maturity, and because he could already out-box anybody in the clique, the younger boy was accepted as an equal.

"That's a great idea, Gonzo," Pat said, "but how are we gonna pay the rent and the heat bills and all that stuff?"

Al Santini was ready with an answer. Al had a good feel for money, and knew how to make it without breaking his *cauziones*. At the moment, he was a "fifty-percent man," running policy for the older guys.

"Easy," he said. "In the beginning, we each kick in about a fin a week. If a guy is tapped out we carry him for a while. That gets us the rent, right? We can rent one of these busted-down stores for a hundred a month, tops. In the beginning, we get some shot-down tables and chairs from our relatives and from the junk pile. Later when we get some dough, we can fix it up real nice."

"How you figure we'll get the dough later, Al?" Pat asked.

He personally liked the idea. Living in the rectory gave him little freedom, and there was a dame on Thompson Street he knew he could bang if only he could get her alone. It was tough finding a place to screw. Most of the guys in the neighborhood had to share rooms with their brothers or sisters, and anyway, the apartments were too small for privacy. He remembered only the week before, he had practically wrecked a good pair of slacks from the tar on the roof of Gonzo's house, and all he got out of it was a bare feel.

"Listen, Pat," the girl had said, "I ain't doin' nothin' on no roof!"

Al waited until he had everybody's attention before he revealed his plans for financing the club.

"First, we take a cut out of the pot in the card and crap games, right?"

He didn't wait for an answer, but went ahead with his listing of projects, which Pat had a feeling had all been planned out ahead. Gonzo, who introduced the idea, Pat remembered, was Al's closest pal.

"Now, that's only for maintenance. Next we put in beer, and we charge for that, and for soda and stuff. We can put in some lockers and if a guy wants, he can keep a bottle of booze there. Then later we can have dances and sell tickets around the neighborhood and start to make some real dough!"

The group was impressed.

"That's really a nitsy idea!" Pauley Federici said. "We could probably make enough extra dough to help out with some terrific neighborhood projects, like fixing up a vacant lot into a playground for the kids . . ."

Santini spit on the sidewalk in disgust. "You stupid *fesso*. We're gonna have enough things to do with the dough ourselves. Let Father Ray worry about the little bastards, right, Pat?"

"Sure!" Pat said, uncomfortable at being singled out as a spokesman for the church.

"So, when are we gonna get started?" Pauley asked excitedly.

Santini flicked an ash from his de Nobili "guinea stinker" and smiled.

"It so happens my uncle Carlo got an empty store around the corner on Grand Street. He says we can have it for a C-note."

"You wise sonovabitch!" Pat said. "You had this set up all the time!"

"So what?" Santini said, reasonably. "It's a good idea, ain't it? We can all get the good out of it."

"But what's *your* angle, Santini?" Pat asked.

"You think I'd screw my own *goombahs*? What kind of a clown do you take me for? Strangers, yeah. I might make a little something off a stranger, but not from my own gang!"

"Okay," Pat said, "I think it's a terrific idea, but if I find out you're cutting in on club money, I'll shove you down a sewer drain, head first. Right, guys?"

There was a mutter of assent.

"Jesus Christ, you guys. You know I can make the dough on my own. I got my own numbers route and everything. Why should I screw around with my own buddies?"

"Because I never saw you, Allie, when you weren't promoting something extra for number one!"

Santini straightened his hand-painted tie nervously.

"Are you trying to start something with me, Conte?"

"What if I am?" Pat said aggressively. He had a gut feeling that this was the time to assert his dominance in the club.

Santini, a half-head shorter than Pat, with a nicotine yellow complexion and narrow hunched shoulders beneath the squared-off padding of his gabardine jacket, obviously was in no mood to tussle with the younger boy.

"Listen, I just don't wanta' muss the suit," he paused, waiting to see if the quarrel would go further. The rest stood watching with interest.

Santini turned to Pat again. "Calm down. We're all gonna have a good thing with this club, right?"

"Yeah, right," Pat said.

"Someday," Paul Ganci said, "we're gonna remember that the Mulberry SAC started right here in front of the Amalfi Coffee Shop."

CHAPTER 8

Pat graduated from Our Lady the following summer. He had made top grades in social studies, and at least passing marks in math and the physical sciences.

The day before graduation, Father Raimundo called him into the cluttered office.

"You've done a good job, Pat. The family is proud of you. You are like a son to me. My brother, too, is pleased with your work for him in the Bronx. You have plans for what you will do next?"

Pat shrugged. "Maybe get a job at Massey Construction. Maybe try for a Civil Service job. I don't really know."

"You ever think about college?"

"What are you, kidding? How could I go to college? I ain't got any money. My folks are dead, you know that. I couldn't even have finished high school if you didn't help me . . . ."

Father Raimundo clasped him by both shoulders, and looked into his face. His breath smelled of Sen-Sen with an undertone of garlic.

"You *want* to go to college?"

Pat grimaced. "I don't know if I want to. I never

thought about it. Most of the guys I know ain't going, except Pauley Federici . . . ."

"You think about it, son. Meantime, on Friday I want you to come with me out to Jersey. It will be a nice party. You will meet some of the family . . . ."

The party was held in Cliffside Park, just across the George Washington Bridge, in a restaurant called Duke's. It was in honor of Willie Moretti, sometimes known as Willie Moore, who had just gotten out of the hospital.

Pat and Father Ray were picked up by Sam Massey's Cadillac, driven by a crew-cut husky kid Pat remembered having seen working in the motor pool at Massey Construction in the Bronx.

"Pat, meet Tommy Saracino. You probably saw him up at Sam's. He's one of our *cugini*."

Pat nodded an acknowledgment and got into the back seat with Father Raimundo. The car rolled across Canal Street to the West Side Highway and then headed north along the river. Father Raimundo sat back, holding onto the strap as though he was afraid of being jolted out of the car, and watched the scenery along the river with keen interest. Neither spoke until they reached a point opposite 125th Street where highway repairs were under way. Father Raimundo reached over and tapped Pat on the knee, gesturing toward the cement mixers and heavy construction equipment on the site.

"That's one of Sam's jobs."

But the equipment was lettered, "FORDHAM HOISTING AND EQUIPMENT CO."

"I thought Mr. Massey's company was Massey Construction."

"Well, he has various interests," Father Raimundo said.

When they got to the turnoff for the bridge, Tommy continued northward. Father Raimundo turned to Pat.

"We are picking up my brothers in Riverdale."

The Cadillac mounted the hill that rose behind the upper reaches of Broadway and stopped before a Spanish-style stucco villa, surrounded by a high brick wall surmounted by shards of broken glass. Iron gates opened at a honk on the Cadillac's horn, and Tommy wheeled around the curving gravel drive to pull up in under the porte-cochere which sheltered a pair of enormous studded oak doors.

They waited wordlessly for a minute or so, and the doors opened to Sam Massey and another taller and younger man who introduced himself to Pat as he got into the car.

"Hi. You must be Pat. I'm Arthur Marseri, the kid of the family."

Pat shook his hand, and following a slight prod from Father Raimundo moved to the jump seat of the limousine as Sam entered and took the right-hand rear seat next to his brother, the priest.

Arthur sat in the adjoining jump seat. Pat looked him over from the corner of his eye. Arthur Marseri was in his early thirties, tall, with straight, black hair and cold gray eyes, though there were humor lines about his lips. He looked as though he might have been athletic a few years earlier, but now was showing an incipient paunch in the slight fold of flesh which punched out the cloth of his blue oxford shirt.

Sam nodded a cool but friendly greeting to Pat as he settled into the lush upholstery.

"How's it going, kid?"

He obviously didn't expect an answer, so Pat just smiled in reply as Sam turned to his older brother.

"We gonna pick up Antonio?"

"No," Father Raimundo said. "He's coming up from Atlantic Highlands."

"With Don Vitone?"

Raimundo shrugged.

It was only a fifteen-minute ride to the bridge, but by

that time it was getting dark. Sam peered up through the window at the shining edifice of Ben Marden's Riviera as they passed beneath it on the Jersey side.

"That place is a gold mine!" he said, apparently to the two brothers. "But I hear there's gonna be a lot of heat on there."

"Is Willie involved?" Arthur asked.

"Don't be stupid. He's involved in *everything* over here. You know that!" Sam growled.

Ten minutes after crossing the bridge, the Cadillac pulled into the parking lot behind a shabby-looking restaurant on Route 505. Pat was interested to note that there were already several big Cadillacs parked there. Sam Massey smiled in anticipation as he looked over the array of cars.

"This is gonna be a good party. I see Joe Jelly is here, Big Al, The Plumber, Gyp. It's a regular convention!"

"Willie has a lot of friends," Father Raimundo said.

Sam threw him a sharp look.

"He got a couple of friends I wouldn't turn my back on if I was him."

Father Raimundo shrugged.

"I don't know anything about those things."

They entered through a rear entrance opening directly onto the parking lot, and found themselves in a large private dining room, decorated with murals in bright blues and yellows of Mount Etna, Palermo, Vesuvius and other Italian scenes.

At one end of the room was a garishly painted Sicilian donkey cart, piled high with melons and wine bottles. The tables had been arranged into a banquet horseshoe. In the middle was a table displaying an overly generous antipasto. In each corner was a table set up as a bar. They were apparently among the last to enter. About twenty men were milling around the room, laughing, clapping one another on the back and drinking.

Standing quietly in a cluster of men in a corner away

from the bar was a small, dapper man with the face of a fox and a wide, cold grin. Pat was amazed to see that as each guest approached him, he would bow slightly and extend his hand which they would grasp and raise briefly to their lips.

Sam saw Pat watching the tableau.

"That," he said, "is Don Vitone. He is a very important man in our family. He knows your godfather and he knew your father. I will introduce you to him."

Sam waited patiently until the crowd had thinned and then took Pat by the arm and led him to the Don.

Like the others, he lifted Don Vitone's hand quickly toward his lips in greeting, but without actually kissing it, Pat noticed.

"Don Vitone, this is Pat Conte. He is the son of Dominic Conte."

"The cop? I remember him. He was a good man. He was killed on the job, I remember."

"That's right. If you remember, Pasquale Gagliano was the boy's godfather . . ."

Don Vitone raised his thin brows and smiled his tight-lipped smile, but did not seem interested.

"The boy is finishing school at Our Lady—that's my brother Raimundo's place."

"Oh, yes. It is in my area. Remind me to send Father Ray a check for the new altar."

"He's here. Maybe you can give it to him later on."

"He's backing the Irishman for mayor, your brother?" Don Vitone asked.

Sam nodded. "It's a good move. I think we can work with him as we have in the past, and one of our own is on the ticket, too."

"Do we have anybody on the other side?"

"There are friends, but I think we can go easy with the opposition this time. The O'Dwyer thing looks very good."

Don Vitone flashed one of his thin smiles and ventured a small joke.

"You see where *he* is? And he started as a cop, like the boy's father here."

Sam smiled politely and said, "I have found him to be a good man, and he can be helpful. You yourself remember in Naples last year . . ."

"There is no question," the Don said. "He is a good man to know, but still he is not one of our own. I never trust those Micks too much. In the end, it is only the family you can trust. Come, let's eat."

And he took Sam and Pat each by the arm and led them to the table.

CHAPTER 9

It was a meal unlike any Pat had seen before. After the hot and cold hors d'oeuvres, which included tiny omelets, stuffed artichokes and mushrooms, little cheese pies, olives, a half dozen styles of sausage and salami, pickled vegetables, cheeses and platters of unrecognizable delicacies, they sat down to bowls of stracchini in brodo, baked tuna, green fettuccine, a steak slit in the middle and stuffed with oysters, sweet cream-stuffed canoli, rum-soaked sponge cake, and finally Sambucca liqueur and cigars. Pat found room for everything.

"You're a good eater, kid," Arthur laughed. They had been seated together at the corner of the horseshoe banquet table to Don Vitone's right. Following the introduction to Genovese, Sam had hardly spoken to Pat, and Arthur had done the best he could to make the youth comfortable with small talk.

"You ever think of going on the force, like your father?" he said, pouring a Sambucca.

Pat shook his head negatively, swallowed the sweet liqueur and said, "I never knew my father, and if you'll pardon me, I'm not too crazy about cops."

Arthur laughed. "I'm not nuts about them myself, but it happens I am a sergeant in the Fifth Precinct. Did you know that?"

Pat stared curiously at his newfound "cousin."

"How come?" he asked.

Arthur shrugged.

"It was Depression. I didn't feel much like working for Sam and the family in those days. I wanted to make it on my own. In the beginning, everybody but Father Ray was against it, but later they felt I could do a lot of good on the force."

Pat looked at him curiously.

"A lot of *good*?"

"You know, for the family. It never hurts having someone in the department to help out. If we don't take care of each other, nobody else is going to take care of us, right?"

And Pat understood from the conversation that he himself was now regarded as one of the family, too.

"You know," Arthur said, pouring another Sambucca for his young friend, "we could use some more bright, ambitious Italian guys on the force. The way things are now, the Irish are running the whole show. What *they* don't control, the Jews have. With two million Italians in the city, we are entitled to more representation in the department, especially at the top."

Arthur was the only one who didn't talk to Pat like a child, and Pat appreciated that, but the subject held little interest for him.

"I got enough to do taking care of my own self without worrying about a couple of million *goombahs*."

Arthur put down the fork and looked at him seriously.

"Kid, you got a lot to learn. We all need help, and

people like us have to stick together more than the others. We got to make our own way, but if we help each other, it is easier. Take yourself. Where would you be if my brother didn't give you a hand? In jail, maybe. Anyway, with an arrest record, and no future. You got a good background. Don't throw it away. You are lucky enough to have had a father with many friends and a godfather who had important connections."

"So?" Pat said, still unimpressed.

"Who do you think paid to keep you in school at Our Lady?"

Pat shrugged. "I don't know. I thought Father Raimundo . . ."

"Don't be simple, kid," Arthur said. "The church needs money like anybody else. You think it was an accident meeting Don Vitone just now?"

Pat looked puzzled. He had thought that it was a simple social gesture.

"You know what it means when he takes you by the arm like that and walks with you to the table? You know what it means to be sitting here with my brothers and me? It means that Don Vitone is showing *respect* to our family, and he is recognizing you as a member of our *family*."

Pat could not help but feel a glow of warmth at being included in this intimate group, a feeling he had not known before.

"Listen, I really appreciate . . ." he started to say. But Arthur interrupted him.

"You're still wet behind the ears, kid. You don't know what the story is. But if you listen and follow instructions, you could have a good future. You're smart and tough and come from good people. These things are very important. So, if I make a suggestion to you, don't give me any smart-ass answers. We are talking about something very serious. We are talking about your

whole future. You want to wind up a cheap hood—a
bum—with no one to stand behind you, with no power
except what you have in your arms, with no respect?
Wise up!"

All of a sudden, Pat saw a side of the sunny Arthur
that he had not noticed before. A steely core inside that
wreath of smiles and a cold light behind the twinkling
eyes. This party, Pat realized, was a lot more than a
simple display of gluttony. It was almost as though it
was a big council meeting of some medieval government.

He began to realize that nothing said at the party was
simply what it appeared to be. That all of the conversations, gestures, winks and smiles were some sort of complex code, which could be learned only after years of
study.

There were many laughing references to a big party in
Havana. Apparently, many of those present had been
down for a holiday, but it was clear, from what they
said, that the trip was more than a holiday.

*Did you see the big guy? . . . Yeah, he looked great.
He's getting to look like a regular nigger with all that sun
down there . . . You work something out? . . . I think we
can do business . . . How was Willie? . . . That guy is
pazzo. He's a great guy, but you never know what he's
gonna say or do next . . . What about the little Jew, was
he there? . . . Are you kidding? The big guy don't make a
move without him. Sometimes I wonder who's really the
boss . . . But he done a lot of things, you know what I
mean? We got to play ball with them guys, too . . . Well,
it's a new thing, not like the old days . . .*

Pat was getting woozy from the wine. Conversation
swirled around his ears in a thick cloud of cigar smoke.
His head began to nod drowsily, until he felt Arthur's
firm hand under his arm.

"Come on, kid. We don't want anybody to think you
can't hold up your end. Let's go home."

Pat slept all the way back as the brothers rehashed the gossip of the party.

The last thing he remembered was being dropped at the rectory as Sam stuck his head out the limousine window.

"Take care of yourself, Ray," he said to Father Raimundo. "And let me know if you need any help with the Irishman. I can be patriotic too, you know . . . ."

CHAPTER 10

Things were different for Pat after the dinner.

Father Raimundo called him into the office a few days after the trip to Jersey.

"Do you remember Arthur talking to you about joining the police department?" he asked.

Pat nodded.

"I want you to think that idea over very seriously. I am sure you will be accepted, and while in the department it will also be possible for you to get a college education. This could be very important for your future. I cannot control you, of course, but you can believe me when I say that this will be a good thing for you to do. Apart from that, I ask you to do this for *me*. In respect for what I have done for you."

"I don't like cops much, father. What I seen of them so far, I don't like. I know my father was one of them, but that's a long time ago."

The priest turned in his swivel chair away from Pat and stared out the window.

"I think you will find you have made a wise choice," he said, ignoring Pat's comment. "You will find the application form on the desk in your room. Fill it out and bring it to me."

It was hard for Pat to analyze his feelings toward the priest. He would not have said he loved him. But there was a closeness he had not felt toward anyone within his memory. Yet, they seldom spoke of personal things, and sometimes the priest didn't speak to him at all for a week at a time. But Pat knew that what Father Raimundo said, he would do, and he knew, also, that it would be in his own best interests to follow the priest's plan.

He took the examination the following week, and three months later was appointed to the December class at the academy, which was on Hubert Street on the Lower East Side, not far from the rectory of Our Lady.

The building was old and dingy, and the rooms reminded Pat somehow of the orphanage in Jersey.

That first week they were all sent down to the jammed equipment bureau near headquarters on Broome Street.

Pat was surprised to find that every piece of gear he was to use had to be bought in the equipment department. Nothing was given away. Even the safety pin he needed to attach his shield cost fifteen cents. The whole deal, including the blue uniforms he would later need, ran more than five hundred dollars. This included two belts—one for the gun and one for the pants, a holster, handcuffs and a handcuff case, an ammunition pouch for the twelve rounds of ammo which each patrolman was required to carry, all sorts of foul-weather gear, gloves, a day billy and a nightstick, and a choice of either a Smith & Wesson or a Colt .38 caliber revolver.

There was no question that when the gun was issued, every one of the recruits felt a strange thrill rising through his groin, like the sensation in a fast-sinking elevator, or the rising lance of genital pain-pleasure you get looking over the edge of a tall building.

Talk over hero sandwiches at lunch that day was all about what kind of "off-duty" piece each recruit was

going to get when he had finished his probationary
period. There were heated discussions about the varying
merits of ankle, shoulder and crotch holsters.

Deep down, Pat knew that this was what it was all
about. The lethal power in hand, the power to right
wrongs, injustices, personal indignities, insults. The
warm, walnut grip was like the hand of a good, strong
friend.

Half the guys were already blowing a fortune in cow-
boy-type quick-draw holsters, Pancho Villa ammo holders, fancy whistles, and jumbo-sized nightsticks.

Recruit Terry Burke was busy buying a handful of
miniature shields in the form of tie clasps and other personal jewelry for himself and family.

"These things are terrific, and it lets people know that
your relatives are, you know, *connected* to the police
force. Ain't you getting any?" The tall, blond rookie was
excited as a slum kid in F.A.O. Schwartz.

"Naah," Pat said. "I ain't got no family."

Privately he wondered how a little crucifix with a
police shield in the center would go over with Father
Ray.

Burke looked at him with pity.

"No kidding. No family at all?"

"My father was a cop. He got killed back in the thirties. Inspector's funeral, the whole bit."

Burke was impressed.

"Cheest! I bet you got some heavy hooks upstairs,
huh?"

Pat shrugged. "I know one guy, maybe."

He suddenly realized that Sergeant Arthur Marseri
was what guys were talking about when they discussed
having "a hook."

Even at that recruit's level, it was known that the
young probies would get the good assignments only if
they had the right connections—a "hook" or a "rabbi"
at the upper levels who could put in a good word.

He was surprised to find himself bragging about his dead and unknown father, but he figured: "Shit, if the old man will ever do me any good, it's right now!"

Pat was embarrassed to hit up Father Ray for all the extra money which the training called for.

"Don't worry, *giovanotto*. You can pay me back later when you are on the job," the priest reassured him.

CHAPTER 11

Pat spent the following weeks holed up with studies of criminal law, police organization, penal code definitions, introduction to the laws of arrest, the lawful use of force, the United States Constitution, and how to cope with accidents and injured civilians. Also, and most important, according to the instructor, was how to fill out the daily memo book which every cop had to keep describing his activities down to the last detail.

"If you take a piss, that goes in the book, too," O'Brien cautioned.

"Do we put how many times we shake it?" asked a voice in the class.

Each night Pat brought home his texts: *The Penal Law, The Code of Criminal Procedure, The Administrative Code, The Traffic Regulations of New York City, The Vehicle and Traffic Laws of New York State,* and *The First Aid Handbook* and locked himself in for the evening, disregarding the jeers of the gang from the club as he passed the corner with no more than a wave and a hello.

"Duck, men! Here comes the law!" Al Santini said.

But there was a new tone of respect in their voices.

72

The gang was impressed, despite their own hatred of cops, that one of *their* group was penetrating the mysteries behind the blue uniform and shield.

"I know Pat," Paul Ganci said. "Cop or no cop, he would never rat on his friends."

Pat was learning the rudiments of police work, but in all that time, Pat noticed, no instructor said anything about graft, free meals and drinks, or roughing up prisoners to get "cooperation." Were these, he wondered, being saved for the advanced courses?

But that aspect of his education was not long neglected.

The locker room and the greasy spoon a few doors down on Baxter Street were in effect auxiliary classrooms.

Several of the recruits had been pulled out of the academy for various special assignments before being returned to finish their training. They had a different version of life in the field than what was taught in the academy classes.

A short course in untaught sidelines by recently reeducated rookie cops:

"Listen, I was sorry I got a coat that fit so good. The first day out we got lucky. Got a call on a radio-electronics store robbery. You shoulda' seen the joint. It was a wreck, and there was all these neat little radios and tape recorders and like that, and me without room in my coat for more than a couple of portable jobs! Still, I made a pretty good score, probably a C-note if I peddle the stuff. But I'm trading in that coat!"

"So, I'm driving for the sergeant, see? And every two-bit, one-arm hash joint, ginmill, cigar store and candy store we pass he says to me: 'Wait here a minute'—and he goes in for a couple of minutes and comes out with a big grin. One time he goes in a saloon and comes out with a flute of booze—you know, in a Coke bottle? So

*he gives me a slug out of the flute and slips me a five at
the end of the tour, and that's all I see the whole lousy
night!"*

"Listen, the first thing you got to do is get out of the
bag. You can't make any real dough in uniform. Too
conspicuous! And the best way to get out of the bag is to
make a good collar, or shoot somebody. Just make sure
you got an extra throwaway piece on you, or a knife or
something so they don't nail you on charges at the
departmental investigation. And one thing more. If you
shoot a guy, don't forget you got to squeeze off a couple
of warning shots after. That's in the rules. Best thing is
make sure you kill a guy if you got to shoot him, otherwise the rat is liable to come back and file some kind of
charge of police brutality!"

*"My pop was a cop. He told me never take no dirty
money—you know, like broads and narcotics. But
things are different now. Anyway, who gets hurt by a little gambling and fucking? As far as narcotics, I ain't
gonna get involved unless it's a big score. If ya get on the
narc squad, of course, it's different. You don't take and
the other guys make your life hard."*

"What I like to try is the pussy patrol! A couple of
collars a night and you're home free! The broads all cop
a plea and you're out of court a lot of times in one session. And you get a piece of nookie here and there just
to make it nice. I'm gonna hide my tin up my ass so I
can get a little before I make my collar."

*"The pussy patrol is crap! Peanuts! Gambling is
where the good score is, and it's clean! Christ! Who
doesn't gamble? Over in nine oh, where they sent me on
that mob-control detail, they had a crap game going in
back of the station house!"*

"Safe and loft is a good deal. You wind up with fur coats, televisions, fridges and all that big shit, and it's clean. Know what I mean? Hell, them guys are all covered up to their fat asses in insurance anyway. What do they care if a few extra pieces go out the door, as long as they get the protection?"

CHAPTER 12

Pat got one assignment in the street before his graduation. He was called out to guard the polls at a schoolhouse in Queens out in the 107th Precinct.

For once the Italians were really making their political clout bear fruit. The candidates were: Ed Corsi for the Republicans, Ferdinand Pecora for the Democrats, and acting mayor Vincent Impellitteri, running as a reform independent on the heels of the resignation of Bill O'Dwyer, who had felt the climate would be far better in Mexico, to which he was handily appointed ambassador after a series of revealing and confusing hearings over multimillion-dollar police payoffs by Brooklyn bookie Harry Gross.

The election duty went without incident, and Pat was invited for coffee by Willie Dugan, the veteran patrolman who had been paired with him at the schoolhouse.

At the diner on Queens Boulevard, Dugan ordered the "T-Bone Special," pie and coffee. Pat ordered a sugar cruller and coffee.

"Ain't you hungry, kid?" Dugan asked.

Pat shrugged.

"Broke, hanh? Don't worry, sport. This one's on me."

So Pat ordered a repeat of Dugan's order.

"You guineas ought to be having a big *festa* tonight, hanh?" Dugan said, shoving a stray french fry into his busy mouth with a black-edged finger.

Pat kept his silence. He saw no need to get into a race-battle with the stupid Mick.

"I bet you think these guys are some kind of tin god, a regular Little Flower, hanh?"

Pat sliced the T-bone into neat squares. It was gray and overdone, but he didn't feel he could send it back. Dugan poked at Pat's rookie shirt with the end of his knife. His breath smelled of bourbon, and Pat guessed that the large number of piss-calls he had taken during the tour had involved some communing with a flute in the men's room.

"Well, I'll tell ya something. I used to work the eight-seven up in East Harlem—that's where your Commie *goombah* Marcantonio is running from. That was last election, back in '46. You know how he got in? Same as those other Commie rats over in Russia. Joe McCarthy knows what he's talking about. They beat the shit out of some slob Republican because he wouldn't turn the vote over to Marcantonio. The guy died. Name of Scottoriggio. You know who gave the word for the rubout? Your *goombahs*, Genovese and Costello and Trigger Mike Coppola."

Dugan leaned over confidentially.

"You know how I know? I was a detective then. I was on the case. But I was just a stupid Mick, and didn't know what the story was. I started lining up witnesses that were leading me right to the guys who did the actual hit. They told me I was on the wrong track—it was probably some Commie radicals, they told me. But I saw Trigger Mike talking to some of these guys only the day before. I was onto a good collar. Next thing you know, I start pushing my idea. I had a stakeout on these hoods and all, even after the loo told me to knock it off.

I was going to go right to Hogan's office with my stuff.
You know what happened? They pulled me off the case.
Next thing you know, they find some entries in my book
that didn't match up with my activities. Next thing,
there's a hearing and I am flopped back to the bag, and
shipped out to East Jesus here to sweat out my pension.
If you ever get the gold shield, make sure you know
what you're buckin' before you start cracking any murder cases, kid."

Pat looked up, wide-eyed. "Gee, Dugan. I thought
you Micks had the whole department in control!"

Next day, Pat read where Impellitteri won by a hefty
margin. Marcantonio, possibly as a result of the McCarthy hysteria against Communists, was defeated by a man
named Donovan.

Pat's graduation from the academy coincided with the
resignation of Police Commissioner William P. O'Brien.
The revelations of police corruption during the previous
years, largely uncovered by the activities of rookie cops,
who had graduated only a class or so before Pat, had
cast a shadow on "the majority of policemen who were
straight, honest, brave and hardworking," O'Brien had
said in his graduation speech to the shiny-new cops and
their beamingly proud parents.

"You men are New York's finest," O'Brien had said,
echoing the brave phrase of New York's last honest
mayor, Fiorello La Guardia. He urged on the young officers devotion to their jobs and their traditions, and
above all, honesty.

Police had been shuffled around like Scrabble letters,
but corruption had continued, and oddly enough, not
one bookie was convicted during the whole shake-up.
But a lot of top cops resigned and one even blew his
brains out after being forced to testify against his fellow
officers.

Under the circumstances, O'Brien told his class, his
situation as PC was "untenable" and he announced his

resignation right there in front of the graduating class.

Pat and the other new rookies crowded around the list of names posted on the academy wall indicating first assignments. Three weeks before, every rookie who knew what was going on had been on the phone to his "hook" or "rabbi" trying to influence that first assignment. Some of them had even invested in a couple of bottles of Scotch or a cash-filled envelope to make sure that they got the right precincts. Considerations were: nearness to home, amount of action, opportunities for promotion, and opportunities for graft.

CHAPTER 13

Arthur Marseri, now a lieutenant in the silk stocking precinct—the one-seven, which covered the swank East Side—was Pat's rabbi, and Pat didn't need to make any special call.

"I could get you up here, Pat, in the one-seven," Arthur had told him, "but it wouldn't look good. Besides, you might as well start out someplace where you feel at home, where you know the lay of the land, so to speak. I'm having you assigned to the Fifth on Elizabeth Street, in your own back yard, more or less."

That was Arthur's decision, and Pat had no objections, though he worried about what would happen if he was called on to haul in one of his own buddies from the Mulberry SAC or something like that.

Still, the precinct was only a short walk from the church, so it was convenient, and Pat was already familiar with the area.

In fact, Pat was already familiar with the Elizabeth Street precinct house. He wondered if that sonovabitch plainclothesman was still there. What would he say if Pat came up to him and asked for the eighty bucks he had lifted from Pat's wallet?

Pat was assigned to a squad and was instructed by a

bored lieutenant to report to the roll-call man for his assignment.

The shift that week was the four-to-twelve, which suited Pat all right. He figured he could sleep late, take it easy in the early afternoon, and maybe bounce around a little after work. He wondered what kind of women he could find who had time to spare after midnight. Show-business broads? Cocktail waitresses? Airline stewardesses? Hookers?

Pat reported early, eager and curious to get started with the real work.

He had a half hour to kill before roll call, so he spent it in the sitting room, which was the social nerve center of the station house.

Idly, Pat looked over the notices posted on the wall. The wanted posters and reports on runaway kids looked tired and dust covered. Those kids probably had runaways of their own by now, Pat thought. In fact, they looked as though they were the same posters that had been there when Pat was in the precinct house last. He noticed that a coin-operated shoeshine machine had been added to the room's decor, and used some of his waiting time to put a gloss on his already perfect black service shoes. Alongside the machine was a full-length mirror which he used for a last-minute check of his appearance.

At first sight, he was shocked to see a *cop* in blue and brass and sterling badges staring back at him from the glass like a recruiting poster. The reflection had no connection with Pat's mental image of himself. But Pat liked what he saw—a tall man, broad-shouldered, strong-looking, dark-eyed, dependable, but dashing. Pat was glad he had invested an extra twenty-five bucks in having his blouse tailored to his narrow hips, with space allowed to fit around the gun and other equipment.

The roll-call sergeant was a studious-looking, round-faced blond man in his late thirties, with horn-rimmed glasses that made him look as though he would be more at home behind the complaint desk at Macy's than at the roll-call desk on Elizabeth Street.

Sergeant Harry Hoffman handed Pat a map of the precinct showing where the various sectors and foot-patrol posts were.

"We're giving you the Grand Street post, Conte," Hoffman said. "Ask one of the older guys. He'll fill you in on what's involved. I just got one piece of advice. Do as little as possible until you know what's going on around here. You got a long time to go before you're eligible for that pension, and you wouldn't want to fuck it up on your first day."

A paunchy and genial older cop fell in step with Pat as they left the roll-call room.

"What post you got, kid?"

Pat told him, and he nodded agreeably.

"I'm on the next post—over toward Centre Street. If you want to meet me when you take your lunch blow, there's a good spot for pasta on Mulberry where they'll give us a break. I can fill you in on what's going on. My name's Lenny Donizetti. They call me Donny. You're Dom Conte's kid, ain't you?"

Pat nodded yes, wondering where Donizetti got his information.

The post itself was no strain. Pat knew every storefront by heart, but he dreaded the first time he would bump into someone he knew from "civilian" days.

Several people whom he had known vaguely in the neighborhood passed and gave him curious looks, as though trying to relate the familiar face to some half-recalled past impression. But nobody said anything.

At eight o'clock, Pat phoned in to say he was taking his break at Paolucci's on Mulberry.

He was a few minutes ahead of Donizetti, but the hawk-nosed waiter acted as though he was expecting Pat and showed him to a small table in the rear of the long, brightly lit room.

"You wait there, son. Donny be along soon. You want a paper to read? A drink? A glass of wine?"

Pat said he would just wait, and sat down to fill out his daily memo book with the uninteresting details of his tour to date.

It seemed that he had done nothing, but noted down conscientiously it looked like a busy, though not impressive night.

He had chased several bums who were sleeping it off in front of restaurants, noted the number of a Cadillac that had circled the block suspiciously three or four times, given directions to a group of tourists looking for Chinatown, warned a super to clear some broken glass from the front of his tenement, helped a kid catch his puppy, checked the knobs on all the stores on his post that were closed for the night and visually inspected the interiors, and advised a husband who was trying to break in the door of his own apartment in which his wife had apparently barricaded herself, that he should go somewhere and sober up, or he would be run in for disorderly conduct. The man seemed impressed by the uniform and went stumbling down the steps, muttering drunkenly under his breath.

"I come back later. I kill that bitch. No-good fuckin' *putana.*"

As the man left, the door, still on a chain, opened a crack and a tear-stained face, framed by dark-rooted blonde hair and streaked with running mascara, peered through the crack. Framed in the narrow opening, Pat could see that she was dressed only in yellow bikini pants and a white bra. The figure encompassed in the six inches allowed by the door chain looked firm and healthy, the midriff smooth, pink and unwrinkled with a deep-cleft naval. Pat wondered if she really was a *putana.*

"Is he gone?" the woman asked.

Pat said he was.

"Well . . . thanks," the blonde said, flashing a dazzling smile. "I guess I'll see you around."

And she closed the door slowly.

Pat did not put that part in his memo-book report.

He had not quite finished noting his break when the door opened and Donizetti lumbered in, his face still lit with what seemed to be a permanent grin of good nature.

CHAPTER 14

Donny was a mine of information on doings in the precinct, and seemed to have been well briefed on Pat's background.

"First thing we got to do, we got to sign you up for the Columbia Association," Donny said, taking a generous swig of the red wine which had been set down in tumblers before them.

Pat already knew that this was the Italian organization in the department, which made certain that national distinctions were not forgotten by organizing the Jews into the Shomrim Society, the spics into the Hispanic Society, the krauts into the Steuben Society, and the Micks into the Emerald Society. It never hurt to have an organization behind you at all times, it seemed, and Pat was beginning to get the message loud and clear.

As they chatted, the waiter brought a plate of *linguini a la carbonara* and a converted sugar shaker of *parmigiano*.

"One thing, you eat good on this post," Donny said, stuffing the yellowish strands into his ample mouth, which he mopped with a wad of fresh Italian bread.

"Now listen, kid," he said, wiping the *carbonara*

sauce from the plate. "I got the word that you're okay, and I should look after you, right?"

Pat shrugged. He didn't think an answer was expected.

"A lot of guys think this is a lousy precinct, because the family keeps things quiet around here—no big collars or anything, right?"

Pat nodded. He had heard that the Italian section of the precinct was kept under a tight lid by the Mafia. Many members of the family still lived in the area, or still had relatives or other interests there. This was where they came to buy coffee, imported olive oil, scungilli, pastry and other Italian delicacies. Crimes of violence were practically unheard of in the area, and when they occurred were often punished by local vigilantes even before the police got word of them.

"Well, don't underestimate *anything*. I shouldn't be telling you all this, being as you're a rookie and all that, but you can do okay around here, and I don't mean just the eating. In the first place, we got Chinatown down here also, and they got a lot of gambling over there. We don't hardly make any collars, but they pay regular, and they take care of their own, same as the Italians, if you know what I mean. Right?"

Pat nodded.

"Then we got all these social clubs and all. They're good for a fin a week and a nice Christmas present. If you get tired, there's a couple of nice coops. They got a good one with a stove in it over on Chatham Square in the men's room. And at night, the school around the corner is good—in the boiler room, right?"

Pat knew that each area had a place where cops could go to rest during their tour of duty. He'd already spotted the patrol cars parked outside the Chinatown public restrooms.

They finished the meal with a plate of Italian sausages and a spinach salad dressed in hot bacon fat.

Over espresso, Donny continued his indoctrination lecture.

"Ninety percent of that stuff you learned at the academy was crapola. Even the forms and all they taught you, we got different forms. In fact, we got so many forms you got to fill out a UF49 before you fart. That's another thing on the gambling collars. Say you spot a KG, and you run him in. Whaddaya got? You got a pile of forms. You got to run downtown to court, maybe two, three times, and the sonovabitch is out on bail as soon as you bring him in, right?"

Pat agreed.

"So it's a waste of time. Besides, those gambling collars ain't worth shit on your record. You need some kind of hassle where your *life* is in danger, maybe somebody takes a shot at you, maybe you shoot somebody, like that. Right?"

"Sure."

Pat reached for his wallet at the end of the meal, but it was clear no bill would be brought. Donny held up his hand in a gesture of negation.

"Forget it, kid. I told you this was a good post. Mario!"

Hawknose ambled over.

"This here is a good kid," Donny said. "He's one of our people, a *goombah*. Not one of these fuckin' Micks they been sending down here lately. You take care of him good, right?"

"*Ma, shur'*," Mario said generously. It wasn't *his* joint.

In the chilly street again Pat buttoned up his blouse collar and was glad he had been tipped off to wear a sweater under it.

"You got any problems, kid, you come to Donny, right?"

Pat said, "Right," and sauntered off to the call-in box to check in.

Pat had been in the job only two weeks when Sergeant Hoffman called him over one night, just before the start of his shift.

"Lemme look you over. Your uniform clean? Ya got a shave?"

He inspected Pat with close attention.

"Okay. You've been selected for a special assignment. Put a shine on those shoes and report to Our Lady Church up the street. They got a dance and a block party tonight, and they asked for someone to handle parking and security."

Pat smiled and snapped a salute at the sergeant.

"Yes, *sir*!" Pat had known that Father Raimundo was planning some kind of a shindig to raise funds for the new altar. But he had little time those days for church functions, so he had not paid much attention.

Church dances had very little appeal for him, anyway.

Pat had never even tried to score with any of them. If he had, he was sure, word would have gotten back almost instantly to Father Ray. Patrolman Pat Conte might find himself married long before his time. Most of the girls that Pat had had anything to do with were short-timers. When a girl he had made love to asked to see him again, it always made him uncomfortable.

He had lost his virginity in the back room of the Mulberry SAC with a fat teen-ager who had befriended every erect penis on the block. She made only one demand. No matter how many men passed between her chubby thighs during the night, each had to intone three magic words before he could enter the soggy portals: "I love you."

The first time one of the guys brought her to the club Pat didn't even get laid, because he couldn't bring himself to say those words. But the next time he had enough bourbon in him to ignore the acned complexion, the slobby lips, the porcine nostrils, the smell of rancid olive oil, and concentrate only on the dark jungle at the juncture of the two fat columns of flesh.

The girl leaned back on the greasy worn plush of the overstuffed couch someone had donated to the club, her lips grotesquely smeared with the pressure of those few who had ventured a kiss as a *lagniappe* to her orgasm. Pat was ninth in line.

"Come on, Pat," the girl said, "you got to say 'I love you' like the rest of them!"

Pat wondered how she even knew his name.

"Okay, I *love* you," he said, spitting the words out like a curse and fell between the waiting thighs.

The street behind Our Lady had been turned into a fairyland of sorts. People in the surrounding tenements had dragged out card tables and decorated them with colorful cloths and crepe paper.

They sat on their folding chairs, watching the crowds in the street and drinking wine and Scotch whiskey. In the middle of the block was a platform on which there cavorted a local rock 'n' roll band, recruited from the parochial school.

There were two vacant lots where the ancient tenements had finally succumbed to the pressures of age and decay, and had been torn down. One was now filled with a gaily decorated ferris wheel. The other was preempted as a parking lot for VIPs. By the time Pat arrived there were already two or three limousines parked against the brick wall of the adjoining building. Lieutenant Arthur Marseri was there in civvies. He introduced Pat to Lieutenant Johnny Behan of the traffic squad who was handling the detail.

"This here is Pat Conte, my little cousin," Arthur said. "I want you to take good care of him."

The lieutenant looked him over with interest.

"So you're one of Arthur's family, eh?"

Pat nodded. "That's right."

"Well, we'll see you don't get in any trouble," the big florid man said, clasping his shoulder. "You go over and watch the parking lot. Make sure they don't dent any fenders on those big shiny cars, and take it easy on the vino. It's a long night. Remember, the lot is only for honored guests. They'll show you a ticket when they come in. Nobody else."

"Yes sir," Pat said, saluting.

"See you later," Arthur said, walking off with the lieutenant toward the tent which had been set up in the play yard of the church school. Pat walked into the lot and inspected the cars that had already arrived. They all had impressively low license numbers. A number of them were from New Jersey.

Turning his back to the cars, Pat looked over the gaily decorated street. Overhead festoons of colored electric lights, arched over the roadway, some of them culminating in a large cross. Near the corner was a plaster statue of Our Lady of the Sacred Heart. Dollar bills were stuck all over the form and casing of the image, and coins glittered around its feet.

Earlier in the day the statue had been paraded up and down the street, carried by a team of selected honor bearers, all of them big contributors to the church.

Stands crowding the edges of the sidewalks were dispensing sausages and peppers, broiled chickens, *calzone* and *zeppoli*, clams, popcorn and candy cotton. Between them were the gambling stands, big numbered wheels, pitch and toss, plates to throw pennies at, shooting galleries and baseball-throwing concessions.

Offered as prizes were plastic bags of goldfish, bottles of whiskey, and the usual collection of plush toys and bric-a-brac.

These were the principal moneymaking concessions. Each of them turned over twenty percent of their night's take to the church. But *eighty* percent went to the concession owners—among whom Pat knew were several close friends of the family. So it worked out well for everybody. The church got its money, and the family got its profit.

Pat leaned against the fender of a cream-colored Lincoln sedan and listened to the strident sounds of the pickup band. A sergeant came around every hour or so to give him a "see," but otherwise the situation was uneventful.

At about eleven-thirty, after the sergeant's third checkup, a tall tousle-haired kid in a seersucker jacket staggered unevenly into the parking lot. Barely able to keep his balance, the young man began trying to insert a key into the lock of the Lincoln. But he had trouble finding the keyhole. Pat, who had been watching him for a few minutes, spoke to the kid.

"Maybe you better take a little rest before you try to drive, fella."

The tall boy looked around angrily.

"Piss off, copper! When I need advice I'll ask for it."

Pat glanced around nervously. The owners of the cars in that lot were all big shots, and he knew enough not to make any unnecessary trouble. But no one had told him how to handle the problem of a snotnosed kid. He slipped quietly off behind some of the parked cars, to think over the situation. It was obvious that the kid would never get that Lincoln out of the lot, but he might kill himself or someone else trying.

Carefully, Pat tiptoed around the far side of the Lincoln, and came up behind the kid in the summer jacket. Gripping his nightstick close to the end, Pat jabbed it suddenly into the kid's back, just below the bottom rib.

With an "oof!" of exiting breath the kid collapsed softly to the ground. Pat smiled in satisfaction. Who could say that the kid hadn't just conked out? The kid himself, of course, never knew what hit him. Pat decided to put the young man into his car and let him sleep off the booze. But when he tried to unlock the Lincoln's door, he found that he couldn't get it to open either.

Attached to the kid's key ring was a miniature license tag, with the letters BX-23. Pat knew then that he had been right not to try to collar the kid. This was the plate of some heavy politician. But it wasn't the number on the license plate of the cream-colored Lincoln. No wonder he couldn't open the door!

Prowling around the parking lot, Pat found the right car two rows away. But it was going to be a tough job lugging the dead weight of the unconscious kid over to the other car.

As Pat was trying to work out this problem, he spotted a group of people wandering over from the tent where the bazaar was taking place.

They were now gathered around the unconscious form of the tall drunk kid—two girls and a young guy in a blue suit with a carnation in the buttonhole. As Pat approached the little group, he realized that both of the girls were extremely pretty in that clean-cut movie-star way. They wore short cocktail dresses with bare shoulders and half-covered bosoms. The sight of that lush pink skin set up a gentle aching in Pat's groin.

One of the girls was a honey blonde with long, straight hair that hung over one eye in a way that must have been hell on her vision, but gave her an oddly vulnerable look. The other had short-cropped black curls, and huge brown sad eyes, like a church madonna. But her mouth was full and sensuous like that of no plaster saint Pat had ever seen.

"Any problem?" Pat asked innocently.

"It's okay, officer, I think we can handle it," the guy in the blue suit said. Pat had not really noticed him up to that point, he'd been so involved in looking over the girls. The man was about six-two, black hair with a heavy jaw and a nose that looked as though the guy might have done some boxing.

The face reminded Pat of the young Jim Braddock, just before he fought Joe Louis. A second glance indicated that the guy was about Pat's age, maybe even a little younger.

The fellow in the blue suit soon realized that he was facing the same problem that had vexed Pat minutes earlier. The stiff in the seersucker jacket was out cold, and he was a hell of a dead weight to carry a hundred feet or so to the other car. He probably weighed about 220 pounds.

The guy slapped the unconscious kid in the face a couple of times, but produced only a sleepy groan.

"Listen, officer," he said to Pat, "you want to give me a hand getting this guy over to his car?"

Between them they managed to sling the arms of the unconscious youth over their shoulders, and drag him, his feet trailing behind him, over to the other Lincoln.

The two girls followed, giggling. Between the two men they managed to get the drunk into the back seat of the car.

The guy in the blue suit turned to Pat with a smile.

"Thanks! That palooka is some armful!" He turned to the girl with the black curls.

"What are we going to do *now*, Connie? You want me to drive you home and send for the Lincoln tomorrow?"

"I don't know," the girl said uneasily. "I don't want to get Marty in trouble. They might ask questions if I don't get home with the car."

Pat stood aside, watching. The girl didn't seem at all upset by the situation. In fact, she seemed to be *smiling*. Pat figured the girl had had a few belts also.

The guy in the blue suit looked at Pat speculatively, sizing him up. Finally he signaled Pat to talk to him on the side.

Away from the girls, he reached into his pocket and pulled out a wallet. Pat thought the guy was about to offer him a tip or a bribe. But to his surprise, the guy flipped open the leather and flashed the tin. He was on the force too!

"I'm Regan Doyle. I'm not really on the job tonight—just out with my girl. Connie, here, is my girl Katie's best friend. That big drunk is just some guy her father fixed her up with so she'd have a date for tonight. Do you drive?"

Pat said he did.

"What time do you get off?"

Pat looked at his watch. It was nearly twelve. Most of the crowd was already leaving. A good many of the cars were being driven by young men hardly more sober than the kid they'd dumped in the back seat.

"Pretty soon now, I guess," Pat said.

"Would you drive the Lincoln back? It belongs to Connie's old man up in Riverdale. He'll really be pissed off if he finds out that that jerk Marty got drunk, when he was supposed to be looking after Connie. Not that I give a damn. I don't even really know the guy."

Pat didn't see anything wrong with the idea. In fact he liked it. It was better than chasing drunks out of doorways or warning janitors about the garbage. Besides the girl was something special.

Twenty minutes later he had cleared himself with the sergeant and was ready to go.

The girl was sitting quietly in the Lincoln waiting for him. The big kid in the seersucker jacket was snoring gently in the rear seat. Pat tossed his hat in the back, next to the drunk, and slid behind the wheel.

The girl smiled at him. She had perfect teeth, the kind only rich people have. The lips were large and soft, and Pat had a strong impulse to lean over and kiss her as she sat there.

"What's your name?"

"Pat—Pat Conte."

"Mine's Connie—Connie Massey."

CHAPTER 15

Nobody had mentioned to Pat the fact that Sam Massey had a daughter, but then, why should they?

"I know your family," Pat said. "I live with your Uncle Raimundo."

Connie laughed delightedly. "We're practically cousins then!"

But eyeing the clinging white fabric around her narrow waist and the warm swell of her half-uncovered breasts, Pat felt very un-cousinlike.

The girl sat close, on Pat's side of the wide seat, and hummed "Moonlight Cocktail" softly under her breath as Pat drove the big car past the ocean liners of the Manhattan docks and up the West Side Highway. The drive reminded him of the last trip he had taken in a limousine, with the Marseri family, en route to Sam Massey's house. It was a trip of forty-five minutes or so, but to Pat it was a journey to a faraway country.

Pat pulled away from the overhead El on upper Broadway and began to ascend the winding roads of Riverdale.

Houses were set back from the street behind wide lawns or high walls. There were no chalked graffiti on the streets or sidewalks. No indicated boundaries for potsy, boxball or stickball. No stoops to bounce a Spalding off.

As they climbed into the hills, they passed a squat, stone building like a medieval castle.

"That's St. Agnes, where Katie and I go to school," Connie said.

There were arched passages cutting through the building, which covered an entire city block. Through the archways, Pat could glimpse a large quadrangle, guarded by stone walls, so that the privileged girl students could stroll to classes without being exposed to vulgar stares from the street. Inside the quadrangle were towering elms, and patches of evergreen surrounded by brown patches indicating flower beds.

"What will we do with your friend back there?" Pat asked as he pulled the car under the porte-cochere of Sam Massey's house.

"Just leave him in the car. One of the men will put it away, and I guess they'll take care of Marty, too."

It was the first time he had ever driven in a car with a girl, but Pat remembered enough from films he had seen to dash around to her side and open the door. Her hand felt hot and dry as he helped her from the Lincoln, and her eyes flashed with mischief. She pressed his fingers in a grip which was more than necessary to keep her balance, and opened her cushiony lips into a luminous, warm smile.

"I don't suppose *you'd* pass out if you took a girl out on a date?" she said.

Pat shrugged. "I never have. But then, I've never dated a girl like you. I might faint from the excitement."

"You'll never know if you don't try." He noticed that she was still holding his hand.

The faint juniper smell of gin reached him through the damp winter air. He wondered if she would remember the encounter the next day.

He leaned forward as though to kiss her cheek, but she turned her head in a birdlike motion, pecked him once with those marvelous, warm, soft lips and skipped up the steps to the main entrance. With a nod of her head, she indicated the upper windows of the huge stuccoed house.

"They're watching," she said. " 'Night!"

And she was gone.

Walking back down the hill to the subway, Pat tingled with a sense of pleasurable anticipation. This was a woman! This was a *lady*! Certainly she resembled nobody he had ever met in the neighborhood. The air of the Bronx seemed to carry an uplifting, purifying quality, at least when it reached the rarefied heights of Riverdale.

The next day, Pat called the Massey house just before he started the four-to-twelve. He figured Connie would be home from school by then, but Sam wouldn't yet be back from work. Somehow, he wasn't sure how her father would react to his seeing Connie.

The phone was answered by a maid with a heavy Spanish accent.

When Connie got on the phone, her voice had the same heavy, slurred, sensual tones that he had noticed the night before.

He had planned a speech of introduction in case she didn't remember him, or wasn't able to place his name.

"I don't know if you remember me. I'm Pat Conte, the cop who took you home last night. I hope you don't think I'm being fresh or anything, but . . ."

Except that it wasn't like that. Connie answered with a delighted laugh of intimacy, as though they were old friends.

"Pat, is that you? I was waiting for your call."

Pat had rehearsed what he was going to ask her. He wasn't off the four-to-twelve until the following week. He wasn't sure it would be a good idea to ask her for a date without checking first with the family. But he was sure that he wanted to hear her voice again, and confirm the strong vibrations he had felt the night before.

Tentatively he suggested that they go "to a movie or something" up in her neighborhood the following Friday, which was his off day. Connie seemed eager to accept the date, but tentative about the details.

"Call me next week. I really want to see you. I'll let you know."

Pat worked the whole next week in a haze of expectation.

He had never had a feeling like this before about any girl, a feeling of enormous distance, and yet closeness, fear and yet confidence. He *knew* she liked him and yet was afraid she'd reject him, even forget who he was by the time he called again.

He knew he should mention something to Father Ray or Arthur Marseri or somebody, but was afraid that if he did, an obstacle would be put in his way. He had to see her again at least once before he risked a family confrontation.

On Wednesday, she told him she would be able to see him that Friday. But the arrangements were so devious, Pat wondered whether she was kept under lock and key like some European princess.

He was to wait near the candy store on Broadway at 238th and she would pick him up in a car.

"Somebody else will be coming with us. Do you mind?"

He minded. It wasn't part of his fantasy to see her in the company of others. And he was afraid that he might not fit in so well with this uptown crowd. She talked differently from him, he noticed, as though she hadn't been raised in New York at all but in some other city where they talked in soft, butterfly strokes with no harsh nasal city twang. Her low voice barely seemed to light on a word before it skipped off in a light wind of sound.

For the first time, he was aware of his Italian Lower East Side accent, and ashamed of it, though it was the way every one he knew talked. Even Uncle Ray and her father, Sam, had those same first-generation Sicilian overtones in their speech. Where had she learned to speak like Katharine Hepburn? In that convent school in the Bronx? Was that a nun's accent she had learned?

On Friday, he put on his only suit, a chalk-striped blue, with wide, squared shoulders and conservatively pegged pants, wide at the knee. It reminded him of his accent. It was wrong, he knew, for that neighborhood, for that girl. But what could he do? Wear his purple lumber jacket with Mulberry SAC in yellow across the back?

The long subway trip—it took almost an hour to get to that rarefied point on the edge of the city—emphasized the gap he felt. In a way, he would have been more at ease in his uniform. In recent weeks, it had become more a part of him than his civvies, and he had not had occasion to wear a suit since he had joined the force.

Now, he was out of that funky, thick, yellow night air of the East Side and into the cold, blue light of the Bronx. The train, roaring out of the underground into the open air of the elevated structure, seemed to stress his arrival in this country of the north, where girls spoke like butterflies.

Nervously, he tightened the wide windsor knot of his tie and shot his starched white cuffs so they showed a half inch below his sleeve.

He ordered a Pepsi at the chilly outdoor counter of the candy store, and watched expectantly for the car to descend the winding hill.

He checked his watch against the Dolly Syrup clock over the fountain. He was five minutes early. He wondered if he should phone again to confirm the date. But then, the car might come while he was in the phone booth and leave without him.

Finally, as he was peering up the hill for the fifth time, he heard a honking from the opposite direction, and a maroon Plymouth convertible pulled up beside him with a woman at the wheel.

"Can I help you, officer?"

It was Connie's voice, coming from the back seat. The girl at the wheel, he realized, was Katie, the one with the long, tawny hair from the night of the dance, and sitting next to her was the Mick, Regan Doyle.

CHAPTER 16

That night was like an adventure in a foreign land to Pat. He had never seen so many non-Italians in his life. They drove across the Bronx and down the Concourse to the Paradise Theater.

Pat had never seen a theater like that either. It was surrounded by towers and columns of a Spanish castle and miraculously, on the ceiling were projected twinkling stars and the shapes of passing clouds.

He sat close to Connie and could feel her thigh pressing against his. On the other side, he could feel Kate's leg pressing against his also. Maybe it was just that the seats were too close together. The picture was *The Asphalt Jungle*.

Pat was particularly interested in Louis Calhern, the millionaire, who kept Marilyn Monroe in a jazzy flat and who was the power behind the throne in city politics. It was Calhern who financed the big jewel caper that was pulled off by Sterling Hayden. When Hayden, wounded, drove crazily down the roads of Maryland and then finally ran across the fields of Kentucky to his horses, Pat felt an unfamiliar ache in his heart, a nostalgia for a place he'd never been. It made him think of half-remembered trips with his mother in Jersey and that time long ago when he didn't know what Little Italy was like or the East Side of New York. Somehow that all connected up with the feeling he had now in the faraway Bronx.

Later, they went to Krum's for sodas. It was full of Irish and Jewish kids, as well as some Italians. You could tell them, each from the other, by the way they dressed and the way they laughed and talked. None of them looked poor.

At about eleven o'clock, Kate drove them home, dropping Connie at the gates of the house in Riverdale. Pat wanted to walk her to the door, but Connie told him it would be better if he didn't.

She held up her face, as if expecting a kiss, and he started to brush her lips with his. To his surprise, she took his head in her hands and pressed her mouth to his with a passion that took him completely by surprise. As he turned to go, she said to him, "Call me soon," and he knew this was the beginning of something.

Kate lived on Valentine Avenue, not far from where they had gone to the movie. The last name was Mullaley, and the block she lived in was an Irish enclave in a largely Jewish neighborhood. Pat excused himself after Kate had parked the car with surprisingly expert moves in front of her two-family house.

Doyle told him to wait a minute, that he'd be right out, and they could walk back to the Concourse together.

Doyle lived west of the Concourse on Morris Avenue, not far from Kate, and they walked back in that direction together to where Pat would get the Independent subway to Manhattan. Doyle told Pat he had a beat in the Silk Stocking district, the Seventeenth, on the Upper East Side of Manhattan, but he lived at home with his parents.

"You must have a good hook," Pat said, "to get assigned to that district. That's one of the big ones."

"Well," Doyle explained, "I got a lot of family on the force. My father's a sergeant in the eight-two in the West Bronx, and all my uncles are cops. I don't guess that did me any harm."

"It's a regular Irish social society, isn't it?" Pat said.

"Well, I gotta admit it's a strong element, but I'm not all Irish anyway. My mother was Italian, but she died when I was a kid."

"You sure don't look it," Pat said. "I bet you don't mention it much around the department."

Doyle looked embarrassed. "I guess I don't, really. Most of the guys think I'm pure Irish."

Doyle invited Pat to join him in a beer before he boarded the train for the long trip back downtown. They compared experiences at the academy and their early months on the department. Doyle had been in the class six months prior to Pat. He was already disillusioned with the corruption he saw around him.

"Seems like everybody in the damned department is on the take, and if you don't play ball, you're marked a scumbag."

"What did you expect?" Pat asked. "Didn't you know any cops when you were a kid? Didn't your family teach you anything?"

"I honestly don't think my family does that kind of thing," Doyle said.

"You must be simple," Pat laughed scornfully.

Doyle didn't get angry, but he shrugged. "If they're into graft, they never told me about it, and I never saw any sign of it, though I'm not too sure about my uncle Seamus."

"You belong to the Emerald Society?"

"What else?"

"Well, you could probably get into the Columbia Association also."

"A fat lot of good that would do me," Doyle laughed.

"I'm an undercover guinea. Anyway, I think I'm getting out of the department soon."

"What for?" Pat asked. "You got a better job?"

"No, but I think I'd like to go with the feds. It's cleaner work, but I'll have to get some college credits first. I was thinking of going at night to Fordham. It's not far from here. My uncles said they'd help out with the money. Besides, I was in the service and I've got some GI Bill coming."

Pat changed the subject. "Listen, what's the deal with Katie? You banging her?"

Doyle's face tightened. Pat thought for a minute he was going to hit him. Then he relaxed.

"Listen, Katie isn't that kind of a girl. I've known her since I was a kid. She's really straight. She wants to be an actress, and she's going to go to acting school after she finishes at St. Agnes."

"You gonna marry her?" Pat asked.

"Maybe," Doyle said with a shrug. "I'd like to."

They finished their beers and walked to the Fordham Road Independent station where they shook hands and parted.

"Maybe I'll see you around again sometime soon," Doyle said.

"Yeah," Pat said. "Maybe."

Actually, he saw Doyle, Kate and Connie again the following Friday. They went bowling at the Paradise Alleys across from the theater. Later, they had coffee in the little bar at the back of the alley. It was the first time Pat had really talked to Connie.

"What do you think your father would say," Pat asked, "if he knew I was seeing you?"

Connie shrugged. "I don't really know. At least you're Italian. He's been upset that a lot of the guys I've been seeing have been friends of some of the girls at school—Irish, Polish, even one Jewish guy. He doesn't

want me to marry out of the family, so maybe he would
be pleased."

"Have you told him?"

She shook her head negatively. "Not yet."

"Why not?"

"If he didn't like the idea, he might do something to
separate us, and I'd really like to see you again."

Pat's face flushed with pleasure. "We'll get together
one way or another," he reassured her.

"What about your mother?" Pat asked.

"Mother is dead," Constanza said. "She died when I
was about three or four. I hardly remember her. She
wasn't with me much. Usually, we had someone to take
care of me, an Irish girl or a Spanish girl. I remember
three or four girls taking care of me. Mother was Italian,
but she was from the north. Everybody says she was
very beautiful, and that's the way I remember her. But
nobody talks about her much anymore, even Dad. I
think he was too hurt by her dying so young."

"Do you have any family on her side?" Pat asked.

Constanza shook her head.

"I don't think so. At least we never see them. Their
name was Bonatti, and I know they came from someplace around Milan."

They talked some more about each other, about their
families. Pat told about his father having been a
policeman, which interested Constanza, and how he had
come to know Father Raimundo.

To Pat, all his relationships with women had been
something of a game, a chase, a hunt.

Now, he felt his conversation with Connie was real,
person-to-person. He felt no need to try and impress her
with his accomplishments, with his masculinity, but felt
a close, warm feeling toward her.

As they approached Broadway, he put his arm
around her shoulder, and Constanza leaned happily
against him.

At the Massey house, they again left Connie at the gate. This time, her goodnight kiss was warm and lingering, and she pressed her body to his.

But it was a different sort of feeling than any he'd ever had before. It seemed very clean and sweet and, at the same time, he found it very hard to picture stripping that cashmere sweater from her slim body and raising that chaste, schoolgirl skirt above her knees. She was sexy, but not in the way of any other woman he had known. He thought of her as somehow having a blank between her legs, like a child's doll.

Later, when they dropped Kate on Valentine Avenue, she pressed Pat's cheek lightly with her lips as they said good night. Although it was only the third time they all had been together, there seemed to be an unspoken understanding that these dates were to be a regular thing.

This time, Doyle didn't go up with her separately, but kissed her at the gate to her house as Pat stood by. It was a fast, respectful kiss. Pat wondered whether they acted more passionately in private.

CHAPTER 17

It took a while for Patrolman Pat Conte's friends at the Mulberry SAC to accept his uniform. As soon as he made it clear that he had no intention of busting anyone and didn't regard minor crimes such as running numbers, shylocking or gambling to be venal sins, he was established more solidly than ever at the club.

Al Santini drew Pat aside and suggested that he accept ten dollars a week to keep an eye on things and tip them off if there was any sign of a raid on the gambling. On the side, Santini was running numbers for Tony Bender, but Bender's territory was over in the West Village and so it had nothing to do with Pat anyway.

Still, Pat felt himself drifting from the club members and spending his spare time with his fellow cops. Sometimes, when he was off duty, he would meet with Doyle and they would have a couple of beers midtown or in the Village. Pat had a feeling that he had to grow out of the narrow confines of Mulberry Street, that there was a lot to learn. The guys on the top weren't necessarily smarter than he was, but they knew more things. They knew more about other worlds. It was time for him to start spreading out also.

It wasn't until he had known Doyle for several months that he learned that Doyle's mother was actually his own mother's sister, Maria, and that they, in fact, were first cousins.

This knowledge came when Doyle, in passing, mentioned the fact that he'd been born in Jersey. From there, it wasn't far to making the connection to their childhood. Both men were extremely moved, Pat perhaps even more than Doyle. In a way, Doyle was now his closest relative by blood. It seemed strange because he couldn't seem to get it out of his mind that Doyle was actually Irish.

"You bastard," he said, pounding Regan on the arm. *"Cugini!"*

"I would not want to have my Uncle Seamus hear you say that," Doyle said.

"Fuck him," said Pat. "You gotta come down to the neighborhood and learn to eat some Italian food, some *scungilli,* some *pastafagioli,* not those cardboard pizza pies you get up here in the Bronx."

And they did go down to Luna's a couple of times, but Doyle was uncomfortable. Little Italy was foreign ground to him. Later, they always met in neutral territory, basically in the Village, north and west of the old Italian stamping grounds on Carmine, Thompson and Sullivan Streets.

That month Doyle transferred to the Sixth Precinct. Pat wondered if he'd asked to have that done so that they could be closer together, but it may have been that he was asked to leave the Seventeenth. Doyle stuck to his ideas about not taking graft and this did not make him popular with the other men on the force. In the Sixth, too, he was soon in trouble for his rigid attitudes.

"Loosen up, you stupid Mick," Pat told him. "You ain't going to change the system. Besides, how's a guy going to live on three or four thousand a year? You want to marry Katie, don't you? You want to have kids? You

ain't going to do it on that stinking patrolman's pay, and
if you don't play ball, you ain't going to get much further
than walking the beat."

"That's why I'm getting out of the force," Doyle said.

The same month that Doyle was transferred, Pat's
"uncle," Lieutenant Arthur Marseri invited him for
a meal at Luna's on Grand Street. They had clams Pos-
ilippo and lobster Fra Diavolo, washed down with
two complete bottles of Barolo. The waiters all knew
Arthur Marseri and treated him like a visiting prince.
Most of them seemed to have known him since he was a
child.

Pat had felt close to Arthur since those early days and
since that first dinner in New Jersey. But it still seemed
unusual for him to be invited for a separate meal by Arthur. Pat knew that there was a serious purpose behind
it all.

Later, over espresso and Sambucca, Arthur finally
got to the point.

"We should get together more often, kid," Arthur
said. "You have to keep in touch. I only found out last
week that you been seeing Connie Massey, my niece."

Pat stiffened with apprehension.

"Yeah, I been seeing her," he said cautiously.

"Don't be nervous, kid. It's okay. But you oughta
know you can't get away with anything without Sam
finding out. He's got ears all over the city and so have I.
What are you being so cagy about?"

Pat stammered, "I, I wasn't sure . . . I thought maybe
Sam would get pissed off at me. Maybe he wouldn't
want me hanging around Connie. I mean, she's going to
school and all. She has an education. I'm just a dumb
flatfoot."

"Well, that's the other thing I came to talk to you
about," Arthur said. "You been on the force now nine
months. That's long enough to have a baby. We gotta
start you moving. We gotta start you doing something.

You haven't had any good collars since you been on the force."

"I picked up a couple of good stolen cars," Pat said.

"Shit!" Arthur said. "That's nothing. You gotta do something that will come to the attention of the brass. You gotta get yourself a commendation or something."

"Listen, are you kidding?" Pat said. "There ain't any violent crime in my district, except maybe some guy wants to stab his wife to death. How in hell can I tell when that's gonna happen?"

"Well, I got sources of information," Arthur said. "Sometimes I hear things. Like you know that candy store on Sullivan Street just north of Houston, it's kind of a luncheonette?"

"You mean Napoli E Notte?" Pat asked.

"That's the place."

"Yeah, I know it. It's not in my precinct, but I'm around that neighborhood a lot."

"Well, somebody's been knocking off cigarette machines and pinball machines and all that kind of thing in that neighborhood," Arthur said. "I got a hunch —maybe you might call it a *tip*—that somebody's going to try to knock that place over tomorrow night."

"The luncheonette?"

"That's right."

"What am I going to do about it? I ain't ever in that district."

"You're off tomorrow night, right?"

"Right."

"Well, you spend a lot of time in the Village. Suppose you're walking around one or two o'clock in the morning? Maybe you had a few beers up the street. You been to Mother Bertolotti's or someplace. Maybe you been to one of those coffee houses on MacDougal Street like Rienzi's. So you're walking around, you happen to pass this place, maybe you see a light inside or maybe you just got a hunch, and you nail this guy, see?"

Pat listened with keen interest.

"What's the big deal? So I pinch a guy for B and E. That ain't going to get me no medals."

"This is different," Arthur said. "This is a bad man. He's got a record. He's wanted by the police. They've got a big sheet on him and he's dangerous. He'll be armed."

"Great," Pat said. "What you want me to do, get my balls shot off?"

"Chadrool! You got a gun, too, ain't ya? And you know where *he* is and he don't know where *you* are."

Arthur squeezed a piece of bright yellow lemon into his espresso.

"You just gotta shoot first and make sure that guy doesn't have a chance to talk when he leaves."

"You mean you want me to cool him?" Pat asked.

"I'm not telling you what to do, but we don't want to hear anything from that guy again," Arthur said.

"Who's *we?*" Pat asked. "The department?"

"Look, you just do the job. Don't ask too many questions," Arthur said. "We're trying to get you ahead in the department, right? You got a throwaway piece?"

Pat shrugged. "I never really had occasion to get one."

"Well, get yourself something, a switchblade, an old Saturday-night special, whatever. You always want to carry one of those things. That way, if you get into a beef and you have to shoot somebody, you're not going to get into a lot of trouble. You just throw down the piece or the knife or whatever, say the guy was carrying it, and that he went for you. Make sure you get a couple of his prints on it. Otherwise, you have a bad time with the grand jury. You'd be up on homicide charges and all that shit. I want you to get ahold of something and carry it with you all the time."

"Okay, okay," Pat said.

He was surprised at the talk they'd had. This wasn't

the Arthur he knew, the genial, smiling, young "uncle." This guy had a hard core of steel in him. He was setting Pat up to knock a guy off and he didn't even blink.

Not that Pat was all that shocked. He'd heard of worse things since he'd been on the force. But he knew there was something more behind this job than catching a petty burglar.

If the guy really broke into the store, how could he go wrong? You can't charge a cop with homicide when he interrupts a man in the act of committing a felony.

But still, he felt funny. He was being sent out to kill a man, he didn't even know his name, he didn't even know what he looked like and he didn't know *why* the man had to be killed.

"Don't forget," Arthur said. "It will be about 1:00 A.M. tomorrow night. Don't fuck it up. You do this job right and we'll see that you get a commendation and we'll see that you get off those big flat feet into a nice soft police car. Deal?"

"Deal," Pat said.

"And one more thing," Arthur said. "If you ever go to shoot a guy, make sure you *kill* him. If he lives, you can have a lot of trouble, but if he's dead, everything will come out all right. There won't be any witnesses against you. There won't be any lawsuits. Get it?"

"Got it," Pat said.

CHAPTER 18

Pat Conte's dinner invitation to the home of Sam Massey, Connie's father, followed the Napoli E Notte incident so closely, that it had to be regarded as a token of recognition.

Pat was surprised when he arrived at the Masseys' house in Riverdale. There were at least half a dozen limos parked in the enclosed courtyard. Most of them had uniformed chauffeurs leaning on the fenders or sitting in the cars reading newspapers. A Puerto Rican maid took his felt hat and his reversible raincoat when he entered. He wore his striped suit again, his only suit.

But Constanza was nowhere to be seen. A black man in a striped vest and bow tie led him into the library, a book-lined room in which eight or ten men were standing around drinking, laughing, talking. Among them were Arthur and Sam and Don Antonio, but Father Ray wasn't there. Pat also recognized the councilman, Philip Dimaio, and a magistrate of the city court.

Arthur spotted Pat in the doorway and ushered him over to the bar where a black bartender in a white jacket was dishing out the booze. Pat took a Grant's and soda and Arthur congratulated him on the commendation.

"You did a good job, kid. You could have a hell of a

future in the department. Just keep your nose clean and don't trust anybody that you don't have to. Remember, those Irish bastards are out to get you. They're going to be riding your ass for a while about that medal."

"I can take it," Pat said.

Arthur took him by the arm and brought him over to meet some of the men that Pat didn't recognize. One was Santo Ganci, who was head of the Italian-American Anti-Defamation League. (He turned out to be the father of Paul Ganci, of the Mulberry SAC.) Another was Guido Paterno, a high officer in some bank downtown.

Each time that Pat was introduced, Arthur would say: "This is young Pat. He's one of our family."

In most cases, the other man would nod without much interest, exchange a few words and turn away. Ganci seemed interested in his work as a cop.

"We need more good Italian boys like you on the force, you and Arthur. The Irish have been running the thing too long and now the Jews are moving in, too. The only way we can get justice for our people is to have some of our own on the top. We should have more boys that are interested in enforcing the law," he said, rubbing his hand jovially on Pat's shoulder.

The talk was mostly about politics. Much of it centered around Carmine DeSapio, who seemed in some way to have offended most of the members of the group. Ganci defended the Tammany leader.

"He's a good man. He's the kind we need now," Ganci said. "I know he worked with Uncle Frank in the beginning, but Uncle Frank gave the okay for him to run a clean show and it's the best thing. People have got to learn that Italian leaders aren't all crooks and mob-connected."

Sam interrupted. "Let's face it. He's a big, slick pain in the ass. With him in the seat, you never know who you can trust up there. We gotta do a lot of business with the city and a guy like DeSapio doesn't make it too easy. He keeps going the way he is, he's going to take a big fall, and maybe Uncle Frank with him."

Pat drank, listened, moved around the various groups and said very little. He was by far the youngest man there, in fact, the *only* young man if you didn't count Arthur. There were no women present.

Later, dinner was served in the big, cream-colored, arched dining room. Huge brass candelabras swayed over the table which was set out for formal dining, with three wine glasses at each place and the biggest array of cutlery Pat had ever seen in one place setting.

Pat was seated between Arthur Marseri and Santo Ganci, toward the foot of the table. The dinner, much to his surprise, had very few Italian touches. There was a crabmeat salad with some kind of dressing like mayonnaise with red coloring in it. Then a huge roast beef was rolled in under a silver dome, and the black bartender cut thick slabs of the red meat for each guest. This was accompanied by brussels sprouts, little brown roast potatoes and followed by a spinach salad with bacon, anchovies and hard-boiled eggs. The salad was the only dish that looked even vaguely familiar to Pat.

After the meal, the waiter passed around with a huge silver humidor of Upmann Havana cigars and they drank Carlos Primero, a Spanish brandy, which was the smoothest drink Pat had ever tasted.

There was more talk about politics, about sports, especially about betting on the big baseball and football games and a little about horse racing. Most of it, except the stuff about sports, went over Pat's head and he decided the best thing he could do was to listen and learn rather than make a horse's ass out of himself by trying to get into conversations that he knew little about.

Occasionally, Arthur would turn to him with some small talk about the department, but it was more or less out of politeness. Ganci talked a lot about Italians who were achieving important positions in government and in the church. He was a great admirer of Father Raimundo, who, it seemed, was away at a retreat at the time. Ganci gave Pat his card and told him to be sure and get in touch, that he wanted him to join the society.

Guido Paterno, the banker, Dimaio, the councilman, and Sam Massey huddled together for a long time in the corner and then most of the guests started to leave. Pat looked inquiringly at Arthur who said, "Stick around a while, kid. I think Sam would like to talk to you."

In about a half hour, all the guests had departed. Sam filled another couple of glasses with Carlos Primero from a decanter on the sideboard and motioned Pat to follow him into the library. There Pat and Sam sat together on a huge leather sofa in front of the fireplace, while Arthur sat in an easy chair facing them. Sam fiddled with a silver cigar cutter, carefully trimming the end of his Havana, licking it sensually and elaborately for its entire length and lighting it, all the time not saying a word.

When the cigar was lit and a satisfactory half inch of white ash had formed on the end of it, Massey finally turned to the young policeman.

"I hear you've been seeing Constanza," he said.

"Yes, I have," Pat answered. "But . . ."

"Don't get upset, kid. It's all right. I'm not complaining. Better you than some of those yo-yos she's been meeting around the school. Those rich kids are supposed to have class, but they don't have no class at all. She's better off with one of her own."

Pat had a strange, suffocating sensation. It was true that Constanza had been something special to him, like no other girl he'd known. But he hadn't given a thought to *marriage*. It seemed too soon. He'd hardly gotten started on what he wanted to do. But, as he sat there,

sipping the fine Spanish brandy and smoking Sam's
Havana cigars, he thought to himself that he could do a
lot worse—a lot worse.

What, after all, was wrong with marrying a beautiful
girl, a passionate girl with plenty of money and plenty of
pull? As far as love was concerned, he wasn't sure that
he *didn't* love her. In any event, he didn't know of any
marriages that had been made for love. All had been
made out of convenience, economic necessity, proximity, family pressure or desperation.

"Does Constanza know anything about this?" he
asked.

"What Constanza knows or thinks doesn't matter.
She likes you. Maybe loves you. She wants to get married very much. You'll see, there'll be no problem if we
show approval of you. Too many girls these days are
turning away from the family. I don't want that to happen with Constanza. It really will be like they say, like
gaining a son. We can work together, understand one
another."

"You mean you want me to come into the construction business?" Pat asked.

"We don't have to talk about that now. There's lots of
ways we can work together. Meanwhile, you're working
with my brother Arthur, right?"

"In a way," Pat said.

When he saw Constanza the following week, he said
nothing about the conversation. But this time, he picked
her up at the house and they were given the loan of one
of Sam's cars for the evening. Constanza had tickets to
South Pacific that Sam had gotten for her. At first, Pat
didn't want to accept them, but she explained to him
that they were freebies that Sam had been given through
one of his contacts.

It was Pat's first time in a theater. In fact, the whole
Times Square area was a strange country to him. New
York, to Pat, had always meant the Village and Little

Italy. Then, with Constanza, he had discovered the Bronx, and now, here he was in Times Square.

Afterwards, they went to Toffenetti's for steak and wine and a baked potato.

Driving back up the West Side Highway, Pat suddenly felt that it would be very nice to be rich, although he had never given it much thought before. When they got back to Riverdale, the house was dark except for a light under the porte-cochere and one in the vestibule. Pat parked the big Fleetwood at the side of the house, away from the front entrance.

Constanza had been sitting close to him on the broad bench seat the whole way up. He had been conscious of her warm presence and of her leg pressing against his each time he moved to brake the car. This had been their first date without Katie and Doyle. Although he had kissed her good night many times, he had never been alone with her in such total privacy. It seemed almost without a conscious move on his part that he found her in his arms. He started to kiss her tenderly, softly, but she suddenly seemed to go wild, holding his head between her hands and kissing his eyes, his nose, his cheek, his ear.

When his lips touched hers again, they opened wide, twisting, nipping and biting at his mouth. Although he'd had sex with plenty of girls, he'd never actually kissed one with this sort of passion. His hands moved around to the front of her breast and felt the warm, pulsing forms beneath the soft, sensual surface of the angora sweater she wore. But as he slipped his hand beneath the sweater to unfasten the bra, Constanza seemed to stiffen, even in the midst of her heavy-breathing passion.

"No, no, please. Please don't!"

Pat, feeling uncertain of himself for the first time with a woman, played the game her way and withdrew his hand. They sat there in the car for another ten minutes, kissing and tonguing each other. But with the barrier

Constanza had imposed, the excitement was gone for Pat.

Necking was okay if it was a prelude to something else, but Constanza seemed to think that necking was the whole game. Or maybe it was just that things were going too fast.

Pat wondered what Sam had told Connie of their conversation concerning marriage. She certainly had not said anything indicating she knew about it, and Pat hadn't mentioned it to her. He also wondered what *she* had said about *him* to Sam to cause him to suggest marriage in the first place.

Probably Sam, whose spies would have told him that Pat was seeing her, simply queried Constanza to see how she felt about things. There was that big ape that had been her date the first night. Perhaps Sam was afraid that his daughter would get involved with somebody like *that*. The fact that Katie and Doyle, her best friends, were Irish probably gave Sam fears that Constanza was drifting away from the family.

After another ten minutes of heavy breathing and necking, Pat pulled away.

"Hey," he said, "we're getting the windows all steamed up. I'd better send you back in the house or we'll *both* be in trouble."

He took her to the door and kissed her again, one long, soulful kiss.

"When will I see you again?" she asked.

"Don't worry," Pat said. "You'll see me again soon. Very soon. I'll call you."

Two days later, had lunch with Doyle uptown at . . . . White Rose on Third Avenue.

"You getting a seat in a car?" Doyle asked him.

Pat shrugged. "Seems like it. I'm waiting to hear. My rabbi says it's on."

"Seeing Constanza?" Doyle asked.

"Yeah, I took her out last week."

He debated how much he should tell Doyle. In the brief time they had known one another, Doyle was as close a friend and confidant as anybody he had ever known. Because they were both on the force, Doyle seemed closer than the friends from the old neighborhood in many ways. And the fact that he was the only one that Pat knew who also knew Constanza inclined him to discuss the matter.

"What do you think about getting married, Regan?" Pat asked.

Doyle swallowed a bite of his corned beef sandwich and washed it down with some beer.

"I think it's great! What else is there? I've been asking Katie for a year now, but all she wants to do is get involved in a career."

"That's a lot of bullshit. She'll grow out of it."

"What do *you* think?" Doyle asked.

"I don't know," Pat said. "I mean, what's the good of it? You get saddled with a broad and a bunch of kids right away. You can't spend your money the way you want. You have no freedom. Every job you take, you got to make more money. You've got to answer to someone for every minute of your time. I'm not sure that I'm crazy about it."

"Then how come you asked me?" Doyle asked.

"Well," Pat said, "I've been thinking, I've been wondering, I thought maybe I might make it, I mean marriage, with Constanza."

CHAPTER 19

Pat took a lot of good-natured kidding about the commendation he had won on Sullivan Street, but most of the other cops seemed pleased and impressed that he got it.

The collar and the commendation seemed to be an initiation rite. He was no longer looked on as a rookie in the Five.

About two weeks later, he got a notice posting him to the Sixth Precinct in the West Village. The Charles Street station had a different mood from the Five. It was in the far west part of the Village, surrounded by dark, dismal warehouses over toward the Hudson River wharves, west of Greenwich Street.

The day before Pat reported for duty in the Sixth, Arthur had called him at the rectory.

"We're moving your assignment and getting you a seat over in the Sixth," he said. "The place came vacant when—ah . . . well, never mind. Anyway, there's a seat there and it'll make less fuss for you to ride regular there than in the Fifth, where they know you."

Pat glowed with satisfaction. "Gee, thanks, Arthur."

"That's okay, kid. Just don't get in any trouble. Keep your eyes open and keep your ears open, too."

His partner, Tom Berkholder, was about thirty—a wiry, compact man with the wise and wary look of a country crow. He had been on permanent shore patrol duty in the Pacific with the Seventh Marines during the war, and the story going around the precinct house was that he had won a Silver Star at Guadalcanal though he never mentioned it to Pat.

"You're pretty young to get a seat like this, kid. You must have some hook. I hear you got the powerhouse behind you."

"Listen, I live with an *Italian* priest," Pat said. "The fucking Irish run the powerhouse. Spellman's *their* pope. But I'll admit I had help."

"And you made a pretty good collar, I hear," Berkholder said.

"That was just one of those lucky breaks."

"Well," the young vet said, "I hope you have better luck than the last partner. You're riding in his seat."

"What happened to *him*?"

"We were rounding up a bunch of fags over on Grove Street. You know that little after-hours joint they got there? They were all juiced up out of their minds, pushing and screaming and shrieking. Fucking creeps! We were just rousting them out a little bit, checking them for junk and things like that. No way we could bring that whole mob in anyway.

"We sent out a 10-85 while we were waiting. Meanwhile, a half a dozen of them got away up Seventh Avenue. Anyway, all of a sudden this car comes roaring down the street. Frank Novak, that's the guy who was my partner, was standing in the middle of the street making sure that none of the fags make a run for it while I lined them up for a frisk, leaning against the wall. Anyway, I hear this car roaring down, and there's a crazy-looking fag in a blond wig leaning out of the window yelling, 'Watch out, girls. Here I come, ready or not.' Next thing I know, the fucking car hits Novak right

in the back and throws him up in the air about five feet.
The car, which is a red Dodge coupe, keeps going before
I could do anything about it. All I can catch is two letters on the plate. The fags all turn around, screaming
and giggling. I fire one shot in the air and I say, 'The
next one of you creeps that moves is going to get a bullet
right up his ass!' Meanwhile, Novak is laying in the gutter and groaning.

"I get back into the car and call in a 10-13, and I
must say those guys came fast, about four cars from all
directions. We get an ambulance, an emergency squad
car over there real fast, but Novak is in bad shape. We
get him up to St. Vincent's and they tell us he's got a
broken back.

"Meanwhile, I book the fags for everything I can
think of—indecent exposure, vagrancy, loitering for
purposes of prostitution, sodomy and disturbing the
peace. I guess you know what happened."

"They sprung 'em the next day, right?"

"Right."

"What about Novak?"

"Poor bastard is a living vegetable. I was up to see
him last week. All he can move is his eyes and he makes
these sounds like, 'ungh, ungh.' It makes me want to
puke. We were partners for about four years and I really
got to know him good. He's got a wife and two kids out
in Elmhurst somewhere, too."

"Christ," Pat said, shaking his head. "That's some act
to follow."

"Shit. I guess it's all in the job," Berkholder said.

Doyle was still working out of the Sixth, working a
beat on Bleecker Street, west of Seventh Avenue. When
their schedules overlapped, Pat and Regan would either
take out Connie and Katie on a double, or, if it were the
late shift, go bouncing around the Village bars. They
had a regular circuit: the Kettle of Fish and the Minetta
on MacDougal Street, Louie's in Sheridan Square, the

Riviera on Seventh Avenue and Chumley's, a dark, secret place on Bedford Street. Then, way up Hudson Street to the White Horse, an old longshoremen's bar, that had become something of a writers' hangout. They could have freeloaded drinks in all of these places, but traveling with Doyle made that more trouble than it was worth.

"I don't see what the big deal is," Pat argued. "We're doing those guys a favor by hanging around. If they have a stickup or anything, we're right there to help."

"Yeah. But it still ain't right. You start in that way, you'll wind up . . ."

"Okay. Can the crap. That's why you're still walking a beat and I've got a seat," Pat said.

Riding the radio car was quite a change from pounding the pavement in Little Italy. Pat rode as recorder while Berkholder drove the car. It took a while to get used to handling the radio and the light switches and all the other mechanisms inside the car and to learn to recognize the various kinds of signals on the radio.

Berkholder seemed to be able to hear them in his sleep (which he often did). There were always a couple of parking lots off under the West Side Highway where they could pull off for a snooze, letting the radio buzz sporadically in their ears. But Berkholder never seemed to fall asleep to the point where he didn't hear the name of their car when it was called.

Pat quickly learned the routine. They were assigned the four-to-twelve shift. Most of the crime took place between eight o'clock at night and two o'clock in the morning. That first tour was a hot weekend, too, with plenty of action.

The first night, they investigated two reports of prowlers on the roof, and one complaint from a woman who said she was being molested by Peeping Toms, although her bedroom window was on the twelfth floor and faced west over an empty row of tenements. She was a tense-looking woman in her forties, still pretty. She had blonde hair with streaks of gray in it, knotted back behind her head in a George Washington bun.

"This man," she was saying in cultured tones used in finishing schools, "has a telescope. He's on one of those roofs, I know. Every once in a while, I see the gleam from his lens."

"Do you see it now?" Berkholder asked, looking out the window across the rooftops.

"He probably heard your car coming and escaped," she said. "You men must be tired, riding around all night. Would you like a drink, or a cup of coffee?"

Berkholder flicked a surreptitious wink at Pat. "No thanks, ma'am. We've got to get back to duty. There's a lot of crime in the streets down there."

"Well, I'll call you again if there's any more problems."

"Do that, ma'am, although I don't know if we'll be the ones to respond."

"Well, feel free anyway to come by for a drink or a cup of coffee or anything," she said.

"Yes, ma'am," Berkholder said, respectfully, as they backed out the door.

As they rode down in the elevator, Berkholder said to him, "Cheez! We get two or three of those hooples every week. Mostly old dames. Cop buffs."

"Ever fuck any of 'em?" Pat said.

Berkholder shrugged. "Once or twice I tried it, but they're all nuts. It ain't worth it."

The next call was from a gray-haired old lady who said that there was a stray dog wandering around in Washington Square Park. She thought they should pick it up and take it to the ASPCA.

"I'm sorry, ma'am," Berkholder said, "but we have no facilities for handling dogs. Why don't you call the ASPCA yourself? They'll come around and take care of it."

"I don't see why the police can't handle this," the lady said.

"I'm sorry, ma'am. We're just not equipped for the job. Call the ASPCA. That's their department."

On the way downstairs, they rousted out an old drunk, sleeping in his own vomit in the hallway.

"Come on, grandpa. Get up," Berkholder said. "This ain't the Mills Hotel."

"Yes, sir. Yes, officer," he said. "Listen, can you let me have a half a buck for a pint of wine? I really need it."

"You had enough already," Berkholder said. "Don't sleep it off on my beat."

"You see? That's what makes criminals out of us!" the old man said, as he slumped off into the night.

The next call was for 95 Christopher Street, a thirties-modern apartment house perched among the brownstones, tenements and seedy storefronts at the corner of Bleecker and Christopher. A balding man in a satin dressing gown met them. He looked a lot like Cedric Hardwicke, the British movie star, but he spoke with a soft, Southern drawl.

"Officer," he said, "I don't like to make trouble, but one of my, ah, guests seems to have taken off with my wallet and my gold wristwatch and cufflinks. It wasn't over five minutes ago. You might still catch him if you look around the neighborhood."

"Do you know the man?" Berkholder asked.

"Well—ah, ah—casually. I just know his first name."

"In fact, you just met him tonight," Berkholder said. "Right?"

The man's hairless head flushed red. "We were casual acquaintances," the man admitted.

"Where did you meet him?" Berkholder asked.

"Well, I, ah, I met him on Waverly Place."

"In the street?"

"We sort of struck up a conversation," the man admitted.

"He was a prostitute, right?" Berkholder said.

The man flushed with rage. "How dare you? You are here to protect the citizens, not to insult them!"

Berkholder sighed. "Look, mister. I'm just trying to find this kid for you. If we know something about him, it will be easier to find him. Maybe he's back at his old post by now. Most guys that get hit like you did don't complain anyway. Do you want to give me a description?"

"Will it get the boy in trouble?"

"Don't you *want* him to get in trouble?" Berkholder asked.

"Well, I don't want the boy to go to *jail*."

"Then, you want us to forget the whole thing?"

The man appeared to ponder for a moment. "Well, maybe he'll bring it back. It wasn't so much anyway. Maybe a couple of hundred dollars' worth of stuff."

"Not much to you, maybe," Berkholder said, "but it'd sure wreck my budget for the week."

"Well, I think he'll come back," the man said wistfully.

"Listen, mister," Berkholder said. "Do me a favor. Next time you're not going to complain, don't call the cops, will yah?"

Toward the end of the shift, at about 11:15, they were sent to investigate a complaint of strange smells in the hall of a plush apartment house at 41 Fifth Avenue. A small, gray-haired man answered their ring. He looked like the last sort of person you'd see in Greenwich Village, Pat thought. But his well-cut flannel suit and manicured fingernails and the fussy perfection of his chrome and leather apartment gave at least a clue to what he was doing down there.

"I'm embarrassed to have called you, officers. I don't

usually like to bother the police. But there's been an odor coming from the apartment next door for about four days now and it's really unbearable. I've rung the bell several times, but nobody answers. It's gotten so I can't sleep. You probably can't smell it now because I've sprayed the place with Airwick."

Pat was sure that Berkholder would tell the old guy to go screw himself, but Berkholder seemed interested and serious.

"Who lives there, sir, in the next apartment?"

"It's quite a nice elderly woman named Eloise Van Houten. I don't know her very well. She stays to herself. But she's always been a lady, and she's never made any trouble. I can't imagine what the cause of that smell is, but I just can't bear it anymore. And at the rent I'm paying, I don't see why I should have to put up with that sort of thing."

The two policemen went down the hall to the next apartment. There was a smell all right, and it was a strong one. It reminded Pat of the air coming up from the sewers on a hot summer night. Berkholder pressed the buzzer and they could hear the loud, harsh ring of the bell inside the apartment.

"That'd wake the dead," Pat said.

Berkholder gave him a funny look. "I think there's a stiff in there," he said. "Let's get the super."

In the cellar, they rousted out a grumbling, sleepy janitor who found a set of passkeys and escorted them back to the corridor. As they pushed open the apartment door, a cloud of vapor rushed from the room like an explosion of hot, stinking breath. There was the stomach-turning smell of rancid meat mixed with an underlying odor of cooking gas. Berkholder grabbed the smoldering cigar stub from the janitor's hand and stamped it out.

"There's a stove on in there," he said. "Wait a minute!"

Holding his handkerchief over his nose, he dashed across the room and turned off the gas. There was the sound of tinkling glass as he smashed out one of the windows.

"He should not do that," the janitor complained. "Landlord, he no like."

"Fuck the landlord," Pat said.

Berkholder came out again and they stood there a few minutes while the cross draft of the night air ventilated the apartment. After a few minutes, Berkholder decided it was safe to go in.

"Okay. Let's get it over with," he said.

Inside, the apartment was all brocade and overstuffed furniture right out of a movie of the thirties. It was one of those one-and-a-halfs with a pullman kitchen. Lying on a chaise was a billowing mass of bruised, purple meat which could only barely be identified as the nude body of a woman.

The neck seemed nearly cut in half with the swelling of the flesh which had tightened some kind of necklace into a noose. And the hands, too, looked like the joints of a puppet where the meat had swelled around bracelets that the woman had been wearing. But the bracelets couldn't be seen beneath the rotting flesh.

"Okay," Berkholder said. "She's going to bust all over the floor. I handled a few of these before. Let's let this room air out while we call the sergeant on this one," Berkholder said.

To the janitor, he said, "You watch that nobody comes in here."

In about ten minutes, the sergeant arrived, along with a unit of the Emergency Service Division. Two emergency men came in, took a look in the door, went downstairs and got gas masks and a plastic body bag, put the gas masks on, went in, tied a tag to the big toe of the right foot, trying to move the body as little as possible. Pat, though half-nauseated himself, stared with fascination. As the men tried to slide the body carefully into the bag, it began to crack at the stomach, oozing a blackish purple fluid.

"Come on. Let's get out of here," Pat said. "We can fill out the papers downstairs."

CHAPTER 20

It took Tom Berkholder a couple of days to check Pat out with some of the boys he knew over in the Fifth. Until then, he went easy on letting Pat know what "contracts" he had in the neighborhood.

"I knew you were okay, being from a cop family and all that," Berkholder said, "but you can't be too sure. They got a lot of shoo-flies around these days. I'll show you the contracts we got while we drive around.

"Like that building we checked out the other day, 95 Christopher. The doorman gives us a hat a month, about a twenty, to look the other way when some of his tenants park a little too long in front of the house.

"We also pick up a couple of sawbucks from the warehouses over by the river for not ticketing their trucks. Then, in back of that barber shop on Christopher, they got a little policy drop. It's a small job, but it's good for about ten a week.

"You can eat on the arm at the Waldorf Cafeteria over on Sixth and Jimmy over at the Horse will run a tab on you, but he usually forgets to collect it and if he does, he only picks up on about one drink in five just to make it look good.

"The doorman over at the Bleecker Street Hotel makes book, and he's good for a couple of presents from time to time. And the rest is the usual stuff, accidents. We get a ten from the highway tow outfit and they give us a boost if there's any repeats on it.

"On a weekend, you can get ten or twenty-five bucks from the after-hours joints and usually I take my morning coffee and read the papers outside that check cashing joint on West Fourth. He throws me a couple of bucks every day.

"Sometimes some of the supermarkets give us a call to escort the payroll, and they usually throw us a fin then, too. There's a lot of other stuff around, too, but I'm just a grass eater. I ain't trying for any big scores. Just pay the rent. Keep ahead of the bills."

Pat nodded. It was impressive. He wondered how much they'd make if they *were* real meat eaters. This way he figured he was good for a hundred to two hundred extra a month above his salary in nontaxable income.

On Thursday of that week, Berkholder suggested that they run over to St. Vincent's and see Novak.

"I wish I could *bring* the son of a bitch something—a book, some playing cards, a bottle of booze—but he can't *do* anything. The only way you know he can hear you is he rolls his eyes a little bit. Sometimes, he's just sleeping."

Berkholder pulled over to the Aphrodite Flower Shop opposite the Women's House of Detention on Sixth Avenue.

"Hey, Pop," he yelled inside to the Greek florist. "I'm taking one of these geraniums. I'll pay you later." The florist nodded morosely and waved him on.

"Don't be worry," he said. "You take."

Novak was at St. Vincent's Hospital. The injured patrolman was in a private room, lying flat on the bed,

covered with a sheet to his armpits. There were four or
five bottles hung from hooks around him, feeding into
his veins.

"He can't eat nothin'," Berkholder whispered. "They
got to feed him through the needle. And when he wants
to take a leak, like they run a pipe into his bladder and
drain him out. I'd like to get the fag son of a bitch that
ran him down. I really would."

Novak, who lying down, looked as if he must be six-
three or -four, rolled his eyes furiously.

"He must of heard you," Pat said. "Look at him
rolling his eyes."

"That's right, buddy," Berkholder said to the prone
form. "We'll get that son of a bitch one of these days. I'll
never forget the look of that red Dodge and that blondie
fag. Wonder if he was wearing a wig? If only I could
have gotten the number. I got a couple of letters. It was
a Bronx car. It had a BX. That's all I got. The guy
probably only comes in like once a month. Maybe if he
knows what he did, he doesn't come in at all. But those
fags can't stay away from here. This is where they get
their action. He'll be back."

"Ungh, ungh," Novak said from the bed.

They sat around for ten or fifteen minutes making
small talk while Tom Berkholder gave his former
partner the news of the precinct and the gossip.

"Harry Martin made plainclothes," he said. "He's
only been in the squad five years. That son of a bitch
must have had some pull . . . Eddie Singer picks up this
hooker over on Eighth Street. He's gonna run her in,
see? So he starts to take her into the car. She says she's
gonna give him a blow job for nothing, so he figures,
'what the hell.' It's not such a big collar anyway. He
takes her into the back of the Van Zawdt Hotel.
And then, he just gets a hunch. He says, 'Wait a minute.'
Then he checks out her boobs. It was a fucking TV! It

was a guy! I nearly split a gut when he told me about it. He gave the kid a rap in the teeth and then he threw him out in the street. I would have beat the shit out of him. But some of them are really good. I mean you can't tell the difference, you know? They squeeze up their tits and they take these injections, these hormones. They shave real smooth. The best way you can tell is the legs and the arms. Some of them got tattoos. And they got these muscles in the arms and veins in the hands. That's the way I usually tell, but, boy I've been fooled a few times. Remember that dame in the caftan, or whatever you call it, coming out of Cafe Society?"

"Ungh, ungh."

"She really had me fooled. She was so little and cute . . . I mean he. I was just thinking. You know, suppose I had kissed her or let her blow me? I mean *him*. Imagine how you'd feel afterwards when you found out? This is the screwiest precinct I ever worked in. You don't find nothing like that nowhere else. Listen, this here is Pat Conte. He's a good man. His old man was a cop. Got an inspector's funeral and everything. Right, Pat?"

"That's right," Pat said.

"He's riding with me, ah, temporarily, till you get on your feet again. Then they got another spot lined up for him. Right, Pat?"

"That's right."

"Well, we'll see you around next week, hey, Frank? You'll probably be getting out pretty soon."

"Ungh, ungh."

"You know," Berkholder said as they left, "I think he really enjoyed that visit and I could see that he liked you."

"Shit. It made me sick to look at the poor bastard," Pat said.

"Yeah, well I saw the doctor last time. You know all that stuff about temporary. That's just for Novak's benefit. He got a bad, serious spinal injury. No way he's gonna be anything but paralyzed the rest of his life. That's if he lives. Maybe the son of a bitch will be lucky if he doesn't. I go out to Elmhurst once in a while to visit his wife and kids. Course, she still pulls his full pay. That helps. And the kids are old enough so she can go out and work a little. Nice-looking head, too. It's really a pity."

They called in to see if there'd been any action while they were gone. They had let the desk know that they were over at the hospital and they'd left the phone number so they were pretty well covered. There was nothing doing, but they had hardly settled in the car when a call came of an armed robbery in a liquor store on Christopher Street.

"Suspects headed west on Christopher," the radio said. "It's a Mutt and Jeff team. Tall, skinny, chocolate colored guy. Narrow-brimmed straw hat. Furry-looking plush car coat. Yellow pants, pegged. Short guy, stocky, light skinned. Might be Hispano. Wearing knitted blue stocking hat. Corduroy fingertip coat. Some kind of pants. The owner watched them and they didn't duck into the subway, so they're headed somewhere west on Christopher. They could of turned up or down Bleecker. All cars be on lookout. These men are armed and dangerous."

Pat flicked the light and siren switch and they raced down Seventh Avenue, made a screaming right on Christopher and headed toward the river. Just on the far side of Hudson, near the Jersey tubes entrance, a car shot out in front of them, tires screaming, and headed west towards the drive.

Berkholder stepped on the gas and started in pursuit. The car wheeled right on West Street and roared up the road against the traffic. Pat loosened his gun and leaned out the window.

"Don't shoot," Tom said. "It ain't worth it. We'll catch the bastards."

There was a twisting, wheel-screaming pursuit up the highway, past the longshoremen and the trucks, loading and unloading from the docks. The patrol car finally overtook the fleeing Pontiac just before the Round-the-Island Circle Line Pier on Forty-second Street and crowded it right to the edge of the stringpiece, almost into the river. Pat was out before the cars had come to a complete stop. The patrol car's doors effectively sealed off the right-hand side of the Pontiac, and on the left-hand side, a man would have to jump out cautiously in order not to land in the water. Pat approached from the left with his gun drawn. An ashen-faced, thin, middle-aged man in a plaid sports jacket and bow tie came out slowly, looking frightened, with his hands up.

"Don't shoot, mister, don't shoot! There's a couple of guys . . ."

But before he could finish the sentence, the rear door of the Pontiac burst open. Pat found himself staring into the muzzle of a big German Luger and behind that, another gun held by a skinny guy in a straw hat.

"Freeze, whitey, or I'll blow you away," the little guy said.

Pat was just starting to drop the gun when two shots rang out and he saw the window behind the two men splinter. The two gunmen turned their eyes to check the source of the shots. Pat raced for the cover of a pile of wooden beams lying to the side of the Pontiac and flattened himself behind it.

The shots had come from Tom, who had managed to crawl across the patrol car's seat and exit on the passenger side. Pat kept his head down and just kept his gun pointing in the general direction of the car.

"Okay, you two motherfuckers, back out!" Pat said. "Hands up! Throw out those guns first or you're going to be all asshole from the neck down. You got them covered, Tom?"

"Right."

"I'm not going to count past one."

There was a moment's delay, and the two pieces came clattering onto the asphalt pavement of the pier. Cautiously, Pat raised himself, keeping a bead on the two men as they backed out of the car. The driver in the plaid jacket was cramped against the fender, his fingers jammed into his mouth in terror.

"Okay," Pat said. "Now lean against that car and keep your feet back."

"Don't shoot, whitey," the little guy said. He seemed to be the talker of the two. "They was only toy guns anyway. We didn't mean nothing."

"Just lean, cocksucker," Pat said.

By this time, Tom was around on his side and scooped up the pistols.

"Son of a bitch," he said. "You know, he's right?"

One of the guns was a perfectly modeled, cast-iron version of a German Luger, but it had no mechanism whatsoever. It was probably made for collectors. The other was a cigarette lighter in the form of a pistol. But as they started to frisk the two men, they found an assortment of penknives, gravity knives, nail files, screwdrivers and other paraphernalia, including a well-sharpened beer can opener.

"Check the hats," Tom said.

Pat reached over and grabbed off the blue knit cap and the straw hat. In the foldup of the knit cap, he found two single-edged razor blades.

"Boy, you sons of bitches, you really come heeled, don't ya?" he said.

"Gonna do a job, do it right," the little fellow said.

As they talked, Pat could hear a sound of approaching sirens. A short, roly-poly sergeant jumped out of the first car and ran toward them.

"What's up?" he asked.

"Well, I'd say kidnaping, grand larceny auto, armed

robbery, possession of dangerous weapons, assault and a few other things."

"You guys are way out of your territory, aren't you?" the sergeant said, noticing the big "6" on the side of the squad car.

"We were in hot pursuit," Tom said. "We picked these guys up on Christopher."

"Well, we'll take it from here," the sergeant said.

"Oh, no, you don't," Tom said. "This is our collar. We're going to have to explain those shots somehow, you know."

"Well, I'll tell you what. We'll give you an assist on it. I mean, you can't take it in the Tenth, you guys are from the Sixth."

"We're taking it," Tom said. "You guys get in the car."

Pat put the cuffs on them.

"*We're* taking the collar," the sergeant said. "We'll give you an assist. This is an order. Looks like you're going to need help anyway to get your car out of here. How you going to drive those guys to the station house? You got a busted left front tire. Your wheel's all out of line. You might as well ride down to the Tenth Squad with us and we'll help you book 'em."

"Son of a bitch," Tom said.

"What was that?" the sergeant said, whirling.

"Nothing. I was just talking to myself."

The sergeant took the two prisoners in his patrol car and started off toward the precinct house with Tom. Pat radioed in a brief report of the proceedings and was told to go ahead with the booking and report in later. A car would come to pick up the damaged patrol car.

As they rode downtown in the car the sergeant had sent up from the Sixth after the booking, Pat turned to Tom Berkholder seriously.

"If those guys had had real guns," he said, "I'd a been a dead man."

"They had you there, all right," Tom said.

"Well, let's just say that's one I owe you," Pat said to his partner.

CHAPTER 21

Miss Katie Mullaley
Radisson Hotel
Minneapolis, Minnesota

Darling Katie:
   Where oh where has your little boy
gone? I suppose you're wondering.
He's gone to the capital to take the
king's shilling. Seriously, becoming
a fed seems to be a grim business.

They work us from morning to
night, around the clock.

I am staying with two guys from
the National Security Administration
in a rooming house on F Street.
There's not much privacy, but then,
I don't need much. Did you know that
there are over one hundred and fifty
violations that a G-man is supposed
to know about and be responsible
for? I feel like I can't even step
out of the door without violating
some federal regulation. But that's
about _all_ I'll violate around here.

Not only don't we have much time
for any shenanigans, but the
department keeps a close eye on us
and I understand anybody even _seen_
going into a pickup bar or any bar
at all that isn't on the approved
list will find themselves bounced
out of here so fast, it would
make his head swim.

But it's a pretty exclusive group
and a serious one. A very different
bunch, I might say, from those I
encountered at the Police Academy.

They have topflight men with
experience in the field teaching
all the courses, such as bank
robbery, extortion, espionage,
sabotage and so forth.

They're very strict and you never
know what it is they're after you
for. During the first couple of
weeks here, they called three guys
out of class and they were never

seen again. Nobody ever knew why
they were let go. A lot of the guys
are very nervous about this, but I
don't think that I will get into
any trouble and I think that my
military and police training will
be very useful.

I'm glad to hear that you finally
got a break in a show and I know
you'll do very well out there in
the boondocks. Don't eat too much
smorgasbord (ha, ha). I like your
figure the way it is. At least South
Pacific is a show that a person
wouldn't be ashamed to take his
parents or children to, unlike much
of the entertainment they have
around nowadays. I hope living in
the Village has not turned you into
some kind of a bohemian, but I know
you, and I don't think that anybody
with your background could ever
go wrong.

I don't think that this is the
time to get serious while we're both
more or less shaping up our careers.
But I hope you will reconsider our
talk about marriage. I know we're
right for each other, and I know
that after I get my permanent
assignment, I will want to settle
down to a more normal life than was
possible for me on the force. I
certainly don't blame you for not
wanting to marry a cop. It is a very
tough life. But I think that the
bureau is a different matter.

As far as your career's concerned,
I sincerely wish you the best of
luck, but you know,"Many are
called and few are chosen," so you
don't have to feel disappointed if
you don't make it and become a big
star. I will always love you,
regardless, as I do now.

I had a good farewell party and
booze-up with Pat and some of the
other guys in the Sixth when I left.
They're a good bunch and I really
hated to leave, but I didn't like
what it was doing to me or to them,
for that matter. As far as I can
see, Pat is a good cop, but there
is a hell of a lot of temptation.

I better hit the books now because
I think they are going to pull a
surprise quiz on us tomorrow.

Good night and love and kisses.
Write soon.

Yours forever,

Regan

            *   *   *

Mr. Pat Conte
Our Lady of The Sacred Heart
(Rectory)
New York, New York

Dear Pat:
You know I'm not much at letter
writing, so I hope you'll forgive

me, but this is the worst grind
I've seen since Parris Island. It is
real GI and strict, but I think
it is all for the best (I better
say that because I think they read
our mail). But seriously, the
training is good and there is an
entirely different attitude here
toward the work than there is in
the department.

I suppose everybody here would be
considered a square by the guys in
the Sixth, but they're all very
intelligent men with good
backgrounds and well mot'vated. Of
course, some of the stuff seems
similar to the training we had in
the academy, but the law is
different here. You would be amazed
at some of the things though that
the feds are responsible for, like
arresting people that set forest
fires in the park.

This is our eighth week, and we
are in temporary quarters in
Quantico, Virginia where we are
taking weapons and combat training.
So far, it's pretty much the same
old stuff, the .38 on the .41 frame,
Thompson submachine guns, and so on.
If you remember, the guys that
taught us at the academy had been
trained here at the FBI, so it's
not very different from what we
learned.

Actually, a few of us with police
experience are pretty much toward

the top of the class in this
training, but some of the judo and
defensive stuff they give us is
pretty rough and a bit more intense
than we got in the department.
There's a real gung-ho marine type
spirit here anyway which is not like
some of the wise-ass attitudes I
remember from police training days.

We spend a lot of time on what the
bureau calls defensive tactics. This
is kind of a mishmash of judo,
juijitsu, karate and all that sort of
thing. We learn how to disarm a man
holding a knife, a gun or a club and
so forth. Again, like what we had
at the academy, but these guys don't
fool around. One guy went to the
infirmary the other day, nursing a
nut swollen as big as a baseball.
All the instructor said was, "You
gotta move fast if you don't want
to get hurt."

We also learned a lot of
come-along holds and things of
that sort.

A lot of the training program
here deals with fingerprint
identification and classification
and methods of lifting prints, that
is, we dust the light areas with
black powder and the black areas
with white powder and we lift the
latent prints. Actually, we didn't
get much of that at the academy,
and I found it interesting.

Also, we're taught a lot about

crime scene searches, the kind of things you do when you're a detective and how to make moulage impressions of tire tracks and footprints and things like that.

I'm glad we had that party at Delaney's before I left because I'm sure not geting any action down here.

Most of the guys are very nervous about making it. We already lost six guys out of our class of fifty and I think there'll be a few more going soon, so nobody wants to risk being bounced after having come this far. I really think that this is a top outfit and that a good man can accomplish a lot here. I know you're thinking of taking law courses and that's a very good idea. It will be excellent background for the work here, also. Why don't you think about joining up with the Fee Bees?

Despite all this, I miss the bunch at the Sixth. Give my love to Tom and Riley and all the rest and keep your nose clean. My sincere love to Connie. When are the nuptials? And if you see Katie, give her a kiss for me, but not too hard.

Your cousin,

Regan

At the end of the sixteen weeks came the toughest test of all. Every agent knew that before he could successfully complete his course, during the last week of training, he had to meet The Director—nobody ever referred to J. Edgar Hoover any other way.

Each future agent had to go in, shake The Director's hand and say a few words as casually as possible.

This was a hazardous duty assignment. The agents took intensive training on just how to handle this situation. Over the years, many potential FBI men were discharged from the service because The Director thought they looked like truck drivers or had clammy handshakes or simply didn't "fit the image" of the FBI.

But Regan had a fair idea of what the image of an FBI man was, and he felt sure that The Director wouldn't bounce him.

Still, he listened carefully as the counselors tipped off the class as to proper behavior.

"The Director likes his men well-groomed," the counselor said.

"Watch out for red ties. He considers them a sign of insincerity, and I suggest you guys pack an extra handkerchief because if there's one thing The Director can't stand, it's somebody with a moist palm. Oh, and listen, I suggest you don't smoke all morning before the meeting because he really hates tobacco and he can smell it on your clothes in a minute. I see you're all wearing dark suits like we told you. Now, take those handkerchiefs and fold them in the breast pocket."

As the counselor talked, Doyle looked around the anteroom, which was in effect a museum of FBI artifacts. On one wall hung a white plaster facsimile of John Dillinger's death mask. Beside it was the straw hat he wore when he was gunned down in front of the Biograph Theater by SA Melvin H. Purvis. Beside that was the Corona Belvedere cigar that had been in his pocket.

On another segment of the wall was a framed list of FBI men who had died in action—about twenty-five of them.

Another section of the room was a revolving rack with dozens of newspaper cartoons, praising the exploits of G-men. The rest of the wall was covered by hundreds of scrolls and plaques presented to The Director by different groups, ranging from bible schools to American Legion posts.

The office of The Director was huge, about fifty feet long and covered by deep-pile red carpet. When the door opened, you had to walk across thirty-five feet of that ankle-deep rug to the oversized mahogany desk behind which sat The Director, his bulldog face thrust forward and challenging.

On his desk was a pair of brass pistol lamps, a small potted palm and a plaque which said: "Two feet on the ground are worth one in the mouth." Also on the desk were two small American flags on standards, with gold eagle tops. In the middle of the desk was a small replica of the FBI seal. Behind The Director were two larger American flags with gold eagles on top and a huge replica of the seal between them.

When his turn came, Doyle sucked in his gut, wiped his palm on the inside of his pocket, and marched in a military fashion to the center of The Director's desk. The Director watched him cross the long stretch of carpet without a change of expression in his ice-gray eyes.

As Doyle neared the desk, The Director stood up and in a jerky movement, reached across the desk and extended his hand. His movements reminded Doyle of a small mechanical man he had seen once on the Steel Pier in Atlantic City.

Regan took the offered hand in his huge fingers and was surprised to find that it was small and soft in texture, and if it wasn't *damp*, it was at least moist. Regan wondered if The Director wiped *his* hand before each candidate came in.

A harsh, strangled voice issued from The Director's impassive face.

"Welcome to the bureau," he said, "and congratulations."

"Thank you, sir," Regan said—and that was *it*.

He turned on his heel and walked back the long length of carpeting. As he turned to close the door behind him, he looked toward The Director for a final nod of good-bye, but The Director was sitting deep in his huge swivel chair, his arms laced across his chest, staring at the door waiting for the next candidate.

After training, each agent was asked to fill out the "Office of Preference List," designating the three offices in which he would prefer to serve. Regan listed New York, Washington, D.C., and Atlanta, Georgia in that order.

Naturally he drew Atlanta.

CHAPTER 22

In an unobtrusive Village steakhouse, a family meeting was taking place to which Pat Conte had not been invited. Present was the entire Marseri family, Don Antonio, Sam, Father Raimundo, and Arthur.

It was, in effect, a monthly council at which the four brothers discussed the affairs of their various relatives and other family business over three-inch-thick steaks.

The brothers were treated like visiting nobility by the red-coated waiters in the small, downstairs restaurant, marked only by a brass plaque, "Julius Lombroso—Steaks and Chops." They were given a table in the rear corner, and the settings were taken off all the tables immediately surrounding their area.

Lieutenant Arthur Marseri and Father Raimundo were the first to arrive. They sat talking quietly and sipping Scotch, waiting for the others.

"How are things in the department, Arturo?" Father Ray said.

Arthur extended his right hand with fingers splayed, waving them back and forth in the familiar gesture of equivocation.

"*Mezza-mezza.* You know, not bad, not good. And you?"

"Things are all right, but the parish needs a lot more money. We didn't raise nearly so much from the festival this year as we usually do. They've got to give us a bigger cut from the gambling concessions. We just can't survive on what they're giving us now. Either that, or we need more business."

"We'll talk to Antonio about that. He probably can arrange it. How about the kid, Pat? Any problems?"

"Well, I guess he's a good kid. He *is* a good kid. But you know, he doesn't come to confession anymore? He doesn't come to mass? He's hanging around with all those *zingara* in the Village. He still comes around sometimes to the club to see his friends on Mulberry Street, but I think he's becoming a real beatnik. He spends a lot of time with that partner of his from the patrol car and with that Irishman, Doyle. It seems that he's drifting away from his people, and now he's talking about getting his own place over there in the Village. I know, I know, a young boy has to have girls, has to have sex. But now he's almost engaged to Constanza, and I think he should be more discreet."

Arthur laughed. "Listen, he's got to sow his oats sometimes, right? Sure, maybe it's a sin. He doesn't want to talk to you about it. You're in the family. Maybe he's taking his confession somewhere else. I hear that he goes to Our Lady of Pompeii over on Carmine Street."

Father Raimundo looked interested. "Is that so? He never mentioned that. I'll ask Father Raphael over there what's going on. I'm not spying, mind you. But it would make me feel better to know that he still goes to mass sometimes."

"Well, after all," Arthur said, "that's where he works now. It's good for him to be part of the community, to go to church there, to know what's going on. He's a smart boy. I think he's going to get ahead, fast."

At this point, Sam and Don Antonio came in

together. Sam wore a Burberry coat and an Irish tweed hat. Under it, he wore a heather tweed jacket, dark gray slacks and soft Gucci loafers. He was holding his older brother, Don Antonio, by the arm. Don Antonio wore the black, wide-brimmed Borsalino he favored with a velvet-collared chesterfield and the dark suit and tie he always wore on his evenings out. He was only sixty-five but he looked ten years older, his face drawn into gray lines of concern. Sam, on the other hand, had the flushed, rosy face of the country squire and the hearty manner to match.

"Well," Sam said. "The two kids are here. I guess we can get going. We got a quorum. Here, let me help you off with your coat, Anthony."

There was already a bottle of Black Label on the table and the waiter, without being asked, poured drinks all around. Raimundo and Anthony took theirs straight in a shot glass, like medicine. But Arthur and Sam mixed theirs with soda.

There was a basket of sesame bread sticks on the table on which they munched as they talked. Sam and his brother, Anthony, usually discussed the more serious family affairs in the limousine on the way down. It had the advantage of total privacy, for one thing. But Don Antonio seemed to still have some unfinished business as they sat down to the drinks.

"You understand about the fuel oil, Sam, for the state hospitals? You'll have the different bids prepared and see to it that the right one is the one that goes to the governor's committee."

"Right. *Bene, bene,*" Sam said, patting his older brother's arm. "Don't worry. We've done it all before. We had the same thing on the sand and gravel contract on the state highway with Dewey's boys. But those upstate Republicans are very hard to deal with. If we didn't have our friends in Buffalo and Albany, we'd be sunk. We just don't pack enough weight there. And to tell you the truth, I don't like what's happening here in the city, either. This O'Dwyer, I don't think he can be completely trusted. He blows hot and cold. And DeSapio, suddenly he's a reformer."

"Well," Don Antonio said, with his slow, precise enunciation, still carrying heavy Sicilian overtones. "You know Costello is acting strange these days. He came up the same as us, but now he's going to some kind of head doctor. I hear he's worried about his reputation, about his friends, the judges and the councilmen. And I know he gave the word to DeSapio to cooperate only as much as necessary. I think we must listen to Lucchese more. You know, I think with that Impellitteri we can do a lot better than with O'Dwyer. Sure, they had three Italian candidates in the last election, but two were Protestants and one a northerner. These are not people you can count on—*amici nostra*. I wish we had a good candidate of our own."

"And, how are things in the department, Arturo?" Antonio said, turning toward the baby brother. "Will we have an Italian commissioner soon?"

Arthur laughed. "I think we have a long way to go. There hasn't been anybody but an Irishman in charge of that department since it started. Still, we're making ourselves felt. The Italians have maybe a quarter of the city already. We're entitled to more representation every place. And we'll get it. The trouble is, none of our people *want* to go in the department. They don't want to join the *sbirro*. But they must learn this is a different country. It's not like the old country. We must have friends every place."

"And you, Sam? I hear Constanza is thinking of marrying Raimundo's *giovanotto*. So, soon maybe we have two cops in the family. Do we need that?"

"He's a smart kid," Arthur said. "I've talked to him a lot. He's ambitious. He's sharp. I think he's going to go places no matter what he gets into. But the department is a good place for him to get a start."

"It didn't do *you* much good," Sam commented sourly.

Arthur grimaced. "Come on, Sam. Don't start that business again. I admit it. I just never had the heart to get involved with family work. When you practically read me out of the family because I wouldn't take a job from you, I just turned in the opposite direction. We've been through all this crap a million times. I told you, I'll give all the help I can, but I'm just not cut out to be one of your soldiers."

"So what about the kid? You gonna make the same half-ass Little Boy Blue out of him?"

"Pat is different. Frankly, he's got a lot more balls than me. I never could have pulled off that Sullivan Street job. I think the kid has a real future."

"Still," Sam said, "I'd like him to be more than a patrolman. Can we get him a promotion? He should have some education, too."

"I'll work on it," Arthur said. "I think maybe we can do something, but we have to give it a little time. He hasn't been in the department a year yet. He's got a commendation. He's got a seat. That's considered good. It will take a while to move him up without causing trouble. But we're watching him, don't worry."

"How much does he know about the family business?" Don Antonio said.

"Officially, nothing. But he's clever. He hears things. He knows who we are, I'm sure of that."

"What about that deal on Sullivan Street? What does he know?"

"Well, you know, that was a favor to Tony Bender. The man was a soldier from the Coppola *borgata* and he was always breaking into the machines, into the stores. I don't know what he needed the money for. But he

shouldn't do that to people who are in the family. This is
Bender's territory. The man must have been *pazzo*. He
was warned several times. If it wasn't for the connection
with Mike Coppola, we could of just had him seen to the
regular way. But this way was better. This way they
can't put the blame on anybody in our family. The man
just made a mistake. Still, I think they'll get the message.
I don't think they'll be having any of these strangers in
our territory anymore."

"Well, it's good, and I'm glad to see that the boy got
good credit for what he did. It will help," Don Antonio
said.

"Listen, that's enough business," Sam said. "Let's order up."

The waiter, who had been waiting for the signal, approached now with a well-dusted, wire-wrapped bottle
of red wine. He diplomatically presented it first between
Sam and Antonio.

"It's a *Biancavilla*," he said. "It's the best from our
country."

"I know, I know, Mario," Sam said. "It's from Etna,
right?"

"Right," said Mario.

"It's a pity that Sicily can't produce the good red
wines."

Mario shrugged. "What can we do? We have too
much sun. But you know, nowadays, a lot of that wine
from the old country, it's never *seen* a grape. They put it
together from ox blood, beet juice, God knows what
chemicals. But this one, *signore*, the *Biancavilla*, it's
made from real *grapes*."

Don Antonio gave a startling laugh in his dry, husky
voice that seldom rose much above a whisper.

"You don't know, Sam. You don't know about that
phony wine, eh?"

"Listen," said Sam. "I may have something to do

with bringing it over, but I don't have to drink it. *This* stuff, though, this stuff from Etna—that's the *real* stuff. That's good. *A salute!*" Sam said, clinking the first glass of the deep red wine against his brother's. They all drank it to the bottom.

CHAPTER 23

Patrolman Pat Conte and Tom Berkholder were bouncing in the Village—having a few beers after a long stretch on the four-to-twelve. They made several stops, walking north from the Charles Street station, heading for the White Horse at Eleventh on Hudson, the only place that showed any action at that time of night.

As expected, the renovated waterfront saloon was jumping. Jimmy Washington gave his usual enthusiastic greeting, and indicated that he would carry their drinks on a tab.

Tom ordered a double J.W. Dant with a beer back.

"Hitting it pretty hard, ain't you?" Pat asked.

"Fuck it. A guy's got to unwind on this job or he'll end up with his guts tied in knots."

Berkholder threw back the shot and ordered another.

Pat found a place at the end of the bar near the Guinness kegs. Tom took his drink and wandered into the back room to check the action.

A round-faced girl with curly ginger hair that made her look disconcertingly like Little Orphan Annie pushed in close beside Pat.

"Could you order a drink for me?" she said. "I'll pay for it."

"What's the problem?" Pat asked.

"That fuck Washington eighty-sixed me. Says I'm a troublemaker."

Pat turned to the girl, and looked into her pale blue innocent eyes.

"I wouldn't mind getting into some trouble with you myself," he said, smiling.

"Come on. Don't give me any of that bullshit. Just get the drink," the girl said, licking her lips nervously.

Pat debated telling her to get lost. But she was an appetizing-looking little piece. He turned to Jimmy.

"Listen, I know you eighty-sixed this broad," he said, "but just give her one drink. I'll take the responsibility."

"You're just asking for trouble," Jimmy said. "I know she looks like Little Orphan Annie, but she's a lush. She's not interested in fucking. She's just interested in drinking."

"Yeah. But right now, she's the only game in town," Pat said.

Reluctantly Jimmy poured a Feathers on the rocks into a stubby glass.

"It's on me," Pat said to the ginger-haired girl, "but don't fuck me up."

"Don't worry about me," the girl said. "I know how to behave."

As they touched glasses in a token toast, Pat looked over the girl's shoulder and saw Tom headed for the door with a short, bright-faced young man—a *pretty* young man. Tom, who was well into his sixth highball, lurched over to where Pat was sitting.

"The guy's a fag," Tom explained. "I just want to have some fun with him."

Pat raised his eyebrows, but said nothing.

"You know what they say," Tom said. "If you can't get a woman, get a clean young man."

Pat wasn't surprised. A lot of the guys in the precinct were switch hitters. Or at least they didn't mind accepting a blow job, if it came cheap, and easy.

Pat turned his attention to the ginger-haired girl again.

He tried to persuade her that she could do her boozing in comfort in his apartment on Christopher Street, where she would definitely *not* be eighty-sixed. They had been talking no more than ten minutes, when the door on the Hudson Street side banged open. Tom stuck his head in. His face was pale and worried-looking.

"Pat, get your ass out here right away! I need you!"

Pat asked no questions. He reached his arm around behind him to see if his off-duty pistol was in its holster under the shirt-tail of his sports shirt, and headed for the door.

"What's the problem?" he asked Tom.

"I think I killed the kid! I swear. I think I killed him!" Tom said, his voice husky with tension.

"What the fuck are you talking about?"

"I'll tell you later. Let's just get over there," Tom said. He grabbed Pat by the arm and pulled him around the corner to Eleventh Street. On the far side of the street was a little courtyard with an iron gate. In it was the pretty-boy fag, crumpled on the ground—but Pat could identify him only by the clothes he had been wearing. Because it was no pretty boy that was lying there now. Blood ran from both nostrils down the chin of the slim figure slumped against the brick wall of the courtyard. A cut had apparently been opened above his hairline, and streamers of blood striped his face in a peppermint-stick effect. One side of the boy's jaw was as red as a slab of raw meat, where his face had apparently scraped along the rough sidewalk.

"Christ!" Pat said. "What happened?"

"I think he's dead." Tom said.

Pat kneeled beside the boy and felt for his pulse. He couldn't seem to find a beat in the slim wrist. But after a minute he noticed bubbles of snot and blood forming in the nostrils which seemed to swell and shrink in an erratic rhythm.

"I think he may be alive, but he's weakening," Pat said. "What did you do to him? That's a lot of fuss to make over some blow job, isn't it?"

"It's not that," Tom said, "This was the sonofabitch that hit Novak!"

"How do you know?"

"His car is parked right around the corner on Greenwich Street. It'd got those BX plates I was watching for—a red Dodge. The kid wanted to blow me in the car. As soon as I saw the Dodge I realized who he was."

"Did he admit it?"

"Shit, no! You don't think he'd admit it, do you?"

"What happened then?"

"I just went out of control. I slammed the kid a couple of times over the car. Then I threw him into the street and kicked him in the gut and the balls and anyplace else I could reach. Then I picked him up and dragged him around here in the alley and slammed him up against the wall. I think I cracked his head then. Anyway I heard a funny noise, and he slid down like that, and it seemed like he stopped breathing."

"You want to leave him here? There's nothing that can tie it to you."

"Yes, there is. *He'll* tie it to me. The little creep queer fag'll tie it to me, if he ever comes to."

"What do you wanna do?"

"You see that building over there?" Tom pointed to a tenement rising five stories behind the White Horse on the Hudson Street side.

"Yeah?"

"I'm gonna take this little creep up there, and I'm

gonna throw him right off the fucking roof! There's not gonna be *any* witnesses to this thing."

"Except me," Pat said.

"Yeah, well I'm not counting *you*. You owe me one, remember?"

"Listen," Pat said. "This is your baby. I don't want to get involved in it."

"It's my job, Pat. I know that. All I want you to do is stand guard in the street while I carry the fag over to the hallway, and make sure there's nobody watching. And then watch the doorway. Give me a signal if anyone's coming up behind me."

Tom Berkholder leaned over and grabbed the slumped figure by one pale hand. He threw the slight form over his shoulder in a fireman's carry.

"If anyone sees us," Tom said, "We'll just say it's some drunk."

It was almost one o'clock by now, and the streets were deserted anyway. Pat cased both sides of Eleventh Street, and then walked to the corner. He saw that nobody was in sight, and he signaled to Tom to hurry over with the body before anybody came out of the bar. Just to make sure, Pat stood in the doorway of the White Horse to block any customers that might emerge. Tom lurched with the limp figure over his shoulders across the street and into the hallway.

A few minutes later, Pat heard a crashing sound, as Tom apparently put his foot through the vestibule door.

"Christ!" Pat thought. "He didn't have to do *that*. Why didn't he just let himself in with a 'loid'?" But it was doubtful in those tenements that anyone would put his head out to discover the source of the noise. People in the Village had a tendency to strictly mind their own business.

As soon as Berkholder and his limp burden had disappeared into the tenement, Pat shifted over to the doorway of the building to intercept any strangers who might try to enter the house before Tom had finished his work.

A few singing and shouting groups emerged from the Horse, but nobody tried to enter the tenement.

Berkholder reappeared panting and out of breath within ten minutes.

"Did you do it?" Pat asked.

Berkholder nodded wordlessly.

"I didn't hear anything."

"I think he landed in a pile of garbage in the back yard. That's what the fuck deserved. The garbage probably muffled the sound when he hit."

"Well, he was still alive when he went over," Pat said. "So he'll probably bleed enough to satisfy the ME."

Both men knew that dead bodies don't bleed, and if it was apparent that the kid had been dead before he hit the ground, there would surely be a homicide investigation. This way it would probably be ruled an accident or a suicide.

"The way he probably looks now," Pat said, "I doubt that anybody will notice the beating you gave him."

"Let's go," Berkholder said nervously, grabbing Pat's arm. "I gotta have a drink on this."

"Don't be an idiot," Pat said, "The less your face is seen around here, the less anybody is going to remember that we were here earlier. We were only in the White Horse a couple of minutes, anyway. You wanna have any drinks, go someplace across town, or better yet, go home and get drunk there, where you're not likely to talk to anybody."

Tom looked at Pat quizzically.

"You're not *happy* that I finally nailed that queer creep? I been looking for him for a fucking year!"

"Sure, Tom, sure," Pat said. "I'm happy, I guess. But if anybody catches wise to all this, you could be up for murder one. Just go home and get some sleep, and let's both try to forget about the whole thing."

"Yeah," Tom said. He seemed suddenly sobered by Pat's remarks. "I guess you're right. I better go home. See you tomorrow."

"Right," Pat said. "I'm going home too."

CHAPTER 24

The next night, Tom and Pat sat in the radio car splitting a container of coffee from Riker's, while passing back and forth sheets of the *Daily News*. Tom made no reference to the events of the night before. There were obviously a lot of things about that night he would like to forget. Pat said nothing either, but he had noted all of the details in a little black book he carefully kept. Not the patrolman's memo book, but another one in which he recorded any information of an unofficial nature which he felt might come in handy sometime.

Pat was reading a story about the investigation of Mayor O'Dwyer.

"I see where our mayor got caught with his hand in the till."

"Yeah," Tom said, without interest. "I guess the climate is nicer over there in Mexico anyway, and he's got the Simpson broad to keep him company."

"Too skinny for my taste," Pat said. "You think all of this television stuff has Costello washed up?"

Tom shrugged. "How do I know? I ain't in the organized crime division."

"I hear both him and DeSapio have had it. That's the word I get," Pat said.

Tom turned to the sports page to check a diatribe by Jimmy Powers against the manners of Ted Williams and his high salary.

"I ain't interested in politics," Tom said. "Jees, you see what they're paying Williams? A hundred and twelve thousand bucks! And here we celebrate a 'hat' that we got to split between us."

"What's *your* batting average?" Pat asked.

He looked idly out the window at Sheridan Square, still busy at 11:00 P.M. He watched a tall girl in a plaid skirt and fur jacket swinging with smooth, liquid movements westward on Grove Street. Something about the mass of taffy hair rolling in counterpoint to the tight, little ass, seemed familiar.

"Hey, Tom," he said, "hang in there a minute. I want to talk to that girl."

He jumped out of the patrol car and ran across the street, hurrying to get enough of a lead on the girl so he could see her face. His hunch was right. It *was* Katie Mullaley.

"Katie, baby," he said. Her face lit up with spontaneous joy.

"Pat!"

He picked her up, lifting her feet off the ground in a bear hug, and gave her a wet smack on the cheek.

"Hey, nutsy! Put me down. You're on duty. You want to get in trouble?"

"With you," Pat said, "it would be a pleasure. What are you doing here this time of night?"

"I'm working," she said, pointing back over her shoulder. "I'm doing a hatcheck thing over at the Cafe Society and I'm taking lessons with the Stella Adler Studio. Acting. I live down here now. Since when are you down here? I thought you were over on Mulberry Street."

"I got transferred a little while ago."

"Oh, yeah," Katie said. "I guess Connie told me. You were a big hero or something?"

Pat grinned. "As long as the department thinks so, it's okay with me."

"It must have been awful," Katie said seriously. "You had to kill a man, right?"

Pat shrugged. "It's part of the job."

"Tell me all about it. Tell me about everything. Can we have a cup of coffee?"

Pat looked over at Tom in the car. "I better not now. But what's your hours?"

"I'm off at 12:30 every night starting Monday," Katie said.

"Great. I start on the four-to-twelve next week. I want to tell you, there's not much to do when you get finished duty at twelve o'clock, except drink. I'm getting awful tired of drinking with other cops."

"Great! Why don't you pick me up any night over at Cafe Society downtown?"

"Terrific. I'll be over on Tuesday. We'll talk over old times."

"Who was that?" Tom said curiously as Pat slid back into the car.

"Oh, just a girl I know from around."

That Sunday he went walking with Connie at the Cloisters in Fort Tryon Park. Connie spent a lot of time trying to educate him, and some of it he found interesting. But now that the deal was made with Sam, their relationship seemed locked in somehow, and no longer had the pulse-pounding excitement he had felt in the beginning.

He had finally given up his weekly wrestling matches with Connie. She was fire and ice. Fire above the neck and ice below. He couldn't understand how anybody could be so passionate and responsive to kissing and not want to fuck.

For some reason, he said nothing about meeting Katie the week before. Doyle was, by now, starting his assignment in Atlanta. Pat wondered if he knew about Katie working in the Village and what he would think about it. Doyle was a good guy but stiff about things like that.

Katie was ready on Tuesday at twelve-fifteen when Pat came by. In the back room, he could hear the twanging sound of Josh White's guitar playing "Evil-Hearted Man." Katie disappeared somewhere in back for a moment to change out of the black V-necked dress she wore in the hat check room into a man's button-down shirt and plain wool skirt, fastened with a giant diaper pin. Her coat was heavy wool tweed, topped by a giant fox collar. It looked expensive.

They went across the street to Louie's. It was still crowded and jumping at 12:30. They ordered beers. Pat decided not to flash his tin, but pay. He was wearing his off-duty pistol in a clip-on holster in the small of his back, so that it wouldn't bulge the new sports jacket he had bought at Barney's, a country-looking, Harris tweed, something like the one Sam wore.

The kids in the bar were young, breathless, excitable, lively. Not that much younger than Pat, himself, but they *seemed* younger.

A tall, golden-haired youth in a fitted suede jacket and a frontier-style shirt came over to their table.

"Hey, Katie," he said. "I hear you did great with that road show. You got anything else lined up?"

Katie introduced the kid, whose name was Steve McQuade.

"And, this," she said, indicating Pat, "is Pat Conte, a real good friend of mine."

"You an actor?" McQuade said to Pat.

"No," Pat said. "I'm not an actor."

Kate giggled.

"What's with you, Steverino?" she asked the kid in the suede coat.

"Oh, a little modeling. I had a gig with the Equity Library Theater up in the Bronx, but that was only for a couple of days. A good part, though. We did *Waiting for Lefty*. I played the title role."

Katie laughed again. "You're a real nut, Steverino."

Pat made circles with his beer glass while they talked. He didn't ask the kid to sit down and he was glad to see that Kate didn't either.

"Well, see you around, Katie, ah, Pat," the guy said and drifted back to the bar.

"What is he, some kind of fag?" Pat said.

Katie smiled. She had the best set of teeth Pat had ever seen.

"A fag?" she said. "I don't know. Not too many of these theater guys are straight, to tell you the truth, but it's different when you're working with them. I understand that Steve's got an uncle in the department, an inspector or something."

Pat raised his eyebrows. "No kidding? You know his name?"

Kate shrugged. "I don't know. I guess it's the same as his. I know they raided his apartment one time and they had a bunch of pot and ammys and all that kind of stuff. Steve made a call while the cops were still there and they just went away. So I guess he's telling the truth about his uncle."

They sat for a moment in silence. Kate drew a face on the circles that Pat had made with the bottom of the beer glass.

"Listen," Pat said, "where's your place?"

"Over on Ninth Street," she said. "Not too far."

"Well, let's get out of here. It's too smoky, too noisy, too many creeps."

Pat threw a couple of dollars on the table and Sal, the waiter, nodded and picked them up.

"See you later, Sal," Katie said, as Pat took her arm and escorted her out.

It was one of those hazy nights you get sometimes in the early spring. The air was damp, but warm, and the mist seemed to press around them, isolating them from the other people on the street. They walked across West Fourth, up Sixth, past the all-night Waldorf, and turned right on Ninth, opposite the House of Detention.

Kate lived in one of those Georgian, four-story houses on a quiet street with no stores except for a liquor store near the corner. There were trees up and down the block and even though it was only a few blocks from Louie's, it was more like a back street in some New England town, like Boston.

Kate held his arm during the whole walk and Pat could feel the firm bulge of her breast against his upper arm.

"Well, this is it," she said, stopping before the red-painted brick house.

"Fancy!" Pat said.

"Well, it's rent-controlled," she said. "Dad has some connections with a real estate agent. It's so cheap that I can afford to keep it even when I'm on the road. That's my window up there with the light in it, on the second floor. I'd ask you up but the place is really a mess."

"Are you kidding?" Pat said. "*Everybody's* place is a mess!"

"Yeah," Kate laughed, "but girls are supposed to be neat. Well, come up I guess and have a nightcap, but don't look around."

They walked up the soft, carpeted steps to the second floor. There were hunting prints on the walls and a long library table on each floor, with magazines and mail on it.

"It's not much, but it's mine," Katie said, ushering him into the apartment.

It was a large, high-ceilinged parlor with a fireplace that had been sealed off with ornamental cast iron. Skirts, panties, blouses and nylon stockings were scattered carelessly around the room which was furnished in an assortment of styles, but mostly with Victorian oak.

A lot of the furniture looked like the stuff in Father Raimundo's rectory, but there, it was simply old-fashioned. This stuff, Pat could tell, had been carefully collected for its character.

Books were piled on all the tables—mostly plays, and there were several play scripts in manila folders. There was a small desk in the corner with a typewriter on it. The walls were hung mostly with Picasso and Picasso-like reproductions which contrasted with the old-fashioned decor, but somehow looked right. Kate raced around the room, gathering up loose clothes and throwing them haphazardly into a large basket in the corner.

"What with working and going to classes," she said breathlessly, "I never really get a chance to pick up."

In the middle of the room was a convertible sofa which was still open. A patchwork comforter lay thrown aside and Pat could see still the S-shaped indentation of Kate's body on the mattress and the pillow.

There were several straight chairs in the room, but the bed dominated the tiny flat. To the left, there was a kitchen which looked as if it must have been converted from a closet. Another door led to a tiled bathroom.

"You sticking with the beer?" Kate said, fussing about in the kitchen. "Or would you like something else? I've got a little Scotch left, some brandy and I think a little vodka."

"A beer's okay," Pat said.

He stretched himself out on the open bed. There really wasn't any other comfortable place. Kate came out of the kitchen carrying two tall, graceful pilsner glasses.

"The beer's cheap," she said, "but the glasses are chilled. I always like to drink a beer out of a chilled glass."

She brought the two glasses to the edge of the sofa

bed where Pat was lying. He made no move to get up. She looked about for a moment for a place to sit.

"Put the beers down," Pat said.

She put them on a small end table beside the sofa.

"Now, come over here." He held up his hands.

Taking both her elbows in his large, blocky hands, he pulled her down onto the bed beside him.

"Pat," she said, in what might have been the start of a protest. But that was all.

He pressed her shoulders till she lay back on the bed, looking up at him with clear, unfrightened eyes, with an expression of open interest. Slowly, with deliberation, Pat leaned over and gently kissed her mouth. Then, in a moment, they were locked together, their legs intertwined, his thigh pressing against her groin, their tongues plunging wildly into each other's mouths.

Pat unbuttoned the white shirt and found that she didn't have anything on underneath it. Her breasts were small and firm, the nipples erect with excitement. Pat lay suckling them like a hungry child. Nothing was rushed, but from the beginning it was clear that the outcome was already decided. Slowly, almost languidly, she reached down and started fumbling with Pat's silver buckle.

"Wait a minute," Pat said. He sat up and unhooked the clip holster from the small of his back and took off his jacket.

"There, that's better. We can go from there."

He put the pistol on the end table beside the beer glasses. Without haste, they helped each other out of their clothes. There were no words of love, but there were moans of pleasure.

Kate seemed completely unashamed of their actions and of her body, and she guided him with interest, helping him to find the spots which gave her the most pleasure. His penis was firm and throbbing. It felt as though it would burst at a touch.

"Here, lie back," Kate said gently.

She bent over him, her mouth on his penis, sliding up and down in soft hot breaths and strokes.

"Cut it out," Pat said. "I can't stand it!"

She looked up. "Doesn't it feel good?"

"It feels *too* good," Pat said. "Come here. I want to finish inside you."

Quickly, she guided him inside her and they climaxed almost at once in strong, pushing thrusts. Afterwards, he lay on top of her, clasped in her arms for a long time with his eyes closed, letting his pulse and heartbeat come back to normal.

He could feel the warm, sticky places where their skin touched, dampened from contact. Underneath him, he could feel her chest heaving and slowly coming back to normal, too. Finally, he rolled over and lay, spread-eagled on the bed. Kate sat up and watched him.

"You've got a funny smile on your face," she said.

"I'm just happy," Pat said.

"Next time," Kate said, "we'll do it slower. I just wanted you so much, I couldn't hold back that time."

Pat nodded drowsily. "Me too," he said.

CHAPTER 25

When Eddie Tobias, the one-two-four man at the Sixth Precinct married, he turned over his one-and-a-half room rent-controlled flat at 95 Christopher Street to Pat. Connie came down to the Village, and along with Kate helped him to furnish the place so that it looked a lot like Kate's, a lot of old oak chairs and a rolltop desk.

They moved a big daybed that had been stored in the garage in Riverdale down from Connie's house, piling it in the back of Katie's convertible.

Whatever had happened between Katie and Pat didn't seem to show up in their relationship with Connie. The three of them had always been friendly and affectionate, and they continued to be that way.

Gradually the pattern of Pat's relationship with Kate had evolved into a once a week visit and date, with an occasional informal drop-in late at night when Pat was on the four-to-twelve. Sometimes he would even take an hour off, leaving the phone number with Tom, when he was on the twelve-to-eight. He found Katie warm, funny and tremendously vital. Perhaps it was the lack of mutual obligation, but he felt more at home and more comfortable in her presence than he had with any woman he'd ever known.

With Connie, now that everything was settled except the date, things were calmer, and yet there was an overlay of strain. Connie seemed anxious to upgrade Pat in education and culture. He appreciated this, but it made him nervous. She was constantly lending him books, taking him to art and experimental films, and arranging for them to go to the theater.

Connie was serene and secure with Pat and flatteringly attentive. Quite often, especially when they went to the theater or movies, they would make up a threesome with Kate. But Connie seemed to suspect nothing, even the overlong greeting and good-bye kisses between Katie and Pat. If anything, she was happy that her friend and her fiancé got along so well.

What seemed funny to Pat was that Katie made no demands on him. She didn't seem to have any streak of possessiveness. She said nothing about love, except in a joshing way. Sometimes she'd say, "You're so crazy, Pat. I really love you," but never was there any serious discussion of the subject.

If she had asked Pat if he loved her, he would have been stuck for an answer. It was a word that *women* used, a word that didn't easily roll off his tongue and never had. To some people, if you say "I love you," it means that you're stuck together for the rest of your life. To others, it's hardly more than a handshake.

Kate saw and dated other men, but it seemed to Pat that most of them were fags from the theater. If she did anything with them, she never told him about it. But they did have a talk one afternoon in Louie's. Jack Lawrenson, one of the first Village moving men, an organizer in the National Maritime Union and now something of a folk hero, stopped by their table. Kate asked him to join them for a beer. Lawrenson must have been near fifty, with a graying, light brown moustache, a lean whiplike build and a way of talking that was a mixture of his native Welsh burr and the West Side waterfront dialect.

It was obvious from the conversation that he had known Katie for a long time, at least since she had moved to the Village. Lawrenson talked with them for only about ten minutes and then left on some errand in his truck. Pat felt a twinge of jealousy.

"How well do you know Lawrenson?"

She looked at him with amused eyes.

"Why do you ask?"

"Just wondering."

"He's an old friend," Katie said. "A *good* old friend."

"You make it with him?"

Katie looked down at her glass and then answered very deliberately.

"You have your life, Pat, and I have mine. Your whole life is set. You're going to marry Connie and you're seeing me and we have a good thing together. But you're only *part* of my life. Not the whole thing. And I don't think it's good for either of us for me to tell you everything. I'll say this, just to make you comfortable. Whatever happened between me and Jack Lawrenson was over a long time ago. But you might as well know, I don't see myself as anybody's exclusive property."

Pat was silent for a long time after this. He really didn't know how to handle this approach. He knew, in fact, that he had no right to demand any more from Kate than she was giving him unless he was willing to break up with Connie. But from other conversations, he knew even that wouldn't make any difference because Katie had no intention of getting married.

"Right now," she had told him, "I'm married to my work. If I had a man I was living with or married to and I got a job offer at Stratford or out in San Francisco, I'd have to go. No matter what he thought or wanted, I'd have to go because work comes first to me. At least at this point in my life. Maybe that will all change some-day."

"What about Doyle?" Pat asked her as they sat one Sunday afternoon on the stringpiece of Gansevoort Pier, watching the cold, distant shore of Jersey.

"Regan wants to marry me. He's told me so from the beginning, and I've told him from the beginning the same thing I've told you. He says he'll wait." She sighed and pushed a lock of her taffy-colored hair back across her forehead.

"There's nothing you can say to a man like that, be-cause you know he *will* wait and wait. It makes me feel good to be loved that way, but it also makes me feel guilty that I don't have the same feeling for him, that I'm not the woman he thinks I am, or the woman he wants me to be. What he really needs is some bright, convent-educated colleen, fresh and pure from the old country."

"*You're* convent-educated," Pat said.

She looked at him with cool eyes.

"There are convents and convents. You'd be sur-prised at some of the things you learn at St. Agnes."

"Still, you'll probably marry Doyle someday," Pat said.

She gave him a twisted smile that barely showed her teeth.

"I have a feeling that might happen . . . but it won't be for a long time."

Pat didn't ask the one question that burned in him. He could accept the possibility that Katie had casual love affairs with the various men she saw, but it would hurt him to feel that he was sharing sex with Regan. Maybe because he knew that Regan was the only one that could offer a real threat.

Sitting there on the dock that spring afternoon, he felt as he had not at any other time, that he had it made.

He was a long way from those hopeless days at the orphanage in Jersey. He had a good job, with respect and power. As a bachelor, the salary was adequate for his needs and the extra money and various favors he received gave him something close to a life of luxury.

He had the use of two beautiful girls, and marriage to Connie would give him an important position, a family and security.

He knew that the family had been the major factor in putting him where he was now. Without it, he never would have applied for the force, he never would have gotten the promotion, he never would have met either of the two women. Probably he would still be hanging around one of those clubs in Little Italy, maybe hustling policy slips, maybe working in Civil Service. Maybe he would have gotten involved with small-time racketeering or loan sharking like Al Santini.

After their discussion about Lawrenson, Pat and Kate sat for a long time with no words. Then, Pat looked at his watch, saw that he had ten minutes to get over to Charles Street, and excused himself.

"Are you angry?" Katie asked him.

"About what?"

"About what we just talked about."

Pat paused and thought before answering and then answered as honestly as he could.

"I'm not angry. In my *mind* I'm not angry. In *principle*, I know you're right. But as far as my *feelings*, the whole thing's a little bit hard to swallow."

And he left to report for duty at the precinct, popping three pieces of chlorophyll gum in his mouth as he went to cover the smell of the afternoon beer.

CHAPTER 26

The two patrolmen sat, drinking coffee in their car. Tom Berkholder was reading the *Morning Telegraph*, trying to dope the races. Pat Conte was looking up Sixth Avenue, past the Waverly Theater to the butcher shop on the corner of West Fourth Street.

Tom looked up from his paper.

"What is this all about, anyway?"

"I don't really know," Pat admitted. "I got an informant I been developing over on Washington Street. He told me to watch for this meat truck. He said the driver's been delivering more than meat around the neighborhood. Like maybe some junk."

"Could be a good collar. I don't know where you get all these tips," Tom said. "I don't get anything like that."

"You don't hang around with the right people. You're too high class, Tom."

"How do we know this guy isn't on somebody's pad—paying off regular to the precinct?"

"My informant tells me he's not covered, an independent operator."

Actually, Pat knew more than he was telling Tom; his informant was Lieutenant Arthur Marseri. He knew that the whole idea of the bust was to get the driver away from his meat truck for a reasonable amount of time. He also knew where the junk would be in the truck.

"Won't this guy be suspicious when he sees the patrol car sitting here like this?" Tom asked.

"I don't think so," Pat said. "He doesn't know we've been tipped off. He'll just figure we're cooping here or something."

They had been sitting there for no more than ten minutes when the gray-painted, boxlike, refrigerated truck with the markings, "Royal Provisions" on its side and "Quality Purveyors" written underneath it in red, pulled up in front of the market.

"That's him," Pat said. "I tell you what. I'll walk up and talk to him and you drive around and come up behind the truck to cover it. Just go around the block. You'll be there by the time I start frisking him."

Pat walked slowly up Sixth Avenue and watched as the driver in his gray coveralls, with the Royal insignia on the back, got out of the truck and went around to unlock the padlock on the rear, insulated doors. The plan was to wait until the lock was open, then make the bust.

Pat stopped to check the comparative prices of liquor at Musante's Liquor Store and sized up a display of door locks in the window of Katz's Hardware. By this time, the driver had unlocked the truck and was beginning to pull down the large handles on the big, rear doors. Pat picked up his pace and came up behind the truck driver.

"Hold it a minute, buddy."

"Shit!" the driver said.

"Just a routine check," Pat said. "Come on around here to the front of the truck."

"Listen," the driver said, "this is a loading zone. Says so right there. I could stop here."

"Forget it. It's not about that. You carrying anything in this truck besides what it's supposed to carry?"

The driver looked genuinely surprised. "Like what?"

"Never mind. Just lean against the hood there with your hands on it and pull your feet out."

"What is this, a shakedown?"

"You don't want to talk that way to the nice policeman, do you?" Pat said, shoving the driver hard so that he fell forward against the steaming hood of the Mack truck.

"Hey, this thing is hot!" the driver complained.

Pat ignored him. He was looking up the street for the arrival of the patrol car. He wanted Tom to be there when he made the find. Just as routine, he gave the driver a perfunctory check. In his back pocket he found a black leather blackjack.

"What's this? You have to kill the cows yourself?"

"Oh, come on. You know they've been roughing up all us drivers on the West Side. This outfit ain't signed up with the Teamsters and the mob don't like that."

"Yeah, well we got policemen to take care of that. This here is an illegal weapon, do you know that?"

"Come on, a blackjack?"

"That's right. You're in violation of the Sullivan Law, 1874 PL. Okay, you can stand up now. Let's see your identification."

The guy fished out a wallet which identified him as Gino Rossi. Pasted to it was a round chauffeur's picture, showing Rossi in a striped suit and tie.

Tom eased alongside the truck in the patrol car and got out, coming around to the driver's side.

"How's it look?"

"Well, we got this for starters," Pat said, holding up the blackjack.

"Oh, he must be a bad boy," Tom said. "How about anything else?"

"I haven't looked yet."

"Anything on the guy?"

"No," Pat said. "Nothing that I could find, but I

haven't given him a real good frisk. Why don't you check him out while I look around inside the truck."

"Okay," Tom said. "Lean against the truck, Gino."

"Christ, I just *did* that."

"Yeah, well it's easier to frisk you that way. We don't want you running away on us."

Gino cursed under his breath and leaned against the truck again.

Pat opened the glove compartment and rummaged through the assortment of screwdrivers, maps, No-Doz and condoms, but his look was perfunctory because he knew just where he was going to find the stuff. He pulled up the floor mats and glanced briefly under them and then loosened the worn, leather-covered bench seat of the truck.

"Hoo ha! What have we here?"

Resting in the space below the bottom of the seat on the floor of the truck was a paper bag with about twenty little glassine envelopes with white powder in them. Gino looked around, his face now white with fear.

"Hey, what is this, a frame? I never saw that stuff! I don't know where it came from!"

"Gee, Tom," Pat said, "doesn't that sound like something you heard somewhere before? I think we better run down to the precinct with this guy. Don't you, Tom?"

"Yeah. Take the bags."

At the station house, it turned out that Gino was in a lot of trouble. He was facing life on the Baumes Law, a three-time loser on charges of assault, assault with a deadly weapon, one stickup and one burglary.

"Well, I'll say this for you," Pat said later looking over his 224 sheet, "you never got busted for junk before."

"I swear to God," Rossi said, "I don't know anything about this."

"You can tell it to the detectives," Tom said, typing out his Unusual Occurrence Report.

"What about my truck?"

"You can call your company if you want to have them send somebody over to finish the delivery and pick up the truck."

It was a good collar because of Rossi's record, but not a great collar, because there was no danger, no shooting, no chance for heroics. Tom was all for keeping a couple of the envelopes in case they needed them to flake some worthy citizen at a later time, but Pat pointed out that they wanted fifty grams—about twenty-five decks—in there to quality the collar for a Class A felony.

The next day as they were cruising by, Pat observed a Health Department car parked in front of the market. A man was nailing up a notice, "Closed by Order of the Board of Health," and Hoffer, the owner of the shop, was standing there, wringing his hands.

"I tell you, I don't know anything about that. I don't know how that stuff got into the meat boxes. It was refrigerated. It just got off the truck. How could it have germs? If there's something wrong, it must have been delivered that way."

"You can tell it to the Board of Health," the man said and walked off.

Hoffer cursed bitterly and took off his apron.

"What's the trouble, Mr. Hoffer?" Pat asked innocently.

"They're trying to ruin me," Hoffer said. "They sabotaged that shipment of meat. I knew there was something funny when those guys came around to the truck after you took off with the driver. What were you holding him for, anyway?"

"Narcotics."

"I know that guy for twenty years. He's a tough waterfront guy, but he never had anything to do with narcotics."

"Yeah, well he does now."

"This could ruin me," Hoffer said. "They warned me not to take off Royal, but I didn't think they'd go this far."

"Well, I'm sure you'll straighten it out, Mr. Hoffer," Pat said and rejoined Tom in the patrol car.

"Did you get a score off him?" Tom said as Pat got back into the car.

Pat looked at him with scorn. "Are you kidding? The guy's about to go bankrupt. Health Department raided him just after we busted that truck driver."

"Funny," Tom said, "how things happen in twos. You don't suppose that informant of yours knew a little more than he was telling."

Pat shrugged. "You want to get out of the bag someday, don't ya? Well, you got to get a good bunch of collars to do that. This was a good one, so don't complain."

CHAPTER 27

Pat Conte was looking at three kings, a diamond run from the seven to the ten, the ten-jack of spades and an ace and a four of clubs. After some thought, he threw the four.

Lieutenant Arthur Marseri looked at it for a minute, picked the next card off the top of the deck, discarded a ten face down.

"I got nine points," he said.

"Oh, for crap's sake!" Pat said and wrote the twelve-point difference across the board in Arthur's column. The twelve points gave Arthur the first game and put him within ten points of the second.

"You take too many chances," Arthur said. "You can't hang on to those high ones so long. That was way too long for you to be holding two pictures."

"Yeah, well I was going to dump them in the next few cards."

"Dump them right away," Arthur said. "You have to know when to get rid of the dead weight."

They were playing in the back of the Mulberry SAC, something they had been doing about once a month for the last several months. In many ways, Arthur was a

185

bridge between Pat and the rest of the family. While he was always aware of Arthur's authority, Pat felt reasonably at home with him. They were almost the same generation and understood each other.

"You like riding in the car?" Arthur asked him.

"Sure," Pat said. "It's a good deal. I like the Sixth better than this one."

"You ever go up around the college much, around NYU?"

Pat shook his head. "I never really had a call there except one time in one of those houses on Washington Square, a faculty house, some professor got his car stolen from in front of it."

"You think anybody knows you up there?"

"No, I don't know any of those kids. What's this about anyway?"

"Well I was talking to Father Ray, Sam and the rest of the family. We all feel that it would be a good idea for you to get more of an education. Don't you think so?"

"Maybe."

"Anyway, there's a plainclothes assignment coming up that I can get you at the university. You'll have two jobs—watching out for Commies and checking out the basketball fixers. Some of those kids have been shaving points for free-lance gamblers. It's been hurting a lot of the books pretty bad and besides the commissioner would like to clean this whole thing up. You're young, you're athletic. You could probably horse around with some of those guys. Maybe you could even get on the team, huh?"

"I'm not *that* good."

"Anyway, you can enroll in the school. We'll see to it that they cut the red tape and meanwhile, you'll be getting credits which you might be able to use and you'll still be on the payroll full time."

"In plainclothes?"

"Of course."

"Do I have anything to say about all this?" Pat asked.

"Sure. You can just forget the whole thing if you want."

"I just wanted to know."

"What about the wedding?" Arthur said. "Any plans for that?"

"Connie wants to do it this summer," Pat said, "and I guess that's okay with me."

"Well, you better let Sam know plenty in advance. He wants to make a big wedding."

"Yeah," Pat said, "I guess I better have a talk with him soon."

Arthur drove Pat back to the Village around midnight. Pat got off at Bedford Street and went into Chumley's for a nightcap. Ray, the bartender, had been teaching him chess and though he was still a beginner, he was beginning to be intrigued with the game. Ray was a small, gray-haired Filipino who seemed to have been in the place since its original days as a stable.

Ray was talking to a stocky man with pepper-and-salt gray hair, brushed back in stiff bristles. The man was wearing a blue serge suit and white shirt. His collar was open, sweaty and stained, and the dark red tie, pulled into a tight knot, hung four or five inches below the collar button. The eyes were gray and wet as though the man had recently been crying. Ray introduced him.

"Barney Morseman, this is Pat Conte. Pat's a cop. Maybe you should tell *him* about your problem."

Ray turned to Pat, explaining, "Barney's my salesman from the Royal Meat Company. Now he tells me that some guys have been coming around and threatening him and leaning on him. He thinks it's mob people who are trying to take over his company."

"I don't want to talk to no cops," Morseman said. "I got enough troubles already."

"He's probably right," Pat said. "You got a complaint like that, you should go to the detectives. I'm just

in a radio car. I don't have anything to do with that kind
of thing."

"He should go to Bill Passanante," Ray said. "After
all, he's our assemblyman. What do we elect those guys
for if they can't help us, protect us?"

Morseman rubbed his rheumy eyes with a cigar-
stained fist. His words were thick and slurred and the
strong smell of bourbon cushioned every word.

"Fucking politicians," he said. "Useless as tits on a
boar hog. Passanante's okay, but he got nothing to say
in the city here. It's all DeSapio—DeSapio and O'Dwyer
and DeSapio and Costello. It's all the mob and that's
just the guys that are after my ass. Hell, what do I care?
It's not my company. Whoever takes over, I could
probably sell for them just as good."

"You right," Ray said. "Just like in Pill-i-feens. Politicians all crooked cocksuckers. Laurel, Magsaysay, all
goddamn crooks. O'Dwyer fucking crook, too. New
York City now nothing but Irish, Italian, Jewish crooks.
Soon, maybe someday, we have nigger crooks, Puerto
Rican crooks. Maybe someday," he giggled in a high
crackling voice, "we have Pilli-feen crooks, too, but we
don't got enough votes."

Morseman pushed over some bills from the pile of
change lying in front of him. "You're right, Ray," he
said. "Buy what's his name, the cop here, a drink and
have one yourself."

Ray took two dollars from the pile, rang up a dollar
on the register, put a dollar in his pocket, gave Pat a
Grant's and soda and drew two ounces of beer for himself in a small glass he kept for that purpose.

"*Mabuhay!*" Ray said, toasting his two customers.

"*A salute,*" Pat said.

"Down the hatch," Morseman said, drinking his
bourbon from the shot glass and following it with a
slight dampening of his mouth from the water glass on
the side.

"Yes, sir," Morseman said, "there's going to be plenty trouble, plenty trouble down over there in the meat market. My boss thinks he can fool around with those guys, but I know he can't. Even the cops, I hear, are tied in with those guys."

Pat put his drink down very hard on the mahogany bar top.

"I don't think I heard you, mister."

"I—I didn't mean . . . I mean there's good cops and bad cops, right, like anybody else?"

"There's only good cops."

"That right," Ray said. "That right. Pat, he a good cop. All good cops here."

Pat left his drink half-finished and exited through the side entrance, into the courtyard and out onto Barrow Street. On the way home, he thought about Barney Morseman and his complaints. He knew that there had to be a good "family" reason behind the bust of Gino Rossi at the meat market and the subsequent closing of the market for sanitary violations.

Having run a certain number of errands relayed to him by Arthur Marseri, Pat was aware that he was already a cog in the giant family machine, with the advantage of terrific connections at the top—connections that would be made really solid by his marriage to Constanza.

Because the family was in many ways just that. While it was possible to work with the Jews and the Irish and anybody else, there was no real trust in anybody except members of the family, preferably blood relatives, or people who came from the same town or the same ancestry, people who are known for generations, people whose history was known.

The family always took care of its own. You had security with the family, maybe more than with Civil Service, and there was opportunity, plenty of opportunity, for somebody ambitious to go ahead, to really get on top.

Pat's thinking had come a long way since that day when he told Father Raimundo that he didn't need any help. He knew, now, that *nobody made it alone.*

CHAPTER 28

Regan Doyle had not been able to get off early for the weekend of the wedding and was only able to leave Atlanta late on Friday night. He landed at La Guardia at midnight and thought about calling Katie then, but was afraid he would wake her. They had agreed on the phone that he would pick her up at noon the following day.

Doyle had already decided that he would not go up to the Bronx and spend the night with his parents. He called Pat at home and at the precinct, but he was not at either place. Doyle decided to have a few drinks in some of their old hangouts, just a nightcap or two, and then sack in at the Earl Hotel.

He had brought a change of clothes for the wedding in his canvas carry-on bag. He thought, now that Pat and Connie were making the move, perhaps Kate would change her mind. Anyway, it looked as though after his stint in Atlanta, he might be able to swing a transfer to New York.

Pat Conte was on the eight-to-four that day. He checked out on Charles Street and went back to Christopher to shower and change. Connie called about five o'clock and filled him in on final details for the wedding. The white jacket and formal pants were to be delivered to the house at Riverdale and all he had to do was to show up around two o'clock in the afternoon. He took off his sports jacket, unclipped his off-duty gun and laid it on the night table and slipped the wrinkled, soiled undershorts over his tired legs.

He turned the shower on as hot as he could stand it and scrubbed himself vigorously, then, dabbing himself lightly with the towel, he lay down, still damp, on the wide bed to let the air cool him by evaporation. He had mixed two fingers of Grant's with a generous serving of soda and now he lay back sipping on the drink and thinking.

Up to now, he had let everything just happen, floating along like a piece of trash caught in the street sweeper's stream of water. But this was really it. Marrying into the Massey family was a heavy commitment, but one that in the end would really pay off.

Connie, in many ways, was what any man would want as a wife: clean, pretty, sweet, devoted. She was also intelligent and could be a lot of fun, but she tended to chatter too much. Occasionally Pat would find himself irritated by her endless babbling about the clothes she had just bought or planned to buy, the books she had read, the shows she had seen. And she was fanatic when it came to the church. Connie was the only woman Pat had every known who would break a date because it fell on a holy day of obligation.

She always asked him about his work, but when he started to tell her, she would interrupt with some anecdote that had happened to her during the day.

He always felt that she was frightened of his work, afraid to hear the details. Of course he never would have told her any of the details of his work for the family, but even the stories of everyday police work seemed to frighten her. As to the family, Pat knew that Constanza had no idea of the range and extent of their business interests or their enormous power.

There was even less sex now than when they had first met. In the beginning, there were the long, helpless, sweating sessions of necking, the schoolgirl passion of Connie and the blue-ball trip home for Pat.

But later, all that had seemed pointless. Most of the time when he kissed Connie good night, she would grab him and press herself against him and open her mouth hungrily. But Pat had very little patience for this inconclusive sort of contact. Always when he held her, he would be thinking of Katie.

Katie was the most giving female he had ever known—giving of herself. No matter when it was that he turned to her, she was moist and ready and anxious.

It was Katie who taught him to kiss her down there, to suck up the sweet-tasting liquor coming from that hot cleft. It was she who had taught him that his very toes were fantastic sexual instruments, or the back of his knee, or the insides of his thighs.

Lying there, thinking about Kate, he began to have an enormous erection. He thought for a moment about masturbating, then he thought about Kate. He twisted around on the bed and grabbed the phone and dialed her number. There was no answer. He wondered where she spent the time, those many times when she was not answering and was not out of town either. Though she had not been willing to commit herself, she had sworn to him that she had no real sexual interest in any other man since they had been together.

"I only wish I *could*, you bastard," she said to him once. "You're ruining my life. I guess I'm only good for one man at a time. But what am I supposed to do the other six nights of the week? Have it off with a banana?"

In other women, that sort of vulgarity shocked Pat, but with Kate, it seemed natural, part of the fact that she was so at ease with him and he with her. He felt closer to her than to any other woman—closer than to any other human being. But goddamn it, where *was* she now when he needed her?

Suddenly, he had an overwhelming, burning desire for sex. His entire body was eroticized from the very roots of his hair to the soles of his feet. Even his own touch turned him on. At that moment, he would have screwed anything—an old lady, a young kid, a big, fat mamma, a skinny spade, a cat, a dog, a chicken, a milk bottle full of liver, anything, except maybe a fag.

Hurriedly, he threw on slacks and a striped sports shirt. He felt certain that if he started on the circuit down at San Remo and worked his way up through the Kettle of Fish, the Minetta Tavern, Louie's, the Riviera, the White Horse, he would stumble on something. He was not in the mood to be too fussy.

Other nights, when you weren't interested or up to it, they'd be all over you.

Still, tomorrow he would be married. Who knows what would happen then? Maybe it would all be over, the great Village roundelay. Maybe he would come home every night and sit down before the television with the sports section of the *Daily News* and get fucked two or three times a month, according to the great Holy Roman Calendar.

Deep down, he knew that it wouldn't be like that. Not as long as he was a cop and working crazy hours. Not as long as he was a *man*.

It was a lively Saturday night crowd in the Village. The college kids were down in force. The night was a warm one with only a slight, fetid breeze from the Hudson to stir the soupy air.

He went up to the Kettle. He had one drink and left. The Minetta was full of tourists who had come to gape at old Professor Seagull, Joe Gould, who conned every passing eyeballer out of a beer as he told the story of his "oral history of the world."

Pat had a couple in there. It was the kind of joint that out-of-towners often came to, women looking for excitement and alone in town. There was a thick-ankled girl in one of those peasant dirndl dresses with the low scoop neck displaying a pair of freckled, melon-type breasts. Pat guessed she would go about one hundred fifty-three pounds, five-seven, long braids tied with a red ribbon, no makeup, buck teeth.

In the barful of gay, laughing, gesticulating, arguing people, she sat alone, reading Henry Miller's *Tropic of Cancer*. Pat could see the title over her shoulder. He slipped into a narrow place beside the girl and ordered a Grant's and soda. The crowd pressed him against her side, but she pretended not to feel the pressure and kept reading intensely.

"It's a pretty hot book, isn't it?" Pat said to the girl.

She looked up at him with a wild, startled look.

"What?"

"I said it's a pretty hot book."

"Oh, that. Well, he's really a very important writer. A friend of mine brought this back to me from France."

"Yeah, I heard about it," Pat said. "You from New York?"

"I'm just here for the summer," the girl said.

"Oh? Where are you living?"

"I'm staying in Queens with my aunt."

Score a minus for the girl. After some discussion, Pat persuaded her to accept a beer. She really wasn't bad looking and she had one of those bodies that would look much better when the clothes were off. But Pat found his pulse-pounding, sexual excitement abating as he talked to her. He knew this would be no easy job.

If he wanted this dame, he would have to spend all night talking to her, buy her dinner and then practically kidnap her to get her up to his place. After the third drink, straining to make conversation, listening to the girl's half-baked theories about crime and correction, Pat was ready to go.

The girl looked around her at the caricatures on the wall of the old-time hangers-on, most of them relics of earlier Village days.

"I hear this is a Mafia place," she said.

Pat laughed and threw a few dollars on the bar to pay for the drinks.

"You must be kidding," he said. "There's no such thing as the Mafia. You been reading too many fairy tales."

When he left, the girl looked disappointed. He wondered if he had overestimated her resistance. Hell, she probably would have been a lousy lay anyway.

Louie's was also mobbed, but it was hard to tell which girls were there alone because the minute one came in and sat down, there would be two or three guys fluttering around like flies around a horse turd.

"Why the fuck," Pat thought, "should I be knocking myself out to get one of these broads in the hay? They want it as bad as I do. I'd probably give them a better ride than ninety percent of the guys here."

He was now on his seventh drink and feeling it. The Scotch was beginning to taste bitter in his mouth and rose high in his stomach, like a vial of acid. The loud laughter, the flirtations, the singing all seemed to drive him deeper into his mood of desperation. He couldn't sustain a conversation for more than five minutes without getting disgusted.

"What a bunch of fucking idiots!"

He cooled off during the five-block walk up Hudson to the White Horse. He always got a kick out of Jimmy Washington, who greeted him with a big blond grin and had his Grant's and soda ready by the time he got to the bar.

The Clancy Brothers were sitting in the back room as was as their habit, singing "The Rising of the Moon." A girl leaning at the end of the bar, munching on a hard-boiled egg, had long, taffy-colored hair that looked familiar. Pat weaved his way to her side and tapped her on the shoulder.

"Katie?" he said.

The girl turned, flashing her crooked-tooth smile.

"I beg your pardon?"

Christ, how could he have thought she was Katie? She was a beast! He fished in the pocket of his slacks for a nickel and went to the pay phone in the corner and dialed her number. The phone rang only two times before it was answered by a sleepy, throaty voice.

"Hello?"

"Katie, it's me, Pat. I'm coming over," he said.

"Pat? Where are you? You sound drunk."

"I'm at the White Horse. I'm coming over in a few minutes."

"Pat," she said, "don't come, please. Not *tonight*, for God's sake. You're getting *married* tomorrow, remember?"

"I don't give a fuck. I'm coming over," Pat said.

"I won't let you in."

"You'll fucking let me in!" Pat said.

He pushed his way through the crowd to the flow of warm, river air on Hudson Street, and began walking in long, hard paces across Eleventh toward Katie's apartment.

CHAPTER 29

Pat pushed the bell in the hallway, but there was no answer. He ran outside and looked at the second-floor window and saw that there was a light on in it. He went inside the hall again and rang several times. Then he took out his celluloid identification card and pushed open the latch of the inner door. Running up the carpeted stairs, two at a time, he pounded angrily on Katie's door.

"Katie, it's me. Pat. Open up!"

"Go away."

"Come on. What is this? Open up. It's me!"

"I *know* it's you," Katie said from the other side of the door. "Go away. You're getting married tomorrow. Go home and rest."

"Katie, if you don't open up, I'm going to bust this door down."

"You're drunk, Pat. Go home. You're waking up everybody in the building."

"I don't give a fuck *who* I wake up," Pat said. "I'm coming in and then I'm going to fuck your little ass off!"

The door opened part way, blocked by the retaining chain. A small bar of light came from inside the room and glared on the rug and Pat's florid face.

Katie whispered angrily, "Pat, go home. You can't do anything when you're drunk like this."

Pat backed up about a foot and hit the door hard with his shoulder, wrenching the screws holding the retaining chain from the doorframe. The door flew open. Katie ran around behind the couch. Pat closed the door behind him and started toward her. She was clearly frightened.

"Pat," she said, "this is crazy! We don't have to be like this. I just *can't* be with you tonight. I don't *want* to be with you. We have to put a stop to all that."

"You bitch," Pat said. "You *want* to be with me. You know you fucking well *want* to be with me!"

He started to unbuckle his slacks and let them fall around his ankles, the gun clattering to the floor along with the pants. He stepped free, standing now, ridiculously, in socks, shoes and sports shirt. Protruding from the gaping opening of the white boxer shorts, was his red, swollen penis, standing out like a policeman's billy.

*　*　*

Doyle had a couple of drinks in Delaney's, looked into Louie's which was now crowded to the point of overflow. He decided to go back to the Earl and get some sleep, but as he headed east toward Sixth Avenue, he thought he would make a detour past Katie's apartment just to look up at the window. Maybe if there was a light on, he would try calling her.

There were very few lights in the windows on the calm, tree-lined streets. The residents were old-line Villagers with money, not part of the bohemian night life. To them the Village meant a quiet place of old homes, trees, antiques, comfort, high rents. Shining through the branches of the ailanthus tree in front of Katie's house, he could see the glow of a light from her second-story window. He smiled with satisfaction. Even if he didn't see her, he could talk to her for a while on the phone.

Then he saw the white translucent drapes move violently as though someone had shoved or tugged them, and shadows looming, moving and dancing against the window. Moving closer, he heard the sound of breaking crockery and shouting voices.

Quickly, he ran into the hall and kicked through the flimsy latch of the outer door with one well-placed blow of his heavy shoe. He raced, stumbling in his haste, up the thickly carpeted stairs and slammed through the door to Katie's apartment without knocking.

The door was still unlatched. The room was weirdly lit from below by the floor lamp which had apparently been knocked over. Broken bits of smashed glass littered the floor. Pat was holding Katie by one arm and tearing at the chenille robe that she clutched around her. One breast peered out like a leering eye. There were big, red welt marks on her cheek where she had apparently been slapped, and a dark red trail of blood ran from the corner of her mouth down over her chin and dripped onto her flushed, pink chest. The lip above it was swollen and cracked.

Looming incongruously between the two struggling figures was Pat's huge, distended member. They all stood frozen in a tableau before the full impact of the scene reached Regan. Then, with an uncontrollable fury, Doyle jumped for Pat Conte, clutching the fabric of the striped sports shirt in one hand.

He caught Conte high on the cheekbone with a roundhouse right that sent him rolling over the sofa back onto the Oriental rug. Pat seemed too dazed, or perhaps too drunk, to even react defensively. Besides, he was three inches shorter and twenty-five pounds lighter than Doyle, who was fresh out of combat training.

Pat started to stumble to his feet and Regan kicked him cruelly in the ribs, knocking the wind from him in a rush. Pat went down, face mashed into the rug, retching and groaning. Katie grabbed Doyle's arm.

"Please, Regan, don't. You'll kill him. It's not what you think."

"That son-of-a-bitch was trying to rape you," Regan said. "I'll kill him! I swear it!"

Pat got to his knees, a ribbon of green bile spilling from his mouth to the rug beneath him. His chest was still heaving in a desperate effort to regain his breath. Suddenly he saw next to his hand, lying like a sleeping animal, his abandoned trousers, and beside them, gleaming dully, the off-duty Smith & Wesson. As Doyle and Katie argued, Pat reached with a compulsive movement for the pistol, unsnapping the holster with almost a single movement and rolled over on his back, pulling the trigger rapidly. The two shots made a deafening sound in the small room and were accompanied by the sound of tinkling glass. They were all Pat could get off before Regan caught his firing hand with his swift toe and kicked the smoking pistol into a corner behind the wing chair. Doyle turned in helpless rage to Katie.

"What's the matter with him? He's gone insane!"

Then, without waiting for an answer, he aimed a massive kick at Pat's groin, the sexual bludgeon he had been brandishing so recently, now flaccid and drawn up into itself. He missed the crotch by inches but landed a heavy blow to Pat's abdomen that doubled him up in agony. Then, in a sweeping movement, Doyle grabbed the huddled, half-naked figure of the injured policeman and hauled him by his shoulders across the floor. He wrenched open the wood-paneled apartment door, dragged Pat to the edge of the carpeted steps and threw him down the flight of stairs.

A vein was pulsing wildly in Doyle's forehead and his

eyes were red and popping with rage. It was the only time he had ever been so completely out of control. He walked back into the empty room, picked up the abandoned trousers and empty pistol holster and threw them down the stairs after Conte, not even looking to see what had happened to him at the foot of the stairs. A red-painted door opened across the hall and a gray-haired man in a satin bathrobe looked out timidly.

"Is everything all right? I thought I heard shots."

"It's okay," Regan said. He flashed his tin briefly so that the man could not see that it was a federal badge.

"I'm the police. We just caught a prowler in Miss Mullaley's apartment. Right, Miss Mullaley?"

Katie nodded, wordlessly, and Doyle shut the door. They could hear Pat at the foot of the stairs groaning in agony.

"Regan," Katie said, "he may be seriously hurt. He may have broken some bones."

"I hope the son-of-a-bitch dies," Doyle said.

"Yes, but . . ."

Then they heard the creaking sound of the downstairs door opening and slamming shut. Regan looked out and down the stairs and saw that Pat was gone. He closed the door and locked it with the sliding bar and turned toward Katie who came into his arms, murmuring, "Oh, Regan, Regan," and it seemed to him that there was pity in her voice and some sort of apology.

"Regan, what can I say?"

He held her close and felt her breath on his chest through his shirt. The robe had come partly open, and he could feel her warm breast, too, pressing into his ribs.

"You poor darling," he said. They sat down on the bed and they kissed.

Katie winced. "Ouch, my lip."

"I'm sorry, darling," Doyle said and kissed her neck and ears and breasts and nipples. Suddenly their excited panting turned from the fierce accents of danger to a slower, deeper, more compulsive rhythm. Tenderly, with dreamlike movements, Katie helped Doyle out of his clothes and lay open the blue chenille robe. Without words, he took her into his arms and they twined together, gently, and then seemed to flow into one another with hardly a conscious movement. Later, Doyle lay there thinking. It was the first time they had been together.

"I always knew that he had too much Sicilian blood in him," Regan said. "He must have been crazy! How could he do that?"

Katie sat up and began to cry into her doubled knees.

"Regan, I have to tell you. It wasn't like that. He's been here before. We've been . . . we've been lovers. But tonight, I just couldn't. Not just before the wedding. Tonight, I felt it was all over and he couldn't stand that."

Regan's mind reeled with montage flashes of all the times they'd been together, the four of them, Constanza, himself, Pat and Katie, over the last year, the camaraderie, the laughing, the tickling, the friendly wrestling, all out of some puppy days. But now, the flashbacks looked like faded pictures in an ancient family album. Suddenly, he was looking at scenes from a past so far behind him that its edges had faded into yellow. He put his arm over the naked shoulder of the sobbing girl.

"Katie, how could you?"

"God, I don't know," Katie sobbed. "I don't know. With him, I can't seem to help myself. He's like a monkey on my back. It's as though my body were acting on its own, and I had nothing to say about it."

She trembled as a sudden, late-night breeze came through the window which had been shattered by Pat's wild bullet.

"I'll have to do something about that window," Regan said. "You'll freeze."

Katie looked at the window in dumb surprise.

"My God!" she said. "He could have killed you! He really could have killed you!"

CHAPTER 30

Pat woke up about nine the following morning, bathed in sweat. His mouth tasted dark with blood and the light hurt, even through his closed lids. He sat up with his eyes still closed and swung his feet over the side of the bed. He felt as though his brain was sloshing loosely and painfully against the inside of his skull. When he opened his eyes, he could see nothing for a moment through the film of mucus that obscured his vision.

Looking down, he was surprised to find that he was still wearing his shoes and socks. His battered jaw felt tender to the touch. He had only the vaguest memory of the night before. For the moment, he was too weary to reconstruct the events. He stripped out of his shorts, shoes, socks and groped his way toward the shower, which he turned on full force and cold. The needle darts of water probed the raw places on his skin and stung in a way that seemed painful and beneficial at the same time. As he was toweling himself off, patting gently to avoid the bruised places, the phone rang. It was Connie.

"Everything going okay, lover?"

"Oh, sure, great," Pat said.

For the moment, he couldn't think of what she was talking about.

"We'll send a car for you about 10:00, all right?"

"A car," he thought. "For Christ's sake, he was getting married!"

"Listen," he said, "how about 10:30?"

"Okay. I guess there'll be plenty of time then. We've got your outfit here. Esperanza will show you where to go. We've got a room set up for you to dress in. I probably won't see you until the ceremony. Everything's going to be beautiful. You should see it. There's a tent, flowers everywhere. It's going to be beautiful. Pat, I really love you."

"Yeah," Pat said. "Yeah. I love you, too. See you later," and he hung up.

He tried to remember the evening as he shaved. He had never before drunk so much that he blacked out, and he had an uncomfortable feeling about the events of the night before. He remembered going to Louie's and then stumbling on to the White Horse. Then he had called Katie and they had some kind of argument. Then things got very blurred, but he had gone over there and there was some kind of a dream.

All of a sudden, Regan Doyle was there. How did he get there? And they were fighting, except Doyle was doing all the fighting. Pat was just holding up his arms to defend himself. And then, he pulled his gun and shot it. He remembered the deafening noise.

Then he remembered nothing except waking up in the cold dark of Katie's hall. He remembered grabbing a cab even for the few blocks and stumbling into the elevator.

He finished shaving, put on a pair of dress slacks and dialed Katie's number, but there was no answer. He went back and examined his freshly shaven face in the mirror. His teeth felt sore, and one of them, the left rear molar, seemed loose. The inside of his mouth was scarred and cut. His jaw was swollen and puffy on the left side. It was obvious someone had landed a right-handed haymaker on him. It had to have been Doyle. The eye, too, was swollen, but fortunately not discolored. His shoulders ached as though they'd been hit with sledgehammers and he felt a sharp stitch in his right side as though a rib may have been broken. Well, if anyone asked, he could always say that he had trouble taking in a prisoner. One good thing about being a cop—you could explain things like that.

As he left the house, Ollie the doorman handed him a brown paper parcel.

"A man left this this morning for you," Ollie said. "Said to give it to you when you came out."

Pat took the heavy bundle from the doorman's hands and thanked him. One of Massey's Fleetwood limousines was waiting for him at the door. It was driven by Tommy, the heavyset, taciturn chauffeur who had driven Pat and the Marseri family over to Duke's restaurant in the beginning, so many years ago. The driver had changed little over the five years, except for letting his hair grow longer and for a deep scar in his neck on the right side, just above the collar line that looked as though it had been cut with a saw-tooth knife.

"This is the big day, huh?" Tommy said, and Pat realized that already he was being treated with the respect of a *padrone*.

"Right," Pat said, and settled back into the deep, gray upholstered seat, leaving the window partition between him and the chauffeur closed. It wasn't a time for conversation.

Pat tore open the brown parcel and found the Smith & Wesson off-duty piece that Doyle had taken from him at Kate's the night before. There was no note and the revolver was empty. He thought that he had to remember to clean it the next day, since he had, as he recalled, fired it twice the night before. He slipped the pistol into

the empty holster that he had put on automatically with
his trousers in the morning.

On the way up the river, he leaned back in the limousine and rested his head and tried to wipe his mind
blank. When he got to the courtyard in Riverdale, there
were already several limousines parked there. Also a
truck from Concourse Caterers and a van from which
they were unloading folding chairs and tables.

Esperanza met him at the door. The Spanish maid led
Pat into a large, bright bedroom on the second floor
overlooking the rear garden. Through the window, he
could see a huge, striped tent with tables being set along
the side with flowers and plates.

On the bed, in a plastic garment bag was a powder-
blue dinner jacket, midnight blue pants, a formal shirt,
midnight blue tie, cufflinks. Everything had been
thought of, except underwear. Pat had been carefully
measured and fit for the outfit two or three weeks
earlier.

It took Pat a while to get the hang of attaching the
suspenders and the cufflinks, since he had never worn
either before in his life. Fortunately, the bow tie was a
ready-made type and simply had to be caught by its
clasp.

There was a full-length mirror in the adjoining
bathroom and when Pat had finished dressing and
combing his hair, he inspected himself in it. He thought
he looked a lot like Humphrey Bogart in *Casablanca*.
He could picture himself passing through the casino,
picking up tabs and throwing out drunks. He had never
been sure he liked the way he looked before, but now he
knew he did. The lump on the chin and the puffy eye
were hardly noticeable when he turned the right side of
his face to the mirror.

The jacket was long, reaching past his fingertips and
the pants were full around the knees in a style that was

popular then, narrowing to a conservative five-inch cuff.
A maroon cummerbund circled his hard, slim waist.

"Pat Conte," he said to himself in the mirror, "you
should have been an actor instead of a cop."

Now, despite the muddle in his mind about the evening before and the feeling of nauseous apprehension he
had felt all day, he felt good. He knew for sure he was
out of the slums forever. There was nowhere to go now
but up, and soon he would have to take very little shit
from anybody. Even if he did have to take a little, he
knew it was because he was going someplace, even
though he wasn't quite sure where.

There was a hearty knock on the door.

"Hey, Pasqualino! Come out. Come down and have a
drink. Let's talk to you."

It was Father Raimundo. He hadn't seen him in
weeks and felt vaguely guilty.

"I'll be right down. Pour me a Scotch and soda."

The men of the family were already waiting, gathered
in the library—Arthur, Father Raimundo, Don Antonio
and Sam. Arthur and Sam were also wearing powder-
blue jackets. Don Antonio was dressed in his wide-
lapeled striped suit and vest with a black tie, as though
he were going to a funeral. Father Raimundo was in
white linen and surplice. Sam poured them each a drink,
and they toasted with a muttered "*Salute.*"

"Well, Sam!" Father Raimundo said. "It's the big
day, heh? For once I feel like I'm not just 'Father' Ray
but a *real* father. That's how I feel about the boy. He's a
good kid. You're not making a mistake. Right, Arthur?"

Arthur nodded. "I think he's got something extra.
He's ambitious, he's bright and he's hard, plenty hard."

"Do you think he understands," Sam asked, "about
the family?"

Arthur smiled. "He's *one* of us. He was raised
amongst us. He's *Siciliano.* His parents are from Sicily.

Could he grow up and not know what everything is about? Of course, I never spoke to him about anything I asked him to do, but he *knows*. Of course he knows. If I would have to spell it out to him, he wouldn't be the kind of boy you'd want."

"Yes," Don Antonio said. "He seems a very bright boy. Clever. He knows how to talk. He shows respect, too. But I wonder, why have we made him one of the *sbirro*? I mean no offense, Arthur. It's been good having you working there, but there are other important things to be done. We need people we can trust."

"That's just it," Sam said. "That's *just it*, Anthony. We've learned how to do a lot of things in this country. I've learned a lot. I went to school. I think it did me a lot of good. In the beginning, our people were all against school. They wanted to stay in the neighborhood. They wanted to protect each other. But now, people are growing up, moving out of the neighborhood. I'm here." He gestured to the richly furnished room with its deep leather upholstery and gleaming wood panels. "This is a big change from Mulberry Street. Right?" He gazed with satisfaction at the room around him. "You think I'm not happier? I am! Sure, I go down sometimes on a Saturday or Sunday to the old neighborhood to buy some pasta. I see the friends. I have a couple *capuccino*. I play some cards. I don't forget the old country. I don't forget our people. But every generation must grow."

"Yes," Don Antonio said. "But sometimes I think that everybody's growing away from us. So many people, they become educated. They marry out of the family. They marry *stranieri*."

"I agree," Sam said. "That's why I like this boy. He was still cut from the old cloth. One of *us*. He can be depended on. I'm sure of it. But what I'm not sure about is how long I want him to stay on the force. What kind of an occupation is that? I'm sorry, Arthur, but how much future is there in it? Sure, you're a lieutenant now, and you'll probably get promoted further before you go. But even you, I feel, haven't achieved what you could have if you'd stayed with us."

"But I *am* with you," Arthur said.

"I mean if you'd worked with me in the business."

Arthur shrugged. "Well, that's the way it worked out. We're arranging now for the boy to get some schooling, even while he's in the department. This will open up some doors. Maybe later, he'll want to change. Meanwhile, he can be very useful to us. And, we'll have a chance to study him and find out where he can fit in best." He turned toward the door. "Here he is now. The wedding boy. Wait, wait, Sam. I'll pour another round. We'll have to drink a toast to the groom." And he poured a round of Scotch in shot glasses which they all held up in a toast to Pat.

"A salute gli sposa!"

Sam grabbed Pat tightly around the shoulders and hugged him in an embrace. He kissed him on both cheeks.

"Welcome to the family, son," he said, and Pat was surprised to see that his eyes were moist.

Sam had always seemed to be a man of stone. But maybe that was only to those outside his family.

By the time the wedding itself came off in the gaily decorated garden of Sam Massey's Riverdale palace, Pat had had six drinks with his future in-laws and was feeling pleasantly vague. It was a crisp, sunny, summer day and the wedding ceremony itself took place outdoors under a canopy of flowers.

Father Ray was the only "family" representing Pat. From Connie's side there were scores of relatives, it seemed—fat aunts, skinny, knobby-kneed cousins, pale and Americanized-looking relatives from beyond the river, from Cleveland, from Buffalo.

The ceremony was performed by Father Bernard Donato, dean of St. Agnes, who was Constanza's confessor and her personal choice. Constanza looked as white and fluffy and unworldly as the cumulus clouds that scudded overhead. She wore a great billowing satin dress with Alencon lace around her flushed, pink bosom. The gown was a handmade copy of the one Elizabeth Taylor had worn in her marriage to Nicky Hilton.

A royal blue carpet had been rolled out on the grass and folding chairs set out on either side of it. Beneath the plush surface of the carpet, Pat could feel the soft, yielding surface of the lawn. He felt light on his feet and seemed to be floating along with the cloudlike child bride as he stood in front of the white-surpliced priest, strange to him, and heard the mumbling and jumbling in the Latin and then, "Do you?" and "Do you?" and "Do you?" and "Do you?"

Father Ray, standing by his side, fished for the ring efficiently and then it was: "I now pronounce you."

Later, Pat stood on the open lawn as armies of cousins and aunts trouped past saying, "My, isn't he handsome?" and the men said, "Welcome to the family," and sometimes something about his being a cop like, "Well, it's a good steady job," or "We got to have cops, too," or, "It'll be good experience for later."

Later there was *pate de foie gras* and capon and sherbet and champagne, lots of champagne, and toasts and dancing, starting out with the *tarantella* and the old dances, but soon switching to the boogie beat and jitterbug rhythms, pounded out by the Lester Lanin Group, hired for the day. They wore matching blue dinner jackets, so that if Pat had gone on the bandstand, he could have been mistaken for a saxophone player.

Pat felt as though it were all happening to somebody else, and as though he were watching it from some window across the lawn through binoculars. He could see himself, tall and slim, with dark, curly hair and broad shoulders in the powder-blue jacket and the shiny shoes.

And the men, as each came up, had an envelope that was gratefully collected, the *porta foglio del sposalizo*.

Besides the relatives, there were a lot of faces that Pat recognized, even in his hazy condition. There were important people from the family and from the other, bigger family, Anastasia, Genovese, Willie Moretti, acting funny and crazy while the others looked at him and tapped their foreheads significantly behind his back. Gambino, gentle, peacemaker, Costello, genial and easygoing, Tommy Lucchese, DeSapio, looking distinguished and distant behind his dark glasses.

And there were congressmen, too, all the many political, business and social friends of Massey and of the Marseri family. Pat had had no idea how wide and deep this power went.

Later, outside, feeling woozy and happy, Sam embraced him again and said, "Now I've got a surprise for you. A little extra wedding present," and he led them to the front yard. Under the porte cochere there was a red Mercury convertible with white leather seats, its top down, gleaming in the sun.

"After all, Pat," Sam said, "you can't be riding around in limousines all the time. You're a working man. You got to have your own wheels, right?"

Pat was stunned. It was probably the most impressive part of the whole day to him. He had never in his life owned a car of his own, and this was a *car*. This was *really* a car!

"You sure you can drive, boy?" Sam said seriously, as Pat walked around the Mercury touching the brightwork, kicking the tries with a dazed smile on his face.

"Don't worry, Sam. I'm all right."

"And you'll remember about the envelope I gave you for Norman Hoffman?"

Pat touched the narrow manila envelope in his inside

pocket. "Sure, sure." He had, in fact, almost forgotten it.

"Remember," Sam said, "when you get to the Nacional in Havana, you call this number at the Sans Souci and let Norman know that you're in town. Norman Hoffman. That's what he calls himself down there. He'll let you know what to do about the envelope."

"Right," Pat said. "Thanks a lot. 'Bye." They zoomed off in the red Mercury headed for the Plaza Hotel where they were to spend the night before leaving for their honeymoon in Havana.

CHAPTER 31

By the time they had driven down to the Plaza, Pat was feeling sober again, even serious. Constanza had changed from her wedding gown to a beautiful white silk suit with a full pleated skirt and a dark, contrasting red blouse that only pointed up the happy flush in her face.

Pat felt vaguely off balance, swept up in a powerful current of other people's plans. He had not really *planned* to get married. He had not *planned* the wedding. He had not *planned* the honeymoon. But he had no complaints. Still, he would like to get his feet on the ground again soon and start running the details of his own life.

It was obvious that the hotel had been advised as to their arrival and all the plans had been made there too. A grinning bellboy turned away the dollar Pat offered him for showing them to their suite, which consisted of an anteroom decorated in Regency antiques, a living room with a sofa and bar and a huge corner bedroom, both of the main rooms looking out over Central Park and up Fifth Avenue.

"Oh, it's gorgeous!" Connie said.

"Boy, this place must go a hundred, a hundred fifty a day," Pat said.

"Well, it's our honeymoon and it's paid for anyway," Connie said, taking off her broad-brimmed straw hat, primping her crisp black curly hair in the mirror. The blouse was of thin, almost transparent silk, and Pat could see the lacy slip underneath it and the bra straps coming up her back. He came up behind her at the dressing table, put his arms around her, kissing her softly on the ear and cupping her breasts in both hands.

Constanza leaned happily back against him, reaching up to run her hands through his hair and pull his face close to hers. He pulled her to her feet and pressed his lips to her open, waiting mouth. She weighed heavily on his arms as her knees seemed to give way in the heat of their kiss. There was a discreet knocking at the door and Pat, sighing, went to answer it. It was a bellboy pushing a cart with an enormous bottle of champagne in a silver bucket, and a huge bouquet of flowers.

"There's a card on the champagne, sir. The flowers are compliments of the house, and good luck to you both."

"Thanks a lot," Pat said.

On the inside of the knob was a sign that said, "Do not disturb," on one side. Pat took it and hung it on the outside of the door and closed and locked the door to the outer room and then closed and locked the door to the inner room.

He took off his linen sports jacket and tie and threw them over the back of a chair and returned to Connie who was now sitting on the bed waiting for him. They both kicked off their shoes and lay back on the thick, satin coverlet.

"Oh, God," Connie said. "I never thought it would really happen."

"Let's go to bed now," Pat said.

"In the middle of the day?"

"It's not the middle of the day. It's almost time for

dinner. Don't forget, we're on daylight savings time," Pat said.

"Do you want to open the champagne first?"

"Bed first, champagne after," Pat said.

Gently fumbling with the buttons on the red silk blouse with one hand while he kissed her tenderly on the neck and the earlobe and in the angle of her neck and shoulder, he could see her ears redden and her breath begin to come slow and deep.

As her hands moved, pressing strongly, with her fingernails digging deeply into his back, slowly and quietly they undressed one another, nibbling, biting and kissing as they did. Constanza was wearing red underwear, a lacy red bra and panties to match. Against her pink skin, the contrast was unbearably sweet.

Pat was now completely nude, his fawn slacks crumpled carelessly with his shoes and socks at the foot of the bed. Carefully, gently, he took Constanza's hand and placed it on his now throbbingly erect penis. Timidly she stroked it. Her hand was cool and damp and the contrast to his hot skin was like the touch of a flower petal. He whispered in her ear.

"I'm so excited, I may come before we even make love."

Without her help, he finally managed to unsnap the fastenings of the red bra and pull it aside to reveal her young, full breasts with their small, pink nipples. Almost reverently, he began to suck the nipples, one by one. Constanza held his head to her chest as though he were a child, feeding. With his free hand, he began to pull down the elastic of the red panties. Connie raised her hips to help him slip the garment down around her ankles. Her pubic hair, which he had never seen before, was sparse and soft, like a baby's hair.

"It's beautiful," Pat said. "You know I've never seen it before."

Gently, he ran his finger among the curly tendrils that feathered up onto her softly, heaving stomach. But as his fingers approached the dark slit, Connie's muscles suddenly went all tense.

"What's the matter, darling?" Pat said.

"Nothing, Pat, nothing, just . . . well, you understand, it's something new. I've never been touched there before."

"Don't worry, Connie," he said. "It's something beautiful. You'll love it!"

Gently, he started to ease his finger into the cleft again. But just as he reached the moist, inner lips, there was a sharp intake of breath from Connie, and she put her hand down over his.

"Please, Pat. Can we have some champagne first? I think I really need it. I know I'll be all right. It's just so new."

Pat stifled his sense of frustration. "I should be glad," he thought, "that I'm the first one."

Suppose he'd married Katie? God knows how many men she'd had. At least Constanza was still pure.

"Okay, honey. We'll have the champagne."

Constanza got up and slipped into a long, sheer peignoir which only served to sharpen the sensation in Pat's groin. For decency's sake, Pat wrapped a towel around him to cover the looming lump of flesh between his legs. Constanza went to the windows and pulled the curtains closed and then the second heavy drapes, creating an illusion of night in the room.

"It's almost dinnertime," she said.

"We'll send down for food later."

They sat quietly on the edge of the bed and toasted one another with the first glass of champagne.

"You have to understand," Connie said, "I love you very much and I want you very much. Please believe that. I've dreamed about this. I've even confessed to the priest that I made love to you in my dreams. But you know, I didn't know how it really *was*—even to dream about. It was just you pressing against me and then this good feeling."

"It's even nicer in real life," Pat said, smiling.

By the third glass of champagne, they were both silly and giggly. Pat began to tickle Constanza and she doubled up in hysterics. Then, finally, he pinned her to the satin coverlet and kissed her hungrily and hysterically on the mouth and then on the breasts and then on the stomach and finally he could feel her leg muscles beginning to relax and her thighs parted, if not passionately, at least willingly. When he ran his hand between her legs again, he could feel that the feathery bush of pubic hair was moist.

"You'd better get a towel," Connie said.

"Why?"

"Well, you know. I hear sometimes that people bleed . . ."

"Oh. Oh, yeah. I forgot about that," Pat said, and ran to the bathroom for a towel.

When he came back, he found he had to start wooing her all over again and it was another half hour before her legs again unclasped. When they finally did, he leaped on top of her, hastily thrust his aching member at that cherished bridal arch. Connie winced with pain as the penis chafed against the still not completely moistened and ready opening.

"You have to help," Pat said, panting. "You have to help see that it goes in right. Lift up your legs."

Obediently she lifted the velvet thighs and with reluctant hands reached below to grasp his member. Then, with a thrust, he pressed in as hard and as fast as he could. Connie answered the thrust with a scream, then immediately threw both arms around his neck.

"I'm sorry, Pat. I'm sorry. I didn't mean to scream. It just hurt. It just hurt for the minute."

But Pat lay there panting. He had already come.

When he caught his breath, he said, "You have to realize, Connie, this is just the first. It's never good the first time."

"It felt nice," Connie said. "I know it will be even better later." She looked at the towel. "I didn't bleed much, did I?"

Pat smiled. "No, but you bled enough. In the old country, we'd have to show the towel."

* * *

The sun at Rancho Boyero Airport in Havana was like a hot, shiny knife. Pat was apprehensive as they passed the gray-uniformed customs agents. The manila envelope in his inner pocket felt large. But the customs men looked only at the pictures in the passports. They chalked marks on their new Vuitton flight bags, (a present from Arthur) and waved the young couple on.

At the stately old Nacional, they again had a corner suite, this time overlooking Havana Bay and Morro Castle. Three bottles of Bacardi Anejo were waiting with a card, "Compliments of the Management." There was a huge basket of tropical fruits with a note saying, "From Norman Hoffman. Come see me," on the stationery of the Sans Souci. Before they could unpack, a waiter arrived with two frozen daiquiris piled high, like miniature breasts.

"Compliments of the management, senor," the waiter said and bowed out.

The drinks were so cold, they chilled the sinuses.

"This is great," Connie said. "It was nice of Dad, wasn't it, to arrange all this?"

"Yeah," Pat said, again feeling the weight of the envelope in his pocket.

While Connie was unpacking and hanging her clothes up, Pat stepped into the bathroom and took out the envelope. He ran the hot water until steam gushed from the faucet and held the flap near the vapor until it became gummy and loose. In the envelope was a sheaf of one-hundred-dollar bills—two hundred and fifty of them. Pat counted and recounted. Twenty-five thousand dollars. There was no note or other document.

Pat resealed the envelope and put it back in his pocket. It was not a surprise to him. He knew from the shape and feel of the envelope that it had cash in it. He also knew enough about Sam's affairs and what had been going on in Havana since Lucky Luciano had established things there four years earlier.

The Sans Souci was one of Meyer Lansky's places, but Lansky was tied into Genovese and Genovese was tied into Sam Massey. He also knew that Sam was certain that Pat wouldn't double-cross him—not for twenty-five thousand dollars.

He knew that being Sam's son-in-law would be no protection if he tried it. But he also had the feeling that this was just a test run, a trial mission. Now that he was in the family, they were trying to find out how far he could be trusted.

But what had he to report to authorities anyway? Just a present of some untraceable cash to a friend in Havana. Pat came back in and finished the daiquiri with Connie and then they got into their swimsuits and went to the pool downstairs.

When they came back, there was a little ivory box on the bureau wrapped with a gold ribbon. In it was one thousand dollars in chips for the Casino Nacional and a card signed simply, "A Friend."

Pat picked up the telephone and made reservations at the Sans Souci for the dinner show that evening. It was late afternoon after the shower and everything was closed for siesta. Pat stretched out on the bed and Connie lay down beside him. Gently, he turned to her and started kissing her eyes and her lips.

"Pat," she said, "you're a good Catholic, aren't you?"

Pat pulled away, surprised. "Sure. Sure I am. What's that got to do with anything?"

"You know, last night I didn't use anything and you didn't use anything. I don't have anything to use. We haven't talked about children or how soon we should have them, but I thought you should know."

"Oh, Christ," Pat said, sitting up. "Kids! I really wasn't planning on kids right away."

"Well, if you don't want to . . ."

"It's a little late for that," Pat said, "isn't it? For all we know, you're on your way already."

"Can it happen after just one time?"

"Sure," Pat said, "it can happen after just one time. Didn't they teach you anything about this at the convent?"

"Mother Rosa told me about the calendar, about the days when it's all right to do it—make love, I mean."

"Well, are *these* the days?" Pat said.

"I think it's just the end of the time when it's all right. There's five days they said when it's sure. Yesterday was the fifth day."

"Oh, Christ," Pat said. "Let's take a nap."

"Are you mad?"

"No, I'm not mad, but we'll have to talk about this. I don't really think God meant people to make love only five days a month."

"No," Connie said. "He meant them to have children."

"Yeah. Well, let's get a little more settled before we go in for that."

That night, Pat put on the white dinner jacket he had brought and Connie wore a long white crepe dress with bare shoulders that showed off her skin, healthy and pink from the afternoon's sun.

"God, you're a sexy-looking broad," Pat said, as they started out the door."

Connie beamed. "Pat, I'm sorry about this afternoon. I know everything will work out anyway."

Pat's expression changed. "Yeah," he said, "I hope so."

The Sans Souci was a huge stucco structure on the edge of the city, almost as big inside as an airplane hangar, festooned with tropical plants and palms.

Pat and Connie were shown to a table at the edge of the huge stage and dance floor. The show was elaborate, equal to anything they'd ever seen in New York and the dancers were spirited, with a way of moving their pelvises that seemed peculiar to the Caribbean and was more suggestive than any amount of nudity. The closest thing to a Cuban dish on the menu was tropical crawfish, a sort of lobster tail and a salad of local fruits mixed with ice cream. Pat ordered these for both of them and they drank daiquiris again.

As they were served the second daiquiri, a tall, slim man with well-trimmed, iron-gray hair and rimless tinted glasses came to the table.

"Are you Pat Conte?"

"That's right."

"I'm Norman Hoffman," the man said, flashing a chalky smile.

"Would you care to sit down?" Pat said, and Hoffman joined them.

"I'd like to thank you for your gift we found in the room. It was very kind of you."

"It's nothing," Hoffman said. "After all, this is Sam Massey's daughter, and you're his son-in-law."

"You know Sam well?"

Hoffman's smile broadened. "I know him *very* well and for a long time. You might say we're family friends, not actually *one* of the family, but *friends* of the family, if you know what I mean."

Pat nodded. "Well, I have regards for you, also, from Sam."

Hoffman smiled and nodded. "Fine. Why don't we just have a little chat in the office? Mrs. Conte, will you excuse us for just a minute? The waiter will bring you anything you need."

Hoffman ushered Pat out of the cabaret and up a small flight of stairs to a carved mahogany door on a balcony overlooking the casino. The place was decorated as a trophy room with heads of gazelles, wildebeeste, rhino, a cape buffalo and a huge stuffed marlin on one wall.

The wastebasket was made from an elephant's foot. To the right of the entrance was a large antique mirror, bound in zebra hide. A huge tiger skin adorned the floor, its teeth a strange match for those of Hoffman.

"Nice, eh?" Hoffman said.

"You shoot these?" Pat asked, indicating the trophies.

Hoffman smiled. "I do a little hunting. I like it. It relaxes me and I have the money now to travel when I want. It's always nice to have money. I believe you have something for me?" he asked politely.

Pat reached into his pocket and pulled out the envelope.

"Ah, yes, very nice. No need to count it. We know Sam. You know, this doesn't go to me personally," Hoffman said. "This is for Batista and his crew. The money comes in and the money goes out," he laughed.

He seemed to assume that Pat knew what was in the envelope and a lot more about Sam's business than Pat actually knew.

"Yes, things are going to open up very big down here in about a year," Hoffman said, "but I won't detain you. You have your wife waiting for you."

Pat stood looking at his distorted image in the wavy, antique mirror.

"It's a beauty, eh?" Hoffman said, "and it's very useful. Watch."

He flicked the light switch and the room went dark but the mirror seemed to spring to life like a TV screen. It was a one-way mirror with a full view of the casino.

"Of course," Hoffman said, "we have men on the cat-walks above watching the dealers, but I like to be able to keep an eye on things myself. A lot of money changes hands here. Some people get sticky-fingered, you know?"

"I guess so," Pat said.

"Well," Hoffman said, shaking his hand, "I have more work to do here. Enjoy yourself. The check is on me. Please call me if you need anything while you're here. I really mean that."

Pat returned through the busy casino to the table.

"I didn't know you had any business down here," Connie said.

"I didn't. It was just an errand for Sam."

They stayed and drank and danced until 2:00 in the morning. Connie was feeling gay but woozy from the drink. Leaving the club, they were met by a man in a cap and a natty brown uniform.

"Senor Conte?" he said. "Senor Hoffman said I was to drive you wherever you wish. My name is Manuel. I will be at your service during your stay here. Here is my card. You can call me at any time, but mostly I will stay in front of the hotel. Now, where do you wish to go? Do you wish to go to one of the other casinos? Perhaps a drive along the *malecon*? It's very beautiful at night."

"No, we'll just go home tonight," Pat said.

"Tomorrow," Manuel said, becoming chatty, "I will show whatever you want. Sloppy Joe's, I will take you to the shopping, to the Hilton, whatever, the Biblioteca Nacional, perhaps to the Morro, if you wish to go.

By the end of the honeymoon, they had seen these things and many more. Manuel spoke excellent English and was a perfect guide. One afternoon while Connie was taking a siesta, he showed Pat to the red-light district at Crespo and Amistad where the girls hissed invitingly through closed shutters or lounged, openly soliciting on the corners.

"These are bad girls. I mean, very low class, but we have some very beautiful houses here. If you like, I will show them to you. And we have, of course, the exhibitions. Does Senora like exhibitions?"

Pat smiled, "I doubt that very much."

"How about Senor?"

"I wouldn't mind, but it would be a little tough to get away."

"Of course. Senor is on his honeymoon."

They went to the new Riviera, to the Tropicana, to the Floradita where Hemingway could be seen dipping his beard into giant daiquiris.

They took a picnic lunch, complete with a giant thermos of daiquiris, to Veradero Beach and came home sunburned and giddy. Constanza was not interested in the gambling, so she went up early most of the nights while Pat stayed on and played blackjack. Basically, he played in the hotel only because he had the thousand dollars worth of chips. The end of his second day of gambling, he was down to two hundred dollars. The pit boss came along and spoke to him.

"How are you doing, Senor Conte?" he asked.

Pat made the Sicilian gesture. "So-so."

"Well, we must have patience," he said, putting his hand on Pat's shoulder, and for the next hour, Pat's luck seemed to turn until he had won back the eight hundred dollars he'd lost and a five-hundred-dollar bonus. At this point, the pit boss reappeared again.

"You're doing better now, I see."

"Yes," Pat said, smiling.

"Well, you have to be careful. You don't want to win too much, do you?"

Pat looked surprised. "Why not?" he said.

"Just joking, Mr. Conte," but Pat noticed that he

started to lose again at that point and something told him that it was time to quit. He dropped out with twelve hundred dollars and cashed it in.

The rum had relaxed him without making him really drowsy and he decided to take a walk in the cool, evening air. He walked from the Nacional down to the Prado, the broad, tree-lined street that ran through the heart of Havana. From every doorway, there came whispered invitations.

"Hey, Joe. You like nice girl? Filthy pictures? You like sleep with black lady? You like see dirty show? You like see superman?"

Pat just kept walking. He turned the corner off the Prado into Sloppy Joe's Bar, a great long mahogany expanse, and bought six Blackstone Cigars, El Productos. A girl with hair too blonde to be true, in a low-cut, black silk dress was sipping a Mojito at the bar. She smiled at Pat.

"You like Havana?" she said.

Pat smiled back. "Sure. I love Havana."

"You buy me a drink?"

"Sure," Pat said. "Anything you want."

The girl ordered another Mojito. Pat sat down at the bar and the girl pulled her stool closer to him.

"I thought you kids liked champagne," Pat said.

The girl made a deprecating gesture. "I don't like to drink at all. It gives me a headache, but men, they no like it if you no drink. Right, honey?"

Pat shrugged. "How do you make your money if you don't drink?"

She smiled. "I no make money selling *drinks*."

"I see," Pat said.

She put her hand on the arm of his jacket. "My name is Betty," she said.

"Betty?"

"Well, my real name is Elizabeta, but for Yankees, I am Betty. You want to come home with me?"

The bleached hair gave her a look of hardness, but actually, she wasn't that old, probably around twenty-three. What he could see of her breasts beneath the black dress seemed full, perhaps a little on the fat side, but tasty-looking. He began to have a warm feeling in his loins, partly due to the rum, partly the sexual deprivation of the past week.

"Fuck it," he thought, "a man can't live without sex. How much is it, baby?"

"For a handsome Yankee like you, it's not much. Fifty dollars. All night. Around the world."

"I haven't got all night," Pat said. "How much for a short time?"

The girl looked crestfallen. "You no have money?"

"I have money," he said. "I no have time."

She grabbed him by the hand. "Let's go."

As they started out the door, she held his arm against her breast and whispered to him. "It is late. You can stay all night for twenty-five dollars."

"I wouldn't mind," Pat said, "but I really *don't* have the time."

BOOK II

CHAPTER 1

The cash and checks in the wedding envelopes had come to fourteen thousand dollars. Pat thought about putting the money into a savings account, but finally he put only a few thousand into a checking account and put the rest into a safe deposit box that he opened up in his name at the Greenwich Savings Bank in the Village.

They rented a three-room flat in one of the new apartment houses in Riverdale, where Connie could be near her family and friends. Pat spent twenty-four hundred dollars of the wedding money on furnishings which Connie picked out at Bloomingdale's.

She did it all in a heavily carved primitive Spanish style with terra cotta tiles and Spanish wool rugs. Connie had a natural flair for decoration and Pat approved. He felt that the new apartment had real class.

He used the red convertible to go to work in the Sixth every day and usually tried to park it far from the precinct house because he was not anxious to call attention to his newfound affluence.

In the beginning, Pat really believed that Connie would ultimately shuck off her shyness in bed. He tried liquor (which had some effect, but required a delicate formulation, because with one drink too many, Connie would fall into a sleep of the dead), gifts (no effect, except resentment that he was trying to "buy" her), soft lights, music, tender persuasion and forceful rapelike sorties. For a while he thought that sadism or masochism would hold the key, but it was a wasted thought.

He drew on his whole repertory of experience for new erotic areas through which to light her fire—the ears, the navel, the back of the neck, the inside of the thighs, the toes, even her lovely rosebud anus. He tried it with the lights on, and the lights off, and a dimly lit in between. On the whole, she preferred darkness.

One night, reluctantly, she agreed to let him bathe her in the shower. The slithery action of his hands over the soap-slick skin seemed to rouse a dormant passion. Her body began to surge and respond to the pressure of his fingers, and as he approached her vagina he felt a shy but positive pelvic thrust.

Gently, careful not to disturb the rare mood, he led her out of the shower onto the thick cotton-shag rug of the bathroom, and laid her, still soapy and damp, on the floor. Her body felt cool and smooth on the outside, but inside, she was hot and moist.

Her mouth, too, was warm and responsive under his lips.

With gentle stalking movements, he moved his hard penis, still slippery with soap, between her legs, but only rubbed the outside of the vagina with it until Connie began to move strongly from the hips thrusting against the stiff and slippery tube between her legs and muttering his name over and over again.

"Pat, Pat, oh God, Pat!"

"Do you want me now, darling?" Pat whispered.

"Yes! Oh God! Yes, please yes! I want you *now*!"

And they combined in a tangle of shining slithering limbs, under the hot eye of the bathroom light in a searing, draining, strung-out orgasm.

Through it all, Connie kept moaning, "Oh, Christ! Oh, Jesus! Holy Mother of God!" and crying until her tears mingled indistinguishably with the damp drying soap tracks on her skin.

But later, she was ashamed.

"I don't know what got into me. I must have been crazy, and I'm sure it's the wrong time of the month."

After that, whenever Pat suggested they shower together, she would give him a veiled, sly look. But no amount of persuasion would induce her to repeat the escapade. Eventually, Pat became bored with the effort of it all.

He settled for sex two or three times a month with Connie, who kept a panic-stricken eye on the calendar and the thermometer. Sometimes it seemed that she would take fire from the lovemaking, but she was always so far behind him that he was through long before she started to move her pelvis in response to his thrusts.

Pat missed Katie deeply, not only for the sex, but for the long talks they would have. Katie had not communicated with him at all after the scene at her apartment, but she had written to Connie to say that she'd gone out to the Coast to train at the Pasadena Playhouse and see if she could get some work in the movies.

Doyle had not shown up at the wedding, but had sent a telegram claiming that he'd been called away suddenly on a case. Pat felt more shame for what he had done than anger at Doyle for having beaten him, but he knew that nothing would erase the bitterness that now lay between them.

About a month after they had settled into the Riverdale apartment at West 246th Street, Pat was given the special assignment as an undercover man at NYU, as Arthur Marseri had suggested.

This enabled him to enroll in the liberal arts course, leading to a law degree at full credits while still pulling duty in the precinct. He was told not to make any collars without checking with the Intelligence Division.

Pat was not much older than some of the students who had been away to the war and were going on the GI Bill. While he was on the assignment, he was told to stay away from the precinct house and report in only by phone or by occasional personal meetings with his supervisor.

He was told to fill out weekly reports on his observations. In a private conversation, Arthur Marseri had told him that what he, at any rate, was really interested in was the game fixing, which was cutting very badly into big bookmakers like Frank Erickson, who was under the wing of Costello.

Players were shaving points just enough to throw the spread off in the betting and the syndicate they had set up seemed to be making some very big kills against the odds.

"Whoever it is," Arthur said, "they're just amateurs, but they're fooling around with the wrong people, so get whatever you can on it and if it's anything that we can't go on officially, let me know about it and maybe we can do something on our own."

He didn't elaborate on that, and Pat didn't ask what he meant.

From the Village grapevine, he was well aware that there was still a fairly close link between Genovese and Costello, although Genovese was gradually taking over as *capo di tutti capi*: head of all the rackets in the area and a unifying link between the five New York families.

This was one time when the needs of the law and the needs of the family were the same. Game fixing had to be stopped. Pat was allowed to look over detective reports and other data which had been gathered to date. Suspicion focused on two or three NYU players, a six-foot-eight colored center from East Harlem, a fast little Jewish guy with a good hook shot and a rangy, simple-looking Polack from Pittsburgh who was murder under the backboard.

Usually, all three were playing on the first team. There was no game in which at least two of them were not active, but the idea was to find out just who was paying them, and how, because the game fixing wasn't limited to NYU but seemed to be going on in Kentucky, Ohio and other schools.

Though he was under no obligation to pass his courses, Pat found himself interested in the schooling and easily able to keep up with the work, and Connie was a big help in a lot of the necessary research and in preparing some of the homework papers. He still had his periodic meets with Arthur Marseri and with Al Santini, Pauley Federici and the gang down on Mulberry Street who now called him "The Professor."

Arthur explained the importance of the undercover assignment to Pat's career.

"You won't get out of the bag permanently on this one, but it will look good on your record, especially if you make some good collars. Then, maybe, you go back in the car for a while and they can use this record to put you up for detective a little later on or at least get you into plainclothes."

The students at NYU were different from anybody he'd known. They seemed aware and tuned in. They were more concerned with what was happening in the newspapers.

In the school cafeteria, he soon found himself a group that seemed to be the most lively and the most involved. This, if anywhere, was where Pat would get clues to any student involved in either the basketball fixing or the Communist plots. Actually, it was the table he would have preferred anyway.

The talk was spirited, the arguments were lively. Many of the older students who were veterans belonged to the Reserve and were very worried about being recalled for the Korean War. One student who had been recalled had been killed only a short time before in the breakthrough at Taejon. Artie Winburg, a tall, thin, balding veteran from Providence, was shook by the news, which first appeared in *The Violet,* the campus newspaper.

"If they call me again, I'm not going, that's all! They conned me into signing into the Reserves so they could hold my rank. Big deal, T-5."

Georgie Wise, the one member of the group with connections to the basketball team, was the assistant manager, a nervous, bright-eyed little squirrel of a boy from Brooklyn who had his ideas on the subject—that MacArthur was a maniac.

"You'll see. He's going to get us into a war with China before we're through over there. There'll be an atomic holocaust. You guys better start learning how to crawl under tables."

The cafeteria special for the day was creamed chipped beef on toast. Winburg looked at his tray with disgust.

"Shit on a shingle!" he said. "Goddamn, I never thought I'd see that stuff again, and eat it too."

A tall, full-breasted blonde girl with straight hair hanging down on both sides of her face came over.

"Mind if I sit down, fellers?"

She was Ellie Vogel, a sometime girlfriend of Winburg's and a graduate student in the biology department.

"Sit, sit, sit," everybody cried in unison.

"Who's this?" Ellie asked, indicating Pat.

"He's a new guy," Winburg said. "He's an Italian, but I still think he can learn something."

"I told you before," Ellie said, "I don't think that sort of joke is funny."

Pat grinned. "Thanks for the defense, but I think I can handle it okay myself."

"I'm not protecting *you*, I just don't like those ethnic slurs."

"That's because your people are krauts," Winburg said, "and you're embarrassed by it."

Ellie started to get up and Winburg apologized quickly.

"Okay, okay. I'm sorry. You're right. That sort of joke is out of line."

Pat had hoped, with Wise at the table, he could steer the conversation around to basketball, but now that Ellie had joined them, they talked more about theater. *Guys and Dolls* was the hottest show on Broadway and he was the only one who had seen it. At last he had something he could talk about with more authority than the rest.

"Well, I think it's stupid," Ellie said. "In the end, a show like that just makes heroes out of gamblers and crooks. That's why we have scandals like Gross in Brooklyn, because people think gambling is funny."

"What's so serious about it?" Wise said. "People like to gamble. So what?"

"So it's all run by the rackets," Ellie said angrily, "and those men are involved in dope and prostitution and every other kind of exploitation of the people. It's all a product of your capitalist opportunism."

"My God," Pat thought to himself. "I'm getting the whole ball of wax in one place!"

He thought it could do no harm to cultivate Ellie. Besides, every time she got excited, her breasts jiggled under her tight white sweater.

"You better be careful," Winburg said, "or McCarthy and his boys will be after you. He hasn't really started on radicals on campus."

"I wish he would," Ellie said spiritedly. "I'd like to get a chance to go before that committee sometime. I'd tell them plenty. It's because of guys like you who won't speak up that the country's gotten into the shape it's in. There's Bailey. He's your campus radical. Why don't you ask him what he thinks?"

Wise called to Jim Bailey, who was passing with a tray, to join them. He was a tall, serious-looking Negro, light brown in color, with a long, aquiline nose and thin lips. Only the skin color and his close-cropped, kinky hair gave away his black heritage. Bailey was introduced to Pat. It turned out he was vice president of the student council and editor of *The Violet*.

"You think the McCarthy Committee is going to come down and investigate all of us campus radicals?" Wise asked.

Bailey looked at him seriously. "I think if they'll let them have their way in Congress and with those movie people, they'll soon be here on campus. I think they're probably here already. I think they're listening to our phones and I think they've got agents all over this campus squealing on us."

The one o'clock bell rang in the middle of the discussion and Pat left the table, heading for the library. Bailey walked along with him.

"What kind of course you taking?" he asked casually.

"Liberal arts," Pat said. "I'm thinking of going for the law."

Bailey nodded noncommittally, but said nothing.

"What about you?" Pat asked.

"I'm in poli sci."

"You planning to be a politician?"

Bailey laughed. "Political scientists don't become politicians, but sometimes they wind up telling politicians what to do, like writing speeches for them and planning their campaigns. I don't think I ever heard of a poli sci major who ever got elected to office, though. Maybe they're not teaching us the right things."

"Yeah," Pat said, "it ain't *what* you know . . ."

"That old saying is right, and it applies here on campus just as well. I know damn well that half the reason that I got elected vice president of the student council is that they wanted to have some spade on the platform. A balanced ticket, just like when they run for mayor."

"Yeah, except last time," Pat said, "we had all Italians." He changed the subject.

"What about these campus radicals they were talking about? Do you think they really exist? Isn't Ellie one?"

Bailey shrugged. "She's active with a couple of groups. She's in the Marxist Society. I don't think any of them know shit from shinola. Most of them get out of here and go into their father's business and forget all about their radicalism."

"You said you figured the FBI or the Senate or somebody had agents here. Don't you think the Communists do too?"

Bailey looked at him quizzically. "I guess I have to figure you're a freshman, that's why you'd ask a stupid question like that. The Communists haven't been worth a shit on campus since the Axis Pact before the war."

They split at the library with Bailey going on to the law building. As he climbed the granite steps, Pat thought that it was the first time that he had ever actually talked at length to a black person who wasn't a cop or a criminal. The odd part was that after the first shock of meeting, he'd forgotten that Bailey was black and he had to admit that while most spades might be stupid, Bailey certainly was the smartest one at the table, and everybody knew it. Later, in the Remington Bar, a cellar off Washington Place where a lot of the students met after class, he got to talking to Wise again.

"How's it look for the team this week?"

Wise shrugged. "We're having a lousy season and Kentucky is very sharp this year."

"You don't expect me to bet against our own team, do you?" Pat asked.

Wise shrugged. "I don't expect you to bet on anybody if you're not going to win."

"Well, there's always the point spread, isn't there? That can balance things out."

"Yeah, it sure can," Wise said, "especially if you

know what it's going to be."

"What do you mean?"

"There are ways of finding out. Sometimes the morning line isn't the right one, if you know what I mean."

"No, what do you mean?"

"I mean that there are some guys that know more about it than other guys. There's some guys that know even more than the professional gamblers."

"Cheeze, I wouldn't mind knowing that," Pat said. "I could use the money."

Wise shrugged. "It has nothing to do with me. I don't play and the players don't tell me much about things like that. I know one guy on this campus, Eddie Scharf. He's driving around in a Mercedes and he takes trips to Florida and Havana whenever he feels like it, and this guy is supposed to be only a student. But he hangs around a lot with the team guys. I got a feeling he knows something. I wish I knew what it was."

Pat filed a report on observations he had made during the week which he felt would be useful in the two lines of his investigation. But he was never clued into what was actually happening. The information was just scooped up by the Intelligence Division and meshed with other information that they had.

He began to feel a certain loyalty toward his classmates and, in fact, found that he liked them better than a good many of the police he'd been working with. He began to leave out parts of the reports which he thought might hurt his friends and which he felt would probably not be important.

In fact, he wasn't sure how important *any* of it was. The Communist stuff did not really seem to be a threat and he really didn't give a shit about basketball fixes, either.

At their next conference, Arthur Marseri made it clear that the thing that interested him was not the Communist aspect, which was just to help him get the undercover assignment, but the basketball fixing. Pat told Arthur about Scharf before he put it in the report. Arthur seemed interested and told him not to bother mentioning it to his superiors.

To some extent, campus life overlapped Pat's old Village life and he was always afraid that he would run into some of the guys from the Sixth, but, in fact, hardly any of them lived in the Village. He still tended to check by Louie's and the coffee houses on MacDougal. In Rienzi's one day, just as he walked in to look the situation over, a sharp whistle split the air behind him and a strong female voice shouted:

"Hey, Conte! Over here!"

The whistler was Ellie Vogel. She was sitting with Winburg at a corner table over a pair of iced *capuccinos*. Pat sat and joined them, but Winburg was silent. Almost before the greetings were over, he turned angrily to Ellie.

"Look, are you trying to say that there's absolutely no such thing as a Communist menace? That Paul Douglas is just a piece of shit?"

"Yes, that's what I'm saying," Ellie said. "I'm saying that the entire Congress is a fascist assembly. Your so-called liberals are just as bad as the rest. There's no real difference between the parties, as far as that's concerned, and until we have a Marxist system, there never will be any benefits for the people."

"Okay, great," Winburg said, gathering up the notebooks that were on the table beside him. "I'll see you after the revolution." He stormed out the door, nearly shattering its glass panel behind him.

"Boy, he's really pissed off."

"Fuck him," Ellie said, and Pat tried not to register his shock. He still wasn't used to women that talked like men but looked very much like women.

Pat started to look over the list of variously adulterated espresso mixtures.

"Listen, screw this," Ellie said. "How 'bout we go over to my place and blow a little gage?"

She lived on Bank Street, west of Greenwich Avenue in a neatly restored brownstone on the fourth floor. The apartment consisted of one huge skylit studio with a laboratory table full of petri dishes and jars at one end, and huge rows of plants near the window and hanging from the ceiling.

"Looks like a regular greenhouse," Pat said, sinking into a sling chair.

"That's right. Botany's my thing, you know," Ellie said. "Here, look at this." She brought him to the window and showed him a tall plant with starlike leaves. "This is where I get my grass."

He looked at it with interest. "You mean you grow your own?"

"Why not? I'm a botanist, aren't I?"

"Is that your specialty?"

She laughed. "No. I didn't want to tell you what that was at first. It might give you the creeps."

She took him over to a tallish plant with what seemed to be a hairy open bulb on one end. It looked like a bristling vagina.

"Carnivorous plants," she said, "that's my specialty. This is a Venus's-flytrap. You'll have to come around some time when I feed them. It's really fascinating."

"What do they eat?" Pat said. "Hamburgers?"

She laughed. "Well, they might eat those, but they like something alive, like a cockroach. They seem to sense its struggles or some scent that it puts out. This causes them to open up and causes their digestive juices to flow. Meanwhile, they give out an odor that's attractive to the insect and the insect flies into it."

She was standing very close. "You give out a pretty nice odor yourself," Pat said. "I don't suppose you'd eat me?" and then he blushed. "I mean . . . I didn't really mean *that*. I was thinking about the plants."

Ellie laughed. "You're really funny. You're really embarrassed by that, aren't you?"

"No, not embarrassed, but it wasn't what I meant to say."

She went over to the table and opened one of the glass jars which was full of brownish, dried weed and began to roll a couple of joints for them from a package of Zig-Zag in the drawer of the lab table.

"You do smoke, don't you?"

"I took a couple of drags a few times at parties. They didn't do anything for me."

"This is different. This is good stuff, and there's plenty in the joint."

She led him to an overstuffed sofa at one end of the room. Behind it was a long library table on which another jungle of plants was clustered. She held both cigarettes in her mouth and lit them with deep puffs, handing one to Pat when it was on fire.

"Take a deep drag," she said. "Hold it in your lungs as long as you can and let it out real slowly."

They sat for a few minutes puffing on the hand-rolled cigarettes, without saying anything.

"Now, just relax," Ellie said. "It will come to you soon."

They both leaned back in the deep cushions. Pat looked lazily over at Ellie. He could see the shape of her high, young breasts through the white sweater which showed that she was wearing only the thinnest of bras, if any at all. He reached over the short space between them, put his hand over hers and was surprised at her quick response. She grasped his hand in her hot, moist palm and squeezed it tightly.

"You're nice, you know that?"

Pat didn't say anything. She leaned back, her eyes staring into space, the smoke coming slowly but in a broad stream from her nostrils. He leaned over and kissed her very softly on her half-opened lips. She looked at him dreamily.

"Wait till we finish the joint," she said. "There's no hurry."

But the look in her eyes caused Pat to stiffen instantly and he could feel his penis straining against the crotch of his khaki pants. Ellie looked down with interest and noticed the bulge.

"My, you do get excited easily, don't you?" she said. "Let's see what you have there."

To his surprise, she reached over and slowly began to unzip his fly.

"You know," she said, "I really *am* a meat eater." And she bent over and placed those virginal coral lips softly and expertly over his erect member.

Pat was surprised, but not about to complain. He leaned back dreamily in the cushions and waited for it to happen. The marijuana made everything seem very distant and slow, almost as though it was happening to somebody else.

Her hand expertly slipped inside the open fly and began to fondle his testicles. Though he usually tended to come very fast the first time with a woman, he now found himself in a state of complete relaxation and just lay against the cushions with his head thrown back. After a few minutes of ecstatic but delicate tongueing, he felt a strange itching and burning sensation on his neck and he began to rub vigorously at the spot. Ellie looked up from her activities.

"What's the matter?"

"I don't know," he said. "There's some sticky stuff on my neck and it's burning and itching."

She pursed her lips in exasperation. "Oh, for God's sake! That's the plants again."

"What do you mean?" Pat said.

"Well, they sort of get the scent of excitement when you make love and that starts their juices going and sometimes they, well, they just drip. I guess a little landed on your neck and now it's more or less digesting your skin. It won"t hurt you. Just wipe it off with a little water. Here, let me do it," and she moistened a pale blue handkerchief with saliva and rubbed his neck tenderly.

It was too late. Pat's penis lay like a limp piece of rope. Trying to seem as casual as he could, he tucked it back into his trousers and headed for the door.

"Listen, I got a lot of studying to do," he said, "but that was a really terrific joint. I'd like to come back again sometime."

Ellie smiled knowingly. "Do that," she said, "and don't forget—the plants don't eat people. I do."

CHAPTER 2

Pat liked most of the people he dealt with at the school, but not Scharf—a sharp-faced dandy, always a little bit too slick, too well dressed, too quick to flash the label from Brooks or Chipps to let you know how much the cashmere jacket cost, or the Gucci loafers.

On campus, when he wasn't wearing imported English jackets and cashmere sweaters, he went around in a white varsity cardigan with a minor letter, gray flannels and white buck shoes. If he had any popularity at all, it was because occasionally he would leak a good tip on one of the basketball games. He also made a pretty good thing out of peddling basketball and football pools, depending on the season. It wasn't clear if he ever went to class.

Pat played up to Scharf's obvious vanity about his clothes.

"Hey, where'd you get that terrific plaid jacket? Have it made?"

With elaborate casualness, Pat baited Scharf with a display of freebie tickets to athletic events, pretending to be fascinated by Scharf's inside knowledge. But according to Arthur, Scharf really did hold some key cards and was worth cultivating.

Arthur fed him all the tickets he needed. Scharf was their best lead at that moment to the key man in the basketball fix, and Erickson, the book, was screaming for justice.

One night, Scharf, notoriously tight despite his obvious wealth, surprised Pat by asking him if he wanted to go to the Ezzard Charles-Joe Louis fight in Yankee Stadium. This surprised Pat because it was the hottest ticket in town that month.

"How much?" Pat asked him.

"Well," Scharf said with some embarrassment, "I got the ticket through friends. It won't cost you anything, but I want to have you along. I'm going to be carrying a lot of money."

"So you want me for like a bodyguard?"

"You might say that."

"Why me?" Pat asked.

Scharf grinned and punched him playfully in the bicep.

"I like the way you handle yourself, kid," he said in a Bogey imitation.

"What's the idea about the money?" Pat said. "You can't be betting at that late hour. You planning on collecting?"

It took about four Scotches for Pat to get any kind of an answer without seeming to press, but Scharf's vanity finally got the better of him.

"Listen, we're getting set up for the basketball season again and we need a grubstake. I've got my end here and it goes into the kitty, see?"

"You mean you're making a betting pool?" Pat asked.

"Sort of. We did it for the last couple of years. That's really where I got all this dough. We've been hitting pretty good."

"Well, I guess if you really study the game," Pat said.

"Ah, that's a lot of bullshit," Scharf sneered. "We've got inside info on the point spread. This guy I feed the money to, he's in touch with some other people and they're in touch with some of the players, like in Kentucky, Brigham Young, even here at NYU."

"So this guy you're seeing is like the key man?" Pat said.

"Well, I really don't know the inside, but I think he's the boss for this part of the country anyway. This is one deal the mob doesn't control, see? I guess they'd be pretty pissed off if they knew what was going on."

"I guess they would," Pat said.

"Anyway, I'm going to have about ten thousand on me and I don't like to walk around without anybody to take care of me."

"I don't want to get involved in any rough stuff," Pat said.

"Oh, there won't be any rough stuff. I did it a couple of years before and I didn't bring anybody with me, but I'm afraid word might be getting around now and it's a good idea to have somebody along. You look tough. I saw you working out in the gym the other day and you were doing pretty good at boxing."

It suddenly dawned on Pat that Scharf was a queer.

Arthur Marseri was very interested when they met for their gin game at the club the next day.

"You know where the meet is going to take place?" he asked.

"I haven't a clue," Pat said, "and I don't think he'd tell me."

"Okay," he said, "meet me again tomorrow and I'll have a plan."

Actually, as it turned out, it took two or three days to set up the plan, but it was a beauty and everybody would come out smelling good—Pat, the department and the family.

Pat met Scharf at the Neutral Corner on Eighth Avenue. There was a lot of subdued mumbling about the fight, but not the usual tension you feel before a heavyweight bout.

Louis was getting fat and he was thirty-six years old.

Everybody wanted him to win. Charles was a colorless slugger, outclassed but younger and stronger.

They drove up in Pat's Mercury, which really impressed Scharf. There was plenty of room in the stadium parking lot that night. Only twenty-two thousand fans or so were scattered through the giant sports area.

Louis looked slow and tired almost from the beginning. In the fourth round, it looked for a moment or two as if he might actually do it. He shuffled in in his old familiar stalking style and caught Charles with a series of stiff lefts, trying his best to set him up for the layaway punch.

But that was it. Charles seemed unshaken. After fifteen jolting rounds, Louis stood with his head down in his corner and heard the judges' decision—unanimous for Charles.

Joe told the radio people, "I'll never fight again."

Pat relaxed, joked about the fight with Scharf, had hot dogs and tried not to be conscious of the weight of the Smith & Wesson pressing against his back. When the night was over, it wouldn't matter whether Scharf knew he carried a gun or not. His cover would be blown.

"Where you meeting this guy, Scharf?" Pat asked.

Scharf looked around him. "In the parking lot after the fight on the 161st Street side."

The meet wouldn't be as anonymous as Scharf's man had hoped because by the time the fight was over, a good many of the crowd had already shoved their way out through the doors and it was a near-deserted stadium without even the usual litter of torn programs and hot dog buns. But they picked their way through.

"He said he'd pick me up by the ticket booth."

As they passed through the iron pipe rails of the exit, Pat's eye caught a short, stocky man about five-foot-six in a narrow-brimmed straw hat and silk suit, lurking behind the octagonal ticket kiosk.

"Scharf?" the man said.

Scharf peered into the darkness. "Is that you, Manny?"

"Yeah. Let's get out of here. Who's that with you?"

"He's a friend. He's clued in."

"I told you not to take anybody."

"You think I'm crazy? I'm not going to walk around with all that . . ."

"All right, all right. Shut up. I just hope this isn't a mistake."

They headed east toward the Jerome Avenue elevated station. The guy wanted to make the exchange in the open part of the lot, but this didn't suit Pat's plan. He peered through the half-light, trying to see where his man might be hiding, but there was very little cover.

"Let's wait a minute," Pat said. "The best place is right here behind the ticket box as soon as this crowd clears away."

"What are you talking about?" the man said. "If we get out there in the parking lot, nobody can get near us."

"Yeah, but did you ever think what a target you'd be walking across that big, open space? You'd be a sucker!"

"Well, maybe you're right," the guy said. "What's the difference? It'll only take a minute to make the change. Let's do it now."

Scharf reached into his breast pocket and pulled out one of those plastic, zippered pouches used by department stores and shops when delivering cash.

"It'll all in there. Ten grand," he said.

"All right. Wait a minute. Let me just check," the man said.

He zipped open the pouch and riffled slowly and carefully through the money, squeezing each bill through his fingers to make sure it wasn't doubled and lifting the corners to make sure the denominations all checked.

The hair on the back of Pat's neck began to prickle as he felt rather than saw or heard a presence coming up behind him and to the left on sneakered feet. A quiet voice came out of the darkness. A man in black pants and a black lumber jacket with a cap pulled low on his face was suddenly standing there and the blue metal of an automatic gleamed in the remote light of the parking-lot towers.

"All right. Everybody be quiet," the man said. "Don't raise your arms and don't move your hands. Just stand there the way you are. Nobody's going to get hurt. Just be calm."

Scharf flashed a terrified look at Pat and Pat shrugged. Manny, the little fat man, in a reflex movement, began to stuff the money into his jacket.

"I told you not to move," the man said.

There were two deafening blasts as the automatic jumped in his hand. But there was no one within a hundred yards by that time.

Manny bucked against the ticket booth wall and slid to the ground in an awkward sitting position. His hat slanted rakishly over one eye. The remaining eye, staring, reflected surprise. The man in the cap reached swiftly for the pouch.

It was the move Pat had been waiting for. He reached quickly around to the holster behind him for the gun which he had already loosened, pointed it at the holdup man and squeezed off four shots—one hitting the neck, one sending the cap flying. The man in the leather jacket spun wordlessly, the money flying from his hand. As he hit the ground, his automatic barked once more, almost by reflex and Pat felt as though one of Charles's jabs had caught him just below the bottom rib. He fell flat on the ground with his pistol trained in both hands on the prone figure of the gunman and squeezed off two more shots. The body jumped as each bullet hit the holdup man's midsection, thunking into the leather, but there was no further movement.

Then there were sounds of running feet. A Holmes guard, fat, paunchy, about fifty, came running up, his gun drawn, his face pasty white with fright. Pat had the tin ready in his hand as the man came up.

"What's the trouble?" the "Pink" asked.

"It's okay. I'm on the job," Pat said, flashing the badge and the man looked relieved. "Call for an ambulance and a squad car. I think we have two DOA's here," Pat said.

He reached over, poked at Manny's eyelid and the body fell over, sideways in an awkward crouch. Blood from the chest wounds had stained everything from his sternum down and was running into Manny's elegant crotch.

"I'll see that nobody touches anything," Pat said. "Go ahead and make the call," and the guard ran with relief to the phone booth. As he did, Pat reached quickly into Manny's inner pocket and felt what he had expected—two thick envelopes.

He knew that Manny had to have made some other stops before he saw Scharf. Quickly he transferred the envelopes to his own pocket. Scharf, who had apparently taken off during the gunfire, reappeared with the guard and several more who were now clustering around along with a small crowd of onlookers and late-leavers.

"They'll be right over," the guard said.

Pat smiled and then he suddenly felt dizzy.

"I think I'm going to need them myself," he said. "This damn thing is bleeding."

In the initial shock, he had hardly been aware that he had been shot, but now the hole in his side was throbbing and he could feel the draft where the clothes let in the cold air.

"Scharf?" he said. The boy looked terrified. "I'm

afraid we're going to have to put you under arrest for conspiracy."

"Oh, Christ!" Scharf said.

"Guard, keep an eye on him," Pat said as he leaned tiredly against the ticket booth.

In the background, he could hear the wail of approaching sirens. He pulled a handkerchief from his pocket and stuffed it against the gushing hole in his side. This had not really been part of the plan, but in the end it would look better. Then he thought about the ambulance and the envelopes in his pocket. He wondered if they would search him at the hospital.

When the first car arrived from four-four, he told them to watch his prisoner while he went to get the keys from his car. When he got to the red Mercury, he opened up the trunk and lifted up the rubber carpeting underneath it and slipped the two envelopes under them, slamming and locking the lid. It was none too soon. The blood was draining his strength faster than he thought and he made it only halfway back to the ticket booth when everything went black.

CHAPTER 3

The publicity, of course, finished Pat Conte's undercover career at NYU, though with convalescent leave and some easy duty assignments, he was able to finish out the semester for credit. He put himself in for a Meritorious bar.

Connie was proud, but terrified. Fein had given him a good play in the *News* and this time all the other papers picked it up because of the tie to the basketball gambling investigation. Fat Manny Toplitz had been a key figure in a syndicate which controlled bribed basketball players on most of the big teams throughout the country. They had been operating for three years and had already taken the bookies for a couple of hundred thousand at least.

There were a lot of flowers in the hospital room, including one huge basket of gladioli with a card signed, "Frank." The wound wasn't a bad one. It had just passed through the muscle between the hip and the lower ribs. None of the organs had been touched. But he'd lost a lot of blood and it took them five or six days to build up his strength before they would release him.

When Arthur Marseri came, Pat had a few questions for him.

"Listen, about that job. You pretty nearly fucking got me killed."

"You got to learn to think fast, Pat. Everything can't be planned, you know."

Pat gestured to Arthur to come nearer. "Tell me something, Art. Why did that hit man have to go?"

"He was a hoople. You know, a little flaky? Maybe something like Willie Moretti. We couldn't have trusted him to keep his mouth shut when the job was finished. This way, it's nice and clean and we solve the case, you get a medal, and you ought to be due for a good promotion pretty soon and everybody else is happy, too. *Very* happy. You'll be hearing more about that soon."

It was more than a week before he had been able to return to his car which Connie had brought back to Riverdale. The envelopes were still there, under the floor mats, gray and speckled with road dust. Each contained ten thousand dollars in fifty-dollar bills. They were added to the growing collection in Pat's safe deposit box on Sixth Avenue.

During those months of convalescence, Pat had time to go to school at the Washington Square campus. His exposure as an undercover cop added measurably to his status, even among his antiestablishment and revolutionary friends.

As far as they were concerned, he had been there only to break up the crooked gambling ring and they were in favor of that. James Bailey urged him to run for campus office in the next semester's elections, but Pat had decided to transfer to the Bernard Baruch School which had courses specifically designed to fit around a policeman's schedule.

Scharf copped a plea and got a six months' term at The Tombs. He wasn't seen on the campus again. Winburg started up a branch of the American Veterans' Committee.

"I hate the idea of a veterans' group," Winburg explained, "but we got more guys coming up now from the Korean War and we don't want something happening like the VFW or the American Legion. We have to have some forward-looking groups. This could be the biggest pressure group in the country."

Ellie continued work on her doctorate. Pat thought at

first the news that he was married would break up their tenuous relationship.

"Don't be stupid, darling," Ellie said. "I'm no more interested in getting involved than you are. I just enjoy your delicious body."

The terms were that they were only together at *her* convenience, not his. If he was feeling sexy and called her up, she was usually busy working on her papers or going to a conference. But when *she* invited *him* for a cup of coffee or a joint or whatever, he knew she was ready and eager.

He didn't mind having it that way. Most of the action took place in the daytime or the early afternoon and saved making a lot of excuses to Connie. Connie was so eager and loving and hard-working as a housewife, that there was nothing in her that Pat could find to dislike, but there were things that irritated him.

She became even more devoted to the church, joined the ladies' sodality and was constantly trying to con him into going to the services or at least taking communion at the church in Riverdale, but Pat preferred to go to Our Lady of Pompeii, where neither Father Ray or Connie were likely to get wind of his confessions. Not that he confessed very much anyway.

But even with school in those months, Pat was home a lot more and he spent more time up at Sam Massey's place with Sam and Arthur. It was almost as though he was going to school there, too. Gradually, as they talked about their various mutual business affairs, Sam and Arthur seemed to open up in front of Pat, almost as though they *wanted* him to learn more—as though this were a *family* night school.

The thing that astonished Pat most about the talks was the range of Sam's interests. He seemed to spread across the spectrum of the business world, casting a shadow on each sector. He had an interest in a Canadian drug company, which was pushing for tests of a new cancer drug and which had a lobby in Washington trying to get the drug approved by the FDA.

"The investment is peanuts," Sam explained, "but if the drug is accepted, it means a fortune."

It had become obvious even earlier that he had some sort of interest in the Royal Meat Company.

"At present," he explained to Pat one day, "we don't actually own anything there, but we've loaned them quite a bit of money and they seem to be falling behind. Of course, as they have troubles, and they've had a number of troubles, it's harder for them to pay and then naturally they must give us more control. Meanwhile, we collect interest when they have it. And if they don't have it . . ." Sam shrugged. "I don't involve myself with the collections, but it's made clear that it's very important for them to pay—*very* important."

Sam laughed suddenly in memory. "I remember Ruggiero. He loaned some money to a man in business. The man said that he didn't have much security. Ruggiero said, 'That's all right. Your eyeballs are your security.' "

Sam laughed again. "You know," he said, "you hear a lot of bad stories about our people, about our business. Actually, they have a lot of crazy laws in this country that don't make any sense. We're just plain businessmen like anybody else, but they've made laws against some of our work. Capone told me once when I was a little boy, he said, 'Son, all I want to do is sell beer. If beer wasn't against the law, then I'd be a perfectly ordinary businessman, but beer *is* against the law, so I have to operate the way I do. But what is wrong with beer anyway?' And you see, he was right because they made beer legal finally, but then it was too late for Big Al. So now, they have laws against so many things that people want to do, gambling, sex, prostitution. I don't have anything to do with that, but why shouldn't people be allowed to have sex and pay for it if they want?"

This was after dinner, and Pat felt that Sam's tongue had been loosened by a good quantity of vino and now the Carlos Primero, and yet he felt that Sam was cold-sober deep down and that much of what he said was said to measure its effect on Pat.

"You see," Sam said, lighting an Upmann, "in many of our enterprises, if somebody does not keep his word, if somebody's dishonest with us, we can't go to the court. We can't ask a judge to enjoin them from doing this and this. So then, we have to do whatever we can do. We try to keep everything fair and we have a commission now, where we decide things. We decide if it's fair what we do. And no person who doesn't mix in our affairs would ever get hurt. It's all business.

"But now we have capital and we can do business like other people and many of the businesses we've been in—trucking, the entertainment business, nightclubs, even gambling in some places—are becoming legal. So now we need more lawyers, more politicians working with us. We have access to more legitimate channels.

"I really think the time for rough stuff is over soon. Even now, as we're moving up, the blacks are moving into the numbers, into the gambling, and the Cubans and the Puerto Ricans are beginning to move up. This is what I was trying to explain to your Uncle Anthony, but he still wants to do things the old way."

Sam dealt a hand of gin and they sat down over two glasses of the Spanish brandy.

"Business is all playing the angles anyway. It's having a little edge, a little jump, a little more influence, somebody to speak for you in the right places, a little extra information. But you must never take the bread out of the mouth of a friend. That was where those people with the fixed basketball games went wrong. That wasn't right, what they did.

"You know, you might wonder why we're so concerned for gambling, but gambling is now more than the liquor business was. Do you know how many bets are made outside of the legal casinos and tracks in a year? I'll tell you how much. Twenty billion dollars! Twenty billion! That's more money than is made in dope, prostitution, loan sharking, the whole business put together."

Sam threw down a ten and knocked with nine points.

"You know, son, there's one thing you have to realize. Everybody takes every edge he can get in life, in business. Now you take when you're playing gin rummy. If you flash the card when you cut it, so that I only know one card, the card that's on the bottom, that's enough. If I know that the ten of spades is the card, for instance, I know you're not saving tens and I know that the eight, nine, jack, queen, king of spades are probably safe. This gives me a big advantage, just that one card. So keep it down when you're cutting next time. Meanwhile, I think Her Highness is ready. Why don't we go to the Copa and see Jimmy Durante? That guy is a scream."

They had gone to the Copa many times together, but here Sam usually left him with Connie when he had his business discussions, or if he had them at the table, no actual names were mentioned. He'd just say, "the little fellow in Brooklyn," or "the Jew in Miami," or "the fat guy in Jersey." Of course, if you knew the framework, and Pat was beginning to learn that, it wasn't hard to identify Gambino as the little guy in Brooklyn, Boiardo as the fat guy in Jersey or Meyer Lansky as the Jew in Miami.

They were sitting in the lounge later that night in a booth. Connie had gone to the ladies' room. A dapper little man with gray hair and a gray face and startling black eyebrows slid in. He was impeccably dressed in a silk suit with conservative lapels, a white-on-white shirt, a white tie. On his pinky was a heavy gold ring and holding the tie was a clip with the seal of the Police Athletic League.

"Hello, Tommy," Sam said. "You know my son-in-law, Pat?"

"Pleesameetcha," Tommy said.

Pat recognized him as Tommy Ryan from the Village, a pal of Tony Bender's and a member of the Genovese family.

"Well, so," Tommy said, "you know about poor Willie."

Sam nodded. "It was a shame he had to go that way. I don't approve of that kind of thing. Very undignified in a public restaurant. How must his family feel?"

Tommy shrugged. "It was an open contract. I think Johnny had it in for him anyway."

"Well, they closed down Duke's. Now, I suppose they'll close down Joe's. Where we going to eat when we go over to Fort Lee?" Sam said.

"Well, you know, Willie was definitely going off. Frank talked to him a lot of times to try and get him to shut his mouth. But like Vito says, you can't have a guy like that going around shooting his mouth off all the time. You know, like Vito said, what are we, men or mice? You know what Vito said to me?" Tommy said.

"No," Sam said.

"He said, 'if I lose my mind like that tomorrow, I would want to be hit so I wouldn't bring harm to this thing of ours, because that's the way it is.' Right?"

"Right," Sam said. "But there should have been more respect. Willie was very well liked."

"Well, there's going to be a big funeral," Tommy said, "and you know, this isn't going to be bad for Vito either. I think Frank is maybe losing his grip a little."

Sam nodded. "I know all about that."

Tommy looked at Pat suddenly as though realizing he may have said too much.

"The kid's—all right—ain't he, Sam?"

"Would I let you talk that way if he wasn't?"

"Well, nice to meet you, kid," Tommy said, and he was off.

"Well, I think we might as well get going," Sam said. "It's too much like business sitting here," and they left.

Pat, of course, knew they had been talking about Willie Moretti. He remembered him vividly, smiling with his goofy jokes at the Duke's and other meetings. The papers had been full of it for the last few days.

As they drove up the West Side Highway, Sam leaned back in the limousine, his eyes hooded to a slit, but still awake as he watched the various construction projects, docks, ships, warehouses that they passed. Every once in a while, he would make a remark like, "I got to remember to take care of that," half to himself. It was clear that there was hardly a mile that went by in which there wasn't some enterprise that touched on Sam's affairs, and even across the river where the high rises were going up, he looked with approval.

"There's going to be big money over there someday, Pat," he said, clasping Pat's knee. "There's lots of room to expand, and now that Moretti's out, it's like musical chairs. Everybody moves up one place."

Pat looked at Connie but she was curled up asleep in one corner of the limo.

"You're going back in uniform, I hear," Sam said.

Pat nodded.

"Well, that'll be good for a while. I'll have Arthur get in touch with you. There's some affairs I'd like to have you look into when you're back down there."

"Anything I can do to help," Pat said.

"And remember," Sam said, "Never tell *anything* to . . ." he nodded his head significantly toward Connie's sleeping form.

CHAPTER 4

In faraway Atlanta, Special Agent Regan Doyle was also learning the rudiments of his craft. Doyle was happy about his decision to quit the department for the FBI, but in one area he was disappointed.

The Director did not believe that there was such a thing as a Mafia, organized crime or a crime syndicate in the country. Furthermore, he felt it was not the proper jurisdiction of the feds.

The Director was more interested in the activities of the Communists and car thieves—Communists, because he felt they were a menace to the country and car thieves because they gave the Federal Bureau of Investigation a fantastic arrest record, since any car that was taken across state lines was deemed to be a federal matter. Cars picked up by local police were usually turned over for prosecution to the FBI.

Burritt, Doyle's immediate supervisor, came from a small town in South Georgia called Headlight, near the Okefenokee Swamp. He didn't like Catholics, Jews, niggers or Protestants (unless they were Georgia Baptists), and especially, he didn't like Yankees. But Doyle just "yes suhed" him to death and found himself acquiring a cornpone accent "right fast."

The local police were pure eagle scouts compared to New York when it came to corruption, although they could be pretty free with their fists and billies when duty called. Basically, the agents learned to handle the local police, either in the small towns of South Georgia or in Atlanta with tact and care and as much southern accent as they could muster.

The Atlanta police department was extra kind to the FBI men, because every time the FBI picked up a deserter from the armed forces, they would turn him over to the local police, and the police officer would get a twenty-five-dollar reward from the governor. A couple of collars a month could keep a cop mighty happy.

After about a month, Doyle was assigned to the Criminal Division under Tom McQuade and got into the type of work he really enjoyed—bank robberies, unlawful flight to avoid prosecution, hijackings and auto theft. Auto theft was the hottest crime in Atlanta because there was a Georgia state law concerning the transfer of papers from one owner to another, which made it very easy for car boosters.

A thief could come in with a transfer written on a brown paper bag and sell a brand-new car and get a good price for it. Some of the auto theft rings, it was suspected, were selling their products on order up north to organized crime buyers, but the car rings themselves were purely local affairs.

Doyle got five commendations in the two years he was in Atlanta for his operations on various criminal matters, but he was proudest of his capture of two white men, brothers from Makey's Rock, Pennsylvania, who had kidnaped a sixty-seven-year-old grandmother from Chattanooga, Tennessee at knifepoint and driven her a few miles across the state border into the Chickamauga Reservation in Georgia.

There they indulged in an orgy of rape and buggery, in addition to poking rifles, bottles, whip handles and a flashlight inside the barely conscious old lady, who required three major operations after being rescued from their hands. The younger brother was found in Atlanta, living in rented rooms behind a pool parlor.

Doyle apprehended him on a tip from a teen-age hooker. He made the arrest personally. Looking at the man's thin but wiry arms and long, horse-tooth face with its close-set bleary eyes, Doyle could hardly believe him capable of the gut-turning atrocities of which he'd been accused. But the description was unmistakable. The man had answered Doyle's knock wearing only a blue workshirt and sucking on a half-empty bottle of Dr. Pepper. Beneath that, he was nude, his penis shriveled and tiny as a Georgia goober.

"Geechy Warren, you're under arrest for kidnaping, rape, sodomy and assault. Get your pants on, you fucking animal."

The older brother was picked up in New York from information gotten from Geechy. They were both tried and convicted as the first white men ever sentenced and electrocuted in the state of Georgia for rape. This, Doyle felt, was what law enforcement was all about.

But the work wasn't easy. Doyle carried a case load of from fifty to seventy cases all at once. In addition to bank robberies, kidnapings and so forth, there were also check passers and deserters.

During his second year, Katie Mullaley came through town playing Marion the Librarian in a road company of *The Music Man* at the Atlanta Civic Center. On Monday the show was closed and they had a fantastic dinner at The Original Fan and Bill's on Peachtree Street.

Later, Doyle took Kate back to the Sheraton Biltmore.

"I'd sure like to go up with you," Regan said, holding Katie's hand between his two giant paws, "but I'm afraid The Director wouldn't approve."

Katie smiled gently. "It would be nice to be with you again, Regan. I know we will be together someday."

"I'm going to want a lot more than that, Katie," Regan said.

Katie pulled him into the shadow of the closed newsstand and blessed him with a long, cushioned, open-mouthed, tongue-probing kiss that left Doyle sweating and red-faced.

"Just let that hold you for now," Katie said, "and try to get yourself transferred out of the boondocks."

CHAPTER 5

As he drove to New York, Stanrilowicz thumped the wheel of the big White Ten-Wheeler, gently keeping time with Kay Starr's rendition of "The Wheel of Fortune" and sang the words with her under his breath. "The wheel of *fortune* goes spinning *round,* da, da, da, da, dum, dum, da, da . . ."

He was making good time on the final stretch of the slaughterhouse run, the big silver-sided refrigerator truck swung slightly in the wind off the river as he cruised down the Deegan, past the darkened Yankee Stadium with its clock, signaling the time, 1:13 A.M.

"Good time," Stan thought.

He was ten minutes ahead of schedule. He could drop the load at Royal Meat and go up to the Market Diner, knock off a few danish and coffee and shoot the breeze with the cabdrivers and the other truckmen before he headed back to Queens.

Buying his own rig had been a good idea and by putting in extra hours, he'd been able to skim off four hundred dollars a week, which was not hay in any man's league.

He whistled happily through his teeth as Patti Page launched into the number-one song "The Tennessee Waltz." As he turned onto the down ramp, leading off the highway at 19th Street, he could see the flashing, revolving light of a patrol car. He wondered if there had been an accident down there and automatically began to

266

downshift, hitting the air brake at the same time. Just as he rolled into West Street, a cop stood out in his headlights and signaled him to pull over, flashing a powerful searchlight that nearly blinded him.

"Son-of-a-bitch!" he thought. "Some kind of a weight check or something. Why'd he have to use such a fucking bright light?"

He pulled the truck to a stop under one of the pillars of the elevated highway and started reaching for his wallet.

"Okay, buddy. Get down."

Wearily he climbed down from the high cab. "Well," he figured, "I guess it's the breaks. You win some, you lose some."

He started moving toward the officer holding the light, but before he could say anything, he suddenly felt a jarring blow from behind that nearly forced his eyeballs out of his head and jammed his lower jaw through his tongue. Then there was a flash of black shoes and cobblestones and that was all.

Pat Conte sat the next day with Lieutenant Arthur Marseri at the Twin Brothers Coffee Shop on Waverly and Sixth. He was on the eight-to-four and having a piss-call while Tom monitored the radio in the car. Spread out in front of him was the *Daily News*.

"That stupid fuck Terli!" he said. "It was a perfect clean job and he had to screw it up!"

The newspaper said:

"NO CLUES IN MEAT TRUCK HIJACK. DRIVER NEAR DEATH

Stanley Stanrilowicz, thirty-seven, of 85-11 37th Avenue, Jackson Heights was near death at St. Vincent's Hospital today. His half-frozen body was found hanging from the hooks of his refrigerator truck under-

neath the West Side Highway early this
morning. Owners of the Rogal Meat Company said that $40,000 worth of beef was
missing from the abandoned truck.

The theft would not have been discovered
until morning had not William Berghoff,
owner of the Rogal Meat Company, noticed
the abandoned truck as he drove to work
at his company's office on West 14th Street.
It was Berghoff who discovered the injured
driver and called the police.

Berghoff said that Stanrilowicz, the
driver, before he lost consciousness, said
that his truck had been stopped by a police
car and that he had been struck from behind as he was talking to the policeman.

The hospital confirmed the fact that
Stanrilowicz was suffering from a subdural
hematoma, resulting from a blow to his
head, and facial lacerations, in addition to
serious puncture wounds from the two meat
hooks which had penetrated his back,
causing serious loss of blood.

Detective Martin Bolinski of the Sixth
Precinct Detective Squad would not comment on the case except to say that he had
been investigating mob pressure on Rogal
Meats for some time.

Berghoff declined to comment on reports
of mob pressure and said that he believed
that it was simply a hijacking. Reports
in the market district indicate that Berghoff
had suffered a series of mishaps and that
several of his workers had been beaten in
the last month but had not reported the
incidents.

"I told that stupid fuck Terli to pull it off down
toward the Washington Market, below the Royal office.
The guy would have been dead in that truck by morning."

"Well, how come you didn't make sure before you
parked the truck?" Arthur said.

"I didn't park the truck. I was redirecting the traffic while they were switching loads. Terli was supposed to take care of the driver, but he recognized him. It was one of the guys he had roughed up a couple of weeks ago. But before Terli got the shots in, this Polack gave him a good kick in the balls and Terli was anxious to get even. I guess he wanted to give him a slow way out. Stupid fuck! Another good shot with the pipe on the head would have finished him."

"Well, he ain't going to make it till morning anyway."

"Yeah," Pat said, "but he gave the tip about the police car. Maybe he saw the precinct number or something, but I don't think so. I had the light right in his eyes the whole time."

"Well, in general, I think it's going to work out all right," Arthur said. "I heard that your old pal Al Santini is joining the management of Royal as vice-president, as of this morning."

"You think Berghoff will say anything?" Pat said.

"Don't be a clown. He's shitting in his pants."

"Maybe I'm stupid or something," Pat said, "but I don't get quite how this thing works. I know the organization isn't in this just for the heist."

"Well, I haven't got all the details myself," Arthur said, "but roughly it's like this. Royal supplies meat, poultry, eggs and stuff like that to the various wholesale houses and markets and to some of the restaurants. It's run by Berghoff. Now, Pride Wholesale Meat and Poultry Company is headed by a guy named Pete Castellana. He's a cousin of Gambino's. So Royal runs out of money and one of the guys working for him, Tommy Bergano, so he's with Vito's family, right? He arranges a loan with an outfit that Castellana's part owner of. You follow?"

"A little bit," Pat said.

"So they charge him the usual one percent a week.

Now a partner of Castellana in the other business is Carmine Lombardozzi, get it?"

"I get it."

"So before you know it, Royal's gotten into a lot of trouble and they can't meet the payments. So the next thing you know, your friend Santini is brought in to protect the company. That's more or less the way it is now. Now, Pride starts to buy a couple hundred thousand dollars worth of meat, get it, from Royal. And Royal goes broke. Only by this time, Berghoff is so into it that he can't squeal on anybody. Meanwhile, there's maybe a half a million dollars split up one way or another."

"Well," Pat said, "I'm just a simple college kid. I can't understand this big business."

"Nobody said you had to understand it," Arthur said.

CHAPTER 6

The Royal meat deal seemed to mark a turning point in Pat's relationship to the family. A few days after his breakfast with Arthur at the Twin Brothers Coffee Shop, Pat got a call from Sam himself.

"Are you free for the weekend, Pasquale?"

"Sure. What's up?"

"A big day for you. I think you can guess. And a day of real pride for me and our family. The car will come by to get you, and we will drive up to Don Antony's place."

"Thank you," Pat said.

"And one thing, of course you will tell nothing of this to Constanza. For her, it is just a hunting trip in the country. *Capish?*"

"Right," Pat said. His voice was calm and businesslike, but underneath he was bursting with joy and excitement.

Massey's limo picked Pat up about nine Saturday morning. Sam and Arthur Marseri were already in the car. Connie seemed happy at Pat's acceptance by her family, but she wasn't happy about the hunting.

"All those guns," she said. "One of you could get hurt."

"We'll be careful," Pat said. "Besides you know how it is on these trips. There's more sitting around and talking and drinking than really hunting."

"Well, I'll be working with the bazaar tomorrow anyway at St. Adrian's, so I guess I'll keep busy."

The big limo rolled up past Hawthorne Circle and on up the Taconic, heading north, through Westchester and Dutchess Counties, past rolling brown hills patched with snow.

After almost three hours driving, they reached a barrier at Philmont, announcing the end of the Taconic and angled off east toward the Massachusetts border.

Pat looked with interest at the rough, undeveloped countryside, laced with white cattle fences at points and dotted with roving bands of Black Angus and Hereford beef cattle.

"It's nice up here," he commented.

"That's right. It's a good place and it's out of the way."

"We're going to Don Antony's farm?"

"That's right," Sam said.

"He got a big spread?"

"All those cows you've been looking at are his."

Now, they turned off the graded road onto a gravel lane, bordered by stone fences which led up to a pair of iron gates, flanked by two Gothic stone arched towers, each of which, in effect, was a sentry box.

A chunky man in a mackinaw with a fedora incongruously perched atop a pair of black earmuffs, came to the gate cradling a shotgun. Recognizing the car, he signaled to the other guard inside the sentry box and the two gates were swung open. Pat gazed curiously at the stone cubicles that had sheltered the guards.

"Looks like a couple of tombstones," he said.

Arthur burst into a high giggle. Sam looked at him with disgust.

"There's a lot of guys say that," Arthur said, stifling his laughter.

The road wound for 500 yards through an apple or-

chard and a grove of cedar. Then it came to a square
enclosure with an iron fence around it. Inside, on
pedestals of colored stone was a cluster of weirdly
realistic-looking busts, mostly of children, and in the
middle, a regal equestrian statue which would have
looked good in London's Hyde Park, except that it was
painted in brilliant colors—the jacket of the rider, a
brilliant brown; the vest, a polished fawn; and the
feathered fedora, brown and beige. The white horse had
one foot lifted as though it was about to plunge down
among the other small statues of the mortals. An
engraved marble plaque had the simple name, "Marseri," on it. The letters were painted red with a yellow
border. Each of the smaller figures of children was
painted realistically, flesh color with corresponding hair
and brightly colored shirts or jackets.

"Holy mackerel!" Pat said, craning his neck as they
drove past.

Sam looked embarrassed. "Nobody ever sees that,
you understand, except the family and close friends.
Well, he earned it."

The road now took another turn. Suddenly there
loomed into view a three-story stone house, capped with
reddish-brown tiles. At each corner there was a stone
tower surmounted by a black gargoyle and chimneys on
each side rose to end in a cupola like a large stone
birdhouse.

In front of the house was a circular flower bed, now
dormant, with shrubs wrapped in burlap. Parked beyond
it were at least eight limousines.

A small, dark, rat-faced man ran out of the house as
they pulled up.

"'I'll take care of parking the car, Mr. Marseri," he
said, but Tommy, the chauffeur, bristled.

"I'll park it myself," he said.

"Yeah," Sam said, "then you go down in the cellar
and play some pool with the other guys."

There was a little crowd gathered already in a chilly

stone room to the right. It was decorated with medieval suits of armor and cases of hunting rifles but the furniture looked homey and comfortable—huge overstuffed chairs and sofas with chintz slipcovers in a flowered print. Pat recognized a number of faces—Genovese, Lucchese, Boiardo, Lombardozzi, Gerry Catena, Tommy "Ryan" Eboli, the guy he'd seen over at the Copa, Michele Miranda, and, of course, Francesco Saveria, known to some as Frank Costello. He was surprised to see in this crowd his old friend, Al Santini from the Mulberry SAC.

The talk was all about sports and show business with occasional oblique references to pseudonymous friends, such as "Potatoes from Buffalo," or "Dandy Phil," who gained fame along with Frank Costello for being cited for contempt by the Kefauver Committee.

Santini greeted him with particular warmth, but made no reference to the Royal job on the West Side. He just clasped Pat on the shoulder and squeezed tightly.

"You're doing a great job, kid," he said.

They had time for only one Scotch when the oak doors at the end of the room opened and Don Antony came in, dressed in a black suit as usual, but in honor of the country atmosphere, sporting a soft yellow shirt and a paisley scarf in lieu of a tie.

"Gentlemen," he said, "to the dinner," and they all put down their drinks and followed after him, like a well-disciplined army troop.

The dining room was like the refectory in a medieval hall, hung with heraldic flags, the table laid out in a horseshoe, with a ceremonial table in the center. In front of every three or four place settings was a chromium napkin holder and salt and pepper, much like those that adorned the tables in Duke's Restaurant in Fort Lee.

"Gentlemen, you all know where to sit," Don Antony said, and they found their places, Pat staying close to Arthur for guidance. At the head of the table stood Don

Antony, flanked on his right by Frank Costello and his left by Vito Genovese. These, in turn, were flanked by Gerry Catena and Tommy Eboli, followed by Michele Miranda. It was obvious that the punctilio of the seating arrangement was as rigid as that at Windsor Castle.

The table was lit with giant antique candelabras and there were wine bottles opposite each group of four. Don Antony stood as soon as the guests were settled. In his high husky voice, still tinged with the echoes of Sicily, he said, "Soon we eat, but first we have a little ceremony, eh?"

The guests nodded. The electric lights were now dimmed, most of the illumination being provided by the giant candelabra. At this point, Pat noticed that somebody whispered something to Al Santini and he was led from the room. Now, Don Antony called in a sonorous voice, "Pasquale Conte, come forward, *vene*."

Pat came up to the table which was set inside the horseshoe, directly in front of Don Antony. A shadowy figure came up behind him and placed on the table a small, thin stiletto of antique design and a Beretta, which Pat recognized with a shock as his own hold-out piece. Don Antony looked solemnly at the twenty-five faces gathered around the ceremonial table.

"This, as you know, is a man of true family. Pasquale Conte. I introduce you to him, though many of you know him. In recent years, we have 'made' very few people and so, each time we do, it becomes very important."

Heads nodded sagely around the table.

"My brother, Sam, tells me times are changing so this time we will conduct the ceremony in Italian and in English."

Pat stood with his legs spread and his hands clasped behind him in a military at-ease position. His face was dripping sweat, whether from the heat of the candelabra or the tenseness of the moment, he was not certain.

All of this antique posturing and gesturing should have seemed comical, but he knew that it was not—that it was deadly serious and the most important thing that had ever happened to him in his life. At this point, Don Antony intoned what sounded like a prayer in Italian, at times gesturing to the gun and the knife. Pat had picked up a lot of Italian on Mulberry Street but not enough to understand completely what was being said in "Scidgie" (the Sicilian dialect) except that it referred to his dedication to the gun and the knife.

In English, Don Antony said, his eyes piercing deeply into Pat's, "This is the gun and knife that are life and death. They represent the strength of our tie to our family. We can live by them or we can die by them, whatever is for the family. Hold out your trigger finger."

Pat extended his right forefinger. Antony gestured imperiously. He was like a priest directing a high mass. Sam stepped forward, his face solemn and picked up the stiletto. He took Pat's extended finger in his hand and quickly and deftly jabbed its point into the tip of his finger. The pain was sharp, but Pat did not wince. When the blood came out, Sam bent forward, and sucked a drop from the finger.

Now Sam whispered, "Hold out your other hand, palm up."

Pat did as he was told. In the hand, Sam placed a colored chromo, such as they gave out in church, of St. Dismas. With a sterling cigarette lighter, Sam lit the edge of it so that if flamed up. Pat stood, holding the burning paper in his hand till the flame died. The pain was not much as the heat went upward.

At this point, Don Antony read out the pledge in Italian and then had Pat repeat in English these words:

"I pledge my honor to be faithful to the Family like the Family is faithful to me. As this saint and a few drops of my blood were burned, so shall I give all my blood for the Family when the ashes and my blood will return to their original state."

"Now," Don Antony said, "by fire and blood, you are one of us."

Then he intoned another speech in Italian and explained again.

"Now that you are one of us, you are in our family. This above everything—your religion, your country, your own family, your wife, your children, if you should have any—is the supreme loyalty. Those who do not obey, those who are disloyal go the way of the knife or the gun. Do you understand, Pasquale Conte?"

"I understand."

"Then you are now one of us and Sam is your godfather."

Sam kissed him on both cheeks, eyes damp with emotion.

"This is the proudest day of my life," Sam said.

Pat stood, smiling stiffly, as the others came up to shake his hand, still stained with blood.

"Now you will sit at your honored place at the table while we initiate the other. Call Al Santini."

CHAPTER 7

At first Pat's official recognition made little difference in his life. Only top members of the family knew of it, of course. It didn't affect his standing much, even in Little Italy, but the connection between certain business concerns and the family became clearer to him—the reason certain garbage-collection trucks got all the private business from all the major nightclubs or certain linen-supply houses took care of all the napkins, towels and tablecloths, or why a penny was found in the rectum of a certain Gianinni when he was found shot to death on 37th Street, the penny being the value that the family put on the man's life—the sign that he had been a double-crosser.

Pat continued his studies at Bernard Baruch and also began to study for the sergeant's exam. No matter how good your hook was, you couldn't get promoted without passing the exam and placing high, although you might get some preference in the sort of assignment you got once you made rank.

Pat was getting tired of patrol-car duty and anxious to get into the Detective Bureau, but for the moment, his advisor, Lieutenent Arthur Marseri, felt that the uniform was more useful.

It was three months after the initiation before Pat was asked to "make his bones" as a "made" member of the family.

The job seemed perfect for someone in Pat's particular position. It involved a formerly reliable "friend of the family" who was showing signs of turning into a dangerous enemy.

Captain Walter Kessel was in St. Vincent's Hospital, suffering from a heart attack, brought on, some said, by certain statements made to the Kefauver Committee by former Mayor O'Dwyer and his friend, James Moran, which came very close to touching on Captain Kessel's high income activities.

Kessel, himself, was on the list of those to be questioned next about his connection with the Italian lottery as it operated in the Village and East Harlem. This was getting uncomfortably close to Vito Genovese's domain.

The word was out that Kessel's name had been found on the list of people receiving direct juice, in addition to the ordinary payoffs of the police pad. There was enough evidence against him for an indictment. There was so much on Captain Kessel, in fact, (much of it gathered by the FBI), that he had few choices left to him.

He could testify for the Kefauver Committee, he could face indictment and ruin, or he could commit suicide. Temporarily, nature, God or ingenuity found another alternative for Captain Kessel. He was stricken by a massive stroke two weeks before he was to be called before the Kefauver Committee. For a year he had been in a guarded room in St. Vincent's, recovering his powers of speech.

Fortunately the family had good access to information in the hospital systems. One friend was Dominic Zevega, who had been appointed Deputy Commissioner of the Department of Hospitals by Mayor O'Dwyer just before he slipped out of office and headed for Mexico, and the word was that Captain Kessel was getting better.

Already, he could move his hands and feet and make

some inarticulate sounds. Pat was acquainted with Kessel, since he'd been on the Honor Board for at least two of Pat's commendations.

Arthur Marseri had a chat at Rocco's Restaurant on Thompson Street with Pat following their usual Wednesday-night rummy game.

"I wonder if you could see Captain Kessel," Arthur said.

Pat had now been around long enough to know what it meant "to see" somebody.

"I understand that his condition is improving, that he's regaining the power of speech and, God willing, may soon be up and around."

"I don't know the man very well," Pat said.

"Well, they're not permitting him very many visitors, but I suppose a member of the force in uniform that went to visit him for old times' sake would be let in and the captain is hardly in the position to say whether he really *is* a great chum of his visitor or not, is he?"

"I suppose not," Pat said.

The following day, a uniformed officer with a pair of silver sixes on his collar tabs was permitted to visit the convalescing captain. Pat Conte brought some magazines, a copy of *Confidential,* an *Argosy* and several new Mickey Spillanes. He also brought a cheap, disposable syringe, which had been preloaded with insulin.

Winburg, his old friend from NYU, had been a diabetic and Pat had many discussions with him about the ailment. One of the things he discovered is that insulin was not a prescription drug and was sold in great quantities.

He managed to have an old-time booze-up with Winburg the following week and it was not difficult to snatch a couple of needles, one for a spare, from Winburg's medicine cabinet while they were having their nightcaps. The insulin he got from Hudson Drug up on Lexington, which was a big discount house, not likely to notice the purchase of a single vial. Anyway, according to Pat's plan, nobody would be *looking* for insulin or for needles.

The duty nurse informed Pat that the police were not allowing visitors, but he explained that he was on the job. The officer slouched in the chair in front of Room 728 barely looked up as Pat came in, indicating the magazines and books he had with him.

Captain Kessel looked puzzled, but not surprised or alarmed when Pat entered the room. Pat smiled and said, "Hello, captain. I brought you some books and magazines."

One-half of the captain's face twitched in what might have been a smile. Pat turned his back and extracted the preloaded needle from his inner pocket. The point had been covered by a plastic cap. Pat hadn't worked out the details of how the shot would be administered, but he knew what the effect would be. The insulin would quickly drain all the sugar from the captain's bloodstream. The brain would get no energy, and the recipient of the health-giving drug would pass, uneventfully, into a sleep, over the borderline to death.

The insulin would be quickly absorbed in the body. There would be no symptoms, nor would there be any other clinical signs detectable by even the most careful autopsy.

As far as the injection site, the captain was already as punched full of holes as a pincushion by the various medications he was taking. One more puncture, more or less, would not be noticed by the ME. The injection would be easy to give since it would be subcutaneous, rather than intravenous. There'd be no need to find a vein—just punch the needle in and press on the plunger.

Pat sat and waited, patiently, in the room, saying nothing to the captain, leafing through the magazine.

The captain, no doubt, thought that he had been detailed in some way by the department and gradually paid no attention.

Pat had decided that he would give three-quarters of an hour to the project, if not interrupted. At the end of that time, he would act somehow. But the problem was simplified when he saw the eyes of the haggard, gray-haired man in the bed close in a doze.

Pat knew that the left side was the one which had been completely paralyzed by the stroke and he was on that side of the bed. It was warm in the room, and the captain was covered only by a sheet. It took less than one second to jab the needle in through the sheet and push the plunger to the bottom. The paralyzed skin, being insensitive, didn't react. Nor did the captain, who continued to sleep.

Pat removed the needle, put it back in his pocket, and left so quickly that the slouching guard had hardly time to register his departure, let alone who he was.

Pat was not concerned anyway. This would be rated an unsuspicious death and would not rate an autopsy in any case.

Captain Kessel's death not only didn't rate an autopsy, it hardly rated more than a few lines in the paper, and probably would not have rated *that* if it had not been for the captain's stormy record on the Vice Squad.

No mention was made of the senatorial investigation or of the probe of the captain's affairs that was being conducted at the moment by District Attorney Hogan, since this was not yet a matter of public record. It was simply indicated that the captain died of complications of a stroke, possibly a blood clot in the brain.

Pat told Arthur Marseri nothing of the details of his job, and in fact, the family never wanted to know details. They just wanted the job done. But Arthur looked at him with obvious admiration.

"I keep wondering," he said. "It wasn't just luck, was it? I mean, it didn't just *happen*?"

Pat smiled and said, "Well, he had terrific timing, didn't he?"

Of course, all of his work was not that anonymous. There were a great many arrests which seemed to be convenient for the organization. Restaurants and bars that didn't understand the value of coming under the wing of Tony Bender or Tommy Eboli in the Village, candy stores that had acquired pinball machines or cigarette machines from sources not recognized by the family, would suddenly find themselves facing summonses and fines.

All of this helped the arrest record of the precinct very much and earned Pat the affection and respect of Captain Kerner, commander of the Sixth Precinct.

Pat placed in the top five percent of his sergeant's examination. He was far more used to examinations than any of the other people taking them, since he had, by this time, been going to school for a year. The questions were uncomplicated and there were no tricks. He was high on the list, and now had nothing to do but wait for the appointment. The additional points added to his score by his several Meritoriouses and commendations lifted him even closer to the top. The wait would not be long.

CHAPTER 8

Pat's work for the family was sporadic. Too much activity would attract unfavorable attention and he was valuable in uniform at the moment. If a crap game was not paying off, an arrest could be easily arranged. It helped Pat's record, the precinct's record and made it clear that all games were to be cleared with the organization, in this case, meaning Tony Bender or his chief, Tommy Eboli.

Eboli was active as a shylock. If the "vigorish" or interest wasn't paid on time, a broken leg, a crushed testicle or a smashed hand might result. But if the borrower ran a bar, an arrest for catering to known homosexuals or drug addicts, or serving a minor, or having improperly heated wash water would serve as a reminder that the payment had to be forthcoming, and quickly.

Sometimes Pat would visit the bar in question or the store and indicate that he had been told that there were threats being made to set the place on fire, smash its windows or strip it in the night.

"Of course, we're keeping our eyes open," Pat would say, "but you can't watch a place all the time. So if you're in trouble somewhere, maybe you better straighten it out."

It hardly mattered if the merchant in question had his suspicions of Pat's motives. There was nothing to be proved, and Pat was only doing his duty.

Pat's chores did not always involve sordid money

matters. Occasionally there were affairs of honor to be attended to. Meyer, The Bug, sent a report from Florida that the daughter of a friend was shacked up over the Pony Bar on West Third Street, with not one, but two "bad-ass spade queens," who were renting her out for dubious pruposes. Pat and Tom caught the "squeal."

Only Pat knew who had made the anonymous phone call, alleging that gunshots had been heard in the flat above the Pony Bar. They made it in ninety seconds flat from Sixth Avenue and Eighth Street, where they were parked outside the Waldorf Cafeteria reading the *News* and having coffee. Tom, as usual, was driving, and Pat was out the door and halfway up the stairs before Tom had the motor off.

In the palm of Pat's hand were two glassine envelopes. It took no time to "find" the envelopes in the purple satin jumpsuit of the tall black man with a goatee. The second spade was a Puerto Rican, short with reddish hair and pale eyes and a broad, flat, freckled nose. He was so enraged at the flaking of his friend that he offered to scratch Pat's eyes out. It was obvious that there was only *one* stud in the house.

The girl was too spaced-out to object. She lay on the couch, her eyes at F22 with her arms pocked like the craters of the moon. Pat wondered what mindless boob would have paid for the use of that pale, worn-out body. About the only clue was the one magnificent breast hanging out of the unbuttoned Indian madras blouse—a pale beautiful hemisphere with a tiny strawberry mountain at its apex. It should have belonged to another girl.

Pat, with a wink, suggested that Tom search the place while he took the goateed spade into the hall to "question" him. While there, the satin-suited saxophone player apparently made a break for it, tripped and fell down the entire flight of renovated iron steps. Tom was neither shocked nor surprised at the unfortunate accident.

The spade had a yellow sheet as long as his beard and the narcotics bust was enough to get him two to five at Sing Sing.

Pat, on the other hand, had a delightful week at the brand-new Fontainebleau in Miami for his part in helping out with "The Bug's" problem.

Connie was concerned.

"Are you sure we can afford this?"

"It's a present from a friend," Pat explained.

"What did you do for him that he should be so kind to you?" Connie asked, folding resort clothes into the Vuitton bag.

"It's just business. There's no point in your getting mixed up in it," Pat said irritably. "And for Christ's sake, get a decent bathing suit and some summer stuff when you're down there! This stuff looks like it was designed by the mother superior. It's not a venial sin to *look* sexy, is it?"

Connie was still preoccupied with the trip.

"This trip has got to cost a thousand dollars. Can't you get in trouble accepting a present like that?"

"Look, I *earned* it. That's all you have to know. You just take care of cooking, cleaning and praying, and I'll handle the finances."

And gradually, Pat Conte was learning the many ways of improving his financial position, while making friends and influencing people.

* * *

There were many places in the Sixth that got special consideration during Pat's patrols. Some of these were places that were on the pad and paid directly to the precinct for extra surveillance and protection. Others were under the wing of Bender and these were surveyed even more carefully.

One night, Pat had hopped out of his car to check on the Casbah, a sailors' bar on West Street near the Federal House of Detention, which served as an informal longshoremen's hiring hall, betting parlor and shylock's den.

Tiny as it was, family rumor had it that Bender was pulling twenty-five to fifty thousand a month out of the shabby premises. Because of the heavy cash inventory needed for shylocking and betting payoffs, the place fell under extra careful scrutiny. Sammy Wein, the proprietor, threw Pat and Tom a hundred a month just to make it sweet.

On an August night, just after the 4:00 A.M. closing, Pat and Tom cruised by for a final check and a couple of "flutes." The front door was already locked. Pat went around West Twelfth Street to the side door. As he pushed the squeaking, wooden door open, he heard the muffled sound of feet scuffling in the sawdust and a strangled, gargling groan. There was a confused muddle of silhouetted figures before him. Pat stepped quickly through the doorway and out of the illumination of the street lamp, reaching for his service revolver at the same time. In the dim light, still shining from the back bar, he could see a man with his knee in the small of Sammy's back, pulling tight on a rope, while another stood guard.

"Take him!" the man with the rope yelled, and Pat threw himself aside as a flash of fire shattered the door panel next to his head. He shot back almost instinctively at the source of the flash and was pleased to see one of the silhouettes disappear like a duck in a Coney Island shooting gallery.

At the same time, he was aware of an overpowering suffocating smell of excrement and the sound of another body falling to the sawdust floor like a sack of potatoes. Another shot from the rear shattered a bottle of Jack Daniels and ricocheted, whining toward the painted wooden booths in the rear. It was Tom, who'd caught the action from the front window after hearing the sound of the shots.

"Okay, freeze," Pat said. He signaled for Tom to

come around through the open door and they turned on the glaring, overhead light. Sammy lay in his wet apron on the floor, his eyes popping strangely from his head, his tongue protruding obscenely, his face purple. He apparently was so close to death that his sphincter muscles had already let go, staining the floor with a messy brown fluid.

"Send for an ambulance and pulmotor fast. He may be alive," Pat said to Tom.

Tom put cuffs on the man on the floor.

"This guy's got one in the shoulder. He'll have to go in the ambulance, too."

Pat gestured toward the other thug, a blond, puffy faced man with blue watery eyes.

"Put your hands up high, real high."

The man did so.

"Okay, now. Spread your legs," Pat ordered.

The man now stood in the strange position of a jumping-jack exercise. Pat leaned his left hand against the bar and with his right foot took careful aim and kicked the man hard between the legs. As the man doubled over, Pat brought his knee up and felt the satisfactory sound of crushing bone as his kneecap hit the falling, pudgy chin.

The two men were booked for armed robbery and attempted murder, but the rope indicated that it was more than an ordinary hoodlum holdup. The rope was the mark of Brooklyn's Profaci gang. Pat knew that it spelled family trouble.

Julie Piacenza, the wounded man, died of blood poisoning in the hospital ward at Bellevue. Puggy Kemelmans, the pudgy blond, apparently became involved in a prison riot in the Tombs and died after having been stabbed with a sharpened bedspring. Because shots were fired by both sides, the job was good for another commendation for both Tom and Pat. It also made another column in the *Daily News,* the *Post* and the *Journal.*

By now, Pat had acquired so many commendations that the newspapers frequently referred to him as "hero cop," which brought a lot of horselaughs in the locker room, but they were laced with envy.

Sammy Wein recovered from the strangulation attack after being given oxygen and artificial respiration in the ambulance on the way to St. Vincent's. There was a sit-down between Genovese's crowd and Profaci's Brooklyn group with Gambino acting as arbiter.

Profaci swore that he knew nothing about the activities of the two dead holdup men, and the fact that they had met such unfortunate ends settled the issue for the organization.

CHAPTER 9

Ultimately Regan Doyle's much sought-after transfer to Chicago came through. To Doyle, the shift from Atlanta's grits and gravy to Chicago's polluted atmosphere was like a breath of foul air. The Chicago police department was famous throughout the country as the most corrupt in the nation. Every captain was picked by a ward committeeman, and if he didn't play ball, he didn't stay.

Coltrane, Doyle's new supervisor, warned him not to share any information with the police department without first checking it out with the bureau. There weren't many cops that the bureau felt could be trusted with information.

If The Director didn't think there was such a thing as organized crime, it might have paid him to spend a little time around Chicago. The Mafia not only controlled gambling, prostitution, narcotics, but also many legitimate businesses such as construction, meat and food distribution, linen services, entertainment and, above all, the hundreds of B-girl bars and twenty-one joints where a sucker could go twenty-five dollars for a bottle of carbonated California wine or get a blow job in a booth for ten dollars.

The First Ward was commonly regarded as the Mafia's own. Sam "Momo" Giancana, the recognized Mafia boss, had relatives all over the First Ward's payroll.

To all intents and purposes, the town hadn't changed since the gang wars of the thirties when Torrio, Capone and Big Jim Colisimo took Cook County over from Dion O'Banion and his pals. But at the bureau, the official word was still, "There is no organized crime. There is no Mafia, and watch out for the Communists."

Doyle was frustrated time after time, turning up evidence of organized crime activities and being unable to make a federal case out of it. Even when he got a tip that a major burglary team was operating, actually within the police department, he couldn't get any support from Washington to follow up on it.

The FBI was authorized to investigate the activities of corrupt police departments. But without support from on high, the project was hopeless. In his gloomier moments, Doyle even thought about resigning or going into private security work.

Katie came through town, this time as lead in an industrial show for the National Plumbing Manufacturers' convention. The name of the show was *Don't Let Business Go Down the Drain*. Doyle wasn't feeling as protective about his job as he had earlier.

He and Katie spent a solid week at the Blackstone. Katie was the most tender, loving, beautiful, passionate woman he'd ever known in bed, but there was a nagging tendril of doubt running up his spine and reaching into the thinking part of his brain about *how* she had learned to make love so well. He was wise enough not to broach the subject, but he did bring up the idea of marriage when they were picking bits of crumbled bacon off the bed tray one Sunday morning.

"Katie, you're the only woman who's ever really been able to get to me, if you know what I mean."

Katie nodded, crunching the stray bits between her perfectly matched and graduated capped teeth.

"It isn't just that we're good in bed together. It's that when I'm with you, I just seem to be happy and everything works right. When we go someplace, people look

at us and *like* us, and funny things happen. Like when
that guy on Wabash Avenue took us to his cellar to that
Dixieland jam session, or that yacht party on the lake."

"It's been really terrific, Regan," Katie said.

"Well, now I've got a good career with the bureau.
Probably my next move will get me into New York and
you've had a good swing through the country and kind
of proven yourself in the theater. Why don't we get married?"

Katie threw her warm, pink arms around Regan's
head, nearly upsetting the bed tray. "Regan, you are *so*
sweet. You're probably the sweetest man in the whole
world," and Regan knew that that meant: "No."

He pressed his nose down into the cleft between those
smooth breasts and left it there for a couple of minutes
so she couldn't see quite how hurt he was. After a while
he came up for air.

"Well, it was just an idea," he said.

"It was a *good* idea, Regan," Katie said seriously. "I
think it would work. I think we'd be good together, but
I'll never be good for *any* man in a marriage till I get this
theater thing out of my system, and believe me, being in
Business Going Down the Drain is not my idea of star-
dom."

They had decided to go to the Brookfield Zoo that afternoon and as they were getting dressed, Regan asked
Katie if she had seen Pat and Connie.

"I catch up with them once or twice a year when I'm
in New York," Katie said. "They seem very happy, and
Pat is really doing very well on the force."

There was a long silence, because Regan really didn't
know what to say when Pat's name came up, but he felt
that in the end it was better not to talk again of that
bruising night.

He put in a memo the next day asking for a transfer to
New York.

CHAPTER 10

When Pat made sergeant, he put in a request to be moved up to the Seventeenth. By now he wasn't concerned with petty police graft. He was into bigger things and the pile in his safe deposit box was growing every year. Of course, moving in the company he did, he had to spend a little now and then.

When he went out bouncing around now, it was no longer in the neighborhood bars of the Village or Mulberry Street, but in the Copa, or Vesuvio, or Jilly's or La Scala, or Manny Wolf's. He also had to show up once in a while in the after-hours places like the Gold Key or the Lilac Club.

Money went, but money came in, too. In many cases, he acted just as a bag man, picking up collections, but sometimes he set up deals for the organization—often deals that had nothing to do with the police department.

The family, this time the *bigger* family, the *Genovese* family was going through some changes, too. Vito was visibly strengthening his hold while Costello was losing his.

Pat's hours were irregular, which meant that he spent less and less time with Connie. When he wasn't actually on the job, he was busy with his extracurricular activities. When they did go on holidays, Connie didn't seem to enjoy the places they went—Miami, Vegas, LA, the Bahamas. She hated the big resorts and the gambling places.

The only happy holiday she had was when Pat took a two-week vacation in Italy. In his pocket was another package for "Mr. Lucania"—Charlie Lucky. They spent only two days in Naples and then took a car north to pass four or five days in Rome where Connie had an audience with the Pope, arranged by Sam Massey.

They drove north to Florence, to Milan and up through the Dolomites to Switzerland. The trip ended in Zurich where Pat had business at the Crédit Suisse. They stayed at the Eden Sur Lac, and to Connie, it was a second honeymoon.

One night, after a fantastic dinner in the hotel dining room, during which they finished two bottles of Dole and topped the meal off with peaches swimming in Kirschwasser, Connie seemed to take fire. And Pat, too, seeing her out of the black frumpy dresses she had taken to wearing, her body still firm and beautiful, with her full breasts pointed and erect, the belly smooth and un-wrinkled, the feathery pubic hairs, transparent as a fishnet, showing the pink skin beneath, felt tender and excited. He kissed her body which seemed glowing and feverish all over. And, when he touched her between the legs, she was dripping with passion. Never had she been so ready. She squirmed and moaned under his touch and reached daringly for his hard penis. When he put it in-side her, she felt slippery and super heated.

He came in long, slow strokes and she, for the second time since they were married, spoke aloud as he slid in and out of her, murmuring over and over again, "Oh, God, oh, God. Oh, God that feels good. Oh, God, please, please."

They fell asleep in each other's arms. It was the first time they had done so in at least three years. The next day they stayed in bed and ordered up an American breakfast—eggs, bacon, orange juice.

"God, I'm tired of that continental breakfast crap," Pat said.

They stood on the balcony and watched the excursion boats cruising across the flat waters of Lake Zurich.

"You know," Pat said, languidly, "it's been a long time since I've had this kind of peace. It seems so far from New York. There's no sense of time. I can hardly remember what day of the week it is, or what month it is."

"Neither can I," said Connie, dreamily. "I left my calendar home—and my thermometer."

Pat felt a moment of panic, but then he smiled. Why not? They had the money now. They had the security and they had been planning to move out of the apartment to a house about five blocks from Sam's place—a nice brown brick house, not unlike some of those they could see around the lake there in Switzerland, with a back yard and trees in the front. It had been Berghoff's house, but Berghoff's Royal Provisions was bankrupt now and he was ready to make a good deal, especially with a friend of Al Santini's.

Suddenly Connie *did* recall what day it was. It was Sunday. They put on their good clothes and went to mass in the Gross-Munster Cathedral built by Charlemagne.

Later, Connie said, "I prayed to St. Theresa. I prayed that we would have a beautiful boy and we would name him Patrick, after you."

"You might be jumping the gun a little," Pat said, sourly. "Besides, my name is Pasquale."

CHAPTER 11

Two months after their return from Switzerland, Connie made her second visit to young Dr. Pileggi and found that the rabbit confirmed St. Theresa's answer to her prayers. She went directly from his office to St. Adrian's, where she lit a candle to the accommodating saint.

Pat was on the twelve-to-eight in the one-seven that day. When he was on the late shift, he often returned home with a bag of bagels that he picked up in Zabar's on the West Side. Connie tried to be awake when he came back and help him with breakfast, but if she wasn't, he would just have the bagels with cream cheese and coffee and flop into bed.

Because of his odd hours, they had separate, but adjoining bedrooms. The morning after she got the news from Dr. Pileggi, Connie set the alarm to be sure she'd be up when Pat returned. As soon as she heard the car in the driveway, she began to squeeze oranges. It would be a treat for Pat. She also set fresh ground coffee to perking. When he took his own breakfast, he always took instant. Pat smelled the coffee instantly when he came in.

"Connie, you up?"

"In here, Pat," she said.

The kitchen was big and sunny with windows on three sides. There was an entrance in back facing the driveway and garage. Pat had come in through that. He brushed her forehead with his lips and picked up the twelve-ounce glass of fresh-squeezed juice with the film of ragged pulp on top.

"Great," he said. "I can really use this," and drained half of it without taking his lips from the glass. He hung his jacket over the chair and sat down with that morning's *Daily News* to check the sports scores.

Connie had never gotten used to the idea of a man sitting in the kitchen in his shirtsleeves with a gun protruding from his waistline, but she was happy. She scrambled some eggs in butter with fresh green peppers, the way Pat liked them. She took the bag of bagels from him and split one and laid it across the top of the toaster to warm.

"This is great," Pat said, absently, turning to Moon Mullins.

Connie brought him the coffee and the little bottle of saccharine he had taken to using in the last year to keep his waistline from ballooning, though his figure was still slim and athletic, showing only a slight fold of flab over the tight belt when he sat down.

Connie sat down opposite him at the yellow formica kitchen table and watched him as he drank the coffee and turned the pages of the newspaper. After a few moments, he became aware of her gaze and dropped the newspaper to look at her inquiringly.

"Pat," she said, "I have some wonderful news."

To Pat this usually meant that the St. Adrian's bazaar had raised eight hundred dollars for Asian orphans or that she'd been able to arrange to paint the bathroom for only twenty-five dollars through a relative. He raised his eyes with simulated interest.

"Yes?"

"Pat," Connie said, reaching over to take his hand, "St. Theresa answered my prayers."

"That's nice."

"We're going to have a baby."

Pat stared at her a full ten seconds in disbelief, trying to let the thought sink into his head. Then he smiled with genuine delight.

"That's terrific, Connie! No kidding, that's terrific! When did you find out?"

She told him the details and he seemed closer and more interested in her than he had since the last trip, two months earlier. He pulled her around the table and into his lap, holding her happily around the waist.

"I'm glad we waited, aren't you?" he said.

"It's good now. We've got the house. We've got enough money. It's a good neighborhood for a kid."

"Did you tell Sam yet?"

"I was going to call him later today."

"Let's call him together," Pat said, and they did.

Sam shouted with delight. "My God, a grandfather! I was beginning to think it would never happen! Let's have a nice party for the family."

"No, *we'll* have the party. It'll be a housewarming, too, but I'd like to wait a few months until we're sure that everything's going to be all right."

Connie beamed with delight.

It was well into June before Pat could find the right time to hold the party. He insisted that it be catered to save Connie the work, since she was already into her seventh month. Sam recommended a caterer who had worked in Bergen County for Willie Moore. Charlie Nightingale would come and set up charcoal pits in the back yard and cook a butcher's tenderloin of pure, aged beef.

A call to Al Santini at Royal insured an adequate supply of the right meat. Connie insisted on making her own version of lasagna as a side dish, and Pat didn't object as long as Esperanza came over to help. He also arranged to have Lewis, Sam's black butler and handyman, come over to assist with the coats and other chores. Altogether, there were more than fifty people, including Art Winburg, Jim Bailey and a few others from NYU and all of the boys from the old Mulberry Street gang—Santini, Federici, Ganci.

To enliven the party, they accepted a "band of music," as a present from Sam—an accordionist, a violinist and a piano player who alternated between "Torna a Sorrento," "Mare, Mare Mezzo Mare" and Montovani classics.

The women talked about babies and marveled over Connie's deft hand with decoration. She had done the new house in an eclectic combination of modern and provincial French.

The men talked about work, sports, politics and sex. Pauley Federici was managing editor of the *Bronx Home News*. Paul Ganci had a funeral parlor on the fringe of the old Mulberry Street district. In the family, they said it was Ganci who had developed the idea of the double-decker bunk-bed funeral in which a body, that for diplomatic purposes had to disappear quietly, was placed in the bottom of a coffin, while a layer of wood was placed over it to separate it from the more legitimate corpse on top.

Guido Paterno, the family banker and financier, was there. He had recently been appointed director of the First American Bank, in which he was furthermore the largest stockholder. The bank had branches in Astoria, Manhattan, the South Bronx, Chicago, Miami and had connections with private banks in the Bahamas, Montreal and Bermuda.

About ten-thirty at night, the party started to break up, in a great flurry of embraces and bright-eyed double Italian kisses. Paterno and Pat went into the ground floor room that had been fixed up as his den with a contour chair, an antique mahogany desk, a leather sofa and a wall of books, mostly texts and law books concerned with Pat's studies. There was also a heavy concrete and steel vault under the floorboards which Pat had built in when they had bought the place. Of course, that wasn't visible.

Pat gestured Paterno to a seat on the leather sofa and took some ice and a bottle of twelve-year-old Grant's from the small, wood-grained office refrigerator. They had left Connie outside to help the guests find their coats and say the final good-byes to those who were left. When Pat finished the drink and they had toasted each other and the baby, they got down to business.

"Guido, this is a deal I'm handling on my own. What can you do with three hundred grand in U.S. Treasury Bonds?"

"I can get you twenty, twenty-five points," Guido said, after some judicious thought. "That's if we sell them here in New York."

"Suppose I've got a Swiss bank account?"

"Well, it would be hard to transfer money from here. . . ."

Outside, Connie was looking for Sylvia Ganci's black diamond mink. It was hanging way in back of the large, well-lit clothes closet to the left of the main entrance of the house. As Connie removed the long, glimmering coat from its hook, she heard a rumble of voices coming through the wall. The closet had been carved out of a larger room, the remains of which now served as Pat's den. She probably would not have listened, but she heard Pat's voice coming through, loud and excited, perhaps a little stimulated by the Scotch he had been drinking.

"You're crazy, Guido!" Pat was saying excitedly. "I could run up to Montreal in no time. We could get the full value. We'll put it through your branch in Montreal. I'll give you ten points on the deal. That's a pretty good return. Then I can hand-carry the cash straight over to Zurich from Montreal and there'd be no record anywhere. Maybe, on my way back, I can drop fifty grand with Charlie Lucky in Italy and put it to work for me. I can turn that fifty into a hundred and fifty in two months."

Guido, the banker, was interested. "Maybe I can help sweeten the pot a little."

"Well, it's the white stuff, you know. Do you want to get involved with that?"

"I thought Frankie said no dealing in the white stuff. No dope."

"Aah! He's *pazzo*. Everybody's into that now. Vito don't tell Frank, but it's a big part of his business and if our family wants to stay afloat, we got to be in it, too."

There was a silence, then Guido's voice, muffled. Apparently, they were pouring another drink, but he said, "My percentage . . . take it with you and turn it over. . . ." and there was some more mumbled talk. As the men moved away from the wall against which the refrigerator was standing, Connie leaned against the closet wall, holding her belly and thinking.

There had seemed to be nothing strange to her in the life that they led. The big Riverdale apartment, she felt sure Sam had helped with it, and the house, well, Pat didn't discuss finances with her, but she assumed the down payment came from the wedding presents.

She had never paid much attention to money details, yet she knew from what she'd heard that the house was worth at least a hundred thousand. Nobody had ever commented on their style of living. She was used to getting presents from her father and to his help.

She had a vague idea that Pat was involved with Sam in some business affairs and so was Arthur, but she had no idea what they were. But even her own limited reading of current affairs in *The New York Times, Reader's Digest* and *The Saturday Evening Post* gave her a fairly clear understanding of what she had heard.

She didn't understand too well about the stocks, though obviously there was something illegal about them. But the talk about "white stuff" was clear enough. It would have to be heroin or cocaine. Didn't they call it "snow"?

Was this the source of those sudden deluxe vacation trips, donated, Pat said, by "a friend"?

Was it because of these manipulations that they had taken that sudden second honeymoon—with stopovers in Naples and Zurich—the same trip that had produced this fecund swelling in her body? Was St. Theresa's gift paid for with the dope in the veins of some sick addict in Harlem?

"Holy Mother, forgive us!" Connie whispered under her breath.

Suddenly, her bulging seven-month stomach felt very heavy and the overhead closet light began to go dim and flicker and flare in different colors. Connie's face was wet and clammy and her breath was coming in short spasms. It seemed as though the enormous bundle of liquid and flesh in her abdomen was trying to force its way up through her throat.

She felt herself sliding down onto the floor and reached out desperately for support. Her hand found the overhead rod, supporting the remaining coats, and she clutched it spastically. But the wooden rod wasn't made for such sudden weight and pressure and the small U-shaped pine support holding it against the wallboards ripped with a splintering sound as Connie tumbled awkwardly to the floor with the mink and cloth coats and Burberries falling atop her.

In the next room, Pat and Guido heard the vagu tumbling sounds and came running out at the same time that Sylvia ran to the closet door which was half-ajar and pulled it open. As she did, she emitted a bone-chilling, high-pitched scream.

"Help! Help! It's Connie! Quick. Help, somebody!"

Pat took one look into the closet and yelled at the top of his lungs.

"PILEGGI!"

He ran into the closet and started pulling the coats off Connie, whose face was damp and dead white, her legs flopped awkwardly apart, with the blue printed silk of her dress pulled high above her knees. Pat took her under the shoulders and began to drag her out into the open air.

CHAPTER 12

Pat managed to shoo the remaining guests out and carry the comatose figure of Connie to her bedroom upstairs.

The doctor peered into her eyeballs with a small pencil-flash, felt her pulse, palpated the bulging abdomen and listened to her heart briefly on the stethoscope. He asked for Pat's help in removing the long, pleated gown from the ungainly figure on the bed.

"Is she all right, doctor?"

He noticed that her eyes were glazed and half-closed, but with bits of the whites peeping through in an alarming fashion.

"She's all right, as far as that's concerned," the young doctor said. (He wasn't the *old* Dr. Pileggi that had cared for the family for so long, but the young one, half-northern, with a tall shock of red hair and a strong belief in Freudian psychiatry.)

"She's had some sort of a shock. Do you know of any incident tonight that might have caused that?"

Pat shook his head in surprised negation.

"Well, I'm just worried that it may induce premature labor. How far gone is she? About seven months, isn't it?"

Pat nodded.

"Well, it would be better if the birth were not premature. We'll see what we can do. Will you excuse me?"

and he ushered Pat to the door before he conducted the rest of the examination.

"I think everything will be all right," he said later. "I've given her a couple of Seconals, but we'd better keep her under close observation for a while. I'll come back tomorrow. Meanwhile, you might try to discover the cause of this shock or upset. It may help. Was she worried about the pain of the delivery?"

"No," Pat said. "I think she was looking forward to it."

"Well, we'll talk to her tomorrow. Has she had any incidences of hysteria?"

"Well, she yells a little sometimes. I wouldn't call it hysteria. She's a little nervous."

"Um hum," the doctor said, leaving Pat to guess what that meant. "Well, how about the sex life? Has that been normal? I hope you don't mind my asking that."

"I don't mind. I just don't think it's any of your fucking business," Pat said, ushering the doctor to the door.

"No offense, no offense," young Pileggi said. "It just might have some bearing."

"Yeah, well you just stick to the medicine, doc," Pat said, as he helped the doctor on with his hat and coat.

In the morning he called the one-seven to tell them he was taking a sick day. Then, he called Sam's house and asked if he could borrow Esperanza for a while. Esperanza came about 8:00 in the morning with the copy of the *News* he had requested, and brought a tray of breakfast upstairs to Connie.

When Pat finished his bagel and coffee, he went upstairs. Connie sat, staring dully at the untouched breakfast tray. She still seemed hung over from the sleeping pills she had taken and barely reacted to his entrance. He kissed her damp forehead and drew up a chair beside her bed.

"It's going to be okay, Connie. The doctor's coming over later. He says everything will be okay."

Connie murmured something but he couldn't make out what it was. He leaned closer.

"Creep," she said. Her voice was flat and without tonality. He wasn't sure what she had said.

"I'm sorry. I didn't hear you," Pat said.

"CREEP!"

He could hear it that time. Pat wondered if she'd gone off her trolley completely.

"You're a goddamn dope peddler and a crook! I heard you."

Pat looked genuinely astonished. "What are you talking about?"

"I was in the clothes closet. I heard you talking to Paterno."

"What are you talking about?"

"I heard you talking about the 'white stuff' and about the stolen bonds and about the trip to Montreal and now I know what all those trips are about, the trip to Havana, the trip to Italy. You're a Mafioso."

"Listen," Pat said, "I think the medicine's maybe affecting your mind a little."

"No. I may be dopey from the drug, but I remember *very well,* and I've been sitting here thinking and I suddenly realized that all this has been happening for years and I just didn't see it."

Her mind seemed to be operating, Pat noticed, but she talked dully as though animated by some small electric motor, a small silent electric motor such as they have in record changers.

"Look," Pat said, "I'm not saying you're right. I'm just saying you don't understand about it. It's *business.* It has nothing to do with Mafiosi or crime or violence. It's just business. You don't want me to be a fucking cop for the rest of my life, do you?"

"Does my father . . . does Sam know about this?"

Pat laughed, a short humorless bark.

"*Know* about it? Are you kidding? He's the *boss,*

Numero Uno. Whose idea you think the whole fucking thing was?"

"What are you talking about?" Connie said, her eyes opening for the first time that morning.

"For Christ's sake, grow up! Don't you know it was Don Antonio and your own father that got me into the family? Don't you know they brought me up like a hothouse flower. You think you get beautiful flowers without soaking their roots in manure? That's what makes things grow. Don't you know our whole marriage was set up by your father so there'd be someone to carry on the family business? For Christ's sake! What'd they teach you there at St. Agnes? You think your Uncle Raimundo isn't in this right up to his starched collar?"

Connie picked up the full glass of orange juice and threw it across the room toward Pat's head.

"You're a creep!" she shouted. "You're a goddamn creep! Get out of here! You're a monster!"

She threw the sugar bowl and the toast at him. Pat ducked them.

Suddenly, her eyes seemed to roll back in her head and she began to scream in long, choked, high-pitched tones, intermingled with sobbing laughs and choked cries. She began to writhe wildly around on the bed, throwing her distended abdomen from side to side and kicking at the restraining blankets.

Pat managed to get the coverlet up over her arms, knocking the breakfast tray to the ground with a crash so that all she could do was roll her head from side to side, biting her lips and screaming. Pat was frightened now. He slapped her face twice but it did no good. Esperanza came running up from downstairs, yelling, *"Que pasa, que pasa, senor?"*

"Call Dr. Pileggi. His name is in the book."

"I no can read, senor."

"Oh, for Christ's sake! Okay. See if you can keep her in bed and calm. I'll call the doctor."

Esperanza sat on the bed and stroked the restless woman's forehead.

"*Calmate, calmate, chica,*" she said and it seemed to have a soothing effect.

Connie lay more quietly now, her chest heaving, but she had stopped writhing and kicking. Pat went to his bedroom and dialed Pileggi on the bedside phone.

"You better get over here pretty fast, doctor. She's in a state of hysteria."

"That's what I was afraid of," Pileggi said. "I'll be right over."

Pat tried to go into the room to see Connie, but it was obvious that his very presence started the whole thing over again, so he went down to the den to think. What had she actually heard? She couldn't have heard much. They mentioned no names. They never did. Just a few phrases. They talked about the trip, the bonds and the white stuff.

Pat often wondered if she didn't realize that their affluent way of life was far beyond their legitimate means.

But Connie had grown up to accept unexpected luxury without question. While she was a wily shopper at the supermarket, she had no idea of the value of things on a larger scale, like cars, houses, travel, servants' wages and so forth. Pat paid all the bills and kept his financial affairs to himself. To Connie this was normal.

Sam Massey had accustomed her to shadowy dealings, and vague "favors" from mysterious friends.

Since her reading was largely women's or popular magazines, romantic novels, or religious epics, she was seldom exposed to popular writings on the family's more nefarious activities. She had long since given up reading newspapers because she found all the violence and tragedies "depressing."

Despite all this, Pat had always felt that *nobody* could be as innocent of the world around her as Connie appeared to be. It was clear that she tended to hear and believe only what she wanted to, and had the capacity to close her mind off from unpleasant truths.

But now certain facts had been practically thrust upon her, it seemed. Exactly what and how much had she heard and what could she make of it all?

Pat jumped up from the leather office chair, ran around to the closet and rapped gently on the wall adjoining his office. Son-of-a-bitch! It was only wallboard. He was always careful about being overheard, but this was in his own *home*. Two of the other walls were on the outside and the third wall was on the corridor where no one could listen without being seen, but he hadn't figured on the closet.

He had always wondered whether Connie could be as simple and unknowing as she had seemed. Could she have lived with Sam all that time without knowing a thing that was going on? Was her constant running to the church some kind of absolution for her of dimly felt guilt?

Pileggi came, went up and talked to Connie and gave her some more sedatives. He came down to talk to Pat.

"Is she going to be all right?" Pat asked. "Is the baby going to be all right? She was like going crazy."

"Well," the doctor said judiciously, "we don't like to use that word, but I would say she may be having a prepartum psychosis."

"You mean she really *is* crazy?"

"Please, it's not that. But sometimes a shock at this stage can precipitate a spontaneous abortion. I think she should have a full-time nurse, or better yet, we could send her up to Rose Briar Acres in Westchester."

"What's that?" Pat said.

"It's a private psychiatric nursing home, but they also have complete medical facilities. I think she may need some shock treatment."

"Jesus," Pat said, "won't that kill the kid?"

The doctor explained that shock treatment, on the

contrary, might bring Connie out of her mental state sooner, and there was no record of this sort of thing having hurt children.

"But we'll have to watch her afterwards. Sometimes there's a combination of neurotic and psychotic behavior after the birth which may lead to suicide attempts or other unpleasantness. I'm not trying to alarm you, but I think you should know the situation. Can you afford to send her up to the home?"

"Yeah," Pat said. "I can afford it. She's been raving. She's been saying all sorts of things. She thinks that I'm some sort of a criminal. I guess that's just part of her craziness, huh?"

"Well," Pileggi said, "people often have strange delusions. Don't pay any attention. I can arrange for a private ambulance, if you'd like."

"Yeah, yeah," Pat said. "Do whatever you have to. The best of everything."

CHAPTER 13

Sam sat brooding in the back of his Lincoln as Tommy sped north on the Sawmill toward Chappaqua.

Connie had called him that morning in an agitated state and insisted that he come out to talk to her.

"Sweetness, I've been planning to come out on the weekend and spend a day with you," Sam had replied.

"I don't *want* you to come on the weekend. I want you to come *now*. You *must* come. Do you hear, Daddy? I'm not fooling."

So Sam brought a huge bouquet of gladioli, canceled some appointments, and set out for Rose Briar.

Connie was in a private room, looking pale and stony-eyed, her swollen stomach now looming enormously, even with her body half-sunk into the hospital bed. Sam had the nurse put the gladioli into a vase and then asked to be left alone.

"You call me if you leave," the nurse said. "My instructions were to stay with her at all times."

"Don't worry. You just stay outside. I'll call you."

"So," he said to his daughter when the door had closed, "well, so, how are you?"

Connie gave no sign of recognition but stared bitterly in front of her.

"What's the matter, dollface?" he said. "Don't you feel well? Is there something I can do?"

"Are we Mafiosi, Daddy?"

"What are you talking about? That's just old people's stories. There's no such thing. Sure we do business with family friends. That's what family is for. Family is who we can trust. There's nothing wrong with that, is there? It's just business, like with anybody else. You don't believe what they say in the papers."

"You *are* Mafiosi," Connie said staring ahead of her.

"You just don't understand it. Family protects each other and that's all. No one is hurt, except maybe some few people who try to hurt the family. We have to protect one another. That's the only time we are ever strong with people. This is nothing to concern you. You have a good husband. He works hard. He's with the police. He's a hero. You don't have to worry about other business."

"But you arranged for Pat to marry me without telling me."

Sam shrugged. "What's to tell, darling? You met him yourself. You loved him. That's the normal way of things. He asked permission like a gentleman. In the old country, all marriages were arranged. This business of falling in love, we never heard of it. We found a good wife, a good husband, we lived together, we made children, we were happy. We didn't know about love. You, at least, had love."

"Jesus, Mary and Joseph!" Connie said bitterly.

"Look," Sam said reasonably, "you're my baby, my only girl. If Pasquale had not pleased you, I would never have allowed the marriage, but he did please you very much. Now, you're about to become a good family and I'll be a grandfather."

"The grandfather of what? A murderer and dope dealer? Oh, your grandson will come into a marvelous tradition! What else do you do? Do you sell dirty pictures to school kids? Do you pass out dope on street corners? Or do you just give the orders and have others do it? Does Pat do your smuggling and murders out of love for his dear father-in-law?"

Her voice rose with every question until it was pitched at a near scream.

"Connie, please, you're upsetting yourself," Sam said, trying to calm her. "It's bad for the baby. Here, have a glass of water. . . ."

Sam reached for the thermos carafe by Connie's bedside, but she swept it from his hands with an angry slap. The carafe fell to the floor with a tinkling protest as the water spread in a puddle under the bed.

"I'll have the nurse clean it up. Try to calm yourself, baby girl," Sam said.

"Is that what you told my mother?" Connie said, her voice still strident and loud. "Is that what you told her before you had her *killed*?"

Sam's voice went rigid and cold.

"Connie, you're talking like a crazy person. If you keep acting like somebody sick, you may never get out of here. You want to get well and have your baby, don't you? Where do you get these crazy ideas?"

"You'll take care of me, too, won't you, if I keep talking about your rotten business? You'll take care of your sweet baby girl and the little grandchild inside, won't you? It wouldn't bother you any more than killing a fly. Tell me, do you talk about your latest horrors when you go to confession on Sundays?"

"Connie, this isn't good for you. I'm going to have them give you a sedative."

"Yes, you'd like them to make me a dope addict too. Why not? You're in the business! Do you confess everything to your brother, so it won't go any further, so it won't reach God? But God is watching you all the time. He knows! And *I* know!"

"Look," Sam said in a measured voice. "God has nothing to do with this. God is for women."

Connie stared at him with hot eyes, her chest heaving

wildly with the force of her emotions. Then as suddenly as it had arisen, the emotional storm appeared to subside. Her eyes went dull and she lay silent, staring into the emptiness of the room.

Sam watched her wordlessly, afraid that anything he said might cause her to flare up again. Finally, he sighed, shrugged hopelessly, and got to his feet.

"Well, I got to get back to the city," he said. "If you need anything, anything at all, let me know and please, don't be upset about the family, about business. This is just what the doctor said, some kind of little craziness from having a baby. A lot of people get it."

Connie said nothing, but closed her eyes, and Sam saw that tears were running down her face. He tiptoed out, closing the door quietly behind him. The nurse dozing in a chair in the corridor outside, leapt to her feet.

"Is everything all right?"

"Yes."

The nurse started to go back into the room.

"Wait a minute, nurse."

Sam pulled a roll of bills from his pocket, peeled one off and pressed it into her hand.

"I want you to take very good care of my little girl—very good care," and he stalked off down the corridor.

The nurse looked down and saw she was holding a hundred-dollar bill.

That night, Connie seemed cheerful in the early evening. She asked for her makeup and put a little powder, rouge and pancake on her face to brighten the hospital pallor. The nurse smiled and continued reading her *True Confessions.*

From the makeup kit, Connie extracted the long-handled ladies' razor that she used to shave under her arms and the few hairs that pushed out under chin. Carefully she unscrewed the safety razor top and took out the thin, blue Gillette blade. The nurse licked her fingers and turned the pages of the magazine. Holding the razor concealed under the bedcovers, Connie dug quickly with the blade into her left wrist and then into her right. Then she lay there, bleeding quietly into the covers, her head thrown back on the pillow with a peaceful smile on her face.

It was five minutes before the nurse noticed the two red blots seeping up through the cotton coverlets.

"My God," she said, "what happened?"

She pulled back the cover and saw the two arms, each lying in a gelatinous pool of running blood. Connie was already in a half coma as the nurse reached for the phone to call the desk for emergency help. Angrily, she took the two wrists in her hand and pressed on the veins to stop the bleeding till help came. She looked at Connie, now slipping rapidly from consciousness and said, "You've been a *very bad girl!* Do you know that? A *very bad girl.*"

CHAPTER 14

Following the suicide attempt, Connie was kept in a constant state of sedation. Her eyes, when she looked at Pat, no longer seemed filled with hate, but simply dull and unfocused. When he told her that he had to be gone for a few weeks on a trip to Canada, she just looked back with her dead eyes and said, "I'll pray for you."

She had, in fact, apparently been doing a lot of praying lately and had requested that the hospital's Catholic chaplain stop by at least once a day. Pat left her a copy of Douglas's, *The Robe,* and the latest issues of *Colliers* and *Reader's Digest* and *Modern Screen*. He also left a flowering begonia on the windowsill, but Connie didn't react to any of this.

She just repeated, "Go if you want. I'll pray for you," so Pat left.

He drove the 358 miles to Montreal and checked into the Ritz Carlton on Sherbrooke Street West.

He had an appointment to meet Al Agueci, Steve Maggadino's representative in Canada, in the penthouse restaurant. Agueci had made dinner reservations for "Mr. Albert," and Pat had been supplied with a complete description. Agueci was tagged as a young, bright ambitious worker, and a man to reckon with in Maggadino's Buffalo *borgata*.

He was only a year or so older than Pat and as Pat approached the table he saw a ruddy-faced, athletic-looking young man in a blue blazer with silver buttons and a striped school tie smiling toward him.

"Mr. Albert?"

"That's right. You must be from New York," Agueci
said, shaking his hand.

Details were quickly worked out for the sale of the
bonds, and rendezvous in Zurich, where a messenger
from Charlie Lucky would pick up the cash. Pat liked
young Al and saw in him an up-and-coming image of
himself. He particularly admired the British cut and
nonmod look of Agueci's clothes and the way he said
"aboot" for about.

After dinner the young Canadian took him on a walking tour of the older parts of Montreal, down Berry
Street to the St. Lawrence River, past old houses wearing brass plaques with ancient dates. Everyone around
him was speaking French and the signs were all in
French. It all made Pat feel even more remote from the
problem in the hospital bed in Chappaqua. They talked
about sports, mostly hockey, which was Agueci's big enthusiasm, a little about basketball, quite a bit about sex
and very little about family business, except to exchange
acquaintances.

Al asked if Pat was traveling alone and this got them
on to the subject of girls. After the walk, they went to
the Chateau Champlain and watched a corny floor
show. The talent was not up to New York standards, but
the girls were fresh and bouncy-looking. Pat expressed a
special admiration for an apple-cheeked brunette, who
sang several Edith Piaf numbers in French.

"That's Mimi Chapelle," Al said. "She's a good
friend. Would you like to meet her?"

"You bet!"

Al wrote a note and gave it to the headwaiter, and ten
minutes later the apple-cheeked young girl was sitting at
the table. Unfortunately she spoke almost no English,
and Al had to act as interpreter.

"Tell her I think she's gorgeous."

"Monsieur dit que tu es tres belle," Al translated.

Mimi smiled and said, "Sank you."

"Tell her I'd like to take her home for a souvenir."

"*Monsieur dit qu'il t'aime.*"

"Sank you," Mimi said, smiling at him with her eyes.

Things went on this way for about a half an hour, then Al yawned ostentatiously and looked at his watch.

"I think we better be going."

Pat looked longingly at the apple-cheeked Canadian girl.

"I wouldn't mind sticking around."

"Don't worry," Al said. "It's taken care of."

Pat noticed that Al simply signed the bill when he left and no questions were asked. Everybody said, "*Merci, Monsieur Albert,*" and "*Au revoir, Mister Albert,*" as they left. Al left him at the revolving door of the hotel.

"What's your room number?" he said, and Pat told him.

"Are you going right up?"

Pat shrugged. "I guess I'm pretty bushed."

"Okay. You may have a surprise a little later. Don't go to sleep right away."

Pat smiled. "I can stay up for that."

About ten minutes after he had crawled into his pajamas, there was a muffled knock at the door. It was Mimi, with a self-conscious grin. Pat ushered her into the room.

"Mr. Albert, he say you like to see me," she said, with a shy smile.

"Mr. Albert is very right," Pat said, helping her off with her coat.

"Mr. Albert said you would like to go round zee world."

"I would love it," Pat grinned.

It was an experience like none other he'd ever had, but frustrating in that Mimi would let him do nothing, insisting on doing all the kissing, licking, biting, stroking and caressing herself. She missed no part of his body.

At about 3:30 A.M., Pat finally dozed off, completely drained. Mimi quietly got up, dressed and left. At 3:40 there was a harsh jangling of the telephone. Pat answered, for the moment not even sure what city he was in.

"This is the desk, sir," the voice on the telephone said. "The young lady is leaving now. Is everything all right?"

"Christ!" Pat thought. "The bonds! The cash!"

He'd been walking around with a quarter of a million in negotiable securities and hadn't even bothered to get up when the girl left the room. Quickly he ran to the closet and checked the zippered inner pocket of his sports jacket. The bonds were safe there. Then he reached into the closet for his leather overnight bag and felt the silk lining where the fifty thousand in hundred-dollar bills had been concealed. Everything was still there. He went back to the phone and said, "Let her go. It's okay," and fell back to sleep, exhausted.

In the morning Al Agueci came by in a rented Cadillac. They had breakfast together in the hotel's coffee shop and in the car on the way to the airport made the exchange of bonds for cash.

"Good luck and bon voyage," Agueci said at the departure gate. "I hope we can do more business again sometime."

"God," Pat thought, "it was all so gentlemanly compared to New York."

In Zurich, he was met at the plane by a blonde named Mitzi Dikler, who was a secretary in the Zurich branch of Paterno's bank. She had made a reservation for him at the Baur au Lac. In view of the current situation, Pat had no desires to revive memories of his weekend at the Eden. Miss Dikler saw to it that he had a good dinner and a comfortable night.

The next day, he went to Paterno's imposing office on the Bahnhofstrasse and completed negotiations for the transfer of cash to Naples and the deposit of two hundred thousand in his bank account at Crédit Suisse.

Pat called the Rose Briar that night to check on Connie's condition, but Connie refused to accept the charges, so he spoke with the nurse who told him that his wife was resting comfortably, but was still under sedation.

"Listen," Pat said, "can't all those pills hurt the baby?"

"I doubt it," the nurse said, "but then I'm not a doctor."

"Well, if she comes around, tell her to behave herself. I'll call again."

As he hung up, he could feel Miss Dikler's warm breasts rubbing against the thin tissue of his pajamas and her warm tongue making circles in his ear.

"Just a minute, sweetie," he said, "till I rinse my mouth out. Tastes cruddy from all that drinking last night."

Pat decided that he would wait three or four days until he got definite word that the transfer had taken place in Naples and that the shipment was all right. He knew he was avoiding coming back to the situation at home, but he had never had such a delicious feeling of freedom and wealth. This was what it was really all about. This was what he'd been working for all this time—women, travel, being treated like a gentleman, eating like a movie star.

His next call to Chappaqua was from St. Moritz, the Palace Hotel. In the gift shop, Pat bought a five-hundred-dollar gold Patek-Philippe for himself and one for Mitzi. The watch would go easily for fifteen hundred in the States, he figured, and yet, did not look ostentatious.

There was no response to the call. Through the muffled transatlantic echoes, he got the feeling that Constanza was not available. He wondered if she were in the process of giving birth.

The next day, they drove down on Route 27 toward Chamfer, passing the Lake of Silvaplana followed by the Silsersee, and Maloja, the small resort town which was Mitzi's natal village. They stopped and had a *raclette* and some of the dry beef which was a feature of the countryside with her sturdy, dairy-farming father, who seemed strangely incurious as to his identity, but served the white Fendant wine and steamy melted cheese with gentle hospitality.

Pat tried to make a call from the village phones, but they all required being switched through Zurich or Geneva and there were always delays of several hours. The white, green, purple and blue mountains, looming dramatically, were what he always had imagined mountains should be in his mind but had never seen.

It was very hard to relate this open, clean world to the crowded scenes of his childhood or even to the pleasant scenic Hudson views of Riverdale.

They finally stopped in Locarno for the night, and Pat was pleased to hear the familiar sound of Italian, although the dialect was far from the "Scidgie" that he knew.

They stayed in a small but luxurious hotel off the Piazza Grande. They had time to do a little shopping before dinner and Pat bought Mitzi a Hermes typewriter and a Swiss embroidered blouse. The blouse was his idea.

Treveling with Mitzi kept him in a state of almost constant excitement because of her habit of touching him on the thigh, on the neck or on the cheek at every possible moment. He might get tired of that someday, but at the moment, it was very stimulating. When they drove in the car, she always contrived to ride with her warm hand nestling in his lap, like a bird sitting on eggs.

The next day, they clocked two hundred beautiful

miles through Brig to Montreux, at the tip of Lake Geneva, where Mitzi pointed out the famous Castle of Chillon, about which Byron had written his poem "The Prisoner of Chillon."

Pat remembered the poem vaguely from high school days but he couldn't remember what the prisoner was in for.

"It was politics," Mitzi explained, "and actually Francois Bonivard was let out from the prison four years after the time of Byron's poem, so it did have a happy ending."

After dinner on the lake, they pushed on to Vevey where they stayed at the Hotel des Trois-Couronnes in a room with a balcony that looked out on the lake. Pat pulled the white telephone out to the small table on the balcony and poured himself a glass of sparkling white wine as he placed another call to Rose Briar.

This time, Dr. Pileggi was there and asked if Pat would be willing to speak to him. Pat said he would. Pileggi got on and said, "Hello, Pat. I guess you're very busy out there."

"Yes," Pat said. "There's been a lot of business to take care of. How is Constanza? Has she had the child yet?"

There was a pause. "Constanza's all right, although still a little nervous."

"And the child? Has she had it yet?"

"Yes, she had it this morning. It's a boy."

"Terrific!" Pat said. "I'll be home on the first plane I can get."

He hung up the phone and whirled Mitzi in a bear hug.

"I'm a father of a boy!" he shouted. "I'm a daddy!"

"Marvelous," Mitzi said. "We should order some champagne to celebrate. I knew you could do wonderful things with your big peter there," she said gaily.

In Rose Briar, they let Constanza recuperate for two

days before they showed her the child. They would have showed it earlier, but she didn't ask for it, and this worried the hospital people. She seemed depressed and worn-out, but finally, in a weak voice, she asked to see the baby.

The small blanketed bundle was brought to her, cradled nervously but gently by a big rawboned nurse. Pileggi was right behind her. The nurse brought the bundle to the side of the bed. Constanza looked briefly at the elongated, sloping head, the slanting eyes and the huge, dangling, obscene tongue, then reached with affection for her son and gently cradled him to her.

Father Maroni hurried into the room, apparently summoned when the child was taken from the nursery. He stood behind the nurse and Pileggi as Constanza stared with a peculiar intensity at the warped bit of human flesh in her arms. She turned to the priest and said, "This is God's will, isn't it?"

"God moves in his own ways, my child," the priest said.

"And God punishes us for our sins, doesn't he?"

"Please, Constanza. You must not think of that. That has nothing to do with it. We cannot understand the ways of God."

"May I have the telephone, please?" Constanza said.

She picked up the small piece of paper by her bed which had Pat's phone number at Vevey and put the call through. A sleepy voice answered. It was two A.M. in Switzerland.

"This is Constanza, Pat. I hate to bother you," she said softly. "I just want to tell you that you're the father of an eight-pound boy—an eight-pound Mongolian idiot!"

Constanza carefully broke the connection.

The baby made a strange high-pitched mewling sound and Constanza began to rock him, gently.

"Hush, my darling. You are mama's sweet baby . . . You're God's own special baby. . . ."

CHAPTER 15

All Pat's familiarity with death and violence had not taught him how to cope with this new experience. Constanza was still being treated at Rose Briar for what the doctor would only call "a nervous condition." Pat went into work for the first week but couldn't concentrate on anything, except that amorphous bit of protoplasm for which he had planted the seed. One of the things that troubled him most was the time that Connie had fainted in the clothes closet after overhearing his conversation with Paterno.

He invited Pileggi to come for a drink and tried to find out if the shock of the moment could have had any effect on the child. He felt he had to know this.

"Many of the child's characteristics," Pileggi said, "result from the modifying influences that it has inside the uterus, as well as the child's genetic inheritance, things like endocrine variations, maternal emotions, oxygen deprivation, drugs taken by the mother. All of these could affect the child, although Down's syndrome is usually not considered to be the product of these things."

"But it *could* be, you say."

Pileggi shrugged and added ice to his highball.

"I'd hate to tell you how much we don't know about all this. Look," he explained, "you know when you get scared or excited or upset or even sexed up you can feel things happening in your body, you can feel your blood

324

racing, you can feel your skin pulsing? Many of these reactions come from your endocrine glands that are stimulated by various emotions. In a pregnant woman, this extra glandular activity can reach the child sometimes. We're not sure, but we think it can have quite an effect."

"You mean, if a woman is upset or shocked?"

"Well, sure," Pileggi said. "An emotional stress or fatigue can definitely alter the fetus. It can cause changes in the blood level, perhaps epinephrine or acetylcholine which can be transmitted to the fetus's circulation. When there is a chronic state of anxiety or fear, the fetus is often very active, and this can have an effect on it, too."

"But I thought that was all old wives' tales about the outside environment affecting the child."

"We used to think that, but we're learning to believe more in old wives' tales," Pileggi said. "Also, she had a lot of sedatives and this could produce what we call neonatal anoxia, that is, it could deprive the infant of the oxygen it needs for developing and it could cause some kind of brain damage to the child."

"Then, why did you give her those things?"

"She was in a state of true hysteria. She's bordering on a psychotic state right now. If we couldn't control her at all, it would have been much worse for the child, and for her, too. In some really disturbed mothers, what's a neurosis before pregnancy can really develop into a psychosis during the childbirth period or right afterwards.

"That's why she tried to commit suicide. The shock treatments helped, but they didn't completely cure her. Now especially, in this postpartum period, we have to watch very carefully for these psychological developments. There could be a lot of personality changes, a sort of a general unhappiness or depression or excitement, an increase in tension, perhaps excessive anxiety or apprehension, agitation, suspiciousness, phobias. She might become very talky, or she might not be able to sleep, or be irritable. Any of these things could indicate some serious psychological problem."

"Why did you ask me awhile back about our sex life?"

"Well, that can have something to do with it. The history with a lot of these cases sometimes shows frigidity or an aversion to sex, a fear of it, especially if there was a strong childhood attachment to the father, which was never gratified. Perhaps if the father was excessively authoritarian, you know, strict, or was away a lot, or if there was not enough sex education. We have to be afraid, too, that the mother doesn't show hostility to the child, but in this case, it seems to be going the opposite way, heh?"

"That's right," Pat said. "The hospital tells me that she won't let the child be taken away from her. She just keeps it there and keeps humming to it and talking to it as if it were a real child."

"Well, he's your child."

"What do you mean *he*?" Pat said. "It's not a *he,* it's an *it*! Am I supposed to take that 'thing' out and play baseball in Central Park with it when he gets to be ten years old? Do I invite the friends and relatives to come and coo over it? Is this the family heritage that Sam is waiting for?"

Pat refilled his drink and this time poured in a good four fingers of scotch. The doctor held his hand over his glass.

"Listen," he said, "I've got to go, but I don't want to have *you* in a mental state also. This is a great tragedy that's happened to you. Nobody knows who's to blame. You can't blame yourself, and you can't blame her. It's just one of those things that happened."

"Yeah, it's 'God's will' like Constanza says, right?"

Pileggi shrugged. "I'm not too inclined religiously, but the fact is that that's as good an explanation as any."

Esperanza, who was now staying full time in the house, showed the doctor out, and Pat poured himself another four inches of scotch. He had almost no belief left in God, himself, but he had an uncomfortable feeling that his actions during those last months of pregnancy could have, in some way, brought on this disaster, and from what the doctor said, it was actually possible, even in a scientific way.

After four weeks, Constanza was allowed to come home from the hospital, provided that she had a nurse in attendance at all times, or at least on call. The nurse, Margo Orten, was found by Pileggi.

She was in her middle or late thirties with long, washed-out straight blonde hair coming to a pointed arch in the middle of her head and a complexion shiny and rough from the remnants of childhood acne.

She was installed in the small room on the far side of Constanza's bedroom that had been planned for the nursery. A crib was set up for the baby next to Constanza's bed. She refused to sleep away from the child. In fact, she usually put it into the bed with her, where it lay, mewling and gargling, emitting its strange, frantic, high-pitched scream, more like the cry of an animal than anything human. If Pat wasn't already drunk when he went to sleep, the cry would drive him down to the den for enough liquor to blot out the sound.

In some strange way, the experience had heightened Constanza's beauty. Her eyes had a feverish brightness that could almost be taken for passion, and her lips, without makeup, seemed redder than they ever had. While her face was dead white, there was a pink flush in each cheek that emphasized her doll-like beauty.

In those days, she never seemed to dress in street clothes or to leave the house. The household was run by Esperanza, with Miss Orten helping where she could. There were few callers outside of the family, except for Father Bernard Donato, from St. Agnes, who came by and held Constanza's hand and talked with her for as much as an hour a day.

Pat, out of guilt and sometimes feeling sentimental from the booze, would come up and try to talk to her, but she would usually respond by either dull evasiveness or waspish remarks about his activities.

"What does that little creep priest come here for all the time?" Pat asked angrily one day. "You can see how much all that praying to St. Theresa did for you!"

He gestured with his highball glass toward the infant lying staring sightlessly at the ceiling.

"I don't pray to St. Theresa any more. I pray to St. Maria Goretti."

"I hope she does a better job than that last one," Pat said, walking out.

Several times Pat tried to kiss her, not with passion, only a good-night kiss before he left the room. But Constanza would always turn her head away and the kiss would land awkwardly on the side of her hair or her forehead. One day, he picked up the missal lying next to her bed and a clipping from *Time* magazine fell out of it. It was bit brittle with age and seemed to be a couple of years old. The headline said "LITTLE MARTYR:"

> In Rome last week, for the first in history, a mother attended her daughter's canonization as a saint. In a place of special honor near the papal throne, eighty-six-year-old Assunta Goretti sat with her two sons and her two daughters and wept. 'My daughter, my daughter,' she cried. 'My little Marietta.'
>
> In 1902 Maria Goretti, daughter of poor sharecroppers on the Pontine marshes, south of Rome, was eleven years old when nineteen-year-old Alessandro Serenelli tried to rape her. She resisted him even though he stabbed her to death. As she lay dying, Maria forgave Serenelli and promised to pray for him in heaven. Serenelli served

twenty-seven penitent years in prison for his crime and is now a handyman and pig tender at a Capuchin monastery. There last week he spent the day of Maria's canonization 'in prayer more intense than ever.'

Fitted with a mask of wax, St. Maria's skeleton had been brought to Rome for public veneration. Calling upon the world to follow the example of 'the little sweet martyr of purity,' Pope Pius XII asked the young people in the crowd whether they would resist any attempt against their virtue. '*Si!*' they shouted in chorus.

"For Christ's sake!" Pat said when he finished reading it. "Is *this* the St. Maria that you're praying to now?"

"She's my personal saint," Constanza said seriously.

Pat went down to the den, got drunk and slept on the leather sofa that night.

The next day, when the child was napping in the crib, Pat made an attempt to make love to his wife, but there was simply no starting point. If he held her hand, she would pull it away irritably. If he stroked her shoulder, she would move.

"Connie, what are you doing? This is crazy," he said. "We're married. I can't go through life like this!"

"You'll find your pleasure somewhere," Constanza said. "Isn't one tragedy of God enough for you?"

Angrily Pat strode from the room and went to the den where he watched the Dodgers night game on television and killed practically an entire fifth of Grant's twelve-year-old. Upstairs, he listened as Nurse Orten brought in Constanza's nighttime glass of warm milk and Seconal and took the baby from her and put it in his crib so that she wouldn't roll over on it in her sleep.

A few minutes later, the nurse, her long, straight blonde hair hanging loose around her shoulders, came downstairs in her flannel robe and Pat could see her go past the open door of the den with her tray and the empty milk glass on it. The robe was hanging loosely open to the waist, where it was tied by a braided cord and under it, Pat could see, the lacy ruff of a cotton nightgown with the deep shadows of an impressive cleavage.

Actually, he thought, if you covered her face, she wasn't such a bad-looking piece. He poured another and turned back to watch the work of Willie Mays on the base path as he heard the clumping of the nurse's fuzzy sheepskin slippers on the stairs again. But he'd lost interest in the game.

Angrily, he switched the TV off and listened for sounds upstairs. He heard the sharp snap of the switch in the nurse's room and the sudden silence of the radio on which she'd been listening to the late news.

He poured another drink and thought of those first dating days with Constanza when she had made him feel so special, and he thought about her bright eyes and black hair against the white sheets. Maybe now in the night with the lights out and the house quiet, and with that goddamn creature in its box, she'd be more receptive. Maybe if he could reach her, touch her, stroke her before she was fully awake again, maybe they could make love. A man couldn't go on like this week after week, living in the same house, seeing those small, perfect breasts through the thin material of the nightdress, seeing the shape of those hills of thigh, leading to that feathery crotch under the counterpane.

He took the glass upstairs and put it on the night table next to his bed as he undressed. Then he put on the silk robe he'd bought in Locarno. He fumbled in the medicine chest for the Old Spice underarm spray and rinsed his mouth with Lavoris. The bathroom was between his bedroom and Constanza's.

Unsteady from the scotch, he turned out the

bathroom light and opened the door to Constanza's bedroom as quietly as he could. He could hear the thin snotty snoring of the thing in the crib and Constanza's quiet, regular breathing. He tiptoed across the blue shag rug and sat quietly on the edge of Constanza's bed, trying to shake it as little as possible.

Then, quietly and carefully, he pulled back the candlewick bedspread and slipped between the warm sheets. He could feel Constanza's hip, hot through the thin cotton nightgown.

Gently, carefully, he ran his hand over the contours of her prone body, brushing gently over those firm breasts down over the smooth curve to the deeply cut navel and then over the slight roundness of that belly to the vaguely defined sunken valley of the crotch.

There was an exciting dimension to feeling that warm flesh through the cloth. He could feel even the fine hairs that surrounded her mons. Gently, he reached down and took the hem of the nightgown and raised it above her legs. It was a warm night and he held the coverlets back and looked at those two beautiful rounded columns, hairless, smooth and glowing.

He rubbed his finger between the lips until he could feel a slight response in dampness there, and the legs parted slightly as Constanza groaned in her sleep. He felt then that her regular breathing had stopped He was sure she was awake and enjoying it.

With his hand still caressing her, he leaned on his elbow and reached around and kissed her gently on the chest, and on her exposed neck. Then very gently he pressed his mouth to hers and slipped his tongue between her lips—and the lips were hot.

He knew that she was feeling what he was doing and was responding. He knew that if he could only get past that crazy subconscious, that weird, Christ-ridden guilt, past the guard of that pubescent child-saint that guarded the portals of her pussy, that he could get something going, that some passion could be drawn from that moment.

Now, he thought he could feel her mouth opening and responding under him. Suddenly he felt her body stiffen and he knew she was awake now—really awake.

"What are you doing?" she said in a whisper as loud as a shout.

"What am I doing?" he asked. "I'm making love to you. That's what I'm doing."

"You're making *love* to me? Love?" she said, and began to laugh wildly, crazily. "Yes, I know about your love. I'm waiting for your love."

In the darkness, Pat could hardly see what she was doing as she reached to the night table beside her. He thought she was going to turn on the light, but then he saw a sudden flash of metallic blur. He threw himself violently to one side as he recognized that the metal in Constanza's hand was a long, sharp pair of scissors.

Leaning on one elbow as he was, with his other hand involved between Constanza's legs, he wasn't able to get his arm up quickly enough to deflect the swift blow and he felt a sudden, sharp flash of pain as the scissor blade lanced into his chest, just below the clavicle.

"If you touch me again, I'll kill you."

"My God," he shouted. "You're really crazy! You're crazy!"

Pat jumped out of bed, blood running down his naked body. Constanza lay there laughing. His blood was now all over the bed.

Pat grabbed angrily, but without fear, for the scissors which now lay loose in Constanza's hand and threw them into a corner of the room. Then he ran for the bathroom where he grabbed a sponge and pressed it against the bleeding wound.

"Orten!" he yelled. "Nurse Orten! Come out here. Hurry up, goddamn it!"

There was a scrambling sound from the next room and the blonde nurse appeared, dazed with sleep, her body outlined in the light from the hall. Her eyes widened when she saw the bloody trail from the silk sheets, across the blue shag rug to the bathroom where Pat was standing, completely naked.

"She's gone crazy," Pat said. "Give her a shot or something, then help me here. I'm bleeding to death!"

The nurse ran to the makeup table where she kept the medications and quickly found a needle and an ampule of sedative which Connie accepted peaceably, almost gratefully, still grinning as though at some enormous joke.

Then, she turned her attention to Pat, who still stood naked in the bathroom, trying to dab at the blood which was gradually coagulating. Deftly she swabbed the wound with cotton and alcohol and pressed a gauze pad to it. Then she ripped wide bands of adhesive tape and pressed them into Pat's hairy chest.

"That's really going to hurt when you pull it off," she whispered.

Pat found the pressure of her cool fingers soothing.

"Press that down a little more," he said, smiling. Nurse Orten smiled back and pressed her fingers down on the tape.

They were standing inches away, their bodies inevitably touching. Pat noticed that she was breathing deeply now. Her face was flushed. Her hand pressed into the tape and wandered a little further into the curly hairs on his chest. Pat held his fingers to his lips, took her by the hand and led her to his room, closing the door.

"Did you give her a good sedative?" he asked. "Is she really out?"

Nurse Orten said nothing but just smiled. In the darkness, you couldn't notice the acne on her face and her teeth shone in the light of the moon coming in through the window. The cloth of her thin nightgown hung in sheer folds from her full breasts. Without any questions or explanations, Pat led her to the bed and lifted the long nightgown over her head and took her in his arms.

"Oh, God," she said, "I've been waiting for this," and reached with practiced assurance for his now stiffly standing member.

She had a sturdy body, with huge, heavy, but firm breasts, enormous brown circles around her nipples, which were large, and a vast area of pale blonde pubic hair below.

"Take it easy," Pat said as she pulled him down on top of her. "You're dealing with a wounded man."

CHAPTER 16

The child was christened Sebastian. The name was Connie's choice, after St. Sebastian, the martyr. Pat could only picture the painting he had seen in the Palatine Gallery in Florence while driving north from Naples. It showed a strong, beautiful man with an athlete's body and a girl's face tied to a tree while an angel floated smiling overhead. An arrow was stuck through the boy's throat and blood ran down both sides of his neck. Another arrow pierced his leg. In the background, vague, silhouetted figures walked and rode, apparently unconcerned.

The week before the christening, a basket of ricotta cheese arrived from the boys in the Mulberry SAC. It was a traditional gift to the father of a firstborn boy. Pat could only believe that they had not heard news of what kind of an offspring he had fathered.

Connie remained cloistered in her bedroom, almost never coming down, tended by Esperanza and the nurse. Father Donato was there at least four times a week, as was Pileggi, the young doctor. Pileggi had suggested a specialist for the child and a psychiatrist for Connie, but Connie threatened to relapse into hysterics every time the idea was brought up, and it was abandoned for the moment. Pat wasn't disappointed.

"Listen, doc. I respect you. I respect your profession. But do you really think a doctor can help that *thing* up there? If God was merciful, he would let it die."

335

Pileggi said nothing.

"And as for Conni͏͏ he thinks she's one of those holy Roman martyrs. She wouldn't accept help from a psychiatrist, only from a goddamn saint. As long as you keep her peaceful, I'll be happy."

"I'll do the best I can," Pileggi said as he left.

The lack of family obligations at home gave Pat more time to devote to his work. Within six months, he was out of the bag and into the Detective Division. He was assigned to the Sixth Detective Squad, covering Greenwich Village.

With some of his newfound wealth, he bought a white Lincoln Capri, but kept the old red convertible for driving to work. It didn't do any good to be seen in the new car. It would only cause talk. In fact, he bought the car in Al Santinis's name, giving Santini cash for it and registering it to Royal Provisions as a business vehicle.

Sam Massey seemed very preoccupied with politics that year. Marcantonio finally died, poor and out of favor, and DeSapio became the leader of Tammany, with Costello's support. Lucchese, who had Sam's support in this and also, *sub rosa,* Genovese's, supported Impellitteri against DeSapio's candidate, Wagner, for mayor in the primaries, but Wagner won easily.

"This is going to be a goddamn nuisance," Sam said bitterly. "We were okay with Impy. You know, we had ways to talk to him. He used to meet downtown with Lucchese and Tom Murphy, your commissioner there."

"I'm surprised they'd be seen together," Pat said.

Sam shrugged. "That's their business. Nobody really knew about it. Who knows what they talked about, but for us, it was better. Frank Costello is not good for the family anymore. I think that shrink is doing things to his head. Vito is right. We got to ease him out somehow, but he's got too much respect now to really be pushed out, if you know what I mean."

Pat was flattered that Sam, more and more, led him

into discussions of the inner workings of the organization. Sam had been deeply disappointed by the birth of his monstrous grandchild. He sent it toys, rattles and baby clothes, as though he were proud of it. But the tragedy actually seemed to draw him closer to Pat.

"What do you think, Pat?" he said one day. "You think she'll have another kid?"

"To be honest with you, Sam, I'll be surprised. She acts like she's really afraid that the same thing will happen again. She thinks God has punished her for something. You know, she heard some talk one tim : about the family. It was just before she had the kid and she was very upset. I told her there was nothing to it, but she just got hysterical."

Sam nodded understandingly. "Just like her mother. Her mother made me plenty of trouble over that kind of thing."

Now that he was spending less time at home, Pat was down in the Mulberry SAC more often, playing card;, shooting a few rounds of pool with the boys and keeping in touch. Paul Ganci persuaded him to attend meetings of the Italian-American League, where he renewed hi; friendship with Paul Federici, who was vice-president of the club and Chairman for Public Relations.

As far as Pat could see, the club was a lot of talk and no action. There were references to the great Italian heritage, plans to build statues in various parts of the city, complaints about prejudice in medical schools, law schools, and housing, but there were only about twenty-five members and most of them seemed to be coming as favors to other friends, just as Pat was. The best thing about it was the social events—an old-fashioned spaghetti dinner in a restaurant on Mulberry Street, a picnic up to Spring Lake in a bus, with kegs of beer and softball games.

Ellie was still studying for her doctorate at NYU and Pat would often sandwich in a visit or sometimes even a night out with her. The sex grew better, less frenetic and more comfortable, but her constant yammering about radical politics sometimes frazzled his ears, especially the clippings she would periodically take from the paper which stressed police brutality.

"Listen," Pat said, "as far as I'm concerned, I don't beat anybody up and I don't torture anybody. But if I go out on a squeal and I know the man is armed, it's him or me—that's all, baby."

Christmas cards started coming in to Riverdale in mid-December. Pat was surprised at how wide his acquaintanceship had grown. There were cards from almost all the members of the Italian-American League, the Mulberry SAC, the friends he still had at NYU or had gone to school with like Art Winburg and Jim Bailey, plus some of the boys at Bernard Baruch College, fellow cops, and assorted family members.

In past years, Connie had taken care of sending out the cards, but she hardly knew what time it was these days and with the kid, snotty and drooling in the bed, it was hard to think about Christmas cherubs and Santa Claus. Pat decided to skip Christmas that year. He spent New Year's alone, drinking scotch and watching Guy Lombardo on television.

He had had plenty of invitations, but knew that going out that night would only stir Connie up. He tried to go up to see her. He opened a bottle of Asti Spumante that he'd gotten from the Sheridan Square Liquor Store as a Christmas gift, put it on the tray and brought the tray with two chilled glasses up to Connie's room at 11:45.

"Happy New Year, sweetheart," he said.

Connie looked at him dully and he could see that she was already sedated for the evening. Gently he put the tray by her bedside and put the glass in her hand. She held it up, looking at him stupidly and the glass tipped, spilling some of the bubbling wine onto the pale skin of her breast.

Pat mopped her with a Kleenex, as though she were a baby and felt himself becoming aroused at the sight of that still-firm bosom and the incredibly blemish-free skin. He held his glass up and touched it to hers and said, "Happy New Year." Connie took a sip from her glass without saying anything, but watching him over the brim like a child.

"Look," Pat said, "it's been kind of a grim year, but there's been good things, too. I got my promotion and pretty soon I'll probably have my law degree. We got a beautiful house here . . ."

Connie finished her drink as he was talking, put her glass down on the night table and snuggled down into the bed, pulling the covers up to her chin. Pat faltered in his recitation, finished the drink and said, "Well, good night and Happy New Year."

"Would you turn out the overhead light when you go out?" Connie said, and Pat did.

As he left the darkened room, Connie called after him bitterly, "Little Sebastian says Happy New Year, too."

Pat called Ellie Vogel from his den downstairs and, to his surprise, she was home and alone. He took a bottle of champagne from the cellar, jumped into the Lincoln and drove down to the Village. She was waiting for him naked in the bed.

Ellie hopped up and got some red caviar, sesame crackers and cream cheese from the icebox and put a Vivaldi record on the changer. Pat let his mind go blank and just enjoyed the pleasures of the moment. There were worse ways to start a new year.

He pulled the car into his driveway about ten the following morning, feeling clean and rested and completely drained. Ellie was really a lot like her meat-eating plants. He had stopped on Broadway at an open market on the way up and bought oranges and fresh Italian bread with sesame seeds, which he dumped in the kitchen.

As he started upstairs, he heard a sound from his office and looked in. Connie was standing there in her wool plaid bathrobe, her hair loose around her shoulders. She was looking out the window into the garden.

"What are you doing up, hon?" he said. "Feeling better?"

Connie turned toward him. "I was thinking I might straighten up around the office here. It's kind of messy," but Pat noticed that she had not brought any cleaning cloths or brooms or vacuum cleaners with her.

"Oh, well," Pat thought, "at least she's beginning to show some interest in things. Maybe it's a good sign."

CHAPTER 17

In the fall of 1954 there was a letter in the large, rounded, feminine hand of Katie Mullaley. It was postmarked Pasadena, and was addressed to both of them. Pat opened it and read it before bringing it upstairs. Katie said she'd been doing a lot of stock work and had a few nonspeaking bit parts in the movies, but that she'd had it with the Coast and was coming East to take a crack at off-Broadway theater, which was becoming the new proving ground for actors.

Pat was glad to see that Connie was as pleased as he was at the news. It was morning and she was less dopey than usual from drugs and looked cheerful and more normal than he'd seen her for a long time, with the rays from the morning sun backlighting her crisp, curly hair.

"I wonder when she'll get here," Connie said. "I know she'll call us. We can't write her there. She'll have left already."

She seemed to be talking and thinking clearly for the first time in months. She turned excitedly toward Pat.

"I wonder if she'll see Regan again, now that he's in New York. Have you seen him?"

"No. We haven't been in touch." In fact, they had not spoken since that night years ago, but Doyle had sent a Christmas card, probably mainly for Connie's sake, so he knew that Doyle was in New York with the bureau.

When Katie came back, she reclaimed her apartment on Eleventh Street, which she had sublet, and within a

month had landed a part as a replacement in a singing
role in *The Threepenny Opera* at the Theatre DeLys
Christopher Street.

She came up to Riverdale for lunch quite a few times
that fall, but it always seemed to be when Pat was on
duty. He wondered if she had done that on purpose. He
called her several times, but never seemed to be able to
find her in and he left messages with her answering service. She always returned the calls to the house and
Connie was the one who answered.

Finally he reached her on the phone early one morning when her voice was still husky with sleep.

"It's me, Kate. Pat," he said on the phone.

"I know," she said, drowsily. "How are you?"

"I imagine you've heard. It's funny, you've been up to
the house so many times, but I haven't even seen you."

There was a pause. "I know."

"Look," Pat said, "I want to see you. I have to talk to
you."

"Pat," she said, "it isn't going to be any good. It was
wrong to start it up again now. This time I think it
really might kill Connie."

"Who said anything about starting it up? I just
wanted to see you."

"I know you," Kate said, and there seemed to be affection in her voice. "You're not the kind that can just
'see me.' "

"Look, it's morning now and you'll probably be going
out to work in a little while. How about if I brought you
a couple of bagels? I bet you didn't get them out in
Pasadena. We can have some breakfast together. I'm
just getting off now anyway."

"I don't see what point there'd be to it."

"Just to talk for old times' sake and find out what
you've been up to. I understand what you're saying.
There won't be any funny business."

"You're sure?"

"Would I lie to you?"

Kate laughed. "That's a ridiculous question," she said. "Okay. Come up, but don't forget. No fooling around."

He was there in a half hour and put his detective plaque in the windshield when he parked the red convertible. He took the steps two at a time.

Katie was wearing jeans and a man's shirt, hanging loose. Her hair was tied back with a bit of red wool and her face was scrubbed and clean, without makeup. The room was filled with the smell of fresh coffee and Kate had set the table near the window, looking out on Eleventh Street, with brightly painted blue and white Spanish dishes. She gave him a hug and a chaste kiss as he came in.

"Pat, it's so marvelous to see you." But he noticed she didn't hang on to him very long. "Come in and sit down. I hope you don't mind canned juice."

"I do, but from you I'll take it," Pat said, smiling.

The blue oxford shirt hung on the points of her breasts like the drapery on an old Roman statue and Pat could visualize that steamy space between the shirt and the naked skin.

He could also feel that great sense of joy and intimacy that he felt whenever Katie was near, something he had not felt in years, not with Ellie, not with any of the other more casual affairs and certainly not with Connie. They chattered like a pair of teen-agers as Katie sliced and toasted the bagels and then smeared them with a thick layer of fresh cream cheese.

Deftly she whipped up a platter of scrambled eggs with just a touch of tarragon seasoning, a couple of pieces of crisp bacon and a slice of grilled tomato.

"Best I could do on short notice," she said.

"Terrific!"

Kate reacted with enthusiasm to the story of Pat's promotion and adventures as detective and laughed at the anecdotes. In turn, she told some hilarious stories about the workshops on the Coast, about the crazy types trying to get into the movies, about all the queer boys in the theater and even queerer women.

"Did you have any boyfriends out there?" Pat said.

"No . . . not really. A few guys, but we never got involved. It's all very unreal out there. I just couldn't get used to it."

Pat felt a tremendous physical remoteness from her. He thought of trying to reach her across the table full of dishes and condiments. He felt sure she would respond if only he could touch her, but every time he moved, Katie made a countermove, keeping a distance or a piece of furniture between them. Finally, she went to the tiny kitchenette and started rinsing the dishes. Pat came up behind her, putting his hands around her smooth waist, touching the warm skin under the shirt.

"Come on, Pat," Kate said. "You said . . ."

"Fuck what I said," Pat said, kissing her on the ear.

"Please, Pat. It's no good."

Pat put his tongue into her ear and wiggled it around and then bit her gently on the lobe. Kate leaned on her hands on the sink, not moving, but not responding either. He kissed her lower, on the joint of the neck and the shoulder and reached his hand up under the shirt to touch the tip of her nipple.

She drew in her breath sharply, as though in pain and he swung her around, facing him, shoving his leg between the two columns of denim. He reached his hand behind her, grabbed the knotted hank of hair, and pulled her head back until her mouth came open, then thrust his tongue hotly between her lips. The mouth opened for the moment in seeming sympathy and then he felt a sharp stab of pain as Kate's sharp white teeth came down on his probing tongue.

"Ouch, you bitch!" he said, and instinctively reached out and slapped her across the face.

"I told you I'm serious, Pat. I don't want to start it again."

"You'll start it, baby," Pat said, and he ripped the shirt from her body with one stroke, scattering buttons onto the top of the sink. He grabbed her head again and lunged down at her mouth.

"I dare you to do that again this time, bitch. I just dare you," and he plunged his tongue into her mouth again, this time scrabbling at the military buckle and the zipper of her jeans with his other hand.

Now, he could feel her breath coming in deep, slow thrusts and he knew he had her, as he felt her legs slowly, weakly come apart under his pressing fingers. Without separating from her, he led her into the living room and laid her down on the shag rug where the Sunday *Times* was scattered in disarray. He peeled the jeans from her as though he were skinning a squirrel. She wore nothing underneath. He got to his knees between her open legs and forced himself deep inside her.

With all the earlier excitement and foreplay, Pat came instantly in deep grinding thrusts that felt as though someone was pulling his insides out with a string, and Kate seemed to be stitched onto that same string, her pelvis glued to his in perfect rhythm.

"Oh, God! Oh, God! Oh, God! Finish it now, now!" she said, and they climaxed together tangled weirdly among the crumpled pages of the *Times*.

"You're the best one! Absolutely the best one," Pat said, as his breath slowly came back to him.

"God, I hate you," Kate said, her legs still wrapped around his back.

Pat was on the eight-to-four that week and when he got home the next night, he found a note from Constanza.

"Pick up your sports jacket at the cleaners. Regan

and Katie coming to dinner on Wednesday. I'm making a rack of lamb, Okay?"

It was signed "Connie," but the word "love" wasn't on it.

Well, Pat thought, life would be a lot more pleasant if there was some semblance of normalcy at home. Maybe Katie's return would stir up some interest in life, aside from the church and the blob upstairs. He wondered what the encounter with Doyle would be like, whether Doyle had been seeing Katie since she'd come to town.

CHAPTER 18

Pat wasted little time consolidating his position as a detective and making it pay off. Within a few months, he contacted Arthur Marseri and suggested that possibly with the help of Frank Costello he might get an assignment with the Intelligence Division working in coordination with the Waterfront Commission.

Arthur and Pat had started to meet at Mogavero's Club on Madison Street in Little Italy, not far from the Mulberry SAC. It was a good place to stay in touch. All of the big wheels showed up from time to time—Bender, Eboli, Miranda, Jimmy "Blue Eyes" Alo, Young Bill Bonnano. It was a good place to pick up information and get vibrations as to what was happening in the organization.

Mogavero, himself, who looked like a bookkeeper in his thick horn-rimmed glasses and neat white shirt and tie, had a record for homicide and income tax evasion that had broken up his own waterfront operation. But he was still a good contact man for anything on the waterfront or in the airports.

They sipped an espresso as Pat explained his request to Arthur.

"I see your point, Pat. A man could do very well down there, but you wouldn't forget your family, would you?"

Pat laughed. "Are you kidding? Naturally you get twenty points off the top. I mean, the family does. But I could get leads to a lot of information there, tip off any of our boys who were really in trouble and still make a very nice dollar. Christ, everybody else is into it. Why not us?"

"I thought you were doing pretty good with floating over the white stuff from Charlie."

"I was," Pat said, "but I don't like that deal any more. There's just too much heat. You know, they made a tremendous bust in August, the feds and the narcos. I hear they made the collar on tips that that fink Gianinni gave."

"Well, you know," Arthur said, "the guys at narco say he got blown away because he tried to screw Lucky and Vito by bringing in his own stuff."

"Well," Pat said, "it was a combination of the two, but I'm getting out of that. It's getting too hairy. Besides, Connie was really upset when she heard rumors that I might be involved in this."

Arthur looked up in surprise. "You mean Connie *knows*?"

Pat regretted having said anything.

"No, she doesn't *know*, but she gets crazy ideas in her head and she's very uptight about white stuff. Why ask for trouble? You know?" Pat said. "We got terrific connections for unloading anything we can pick up on the waterfront—some of those discount stores that Sam's got over in Jersey, the restaurants for fish and meat, and the TVs and imported cars—those can be unloaded directly."

"Yeah, it sounds like big business. Frankly, it's over my head," Arthur said laughing.

"Well, I been talking to Sam about it up at the house and he agrees with me."

"Okay, okay," Arthur said. "I get the picture. You'll get the assignment. The way you're going, you're not only going to be a lieutenant soon but a *capo*. You'll be kind of a double lieutenant."

"Very funny," Pat said.

Pat got the word that the new assignment was okay at Bill Bonnano's wedding at the Astor. It was the biggest wedding that Pat had ever seen. There were more than three thousand people at the reception, with Tony

Bennett entertaining.

Bill was marrying Rosalie Profaci, so it was a marriage of royalty, and everybody who was anybody was there—Vito, of course, and Frank Costello, Al Anastasia, who was in trouble with both of them, and a lot of people from all around the country, like Joe Barbara, from upstate, Joe Zarilli from Detroit, and a Chicago delegation headed by Sam Giancana and Tony Accardo. Old Stefano Maggadino was down from Buffalo. He was a cousin of Bonanno's and had an honored place on the dais. Pat thought, "It's a shame that the FBI still doesn't believe that there is such a thing as the organization because they could really make hay with this bunch. Just the guest list would shake them up.

The way Doyle told it, The Director insisted there was no such thing as organized crime.

Pat ran into Al Agueci again and they had a couple of drinks together. It was, in fact, quite a time for weddings. Down in Newport, Kentucky, Trigger Mike Coppola married a dame from the outside named Ann Drahmann in Frank Costello's Beverly Hills Club. Sam, who knew Coppola from the old days, disapproved. In the first place, he told Pat over a drink, the guy should never marry an outsider. They can't be trusted. In the second place, Sam said he had a hunch that that dame would make trouble for him. Sam had had a few drinks.

"You always have to watch out for women in this business. Never tell them *anything*. That includes you, son," he said, looking directly at Pat. "I can tell you, I had plenty of trouble with Connie's old lady, plenty, may she rest in peace."

"Well, to tell you the truth, Sam," Pat said, "aside from Connie's health, that was one of the reasons I didn't have her come down here. I just don't like her attitude lately toward the whole thing. She doesn't really know anything, but she makes a lot of remarks about the family business."

Sam nodded understandingly. "Yeah, I know.

That's a tough thing. Well, they're cutting the cake I see. Let's go over and watch."

Young Bill Bonnano, a tall slim, handsome college type was standing next to Rosalie, who looked a lot like Connie, only plumper. The cake was nine feet tall and had seven layers separated by giant columns and topped by an enormous cupola, like the top of a church. Sam stood looking sourly on.

"You know, Big Joe has that kid in mind to take his place, but I'll tell you one thing. He's not half the man you are. He spent too much time in college, if you'll excuse me for saying so."

Pat was pleased to note that he was seated on Sam's right hand, while Arthur was seated a little further down at their table. Don Antonio, of course, in an old fashioned tuxedo with one of those U-shaped vests, was at the head of their table.

There was a lot of cheering and drinking and more gossip than usual since everybody knew everybody at the table and knew they could be trusted. Don Antonio teased Father Raimundo over the time Joe Profaci had been named Knight of St. Gregory by Pope Pius. The old man nearly choked laughing.

"You know, Profaci was eating a plate of spaghetti down at Luna's when he heard that the Pope took back the Knight of St. Gregory. You know what he did? He puked all over the table. Right in the restaurant! This is supposed to be a man of respect?"

"Well," Sam said, "I don't think he's getting so much respect anymore. He's not moving with the times. He's squeezing too hard for the buck. He's getting very unpopular down there in Brooklyn. If he don't watch out, he's going to be in a lot of trouble."

Pat kept quiet and absorbed all the information he could. Agueci told him, as they were leaving, that John Montana, Steve Maggadino's front man, had been named Man of the Year in Buffalo by the Chamber of Commerce.

"You see," Agueci said, "little by little, things are changing. Everything is becoming legitimate, and that's the way it should be. By the way, you making any more runs?"

"No," Pat said. "I'm staying close to home for a while."

"Well, I'll see you around. Don't forget to look me up if you come up to Montreal."

"I will," Pat said.

On the way up to Riverdale in Sam's new Chrysler Imperial, they reviewed the events of the wedding.

"It was a nice affair," Sam said, " a nice one. I have to admit it was better than yours, but you weren't such a big deal then."

"No," Pat said, "and I'm not such a big deal now."

"You're coming along very nice, son. I'm proud of you."

Pat flushed with pleasure.

"Tell me, do you want to move out of the department? When are you going to get your law degree?"

"It will be a few years yet," Pat said. "It takes a long time going at night and I've been busy with a lot of other things."

"Well, I'm beginning to believe that an education's important in the way we do business now, so keep with that. You know, things are changing very much, but a lot of people are not keeping up with it. Costello seems to be out of things entirely. On the other hand, that crazy Anastasia, that's all he knows, hit, kill, blood. We finished with that in the Castellammarese days, at least I hope we did. It's terrible that we can't settle these things peaceably. I only hope our family can stay out of it."

"I hope so, too," Pat said, getting out at his brown brick house, a quarter of a mile from Sam's mansion.

Sam looked embarrassed. "How's the ah . . . kid?"

Pat shrugged. "He'll never be anything but a freak, Sam, let's face it."

CHAPTER 19

The dinner with Katie and Regan Doyle had turned out to be surprisingly pleasant. Connie put on street clothes for the first time in months. She wore a long plaid skirt with a ruffled deep-necked blouse.

Katie wore a shirtwaist dress in a clinging knit fabric that emphasized her lush figure, with a collar, opened down to the cleavage and a wisp of a chiffon handkerchief around her neck. Doyle looked easy and comfortable in a plaid sports jacket, slacks and loafers.

"I see you left off your FBI hat," Pat said, smiling.

"Only need it when I'm on duty," Regan said, without any trace of tension.

It would seem that the years had erased the bitterness of that last incident, at least Pat hoped so. They ate in the big dining room that Constanza had decorated in Regency style with pale green and white paneled woodwork. There were gardenias as a centerpiece and candles at the table.

"This is elegant," Doyle said, sitting down.

"Yeah," Katie said, "it's a far cry from Krum's on the Concourse."

After dinner, they sat in the living room and drank

brandy and remembered old times. Doyle told funny stories about the Georgia crackers.

"Tell us about Chicago," Katie said.

"Yeah, well that was something else. I mean the cops there . . ." He cast a sidelong glance at Pat. "Well, forget it. Anyway, it's different from here."

It was obvious that Doyle wasn't looking for trouble, because Pat knew that Chicago had the crookedest police department in history. Even the New York cops had to give them cards and spades in chicanery. But in Chicago, the mayor and the pols told the cops what to do. In New York it was often the other way around.

They planned to get together again downtown in the near future. As they went for their coats, Katie said to Connie.

"I'm dying to see the baby. Is he asleep?"

"Yes, but he won't mind. Come on, I'll show him to you."

Pat was relieved when Doyle said he'd stay in the living room and keep him company. Katie came downstairs again in a few minutes, looking pale and distressed, but Connie seemed not to notice.

"He's a darling, isn't he? And so good."

"Yes, he is," Katie said.

As it turned out, 1957 was one hell of a year for the family. There was trouble in the air, almost from the beginning of the year. Genovese was busy lining up allies, among them Profaci and Lucchese, in his campaign to take over as recognized *capo di tutti capi*—boss of bosses. There wasn't anybody to stop him except for Costello, who nominally shared control of the old Luciano family with Vito. But Costello's main power was in politics, and with DeSapio's lessening influence and Costello's reluctance to involve himself in any of the action, there was a gradual loss of prestige.

In the end of April, according to some people, Don Vitone met with Tony Bender and Vinnie Mauro, and said that he had definite information that Costello had been talking to the feds. Why else had Costello been released after his arrest for tax evasion?

It was clear that Costello was a stool pigeon. He was too old and sick to stand the idea of going to jail again, and so he had talked.

Don Vitone made the decision on his own without going to the commission. A huge dim-witted ex-boxer named Vincent (the Chin) Gigante was given the job of pulling the trigger. Tommy Eboli and Dominic (the Sailor) DeQuatro were to help.

Frank was dining with his wife Bobbie and friends at Monsignore on the East Side, when he got a call. After listening to the voice on the phone, he excused himself and said he had to go back to the Majestic, where he maintained an enormous apartment. He tipped the cab driver lavishly as he pulled up at the elegant old apartment house at 71st Street and Central Park West and left his friend, Phil Kennedy, in the cab. As he walked through the lobby, a hulking, big-chinned man in an overcoat stepped from behind the pillar.

"This is for you, Frank," he said, and from a distance of only five feet fired a single shot into Costello's head. The shot reverberated through the marble halls of the lobby, but before the doorman or anyone could move, the huge man was out and a black limousine was seen to drive away from the curb, through a red light and up Central Park West.

In it sat the huge Gigante, tired and happy, convinced he'd pulled the hit of his life. Inside the lobby, Costello wasn't even on the floor. He was sitting on the black plastic bench, holding a monogrammed linen hankerchief to his head and insisting that he was okay. Kennedy helped him back into the taxi and they raced to Roosevelt Hospital. Kennedy, aware that Frank's clothes might be gone through when he got to the hospital, offered to hold anything that might be incriminating, but Frank shook his head in confusion, certain there was nothing. Actually, it turned out that the injury was nothing—a superficial wound that grazed the scalp; but the slip of paper in Frank's pocket, that was really *something*.

Gross casino wins as of 4/27/57,
$651,284 (CHECK)

Casino wins less markers (IOU's),
$434,695

Slot wins, $62,844

Markers, $153,745

Mike, $150 a week, totaling $600
Jake, $100 a week, totaling $400
L. — $30,000
H. — $9,000

The trouble from Frank's handwritten memo reached all over the country, to Las Vegas, New Orleans, Miami. The police and everybody else were very interested in that little slip of paper. There was hardly time for a scab to form on Frank's head before District Attorney Frank Hogan had him up before the grand jury. Frank said he didn't know anything about anything and took the Fifth on all questions concerning the little slip of paper. In the end, he served fifteen days in jail for contempt of court, but that was nothing compared to what would have happened to him if he had talked. Meanwhile, Gigante had been identified by the doorman. Everybody in Don Vitone's family took a very sudden vacation. There were fears that there'd be another night like the night of the Sicilian vespers.

Uncle Frank was at the end of the line. He just didn't have any guns. He had preached peace for so long that he had no torpedoes on his payroll. But crazy Albert Anastasia, the Mad Hatter, was still around and there was no telling what *he* would do.

Don Vitone retired to his $250,000 mansion in Atlantic Highlands and surrounded himself with thirty topflight gunmen. Bender called his regime together at the Manhattan Hotel and assigned about thirty soldiers to various parts of the city to be ready in case of retaliation from Anastasia. There was always a chance that another big war like the Castellammarese war would break out. Don Vitone contacted all of the important family lieutenants for a show of loyalty, including Sam Massey and Don Antonio. The only one who didn't show up was "Little Augie" Pisano.

Pat Conte didn't attend these meetings, and he got word from Arthur to simply sit tight and keep his ears open. There were very few people that even knew that Pat had connections to the Marseri family.

Meanwhile, Don Vitone with his foxlike smile, explained that the hit on Costello had been necessary because Costello had actually been plotting to kill Don Vitone.

In a month or so, the heat died down. Obviously, there was not going to be any retaliation. Nobody wanted to stand up for Costello against Genovese.

Five months later, a hood named Joe Scalice was reported missing by his son. Word came down through the organization that Scalice had been invited to the home of Vincent (Jimmy Jerome) Squillante. There, he was shot in both eyes, blowing out the back of his head, and then cut up into 150 tidy one-pound packages with hacksaws and an ax and disposed of through Squillante's garbage-collection service.

Anastasia swore that the reason Scalice had been killed was that he'd been trying to sell memberships in the organization at $50,000 apiece. But Don Vitone said that it was *Anastasia* who was selling the memberships, and that Scalice was killed because he might talk.

Don Vitone was well aware that Anastasia had been meeting with Costello in various hotels around the city. He had a good source for his information. Carlo Gambino was Anastasia's *braccio destro,* his right-hand man. But Carlo Gambino wasn't happy with his boss, who was getting crazier all the time, more vicious, more careless and more violent. It definitely seemed it might be better for Gambino to work with Don Vitone, and so he did.

Gambino decided to take the contract on Anastasia, but rather than doing it himself, he passed it on to Joe Profaci, who was ambitious for more action in Brooklyn.

On October 25, Pat Conte was sitting in an unmarked squad car outside of the Park Sheraton Hotel on Sixth Avenue and 58th Street. Inside, Anastasia was getting a haircut. Al came in that afternoon and sat in his usual chair as the barber wrapped his face in hot towels to soften his heavy blue beard.

He had been in the chair ten minutes when two men in caps and masks moved into the barber shop with quick but calm movements. They went directly to Anastasia's chair, shoving the barber to one side, and emptied their revolvers into Big Al's ugly head. Then they turned on their heels, went out the door with casual speed and drove away.

Pat watched the car leave and rushed into the barber

358   *The Family Man*

shop, answering to the sound of the shots. When he saw
that the job had been well done, he didn't bother to identify himself, but left. There was no point in being on
record as having been on the scene.

There was no question now that Don Vitone was the
capo di tutti capi, but there was a lot of business to be
straightened out before all the territories could be
reassigned and responsibility divided up for various activities. A big sit-down was scheduled for November 14,
1957 at the estate of a member of the Maggadino mob
named Joseph Barbara in the Catskills, a place called
Apalachin.

"That's a funny name for a town," Sam commented
to Pat when he got word of the meet.

"You want me to drive you?"

"No. I'll take Tommy. The less you see and are seen,
the better."

"Listen, 'Ba," Pat said. (In recent years he'd come to
regard Sam as a kind of a substitute father and called
him by the Sicilian diminutive for "papa.") "There's
something I think you should bring up at that meeting.
You know, they've passed the new Federal Narcotics
Act in '56 and it's a stiff one. We can't fix the judges
anymore because there's a mandatory sentence of five
years. Big John Rometto already got forty years on one
of those. You know, I stopped handling the white stuff a
long time ago and you agreed."

"That's right," Sam said. "You can get into a lot of
trouble with that. I don't like the people you have to
deal with."

"That's just it. You always wind up dealing with
hopheads and none of them are to be trusted. Now, with
the new mandatory sentences, I just think it's too hot to
handle, and I think we should get out of it, especially the
import side. If we have anything to do with it, it should
be strictly to finance some of those guys, but don't touch
the stuff itself. I think that's going to be one of Don

Vitone's weak points at that meeting. And another thing," Pat said, "I think the whole meeting is a lousy idea. Up to now, none of the authorities really know if there is an organization or if there isn't and if there is, who's in it. The FBI doesn't even think there is such a thing. About the only guys in New York that know anything about it is the pizza squad, and a lot of those guys are a bunch of *chadrools*. So, why give them something to work on? You know, since I've been in the Intelligence Division, I realize how, with a little bit of information here and a little bit of information there, even the feebees can put together a story. So don't give them any information to work on."

"What can I do?" Sam said, shrugging. "They called a sit-down. I gotta go, right? I gotta look out for my interests."

"Well, don't forget, Sam," Pat said, "you're one of the few guys that are connected with the whole business that doesn't have a record. They don't have your name down anywhere, so keep it clean. Don't even take a gun with you."

"I leave that to Tommy," Sam said.

"Okay, then, that's Tommy's problem."

They shook hands and embraced on parting.

"Have a good trip," Pat said.

"You got a good head on your shoulders, Pat," his father-in-law said. "You could be a *consiglieri* soon, especially when you get that law degree. You're smarter than the whole bunch of them, and that stuff you said, that gave me a lot to think about. I'm going to bring up some of those points when I'm over there."

The meeting at Apalachin and the inopportune alertness of State Police Sergeant Edgar G. Crosswell gave all of the big shots invited to the upstate mansion plenty to think about. Fifty-eight of them got caught, either running through the bushes or trying to drive out of the estate, which was surrounded by Federal Alcohol and Drug people and state police.

Another forty, including Sam, managed to keep their noses clean by staying in the house until the heat died down. Sam was wise enough to know that the cops couldn't invade the house without a warrant and there were no grounds for a warrant. It was just a family meeting of friends from the old country.

But the big Apalachin bust caused more unwelcome attention in the newspapers than the organization had gotten since the Kefauver Committee hearings of 1951, especially following on the heels of the Costello attempt and the Anastasia murder.

It was the kind of break Special Agent Regan Doyle had been waiting for.

CHAPTER 20

Special Agent Regan Doyle settled his large frame into the swivel chair in the tiny cubicle assigned to him at FBI Headquarters on 69th Street near Third Avenue. Before him he had spread out a heap of newspaper clippings which he had been accumulating for a week following the raid at Apalachin.

The *Post* had a feature headed, "THE MAFIA, FOLKLORE OR DEATH SYNDICATE?" by Sid Friedlander. Mentioned in the article were Lucky Luciano, Frank Costello, Vito Genovese, Three-Finger Brown (ne Lucchesei), Willie Moretti, Joe Adonis, Jack Dragna and Albert Anastasia. The big head on the page was, "*Mobsters Meet and Cops Fear a Brand-New Gang War.*"

On page 4 of the same paper was an analysis of the Apalachin raid under the headline, "*Gang Bigshots Fear Upstarts,*" and on the facing page another article called, "*The Old Gray Mafia Ain't What It Used to Be.*"

U.S. Attorney General William Rogers came to New York and approved a probe of the Apalachin meeting. This included opening the FBI records on any of the people there, but when Milton Wessel, who'd been appointed by the attorney general to set up a regional office to investigate the Apalachin hearings and get grand jury proceedings concerning them asked for FBI men to be assigned to his special group, Director Hoover refused the request. He said the whole program was a "fishing expedition," and he explained it all to Congress by saying:

"Obviously, we have neither the manpower nor the time to waste on such speculative ventures."

Wessel suggested the organization of a Federal Criminal Intelligence Unit to bring together prosecutors and investigators with people best qualified to help them. Attorney General Rogers carried this suggestion to Congress, but Congress ignored it.

Regan, having served as a policeman in New York in Tony Bender's territory, knew more than the average agent. He knew what every cop in the Sixth Precinct knew—which places were under Tony Bender's wing, which unions were controlled by the mob and many other points which couldn't be proven but were common gossip in the district.

He was sure that Pat, who had stayed on much longer than he in the district would know a lot more about these things. But what was the good of pushing it when the chief of the bureau simply didn't believe in it? Still, he kept accumulating his private file and submitting memos.

Because of Regan's interest in the subject, he was assigned to the hijacking squad and, here again, he found his informants feeding him reams of information about organized crime, most of which was put into the "File and Forget Department."

In fact, orders came from Washington to tell some of the informants to stop feeding so much information about the organization and just get down to brass tacks with the hijackings.

Still, in checking out hijackings, it became clear to Regan that each type of hijacking was the responsibility of a different Mafia family. For example, the Gambino family and the Profacis had a big hand in the meat and produce capers and also in stolen shrimp and lobster. Bender and the Genoveses had a lot of interest in television sets, radios and washers and dryers, plus anything that came off the waterfront. Cigarettes went to Profaci in Brooklyn.

Regan felt that at least with the hijacking squad, he was on the right trail. He was no longer involved with catching AWOL's or checking on the politics of college students. At least he was dealing now with real crimes.

Someday, the bureau would have to recognize the organization as the main factor in crime in America. Meanwhile Regan was building his own records.

Life in New York on the hijacking squad was a lot different from his duties in Chicago. He tended to work both days and nights and spent a lot of time in places like the Copacabana, which was widely known to be partly owned by Costello, and the Playmate Club on 55th Street which every cop and reporter in New York knew belonged to Vinnie Mauro of the Genovese crowd.

There was also a string of less-known and seedier places where the growing list of informants that Regan was developing would meet him. Sometimes, it would be the Automat in Times Square, where strangers could sit at tables together without being noticed. Other times it would be in the crowd emerging from the fights at the Garden or Hector's Cafeteria at 43rd and Eighth.

Mondays were a big night at the Copa. It was the night when all the mobsters paid up and settled their various affairs—shylocking, betting and other activities. It was not easy to get close to anything that was happening, but Regan was anxious to familiarize himself with the faces that appeared—some of them were of important people in the mob. He was also on the lookout for PCI's (potential criminal informants) to put in his official reports.

Sometime during his second month in New York, Regan was surprised to notice a familiar back several stools down at the bar in the Copa. It was Pat Conte, wearing a stylish brown gabardine suit with a tan tie, dark brown shirt and gold cufflinks. It was clear that Pat was doing a lot better than he had as a patrolman in the Sixth. But then, he had made sergeant, and Regan supposed as sergeant one could afford to dress better. Also, he knew that Pat was not above taking a few bits of small graft. He probably got the suit wholesale from someone in his territory.

Regan threw a bill on the bar and told the bartender to send a drink to Pat. Pat looked up in surprise as the Grant's was placed in front of him. The bartender pointed at Regan. Pat's face lit up in a smile. He brought the drink over and took the stool next to his old friend.

"Well, doing the town, heh?" he said to Regan. "I didn't think you guys got into this territory much. You working?"

Regan shrugged. "It's more or less on my own, you might say. What we call VOT—voluntary overtime. I'm just soaking up the atmosphere."

"Yeah," Pat said. "Me too."

"What are you on now? I heard you were with the Intelligence Division."

"Well, I been attached to the Waterfront Squad."

"Good duty?"

"So-so."

"What are you doing up here?" Regan asked. "Just bouncing around?"

"Yeah, well, you know. Same as you."

"Listen," Regan said, "why don't we get together sometime, someplace where we can talk a little more? I don't like to talk too much in this place."

"Yeah," Pat said, "I know what you mean."

"I'm working on a few ideas. Maybe we could get together."

"Sure. That's a terrific idea," Pat said. "Why don't we have lunch at Manny Wolf's tomorrow? Can you get away?"

"Yeah, but I can't put that on my expense account."

Pat smiled. "That's okay. It's on me. I can always put down an FBI guy as an informant. Nobody's going to kick about that."

"They give you that kind of expense allowance?" Regan asked in surprise. "I didn't think . . ."

"Oh, yeah! The Waterfront Squad is a hot spot. They give me a lot of leeway," Pat said. "I hear you're working hijacks."

Regan was surprised. "Where'd you find that out?"

"Listen," Pat said, "it's not as big a town as you think. Word gets around."

They sipped on their drinks for a few minutes and looked at the swirling crowd around.

"Lot of big men in here," Regan said.

"I guess so." Pat called for another couple of drinks. "But I'm only interested in the ones involved with the waterfront jobs. You hear a lot of things hanging around here I guess," and then he changed the subject. "How's Katie girl?"

Regan's eyes narrowed for a fraction of a second and opened again, clear and guileless.

"She's great. She's still playing in *Threepenny Opera*. . . . Don't you ever run into her when you're down there doing the waterfront thing?"

Pat smiled. "Between the job and the family, I'm just too busy for that kind of thing. Besides, I got a little action going over there at NYU and that takes time, too."

"Well, nobody ever said you were a straight arrow," Regan said, laughing.

"What about you?"

"Well, I don't fool around that much in the first place, and then the bureau is pretty touchy about our personal lives. Even being seen in a bar like this would probably go against me, except I checked it out with my supervisor earlier. I don't know how in Christ they expect us to find anything out if we can't go into a place where things are happening. Sometimes . . ."

"Yeah."

"You know, I asked Kate to marry me a couple of times, but she's too hung up on her career. She says maybe after she's a star . . ."

"Well, the way she's going, that may not be long, right?" Pat said.

"Yeah. You know, I think she'd be willing to live with me without getting married, but J. Edgar would be very down on that idea. He's thrown guys out of the bureau for a lot less than that."

Pat finished his drink and patted Regan on the shoulder.

"Well, take plenty of cold showers. It helps a lot," he said, and left.

From his position at the bar, Regan could see through the revolving door that Pat was climbing into a white Lincoln Capri convertible which the doorman had pulled up for him.

CHAPTER 21

With Regan assigned to hijacking and Ten Most Wanted squads and Pat in the Waterfront Division (and having a number of family obligations that Regan knew nothing about), it was inevitable that they would continue to cross paths. As far as Pat knew, nobody in the department was aware of his family connections, and he planned to keep it that way.

Much of what he did for the family consisted of simply keeping them aware of events that took place on the waterfront and in the city in general. Also, in the intense Machiavellian internecine power plays in the organization itself, he could be tremendously useful while building up his police reputation.

For instance, he did, in fact, feed Regan a number of legitimate tips on hijacks. They were hijacks pulled by the Profaci mob, which at that time was at odds with the Genovese family. Not only did this result in a lessening of income for the Profacis, it also caused deep mutual suspicion within their group as to who had actually given the tip.

Pat was slowly becoming a respected and senior member of the family, and was not asked to actually participate in any rough stuff anymore. But because of his access to police cars and his ability to set up barriers and close off roads, he often lent a hand when necessary to make sure the job went off right.

At Sam's suggestion, Pat also bought a farm in Ancramdale in Columbia County, about a hundred miles north of New York, not very far from Don Antonio's place. Sam had located the spot, which had on it a num-

ber of limestone caves, a quarry and an abandoned lead
mine.

"You know, Don Antonio's place is getting too
popular," he said. "Too many people know about it. It
could be very useful to have a bit of land that nobody
knows about. Of course, we'll put it in Paterno's name.
Meanwhile, I guess you're getting a good investment,
putting your money out with the shys."

Pat smiled. "I'm getting five percent a month. It
mounts up. I'm glad to see, Sam, that you gave up the
dope. I got a bad feeling about it in my bones."

The bad feeling was justified. In September, Don
Vitone and thirteen others, including Vincent (The
Chin) Gigante and a Genovese soldier named Joe Valachi were indicted for conspiracy to violate the new
Boggs-Daniel narcotics law. Genovese got the best legal
brains in the business and managed to stave off disaster
for almost a year. During that year, he did more than
fight a trip to the federal pen in Atlanta. He worked
hard at consolidating his empire and his authority as
capo di tutti capi.

If Luciano could run the mob from Naples, then
Genovese could run it from Atlanta, but there were details to be cleaned up. Don Vitone trusted nobody, even
in his own family. Tony Bender was obviously getting
ambitious and was spending more time with Little Augie
Pisano than Don Vitone liked. Little Augie was a big
deal in the organization and had very heavy connections
in Florida with the Lansky group. He was a lot smarter
than Bender, and some of the others too.

Early in September 1959, Sam Massey delivered a
message of some importance to his son-in-law.

"I don't know what it's about," Sam said. "but Don
Vitone wants to meet you down at Alto Knight's tomorrow night."

"What do you think it is, Ba?"

Sam looked puzzled. "I don't know, but Don Vitone

knows that you've pulled a lot of jobs and managed to keep it all very quiet. He doesn't even know some of the work you've done, but he hears things. It must be that he's got a very important job, but very confidential. I think he's showing you a lot of respect with this."

Pat met the fox-faced man the next night. Don Vitone sat huddled in a big blue overcoat that rose around his neck like a cape and never removed his white fedora. Don Vitone didn't furnish any plans, but he made it clear what the job was that had to be done. Pat put the wheels in motion.

On September 25 Little Augie was having a big night on the town. He was at the Copa having drinks with Janice Drake, wife of comedian Alan Drake. Alan was somebody whose talent Augie appreciated and supported, but he expected a lot of gratitude for his help. Janice was the kind of statuesque, voluptuous blonde that a little guy like Augie liked to be seen with. At the Copa, they ran into Tony Bender and a few other people and they all retired to San Marino's on Lexington Avenue for dinner.

Little Augie had big ideas. He planned not only to replace Genovese as *capo di tutti capi*, but to displace Lansky in Miami. He had spent a lot of time trying to recruit people from the organization to his side. When a telephone call came to him at the bar of the San Marino, Augie was very interested. The call seemed to be from Jimmy (Blue Eyes) Alo. Augie had been trying to win Alo over to his side for a long time and now it seemed he was willing to talk. Augie returned to the table and threw down a hundred-dollar bill.

He said, "That's for my part of the party. I got a heavy appointment in Queens. I gotta go right now."

"Can I go with you, Uncle Gus?" Janice asked.

Augie looked at her for a moment in doubt and then said, "Sure. Why not?"

Near La Guardia Airport, according to instructions,

Little Augie was met by two men, both wearing trench coats and brown fedoras. They explained that Jimmy Blue Eyes had gone to his apartment a few blocks away and they were supposed to take Little Augie along.

"It's not far. We'll show you the way," one of the men said and Augie threw open the back door of his new black Cadillac and let the two men in. As they drove onto the service road alongside of La Guardia, he didn't notice that another car was trailing from some distance with its lights out. They drove a couple of hundred yards along the dark service road when Augie began to get an uncomfortably suspicious feeling.

"Hey, Jimmy Blue Eyes doesn't live out this way. . . ."

"Take it easy, Gus," Janice said, laughing. "It's probably a short cut."

"That's right, lady. It's a short cut," the man in the brown hat said.

The second man was looking out the window for signs of other cars and then back through the rear window to see if the covering car was behind them.

"Okay," he said. "This will do," and the other man pulled his hand from the coat pocket. He was holding a nickel-plated .32 automatic.

"Stop the car, Augie," he said. Augie eased the car over onto the gravel shoulder.

At this point, the other man pulled a gun from his pocket, reached over and snatched Little Augie's car keys and threw them on the floor of the car.

"Now, roll down the window," the first man commanded.

Augie did as he was told. The two men got out of the car, one on either side, and with deft movements, almost simultaneously, each fired one shot behind the ear of the passenger nearest him—one shot behind Little Augie's left ear, one shot through the beautiful blonde hair and just over the lovely pink ear of Janice Drake. The bodies twitched in unison and fell toward one another and the couple sat there, their heads together like a pair of necking high school kids, their lives draining down into the seat cushions.

The man on the road side held up his hand and the car trailing behind rolled quietly alongside, its rear doors already unlatched. The two men jumped in, one on either side and the car took off, not putting its lights on until it was off the approach road and on to the parkway.

The curly-haired man at the wheel flashed a brief bright-toothed smile. It was Pat Conte.

"Everything okay, I guess. Right?"

"Right."

"Okay. Look on the floor. There's two envelopes. You can check them if you want."

"No, that's okay, eh, 'Mr. Conrad.' We trust you. We know where to find you."

"Okay," the curly-haired man said, pulling up to the Independent Subway station at 74th Street and Roosevelt Boulevard. "I suggest you take the subway from here and stay away from the cabs until you get into town."

"Right."

Pat sat in his unmarked detective car and watched until the men descended into the subway station. Then he pulled the car fifty yards down the road, stepped into a street phone booth and made a call. It was brief and mentioned no names. Then he made another call. It was already almost 1:00 in the morning, but the phone rang only a few times before a drowsy voice answered.

"Hello, Katie," Pat said. "It's your ever-loving blue-eyed boy."

"Okay, I'll be here," the voice said.

Pat jumped back into his car and drove back to Eleventh Street, whistling "Mack the Knife." It was Katie's favorite song from the show.

CHAPTER 22

The killing of Little Augie and his girlfriend made sensational headlines. It also made for a lot of trouble between Profaci and the young Gallos, who were already unhappy about the stingy old man's rule.

In Riverdale, in the den, Sam Massey smiled and poured a Carlos Primero for his son-in-law.

"Beautiful, beautiful," he said.

Pat took an Upmann from the sterling silver humidor on the coffee table and lit it.

"You're sure they didn't know who you were, who ordered the hit?"

Pat smiled. "They were from Detroit. They didn't know me. They didn't know anything. They came to town for one day, they took their money and they went home. It's the only way for a job like that. I didn't even go through any of the organization people in Detroit. I used some of the contacts I learned about on the job."

"Beautiful, beautiful," Sam repeated. "That son-of-a-bitch Little Augie had it coming to him for a long time, but this way Don Vitone kills two birds with one stone, right? He hits Profaci where it hurts, and he gets rid of Little Augie."

"I think Don Vitone must be a student of Machiavelli," Pat said, building a long white ash on his cigar. "In a book of his I read he said 'Wounds are not cured so properly by words as amputation . . .' "

Sam smiled. "You're learning, you're learning. I'm glad you're going to school. You're learning a lot."

"It's your brother, Father Ray, who's been coaching me on Machiavelli. He's a fan of his. It was Machiavelli who first realized that Italy could only become great by uniting under one prince. It's a shame everybody didn't listen to him at the time. He taught that the first thing we must do is to divorce politics from ethics."

"Yes, yes. He was a wise man," Sam said, swirling the fine brandy around in his snifter.

Pat, on his third brandy, felt strangely light-headed. It was only one night since the Pisano job, but sitting there with the newspapers in front of him . . . the headlines screaming . . . the weird, even comical interpretations of motive, misdirected suspicions of guilt . . . gave him a heady feeling and for the first time, a sensation of power which he seemed to enjoy for its own sake: not for the money, not for the position he gained, but just for the feeling that he could make things happen.

"But you know," Pat said, "we've got to get away from this violence, this bloodshed and killing, especially in the family itself. It's bound to attract a lot of bad attention. First the hit on Anastasia, then the godawful bungled job on Costello and Apalachin, now this. Eventually we're going to have the feds on our backs, and they're going to be a lot harder to shake off than the New York City Police Department. You oughta hear Regan Doyle on the subject. He's like one of those Doberman Pinschers on a leash, trying to break loose and tear things up.

"The other day I spoke to Father Ray and he was talking still about Machiavelli. He said there are two kinds of of people—foxes or lions. The foxes live by their wits. I can even remember the way he phrased it: 'They put their reliance on fraud, deceit and shrewdness.' The lions used force instead of brains. He said that they are, 'conservative, patriotic, loyal to tradition, to the family, church, country. They don't trust anything new and they prefer duty and character to brains.' Don Vitone's a fox. He always has been. If he'd stayed away from the white stuff, he'd still be on top. Now it's time for some new fox to move up."

Sam looked up with a worried expression on his face.

"Better watch that brandy, kid. You're talking a little strong. That's the way our friend Augie was talking before . . ."

"Yeah, well I'm just talking theory."

"I sure hope so," Sam said.

"Anyway, you know who the real fox is. It's not Lucky. It's not Don Vitone. It's that skinny Jew in Miami, Lansky. He never gets his hands dirty. He just sits down there and rakes it in. He's the guy Machiavelli would have admired. With us, we got a little of the fox and a little of the lion. Maybe too much of the lion."

Pat finished his drink and Sam quickly reached over and poured another.

"Stay, stay. You know, I really enjoy these talks. It's something I never had in my life—somebody I could talk to and still respect, but not afraid he's going to stick a knife in my back sometime. I'm sorry about the child . . . but I'm very glad that Connie picked you."

"And I'm glad I was adopted by your family," Pat said.

He knew they were both getting sentimental from the brandy, but he enjoyed it.

"If I'm gonna to stay a while longer, I better call home and tell Connie I'm going to be late."

He picked up the phone from the small coffee table next to him and dialed his number. Esperanza answered and put Connie on.

"I thought you were coming home tonight," Connie said, dully.

"You been taking those tranquilizers again?" Pat asked.

"Why not? Is there something so great in life that I'm missing?"

"Look, I told you to knock those off."

"Watch your step, Conte. You're gonna slip one of these days."

She's getting flakier every day, Pat thought.

"Listen, what are you so upset about now?" Pat said.

"You've been up to something again. I know it. I don't want any blood on my doorstep. I don't want to be ashamed to go to church."

"Oh, for Christ's sake," Pat said. "Take a glass of warm milk and go to bed. I'll be home soon."

"Drop dead," Connie said and hung up.

Pat could picture her crossing herself after she said the words.

"You know that daughter of yours," Pat said, picking up his glass again, "I think she's a *strega*. I don't know how, but every time something's up, she picks it up on those weird antennae of hers. She never knows *what's* happening really, but she always knows *something's* happening."

"I know, I know, Pasquale. Sometimes I think she's really her mother's daughter, her mother's daughter alone. Look, drink up," he said and poured another glass of the Spanish brandy.

CHAPTER 23

Regan Doyle was beginning to feel like a rebel in the New York office. He had always thought of himself as being the clean-cut, conscientious agent that The Director liked to see in his service, but the places he had to go to develop his PCI's were not the sort of places for the kind of shirts, ties and haircuts that the bureau favored.

New York was the top bureau outside of Washington and the SAC—Special Agent in Charge—Harvey Foster, was regarded as not only efficient, but a smooth operator and a top public relations man. He helped a lot in keeping the image that The Director wanted of the agency. Regan got the feeling that the bureau was more interested in statistics, rates of conviction or recovery of stolen objects than they were in actually breaking up crimes. There wasn't much actual investigative work done. Most of the work consisted of developing reliable informants, since there were no real undercover men who were SA's themselves. Still, one of the best ways an SA could get a commendation or a recommendation was to develop informants.

Sometimes Regan wondered if he had made the right move in leaving the police department. The one thing he could say was that there was no sign that any of the SA's were on the take. And there was no such thing as cooping in the bureau. Every agent had to fill out a form FD-256 every day. It was usually called the "number-three card." The number-one and number-two cards were the sign-in and sign-out registers, more or less the equivalent of a time clock. On the number-three card, the agent was supposed to list any place that he might be so that he could be located at all times in case of an emergency.

At the bottom were a lot more initials—VOT, TIO, ATIO, TOPSI, TOPRI. VOT (voluntary overtime) was something that The Director was crazy about because he would list these hundreds of thousands of extra hours to boost appropriations from Congress. But an SA soon learned how to pad the VOT. He would simply list as "voluntary overtime" eating supper, watching a flick, or even having a few in the Copa while developing a PCI—Pat Conte for instance.

The best way to develop an informant was the way the police did it—arrest him and threaten him with a big jail sentence unless he rolled over. This was tougher for the FBI, which did very little actual law enforcement and had to get an okay from the U.S. Attorney General's Office to make an arrest. Still, they could often bluff their way by threatening federal charges even when there was no actual violation.

As far as Regan knew, nobody in the bureau resorted to flaking a suspect by planting narcotics or other incriminating evidence on him the way the New York cops did, but it sure was a handy way to develop informants, Regan thought.

In fact, shortly after the Apalachin thing, there was a lot of heat on the FBI to start developing information and making some arrests on organized crime, despite The Director's denial that such a thing existed.

The bureau's response was to start up a secret operation called The Top Hoodlum Program. The existence of this group was not supposed to be told to anybody outside the bureau, even to the police or other law enforcement agencies. The idea was strictly to gather intelligence on the top mob leaders in each major district. Up to that point, organized crime information had been simply dropped into a catchall file which was called the GIIF (General Investigative Intelligence File).

In the beginning, almost all of the information in the new file came from the New York City police, the informants in this case being detectives. It was a one-way street of information, and it was something the police objected to. The FBI had access to New York City Police files, but the police had no access to FBI files, so cooperation tended to be official and formal rather than enthusiastic.

In this situation, Regan was ahead of the other agents. As one of only five agents among four hundred or so in the bureau who were actually assigned to looking into organized crime, he was the only agent that had police experience in New York City itself.

Tom Donovan, the ASAC, gave him a lot of encouragement. Once, over a hamburger at P.J. Moriarty's, Donovan unbent a little to the new SA.

"You know, Regan, I'm not saying that what you're doing isn't right. It's the kind of thing I've been thinking about for a long time, but to tell you the truth, it won't do you much good in terms of promotions in the bureau. The way you get promotions in the bureau is to put in plenty of VOT, keep your nose clean, dress neat and don't offend anybody with political influence."

Regan noted that Donovan was on his third Heinekens or he wouldn't have talked that freely. He was a tall whipcord of a man, who looked like Randy Scott, the old Western movie hero, with close-cropped blond hair and an outdoor face. Regan wondered if he used a sun lamp to keep up that tanned appearance, as he certainly didn't get out in the sun much during the week.

Donovan leaned confidentially over the table.

"I wouldn't want anybody to hear this, especially anybody in the bureau, but The Director is getting, well, *old*. He still has tremendous power in Washington. You know, he's got files on every congressman and every senator—personal dossiers that are not part of the bure u's files.

"I found out all about that when I was working in the Washington bureau. But with all this shooting that we've been having around here and now the Apalachin thing, he's got to yield a little. What he's really afraid of is that they'll appoint some other federal outfit like this new OCR to take away some of the power of the bureau . . ."

Regan listened without commenting. Donovan might be leading him on. For all he knew, there was a goddamn microphone up Donovan's ass.

"You know," Donovan said, seeming to read Regan's mind, "I've put in a request for more technical equipment. Mikes, transmitters, bugs, things like that. We've got to have ways of checking out some of these informants. We can't just go with some junkie or pimp that we meet in some Eighth Avenue bar."

"Well, I *have* been checking them out," Regan started to say defensively.

"No, no, your informants are fine. We haven't made any arrests, but we're building up a beautiful file, for whatever reason I don't know. But there are ways, you know, of getting bugs on somebody's phone or even planting mikes in a room without going through the whole rigamarole of getting a *legal* okay. You have a lot of friends in the police department, right?"

Regan shrugged. "I know a lot of guys."

"Well, you know, a lot of times they have bugs or they can put them on easier than we can. We can just get the information from *them*. That way it doesn't show up on our record that we wired anybody."

Regan nodded.

"You get the idea?"

Regan nodded again.

"A lot of that stuff isn't any good in court, but it

could still give us leads and means of checking on the information that's coming in. We're just going to have to do more work like that in the future. That's the trend now."

Regan began to turn more and more to Pat for inside tips and support and was even willing to leak a little of what was going on in the bureau on an unofficial basis to Pat as a repayment. Regan was fairly certain that he was the only member of the bureau to have good connections in the force, and with Pat now working in the Intelligence Division, the contact was all the more valuable. But Pat was openly skeptical concerning the value of the bureau in deterring criminals.

"You got a bunch of farm guys there. They don't know anything about the city. They don't know what makes it tick. They never even heard of 'street sense.' They're still chasing Dillinger in the cornfields in Kansas. You know how many real crime cases the bureau's been involved in since it started? Maybe two. Back in '29 in Chicago, they got up some kind of a contempt rap on Al Capone and then in '39 when Lepke decided to turn himself in to Winchell, the FBI helped to set up the meet, but that was all Lepke's idea because he didn't want to turn himself over to Dewey. Dewey had a murder rap going on him, but the feds only had a narcotics rap."

"Yeah," Regan said, "but Lepke finally got the chair, right?"

"Big deal. It was still a state rap, right?"

"Okay, okay," Regan laughed. "Right, right. But it wasn't a New York City rap either, right? Listen, are we on the same side or aren't we?"

"I don't know," Pat said. "Are we on the same side? I've been making tapes available to you and files and handing over informants to the FBI and what am I getting out of it? How 'bout letting me in on something that's going on over at the bureau, if you have anything."

"Well, we've got a few tapes I think you'd be interested in," Regan said, "but it's going to be tricky getting you to hear them. Maybe I can get hold of the transcriptions and sneak them out of the office."

"Shit, sneak the *tapes* out and I'll copy them."

"Well, I'm really sticking my neck out," Regan said.

"Sure you are. We all do that. You can never develop anything going strictly by the book. So maybe we drop a little horse in a guy's pocket once in a while. What's the big deal? He's a known user, he's a known dealer. Just because he happened to have flushed the stuff down the toilet when we catch him. . . . Shit, I say that that's as legal as anything. The idea is to get crooks, right? So maybe you guys once in a while have to resort to a suicide tap."

"I haven't chanced that yet."

"Look, *we* take chances all the time. Why can't you guys stick your neck out?"

"Well, I don't like to put an illegal tap on. There's a lot at stake and frankly, we don't get any protection upstairs. If you do it on the force, you can always have some rabbi interfere for you. But in the bureau, it's different. You just step out of line once, pow! You've had it—'dismissed with extreme prejudice.' You know what that means? It means you're fucked, not only in the bureau but in getting a job anywhere, since everybody goes to the bureau to check on people's qualifications."

"I guess you'd have to join the other side, right?" Pat said, smiling.

Regan turned serious. "I'll say this. I never heard of an agent crossing over, but I've heard of plenty of cops."

Pat smiled again. "Okay, okay. Let's not start comparing jobs. You picked your spot and you've got it.

Meanwhile, I'd like to get a listen at some of those tapes. I'm trying to develop some stuff on organized crime too."

"I thought you told me there *wasn't* any Mafia," Regan said.

"Listen, Italians aren't the only criminals in the world. There's a lot of spades and spics and Jews and other people in it now, right? And if there aren't many Irish, it's because they got shovéd out."

"Or maybe they got smart."

"Well, anyway, if you've got any of these tapes, I could use them about now. You know, I passed the lieutenant's exam and I'm on the list now. A couple of good collars would really help."

"Well, I'll see what we've got. There's something that I've been listening to that sounds interesting. It involves a couple of kids that are soldiers in the Profaci mob. I never heard of them myself, some brothers called the Gallos. You ever hear of 'em?"

"No," Pat said. "I never heard of 'em either."

CHAPTER 24

Pat was as good as his word with Regan, and how good his word was depended on what kind of action Pat was interested in. He gave Regan an excellent tip on a shipment of automatic weapons on one of Tony Anastasio's docks in Brooklyn. These pieces had been resting at the Bush Terminal awaiting shipment to Miami and then on to Castro's newly founded government in Cuba.

It didn't bother Pat to rat on Anastasio, who was Big Al's brother. Anastasio was having trouble maintaining control of the International Longshoremen's Association after the death of his brother, Al. Since this section of the waterfront was actually in control of the Profaci family, Pat felt he would actually be doing a favor to Sam Massey and Don Vitone. It was part of Pat's theories as derived from Machiavelli that it was better to dry up the sources of income of opposing factions than to indulge in a constant shooting war.

The knockoff of the weapons shipment by the FBI served a double purpose. It confirmed Pat's credentials with Regan and it struck a blow for the family against the Profacis.

Sam was concerned about Pat's friendship with Doyle.

"You know," Sam said, "I never liked the feebees, even though so far they don't give us much trouble."

"That's the point," Pat said. "There's a lot of heat on them now. Eventually they're going to start nosing around, and I like to keep my own hand in their business so I know just what's happening. We can use these guys the same way we use the police department, to hit anybody that's out of line without having to go through big discussions with the commission.

"Mind you, though," Pat said, "I'm not saying we'd give them information about our own family or about the organization. But when you explain to Don Vitone, he's going to understand what I did. After all, he's the original fox himself, right?"

"Right."

The tip worked out well. Regan was able to lead a raid on the Bush Terminal and intercept the shipment before it was loaded on the boat. He also took along agents of the Treasury Division, charged with enforcing the code against automatic weapons. The information concerning the arsenal from which the shipment had been stolen was sent on to Washington. Information concerning illegal shipments out of the Bush Terminal was acquired from Frank Madden and Billy (The Hook) Giordano, two ILA toughs who took the rap for the gun job.

Regan had lunch with Pat the week afterwards at the Schrafft's on Fifty-seventh Street and Third. Pat looked around the place with distaste.

"Why'd you pick this place?" he said. "All these fag businessmen and little old ladies with flowered hats . . ."

"Look," Regan said, ordering a double bourbon, rocks, "the bureau's on my ass enough about the places I been hanging around trying to pick up stuff on this organized crime thing. This way, I go into Schrafft's, they figure I'm having an ice cream soda. Actually, they've got the biggest drinks in town here for the money."

Pat smiled in approval. "Smart, very smart. But it must be a pretty cheap outfit you're working with if you got to worry about the price of a couple of drinks."

"Well, Pat," Regan said with a bitter note underlining

his voice, "we don't get the chances *you* do for extra money."

Pat laughed. "Listen, I don't get the chance for extra money. I just happened to marry a rich girl. I got a kindly father-in-law."

"I heard a rumor about your father-in-law," Regan said. "I heard that Sam Massey's Riverdale Sand and Gravel Company and a few other enterprises were tied in with the mob."

Pat flashed his big, square, shiny teeth in a deprecatory laugh.

"Old Sam? You got to be kidding. What does he need that kind of connection for? He's cleaning up in legitimate business. You know, when I was a kid I worked for his construction company in the Bronx."

"I didn't know that," Regan said.

"Sure. That was back before I even ever met Constanza. Anyway, just because the guy originally had an Italian name doesn't mean he's in some kind of a racket. Look at me. Look at all those guys on the pizza squad. Look at Ralph Salerno. There's plenty of guys on the law side, too, that are Italian. Look at you. You're half guinea yourself."

Regan smiled. "I never heard of a guy that was in love with his father-in-law."

"Well," Pat said, "I haven't *got* a mother-in-law, or a father or mother either. Seriously, I'd be glad to have you check out Sam's record. I checked it out myself just to see what I was getting involved with. It's clean. He's never had a bust for anything. The man probably wouldn't know what you were talking about if you mentioned some of these mob things to him."

Regan grimaced. "Oh, come on, Pat. You can't get to where he is in the construction business without knowing *something* about it."

Pat shrugged. "Well, so he *knows* something about

it—like anybody who reads the papers. Believe me, if he was into anything, I'd know it."

"I suppose so," Regan said. "But I notice every time Sam gets a job, one of those phony mob-controlled pocket unions is in on the contract."

Pat looked at him speculatively.

"You been doing a lot of homework on my father-in-law, haven't you?"

Regan shrugged.

"Why not? Nobody's above suspicion."

"Well Sam Massey is, as far as I'm concerned, and you better lay off him if you expect any more cooperation from me."

Regan held Pat's gaze for a full ten seconds.

"*Nobody's* above suspicion, Conte," he repeated. "Not even *you*."

Pat debated taking him up on that one, but decided the time wasn't right.

"I gave you a good one down at Bush Terminal, didn't I?" he said finally, letting Doyle's challenge pass.

"Right."

"So now you owe me one. What have you got for me? This ain't a one-way street, you know."

Regan scratched his head. "Well, we got a piece of tape we picked up out in Brooklyn. We had a bug on this telephone in the Sahara Lounge. It's a mob hangout down there."

Pat nodded with interest.

"You know, the bureau has been helping out a bit with the McClellan Committee. This Bobby Kennedy kid is really out to get Jimmy Hoffa's ass, and he's getting there. So we were checking out some of the teamsters that hang around in there. It was strictly a suicide bug that we put on it, but we paid off a telephone company guy, and there's no way of tracing it to us. We got a transmitter on it so they can't trace it by wires. We just pick it up with a radio in a car nearby and put it on the tape."

"Yeah, that's a good way," Pat said.

"That's what I figured," Regan said.

"Can I hear the tape?"

"Well, I had it transcribed. I'll bring you the transcript next meeting."

"I'll come back to the office with you and pick it up right now," Pat said.

Regan shook his head negatively. "The bureau doesn't trust New York cops. If I bring you back to the office, there'll be a lot of questions. We're not supposed to give you any information. You're supposed to give *us* information."

"I *gave* you some, didn't I?"

"Right, but I'm not supposed to give *you* any."

"One hand washes the other, right?"

"Right," Regan said.

The next day at Schrafft's, Regan slipped Pat an unmarked manila envelope. It wasn't exactly a transcript of a tape, but a copy of a summary report.

```
TO   : SAC, NEW YORK, (2473420)
       DATE: 9/12/1960
FROM: SA REGAN S. DOYLE
SUBJECT: ILA SURVEILLANCE


The following information was
excerpted by this SA from date
furnished on 9/11/60 by NY 1407-M.
Any dissemination of this
information outside of the bureau
must be adequately paraphrased in
order to protect this highly
sensitive source.
During the conversation between
```

JOEY GALLO and unkown respondent
referred to as TONY, Joey complained
of poor treatment from "The Old
Man."

GALLO: That fuck is tighter than a
jar of olives. You know, after the
Frankie Shots deal, I thought he'd
really take care of us, but he gives
us nothin'. A couple of machines,
that's it. Son of a bitch sets up
one of those Moustache Petes in a
grocery store, lays out fifteen,
twenty grand. To us, nothing. What
are we, orphans? We laid it on the
line for him so where's the action?

VOICE (TONY?): I know, I know. He's
always been that way. He still
operates the old way, you know? He
never learns nothin', that fuck.

GALLO: You know, they tell me the
other day, Frank Costello has
Louisiana. Who the fuck gave
Louisiana to Frank Costello?
Eisenhower gave it to him? Any son
of a bitch that's strong enough to
take something and hold it, he ought
to get it. If he's not strong enough
to take it, than nobody can give it
to him, whether it's Louisiana or
anyplace else, if you know what I
mean.

VOICE: Yeah, I know what you mean.
It's the same with you guys down
there, huh?

GALLO: That's right. They can't give
a territory away. We laid it out
down here in Brooklyn from President

Street all around the neighborhood.
What do they give me? They don't
even give me a lousy crap game.
What do you gotta be, some kind of
a star to get a crap game? You know,
we're good enough when they want the
job done, you know, like a hit. Like
(inaudible).

VOICE: Watch out what you're saying.
There could be a bug or something
on this phone.

GALLO: Yeah, right. Well, when they
want some work done, we're good
enough, right?

VOICE: Right.

GALLO: But we're not good enough to
come to his fucking house. You know,
I never been to his house?

VOICE: That's not right.

GALLO: Look, to tell you the truth,
I think I could use some
advice. Can we have a meet? I don't
like to talk on the phone. You know,
Tony, you're the only guy that knows
what's going on. You got the same
kind of operation over there in the
Village. That's all we want. Some
machines, a couple of games. You
know what I mean. But we gotta
have support.

VOICE: Okay. Save it, save it . . .
How about, you know the place we
always meet? You know the place I
go to on Thursdays? You know what I
mean? The place that has the good
spedini?

GALLO: Yeah, you mean the place that

begins with L, right? Down in the
neighborhood.
VOICE: Right, you got me. I see you
there Thursday the usual time.
GALLO: Okay, Okay.

The last page of the transcript was short and the
paper ended in a ragged edge, as though it had been torn
off against a ruler. Pat smiled. It was obvious that
Regan didn't trust him *that* much.

The interpretations and evaluations on the report had
been ripped off, but, on the other hand, he was sure that
Regan didn't completely understand the conversation.
The name "Tony" and the references to crap games and
machines in the Village made it clear that the "voice"
was that of Tony Bender.

The "Old Man" was Profaci. It was fairly well known
that the young Gallo boys had been responsible for the
Frankie Shots job. "Frankie Shots" Abbatemarco had
been a sixty-two-year-old enforcer for Profaci. He was a
top soldier in the family who took in almost a million a
year from his policy bank. But Frankie Shots wasn't
paying his regular tax to Profaci, the boss. Frankie complained and postponed, but didn't come up with the
money. Profaci hated that kind of thing.

On November 4, 1959, two men with red bandannas
over their faces intercepted Frankie Shots as he was
leaving Cardiello's Bar and Grill on Fourth Avenue in
Brooklyn. They caught him with four slugs in the belly,
the throat and the face. The force of the bullets knocked
Frankie Shots back into the saloon where he made a last
wild grab for the bar and then slid to the floor. The gunmen followed him in. One of them, a short, fat man
reached inside Frankie Shots's coat, pulled out his pistol
and shot him three more times in the belly with it.

When the cops arrived, Frankie Shots was dying and
unconscious. He was on his back in the sawdust of the

bar floor, his white fedora lying neatly next to his head, where it had fallen off, its brim gradually turning red from the blood it was soaking up.

Pat's division of the department, the Criminal Investigation Bureau, was convinced by unofficial information that the short, fat gunman had to be Joe Jelly (Joseph Gioelli) an associate of the Gallos. Brooklyn cops picked up Joe Jelly and grilled him, but they could get nothing on him. They finally booked him for carrying an unidentified key.

Jelly stubbornly insisted that he had no idea what the key was for. The detectives knew that the key was for his girlfriend's apartment, but Jelly had a very tough wife and was not about to admit that, so they booked him for possession of a burglary tool (the key).

It was obviously a contract job by The Old Man, but nobody could prove it. But it was not hard to guess from the actions of "Crazy Joey," the big-mouthed member of the Gallo family. Informants on President Street said that when John Scimone, Profaci's personal bodyguard, came down to see if he couldn't calm down Crazy Joey, Joey responded by spitting on Scimone's shoe and there was almost another gangland killing on the spot.

Pat's inside knowledge was useful in interpreting the tape, as was his close, personal knowledge of Tony Bender. It was obvious that Bender was talking about Luna's Restaurant where he liked to go on Thursday nights for a quiet plate of *spedini* with a tumbler of good dago red.

Of interest to Pat was the close bond that seemed to be growing between Gallo and Bender. This was definitely something not known to Don Vitone or Sam Massey. The day after he got the memo from Doyle, Pat met with Sam and Don Vitone, whose face was sharper and paler than ever beneath the wide-brimmed fedora.

"You going to do anything about this, Don Vitone?" Pat asked.

The *capo di tutti capi* shrugged. "We'll take care of it when the time comes. Meanwhile, I wouldn't mind putting on a little heat. Can you do that?"

"Sure," Pat said. "We'll just bust the meeting."

"Okay," said Don Vitone, "but make sure nothing comes out that we don't *want* to come out, eh? I mean, if there's any searching, you be there and check everything."

"Listen, they won't be able to hold them on anything. It will just shake them up a little,—especially Tony."

Pat gave a guarded report the next day to Deputy Chief Inspector, John Brady of the CIB and got an okay to raid Luna's that Thursday. Promptly at 8:30, four burly detectives of the CIB and Pat entered the crowded restaurant. Seated around a large table in conference, was his lean, scholarly looking friend, Tony Bender. Next to him was Crazy Joey, mopping up the remains of a plate of *linguini aglio-olio* with a piece of Italian bread. Also present were Frankie "The Bug" Caruso, from Bensonhurst, Joey Agone, business representative of the "Union of Affiliated Unions," Phil Albanese of Valley Stream, and Georgie Gilippone from Brooklyn. They were all charged with consorting with one another, since every man at the table had a considerable police record.

Bender looked up with resignation, then his eyes widened for a fragment of a second as he caught sight of Pat, standing there in his civvies, directing the operation. Pat tipped Tony a very slow and wise wink and left him to figure out the meaning of it. Tony, of course, knew that from time to time Pat had to make a collar, even amongst the family, but never had he reached so high into the organization. It must have given him a *lot* to think about. All of the men were questioned and released and the charges ultimately were dropped.

But apparently Bender still didn't get the message.

CHAPTER 25

Nineteen-sixty was a good year for Pat Conte. The money had been better, he'd placed high on the lieutenant's exam and had only to wait for a spot, and that summer he finally finished the last course in ten years of night-time and afternoon studies at Bernard Baruch.

Late in June, he got the word that he had passed the bar exam. Pat and Connie had done very little large-scale entertaining since the birth of the baby seven years earlier. But Pat felt that this occasion called for a celebration and he decided to hold an outdoor barbecue at the farmhouse in Ancramdale, where he had been spending what little spare time he had on weekends and during holidays.

Basically it would be the immediate family and a few close friends. Pat would have liked very much to have invited Katie. Constanza was in favor of that, but inviting Katie would have meant inviting Regan Doyle and though he had been friendly with Doyle during the last year or so, he was not anxious for Doyle to get a look at some of his family associations.

Gradually, the FBI, at Doyle's prodding (in the New York Bureau anyway) was getting more and more interested and even a bit knowledgeable about family activities. If Doyle came, then certain members of the family certainly couldn't be asked.

Sam Massey's connections were still almost unknown to the outside world, but Doyle could put two and two together if he saw some of the other guests.

Pat and Connie had a big fight over that. She insisted

that he was excluding Katie and Doyle because he was ashamed of the child, who at seven years of age was the size of a two-year-old and could neither walk, talk nor control its bowels. It could only sit up in its crib, rocking back and forth on its haunches, making strange, unintelligible noises over its dangling tongue.

"Look, Connie," Pat said with exasperation, "I'll admit I don't carry the kid's picture in my wallet, but that isn't the reason I haven't asked Doyle and Katie. I just like to keep this a family affair."

"Then why are you asking Paterno and Ganci and Al Santini and all those people from Mulberry Street?"

"Because they're practically my family. Besides, I'm very involved with the Italian-American Defense League and it's becoming more important now that I'm getting out of school. I'll have more time to give to it."

"God will punish you for being ashamed of your own child."

"God punished me by *giving* me that child."

"God had a good reason, and someday you may know what it is."

"Jesus, I can tell you're still talking to that loony priest of yours," Pat said with disgust. "Will you look at that thing?"

"Sebastian," he said. "His name is *Sebastian."*

"Well, *look* at him. Look at that big space between his toes. He's got webbed feet, for Christ's sake."

Connie leaned against the side of the crib, tears running down her face, soundlessly.

"Okay, okay, I'm sorry," Pat said. "I'll tell Nurse Orten to get some help from the registry and we'll drive up to Ancramdale in the morning."

"Pat, can't we take Sebastian? He loves the country and the family will want to see him."

Pat grimaced with disgust. "Look, Connie. Get it through your head. The family doesn't *want* to see him. The family wants him hidden away. The family is *embarrassed* to see him, and he doesn't know where he is half the time anyway. What's the difference if he's in the country or in the city? The nurse can read him one of those dumb picture books. He seems to like the sound of her voice."

"You're the cruelest man I know," Connie said bitterly, "and as far as I'm concerned, you can go to your goddamn picnic alone."

That Saturday, Pat drove to the picnic in the new Capri. (He had traded the old one in only six months before.) Arthur Marseri rode with him for company. They traveled up the Taconic to Ancramdale with the top down.

"You ought to be glad you never got married, Art," Pat said. "If it wasn't for the family . . ."

"Well, you got a tough break there with the kid," Arthur said sympathetically, "but you're right. I am glad I never married."

"You ever think how much a kid costs? You know, colleges, vacations, extra rooms? My kid ain't going to college," Pat said, laughing wildly. "I think we might get him into kindergarten by the time he's twenty-three, if he lives that long."

Arthur changed the subject. "I think before Christmas you may have something else to celebrate."

Pat looked interested.

"I been checking it out and I think there's going to be some vacancies for lieutenant by then."

"That will be terrific. We better get together sometime soon and talk about what kind of assignment we can land. What about you? You making captain?"

Arthur grinned happily. "Next month. About time, isn't it?"

"So you're always keeping a few steps ahead of me," Pat said, smiling.

Arthur Marseri looked at him seriously.

"You'll pass me standing still one of these days, Pat. I don't know if you realize it, but I've only been a disappointment to the family. They thought that I'd be the bright one, leading us all into a new era. But somehow I didn't inherit the right kind of aggressive genes. Maybe I had it too soft when I was a kid. The best thing I ever did for the family was taking you under my wing in the department. They've all told me that many times. Captain is *it* for me. That's where I stop. But you've got a big future in front of you. *You're* the hope of the family now."

Pat was moved by Arthur's speech. He had felt his growing influence, and he had known all along that Arthur would never have had the balls to pull off the jobs that Pat had handled. But the feeling of belonging finally to a real family gave him a warm feeling inside.

"It take all kinds, Arthur. It's no crime not to be aggressive."

"Thank the Lord for small favors," Arthur said.

The farmhouse was an old, clapboard, Dutch Hudson Valley cottage. It was small, but the party was to be held in a brick building on the edge of the limestone quarry which was one of the selling points of the land. The building had once been used for dressing the stone, but Pat had had it redecorated into a large, comfortable game room.

Behind it was the quarry with its steep, marble-white stone sides. The quarry had filled with water long ago, and made an attractive swimming hole and landscape feature. On the water side end of the brick building, Pat had broken through the wall and made a pass-through bar and patio. There was a large, outdoor brick fireplace with heavy grills over it.

Sam's chauffeur, Tommy, had taken responsibility for the meal, which was to consist of grilled Italian sausages, hot and sweet, with peppers and onions, chickens roasted on the coals, steaks and chops. There were kegs of beer set up at both ends of the patio and

Tommy's younger brother, Georgie, was working the bar for hard drinks.

When he finally realized Connie was not going to come, Pat decided to make the whole thing into a stag affair. All together, there were about twenty guests—Father Ray and Sam Massey, of course, and Ganci and Paterno. He would have had Don Vitone, but unfortunately, Don Vitone was very busy playing *bocce* in the exercise yard at Atlanta Federal Penitentiary. Tony Bender begged off, saying he had a meeting in Brooklyn. But Jerry Catena showed up as a surrogate for Don Vitone and to give the party a little cachet and Don Antonio, of course, the aging prince of foxes.

Jim Bailey, who was now a leading feature writer on the *New York Post* showed up with a small group from the school. Pat greeted him effusively with an Italian embrace when he joined the crowd around the brick bar.

"Jim, boy, how've you been? It's been a year or two, hasn't it?"

"Just about."

"Well, I've been watching your stuff and it's real good. We all knew you had it in you."

"And I've been watching yours. You've been getting your name in the paper quite a bit. Hero cop and all that shit."

"Well, I got good press agents," Pat said, laughing.

Father Ray came over beaming and put both of Pat's hands in his.

"So, you're going for the law now? Isn't that marvelous? I remember when you were just a kid fighting in the streets."

"Well, Father Ray, I've been listening to a lot of the things you say. Maybe the time for fighting is over, right?"

"Yes. It's time to be a fox now. The lions are out of fashion. Maybe you could give some thought to politics," Father Ray said smiling. "Who is your Negro friend?"

"Oh, he's a guy I know from school."

"Good, good. We need everybody." Father Ray seemed pleased.

It was a perfect day. There were still blossoms left on the fruit trees, but the air had enough spring chill left in it to keep things from being muggy. Sam looked around the property with approval.

"You know, Pat," he said, "I was thinking of buying this myself at one time. It's a beautiful piece of land, and I like what you've done with it."

"I like it too," Pat said. "It makes me more able to stand the city, getting out here once in a while. I'm thinking of buying some cows from Don Antony if I can get somebody to look after them."

"That's nice. You'll be a regular *gregna*. I'm really proud of you, son."

Sam draped his gray flannel jacket over his shoulders and took Pat's arm as they walked over to the edge of the quarry and stood looking at the water. Pat thought it was funny, because Sam had shed almost all of the old country mannerisms in his clothes, his speech, his food, but he still hung his suit jacket over his shoulders like the Moustache Petes from the old country.

"This is a beautiful piece of water," Sam said. "You know, any property with water on it now is worth a fortune. Everybody wants to get out of the city."

"I like it and it's nice and cool for swimming," Pat said.

"You know, I had this whole property surveyed," Sam said. "You know how deep that quarry is? Three hundred feet, straight down. You see how the sides go straight down there where they used to take the rock out. That rock, it's like marble. You can build houses with that. It's like Carrara and, of course, it gets deep right off the edge here. It just goes straight down.

Straight down, three hundred feet. I dropped a line down there one time just to see. My God, if anything ever fell in there all the way down to the bottom, nobody would ever find it! You know, that's deeper than most divers could go."

Sam was not given to small talk or poetic expression. It was clear that he was making an important point here. He surveyed the overhanging ledge of white limestone.

"You see, if you should want to get some more stone sometime to build up your property, you know, add to your patio or make a nice limestone wall, you might blast a little in that wall and get out some nice pieces of stone. Of course, a lot of stone would go down to the bottom also, but you have plenty."

Pat nodded with interest.

"If something were on the bottom, of course, and the stone covered it, well, there'd be no way to get it back, would there?"

The picture was becoming clearer to Pat.

"Well, there's lots of ways in which things or people can disappear," Pat said. "I know there's a junkyard up on the Bronx River, there. Sometimes, something falls into the big metal press there, the one that takes a whole car. If something falls in there, it's never seen again. It just gets squashed into a little cube and then it goes down to the steel mill on the railroad cars."

"Sure, sure, I know," Sam said, "but you know that's an old-fashioned kind of operation, and besides you need an operator for the hydraulic press, a truck driver, you need men to load the car in the crusher and to run the crane. That's a lot of people to have around when you just want to crush up one car. Now, it always seems to me that if you want a job done and you don't want anybody to know about it, well, then the less people that are around, the better. Maybe there shouldn't be any at all because sure as hell, it comes back to haunt you when you got too many people on a job.

"You know, in the old days, we had *omerta,* we had honor, we had respect, but things are changing very much now. People change sides, right and left. We can't depend on them."

"It's not just now," Pat said. "That's the way men have been through history. Here's something I learned by heart from Machiavelli:

> It may be said of men in general
> that they are ungrateful and fickle,
> dissemblers, avoiders of danger and
> greedy of gain. So long as you
> shower benefits on them, they are all
> yours; they offer you their blood,
> their substance, their lives and
> their children, provided the
> necessity for it is far off; but
> when it is near at hand they
> revolt.

"You're a regular professor," Sam said, laughing. "But he was *something,* that Machiavelli, eh? He was the number-one *consigliere.*"

They sat down on the redwood bench that Pat had had placed alongside the diving platform and lit an Upmann.

"These are getting hard to get now since that Castro took over," Sam said, "but they still send me a box up from Miami once in a while. I'll get you some."

"Thanks," Pat said.

Sam blew a big cloud of smoke out over the black waters. "Yes, yes, what he said there, Machiavelli, they are ungrateful and fickle, avoiders of . . . avoiders of danger . . . greedy. Yes. You know, there's a lot of truth to that. By the way," he said, "how come your *compare* from the Village, Tony Bender, isn't here?"

"I asked him," Pat said, "but he said he had to go to Brooklyn for a meeting."

"Brooklyn, Brooklyn. He goes to Brooklyn a lot. He has a lot of meetings. We don't see him down at the Alto Knights so much or down in the club. Who is he meeting with? He seems very friendly with those young punks from President Street, those Gallos. I don't see what benefit there can be for us in that relationship."

Pat squinted into the birch grove that fringed the far side of the quarry crater.

"Has anybody been in touch with you about all this?" Pat said.

"Yes, I been in touch with the Jew in Miami. Believe me, they know everything that's happening. There's plenty of communications, if you know what I mean."

"What you're talking about, it would be a very big move," Pat said. "It might cause a lot of trouble."

"First, they would have to know who did it, right?" Sam said. "Now, if even the most thorough search and questioning of everybody in the organization couldn't turn up anybody, well then, nobody would *know* who did it, would they? It's not the kind of thing you could trust to an outsider."

"When do you think such a thing might take place?" Pat said.

Sam blew another cloud of fine Havana smoke. "Oh, we can afford to watch and wait a little. There's going to be a lot happening down there in Brooklyn. Who knows? God may grant our wishes by accident. I see a lot of bullets flying over the river there before they settle that matter."

"Well, sometimes I think Profaci brought that on himself. You have to go with the times and you have to be more generous than he is. He gave those Gallo boys nothing and they took some big chances."

"Yes," Sam said, "but between the two factions, I don't like either one of them. I think in the end it's going to be Gambino who benefits."

Sam was right in his prediction. There was violence in

the air, and it broke out in Brooklyn barely six months later. The Gallos planned it to be a devastating blow that would knock out the Profaci faction in one day.

"We will do it like Fidel La Barba," Joey Gallo was heard to say on one of the many police bugs that infested the President Street headquarters.

In one afternoon, in a series of coordinated raids, the five top leaders of the Profaci family were hunted down in their clubs and bars and kidnaped at gunpoint, but the wily old man, Profaci, was not home when the kidnap team turned up in Bensonhurst to snatch him.

Larry Gallo's idea was to hold the team hostage for a settlement with the Profaci mob. Up to this point, the Gallos had not been strong enough, not commanded a big family of their own to get a sit-down before the commission to discuss their grievances. But now, with four of the five leaders, the Gallos and their coleader, Joe Jelly, felt they had the upper hand. Larry felt that once their grievances were heard and fairly acted on, they could release the captives unharmed. But Joey had a different idea.

"We kill one of 'em, you see, and we tell 'em we want a hundred Gs cash as a good-faith token before we sit down and say anything," but Larry and Joe Jelly talked the excitable blond out of that, although Larry had to actually slap his brother to convince him that such bloodshed was not necessary. And, in fact, to avoid a premature blow-off, he sent Joey to California on a vacation to cool down.

Through neutral ambassadors, a meet was finally set up and the hostages were left unharmed. It wasn't that Larry was against bloodshed, but he felt that as long as they couldn't wipe out Profaci at the same time, the situation wasn't wise.

If any of the captives were killed, Profaci still had enough guns to wipe out the whole Gallo mob. The idea was to use the captives as pawns. Word came from Profaci that he'd deal with the Gallos and two weeks after the kidnaping three hostages, Joe Magliocco, Sally "The Sheik" Mussachia and Frank Profaci, the boss's brother, were released.

But John Scimone, the toughest and coolest of them all, was detained. This was partly because, while he was being held in an East Side Manhattan hotel, Scimone had convinced the Gallos that he was thinking of switching to their side. In order to avoid suspicion, they kept Scimone an extra week. In the end, the matter went before the commission, the leaders of the top five families.

The meeting was in the basement of a restaurant on Long Island. Crazy Joey was back by this time and it was hard to keep him from wisecracking his gang into trouble, but Larry used his superior personality and diplomacy to squash his impetuous brother and argued the case of the injustices that the gang had been subjected to by Profaci.

Tony Bender stood up and supported the Gallos' point of view. Above all, he said, peace was needed. There was no need to attract outside attention by more killings and violence. Gambino and Lucchese said nothing, and finally the commission decided that Joe Profaci and the Gallos could fight out their differences any way they wanted to.

The Gallos were confident. They had Scimone as a secret fifth column and feelers of friendship had been extended to them by Carmine "The Snake" Persico, a Profaci hit man. The day after the meeting, Pat met with Tony Bender for a steak at Lombardi's and got the whole story on the commission meeting.

"If they really wanted peace," Pat said, "they wouldn't have left it up to those young punks. There'll be no peace."

"Well," Bender shrugged, "*que sera, sera*. You know what I mean?"

CHAPTER 26

Pat was feeling good those days about most things—the promotion, his assignment back to the Sixth, the comfortable relationship he had settled into with Katie. He would see her, generally speaking, on Mondays and Thursdays. There was no planned schedule, but often he was home for the weekend or away in the country, so that by Monday, his frustration quotient was nearing a peak. Also, Katie didn't perform on Mondays so that often they might go out to dinner together or to a movie. He enjoyed Katie's company, aside from the sex, which continued to be the best he ever knew, and got even better.

Thursdays he would see her more or less in preparation for the long weekend, since he and Connie often drove up to the country on Fridays with little Sebastian, stinking and gargling, swaddled into a padded box in the back seat of the Capri.

One Monday in September, Pat was heading for an early date at Katie's, having spent the afternoon going over Election Day assignments with the captain. Pat was thinking about the forthcoming election as he strolled east on Christopher, past Katie's theater, his old house at the corner of Bleecker, past endless rows of streamers and posters and graffiti for Kennedy or for Nixon. There was one thing the family felt united about and that was that Kennedy was bad news for the organization. The candidate's activities and that of his brother, Robert, on the McClellan Committee had indicated which way things would go if the Kennedys won. Already, they had been putting heat on the FBI to spend more time on organized crime and less on stolen cars and hillbilly bank robbers.

Doyle was rooting all the way for the Kennedys and "It's not just because they're Irish," he told Pat. "It's because that other guy's a crook. We got stuff on him in our files going back to the Bahamas that you'd be surprised at."

"I thought the bureau was crazy about him because he kept the Commies out of government," Pat said.

"Yeah, well the bureau may be, but I'm not."

Pat let the discussion go at that. If he had any interest in politics himself, it was on a local level. He was more interested in what was happening to DeSapio's power in the Democratic party then he was about what was going on in Washington, D.C. One thing that was certain, whether Nixon won or not, the Republicans would never control New York City. So, it was a question of which faction in the Democratic party to back. If possible, both.

That fall, Pat won still another citation for valor when he stumbled into a holdup at Riker's Coffee Shop in Sheridan Square. There was a hostage involved, a black professor from NYU who complicated the issue by complaining that Pat had killed the two holdup men unnecessarily and had also risked the life of the hostage. But the Honor Board supported Pat's claim over the protests of the NAACP, and Pat benefited from another spate of newspaper publicity. Fein, the news reporter, even suggested that there would soon be enough material in Pat's publicity file for a book.

Winburg, too, was impressed with his friend's growing fame.

"It's really a shame to let all that notoriety go to waste," he said. "You ever think of trying for politics? With your record, you would make a helluva candidate, and you've got the presence and personality for it, too."

"Are you kidding? I'm a flatfoot, not a pol."

"I'm not kidding one bit," Winburg said. "Give it some thought. You don't want to be a copper all your life, do you? And one of these days, you may *lose* one of these shoot-outs. You could have the support of a lot of important groups—the PBA, the Columbia Society, the Italian-American League. There's a great fear in the city of the increase of crimes of violence. A law-and-order candidate could be just the ticket."

Pat mollified his friend by telling him he would think it over. It was a whole new concept to him, but there were aspects of it that appealed to him.

He tried the idea out on Father Ray over a glass of Cinzano in the rectory.

"Your Jewish friend has a good mind. I have never felt that you should spend your entire life in the police department. That's all right for Arthur. His ambition is small. But you, I say think about it, seriously. The time may still be early, but even now you could be preparing the groundwork. If you decide to take that path, you know the family will be behind you, and we are not without political influence. Right now we are still concerned about how to handle the DeSapio problem, but things will change soon, and open up for our people."

"It sounds as though you already have given this some thought, Father Ray."

"I have. I have. Just take your time. Stay out of trouble. Wait for the right moment."

Shortly after that he won a citation in a shoot-out at Riker's Coffee Shop. The Deputy Commissioner in charge of Public Relations, suggested that Pat might be of use to the department lecturing at high schools and to civic groups. He had already shown a considerable aptitude for public speaking at the Columbia Society and in the Italian-American Defense League, word of which had reached the public relations section.

The commissioner requested a leave of absence on

the basis of the fact that the department was in desperate need of improved public relations. Pat was glad for the rest, and enjoyed the adulation of the crowd. The second week in November, he had lectured at Julia Richman High on the Upper East Side and he took the chance to meet Doyle for a drink at Schrafft's.

"I'm buying," Doyle said. "This is to celebrate the election. Here's to our new President, Jack Kennedy, and to the new Attorney General, Bobby." There was a pause. "And to all our brave policemen," he said.

"I'll drink to that," Pat said. "In fact, I kind of *like* Kennedy."

"What about Bobby?" Doyle said.

Pat shrugged. "We'll see. I know one thing. Your boss doesn't think much of him."

Doyle looked all around carefully and started to say something. "Screw . . ."

"Yeah?" Pat said.

"Never mind. The place may be bugged," Doyle said.

CHAPTER 27

While Police Lieutenant Pat Conte was on the glory road, Doyle was still struggling to get the FBI to realize that there *was* such a thing as organized crime. He began to feel that he might be getting somewhere when Supervisor Jones informed him that he was to go back to Washington for a three-week course in the theory and practice of wire tapping, bugging and lock picking. The course was a hush-hush operation and was held in the attic of the Identification Building in an area where tourists taking the FBI tour seldom strayed.

A mock room had been built in a corner of the third-floor area and here Doyle was taught how to pick a hole in a plaster wall or wood paneling, plant a bug, cover it up and repair the paint and plaster so that there were no signs left.

On Saturdays, when the Justice Building was practically deserted, they made the "spaghetti run." This was practice in finding a particular wire out of the incredibly tangled maze of filaments that ran through the conduits in the room. But the segment of the course that was most hush-hush was lock picking. Each agent taking the course—and there were not more than a half a dozen at a time—was given an unlisted set of lock-picking tools and instructions in their use, but they were warned that if they were caught with the tools, they could get up to ten years for their possession.

Doyle was well aware that this training was given only to special and trusted agents. The combination of burglary and planting the bugs were usually called a black-bag job because of the equipment that had to be taken along. The technique they were taught was first to check by phone or observation to make sure that the occupants of the place to be bugged were away and to put a tail on them with a two-way radio to make sure they didn't double back and surprise the agent. One agent would sit nearby with a police radio and listen to the calls to make sure there was not a report of a prowler. If the agents were caught by the cops, there would be a lot of explaining, because on a black-bag job the agents carried no credentials nor anything else that would identify them with the FBI.

Doyle was having lunch in the commissary with Jack Keller, one of the other agents in the course, a long stringbean of a man from the Butte, Montana bureau.

"I thought that was supposed to be Siberia up there," Doyle said. "How come you got this special assignment?"

"Shucks, man," Keller said. "I *like* it up there. I'm from the Rockies, and I wouldn't want to be anyplace else."

"You must be the only guy who's ever picked Butte as an office of preference," Doyle said, shaking his head.

"Listen," Keller said, "I've been thinking of something about these black-bag jobs. Hell, you get caught on one of these, you're just fucked, right?"

Regan took another bite out of his paper-thin commissary ham on white and shrugged.

"That's the name of the game, I guess."

"Well, what would you do if you were caught?" Keller prodded him. "I mean if the cops busted in on you right in the middle of one of these jobs?"

"I guess I'd hit the fuck over the head with a chair or a crowbar or anything handy and run like a son-of-a-bitch. What else could you do?"

"Yeah," Keller said bluntly. "I guess you're right, but

that wasn't the kind of thing I had in mind when I joined up."

When Doyle got back to the New York bureau, he was well aware of the infighting that had been going on since Bob Kennedy had been appointed Attorney General. Kennedy had gotten the idea in his head that the FBI was a branch of the Justice Department, which, of course, it was, but nobody had ever treated it as such. It had always been considered the private domain of "The Man," J. Edgar.

Both the Attorney General and his brother, the President, were interested in setting up some form of National Police Division or at least a coordinated crime information bureau. Hoover was absolutely against it. Finally, with his back to the wall, The Director yielded a few steps and organized something called the Special Investigative Division.

Doyle was one of the three or four men in the bureau with recent black-bag training, and because of his interest in organized crime, was rapidly integrated into the new division. He was often sent out on black-bag jobs which made him very nervous but had compensations. For every successful black-bag job, the agent was given a cash bonus of between $500 and $1,000. Doyle made an extra $5,000 the first year.

Sometimes the agents would get wind of a building or a repair project for a known organized crime figure and would come in as workmen and install the bug while the operation was going on. A couple of times they were even able to install bugs on houses that were still being built. Those were later completely undetectable.

Phone taps were another matter. They were more difficult because they had to be authorized, but the bugs

Doyle was having lunch in the commissary with Jack could be authorized on the bureau's own say-so, with approval of the attorney general even though the installation sometimes involved cutting a few corners.

Doyle was selected as one of the few agents with ready access to a small concealed room in the rear of the office called BUGOUT—also called the Technical Surveillance Room. This was where most of the monitoring was done and the information taken off the bugs and taps. If the information came from an illegal tap or bug, it was simply assigned the number of a fictitious "informant" and reported in that fashion so that the existence of the bug or tap never showed up on the records.

It was inevitable that Pat Conte, during their occasional meetings, would detect the fact that Doyle had special and excellent training in some of these areas, and while Doyle admitted nothing, Pat would often tease him.

"You know," he said, "I think you're listening to so many tapes, you're beginning to talk with an Italian accent."

Doyle smiled. "I'm learning plenty," he said.

"I don't see you making any arrests."

"Don't worry. This Kennedy kid is gung-ho. There's going to be plenty of action pretty soon."

"Not as long as you got old Fearless Fosdick on top in Washington. Don't kid yourself. He's still running the show."

Somehow, Regan Doyle began to get the feeling that his old buddy, cousin Pat Conte, was pressing a little too hard for information about the FBI bugs. Whether this was to get the jump on a good collar or for whatever reason he didn't know, but he was becoming more circumspect with his information.

It was hard to interpret some of the material that was coming in on the taps, but it was clear that more trouble was brewing involving the Gallos in Brooklyn. The police knew it, too. South Brooklyn Commander Raymond Martin assigned eight of his best detectives to the Gallo territory, and they made sure that everybody knew that they were around, in the hopes that this would keep the situation quiet.

Pat stayed away from President Street. He wasn't anxious to have his face that well known to the Gallo mob. But he kept in touch with Ralph Salerno, Kissel and other cops that were on the beat, and he checked from time to time with Deputy Commissioner Martin's group.

While Doyle's bugs didn't tell him exactly what was going on, it was obvious that the Gallos were trying to keep their tie-lines to Tony Bender and were wooing Carmine "Junior" Persico and another Profaci soldier, Salvatore "Sally D." D'Ambrosio. Persico was a feared killer, even in that tough mob and had been first indicted for murder at the age of eighteen.

The Gallos felt that their alliances with the younger Profaci men were growing stronger when Persico and Sally D. invited Joe Jelly on a bluefishing trip aboard Sally D.'s thirty-two-foot cruiser, anchored in Sheepshead Bay. Nobody even noticed at first that the fat man never came back from the fishing trip.

The next day Larry Gallo got a call from John Scimone and he was very pleased. Scimone said he had some good news for Larry and suggested that they should meet to celebrate with a few drinks at the Sahara at around 5:00 P.M.

The Sahara Lounge was a favorite spot for the Gallos. It was at Utica Avenue and Clarendon Road in Flatbush.

It was noted as a hangout of the Profacis, but then, Scimone was supposed to be close to Profaci, so there was nothing suspicious about that.

When Larry arrived promptly at 5:00 P.M., Scimone was waiting for him outside. The place wasn't open yet, but as a sign of good will, Scimone handed Larry a hundred-dollar bill as soon as he got out of the car. Larry felt that this was going to be his lucky day. People don't pass out hundred-dollar bills for nothing. Scimone rapped on the window and got Charley Clemenza, the manager, to let them in even though the doors weren't officially open yet. Even the lights weren't on, just a few behind the bar.

Clemenza smiled and poured them a couple of drinks on the house. Gallo was really anxious to hear the good news but Scimone was taking his time.

"I'll give you the whole pitch, kid, as soon as I take a leak," he said and left Larry alone drinking at the bar.

Larry was so happy talking to Clemenza who was polishing glasses behind the bar, and trying to figure out what the good deal was that Scimone had asked him to cut in on, that he hardly flinched when two men jumped out of the shadows of one of the booths, threw a rope over his neck and tightened it like a noose. It was Carmine "The Snake" and Sally D. They twisted the rope until Larry saw pinwheels of color before his eyes and just began to slip from consciousness. Then they loosened it up enough to suggest that Larry should call his brothers to come over to the Sahara.

"Fuck you!" Larry said, strangling on the rough rope.

"Well, that figures," the Snake said. "Let's just finish it," and he tightened up on the rope.

Larry went limp and his sphincter released his bowels in a noxious rush, but before the job could be finished, the door in the rear of the bar opened and Sergeant Edgar Meger, who had been cruising on Utica Avenue, stepped in. He had noticed that the side door was ajar and was coming in to check. There was no one in sight except for Clemenza, and Clemenza said everything was fine, but before he left, Meger saw a pair of legs stretched out on the floor.

As he bent over to get a closer look, three men jumped out and rushed for the door.

Meger yelled, "Blei, watch it!" and Patrolman Melvin Blei, who was waiting outside, tried to block the escape. One of the running men fired sideways at him and the bullet ripped through Blei's cheek. The men escaped in a white Cadillac before any action could be taken.

A few days later, a Cadillac slowed down outside of Joe Jelly's favorite candy store in Bath Beach and someone tossed a cloth bundle on the pavement. It was Joe Jelly's voluminous blue cashmere overcoat, wrapped around a dead fish. The truce was over.

Pat dropped in on Bender that Thursday at Luna's.

"Well, Tony," he said, softly, "it looks like your boys are having their troubles over there on President Street."

Tony looked up, tense, almost frightened.

"What do you mean 'my boys'? I hardly know those kids!"

"Oh, is that right?" Pat asked with surprise. "I thought they were pals of yours. That's the word that's going around."

"Nah, nah," Bender said, cutting into his *spedini*. "I hardly know those punks."

Meanwhile, on East 69th Street, Doyle was trying to put together the pieces of the puzzle, but he was starting out far behind Pat Conte, who knew the names and numbers of all the players from the start. Doyle piled up many hours of VOT, not only checking the tapes, but going back to some of the earlier federal crime investigations undertaken by the Kefauver and the McClellan committees. Somewhere, he was sure, he would find a link to the Marseri family.

Going over the transcripts of the McClellan Committee, Doyle stumbled on a segment of an interview involving a man named Charles Lichtman. It seemed that Lichtman had some jukeboxes in Westchester County that he'd been having trouble with.

Doyle's interest in sneaking out the transcript was his attempt to find out what connection Bender had with the activities now going on in Brooklyn. He was also interested in the history of jukebox unions as they affected the Gallos, who controlled Local 266 of The Associated Music Operators Union, a branch of the Teamsters. This was a union with no members and no union activi-

ties, but bar owners either paid dues to it or faced bad
blood with the Gallos. It was a convenient thing for the
union that Joey Gallo also owned the Direct Vending
Company at 51 President Street, which happened to
control both jukeboxes and pinball machines, a handy
service for the union.

In the McClellan file, Doyle found this passage,
which he Xeroxed.

KENNEDY: Now you still decided you
wanted to get your jukebox union
back and did you go back up there?
LICHTMAN: I went back there a number
of times but I found out that Mr.
Getlan had a pretty good hold on it
because he had brought some mobsters
into the picture.
KENNEDY: You talked to a man named
Valachi?
LICHTMAN: Yes, sir.
KENNEDY: Who is Valachi?
LICHTMAN: I happen to know Valachi
from around Harlem. He thought he
could straighten it up for me.
KENNEDY: He is an associate of
Anthony Strollo, alias "Tony Bender"
and an associate of Vincent Mauro.
He was convicted of violation of
the federal narcotic laws in 1956
and sentenced to five years. He has
seventeen arrests and five
convictions. He told you he could
straighten it out?
LICHTMAN: Yes, sir.
KENNEDY: What happened then?
LICHTMAN: So he had me go up to a
bar on 180th Street and Southern

Boulevard. I sat out front at the
bar.

KENNEDY: Who met at the bar?

LICHTMAN: Well, I met Getlan there
and I saw this Blackie. Then Mr.
Valachi came and they went into the
back room and they had a meeting.

KENNEDY: Who was in the back room?

LICHTMAN: I don't know who else was
there.

KENNEDY: Did you know Jimmy "Blue
Eyes" Alo was in the back room?

LICHTMAN: I didn't see him myself. I
saw Tommy Milo.

KENNEDY: A notorious gangster in
New York?

LICHTMAN: I imagine so.

KENNEDY: They had a meeting as to
who was to control the jukebox
union in Westchester?

LICHTMAN: Yes.

KENNEDY: What did they decide?

LICHTMAN: From what they told me,
from what Valachi told me at the
time, my partner, Jimmy Caggiano,
took $500 and sold me out and for
that reason I couldn't get anything
back no more. You have no racket
connections so you are nobody. You
are out.

KENNEDY: You had Mr. Valachi who has
a pretty good record . . ."

Doyle wondered if he could ever get a chance to connect with Kennedy directly without getting in dutch with
the bureau, and he decided to dig further into Bender's
connection with Vito Genovese, whom he knew fairly

well from his days in the Sixth, and Sam Massey, whose connection with both Bender and Genovese seemed less clear, but whose companies seemed to do a lot of business in the same areas as the two mobsters. Of course, he also had a personal interest in the doings of the Marseri family and their member-by-marriage, Police Lieutenant Pat Conte.

CHAPTER 28

In many ways, Sam Massey, and Pat Conte, as his *braccio destro*—his right arm—were Tony Bender's only solid connection left to the top, that is, to Vito Genovese in his palatial cell in Atlanta, and through Vito to Lansky in Miami and Charlie Lucky, without whom no big deal could be completed.

Bender was probably well aware by now that he was under a shadow for his dealings with the Gallos. Also it was one of his unauthorized dope operations which had led to the arrests which put Don Vitone in Atlanta, along with Valachi, Vinnie Mauro, the Agueci brothers and a few others. Bender couldn't talk to Gerry Catena or Tommy Eboli or Mike Miranda or Jimmy "Blue Eyes" or Richie Boiardi because they were all after the same thing—Don Vitone's seat on the commission, and control of the Genovese family. Each was extending feelers to build up reliable allies when the trouble came.

Of all of them, Sam Massey was probably the cleanest and most respected. He had crossed no one. He was close to Don Vitone. He was friendly with Profaci and Gambino, and he didn't muscle into anybody else's territory. While there had been no official announcement, it was becoming increasingly clear that Pat Conte was *consigliere* to the Marseri family.

Bender, technically, was higher in rank in the organization, but Pat's connections to Don Vitone and to Lucky made him potentially more powerful. Bender was desperately anxious to repair fences at the top level.

The scholarly *capo* invited Pat to join him in one of his Thursday dinners at Luna's.

Pat had already reached a point with Bender where he definitely would not have met him in a dark alley or even in a well-lighted but deserted street. He wasn't sure where Bender was going with his operation, but he was sure he didn't want to be anywhere where he might be under Bender's guns.

Luna's was by tradition a safe spot. It was an accepted thing in the organization that no hits or actions were undertaken in Little Italy. Pat knew that the CIB had a tap on the phone booth at Luna's, and he suspected that the FBI might have run a few suicide bugs into the place. In all probability, Regan Doyle had access to hours of tape recorded in the booth at Luna's. How long, Pat wondered, before his own name was mentioned in some embarrassing context?

Since Bobby Kennedy's takeover of the Attorney General's office, the FBI had been paying much closer attention to the Mafia. They had also been cutting corners on things like illegal bugs in a way that they never had under J. Edgar.

Pat had a feeling that there were stakeouts all over Little Italy now, and he had noticed suspicious trucks on Mulberry Street near the Mulberry SAC. He made a mental note to do research in that area. If Doyle wouldn't leak the information, perhaps he could find out from other sources.

One thing was certain. In a very short time Doyle had become knowledgeable about their operation.

To be on the safe side during his conversation with Bender, Pat brought along a small plastic transistor radio which he kept tuned to a brassy top-ten rock station during the important parts of their conversation.

Bender, scholarly looking, almost aristocratic in his glasses, with a neatly tailored, light gray, glen plaid suit and flowered tie, still ate with the table manners of a fieldhand. He bent over his green fettucine and sucked it into his mouth in a continuous bile-colored river, vacuuming up vagrant strands so that they snapped against his upper lip like rubber bands. Fortunately the white clam sauce gave only a light stain to his jowls. Pat ordered a half bottle of Barolo and a large antipasto.

The lessened physical activity of his new rank had caused him to start bulging slightly at the waistline and he was anxious to avoid the giant portions of pasta that accompanied meals at Luna's.

Pat and Tony Bender made small talk about business and mutual friends, but carefully avoided sensitive areas such as the activities of the Gallos in Brooklyn.

"How's the wife and kid?" Bender said, then blushed. "I mean, everything okay at home?"

Pat smiled with tight lips. "Sure. Everything's great. The wife stays home and looks after the kid and I do what I have to. She tells me next year the kid may learn to wave bye-bye and he's only eight years old."

"Yeah, that's too bad about that," Bender said.

Pat cut the small talk short.

"I got to give a speech on juvenile delinquency at PS 3 a little later," he said, looking at his watch. "Did you want to talk about something?"

"Well, you know," Bender said, "all this trouble everybody's having, it's using up a lot of money. I know Don Vitone must have spent a lot on legal fees and so on, bail money."

"Yeah, yeah," Pat said. "You got some kind of deal?"

"Well, you know that stuff that we brought over, the stuff that's involved in his case?"

"Yeah, I know."

"I got the docket number right here of the evidence. It's only a couple of blocks away over there on Broome Street in the property clerk's office. I got the name of the detective, his badge number and everything on the case."

"Sure. That figures," Pat said. "Wouldn't he take?"

Bender shook his head in disgust. "Lousy fifteen-grand-a-year dick. He could have been set for life."

"So what's this got to do with me?"

"Well, if somebody was to check out that stuff, they could maybe replace it in a few days. I hear what's in the bags doesn't have to be pure to check out as evidence, so who would be hurt?"

Pat speared a hardboiled egg and laid an anchovy across it and popped the half-hemisphere into his mouth. The announcer on the transistor was screaming, "And now for an oldie but goldie! Elvis sings 'You Ain't Nothing but a Hound Dog!'" The pulsing howl of the Memphis wonder made conversation all but impossible except in staccato bursts.

"What kind of money you talking about?"

"Five hundred big ones."

Pat laughed. "You're not even in the ball park. You know what that stuff goes for. Besides, we don't even like to handle white stuff."

"This is different. You're just moving it maybe a couple of miles and there'll be no record of anything happening."

"One big one is the price," Pat said.

Both he and Bender knew that that was the price in the first place. It was just part of Bender's game to try to undercut it.

"All cash, right?" Pat said. "Clean money."

"Of course."

"Okay. Where do we make the switch?"

"How 'bout that little park near Grand Army Plaza in Brooklyn at the foot of Flatbush Avenue?"

"You bringing it?"

"No, I'll send somebody. You pull up on the right

hand side on that block, just before the arch. About 2:00 A.M. tomorrow, okay?"

"Yeah," Pat said. "I don't want to hang onto that any longer than I have to. Who's handling the switch for you?" Pat said. "I want it to be somebody I know."

"You'll know him," Tony said. "It's Hal—you know the guy that works at Louie's sometimes."

"Yeah, I know the guy. Will he be alone?"

"He'll have a driver with him. They'll pull up behind you and blink the lights three times. You'll know it's them and, of course, you'll recognize Hal."

He wiped up a bit of olive oil with the fresh Italian bread and stood up, leaving most of the tuna fish and pimentos on his plate.

"You didn't finish," Bender said. "That's good stuff."

"That's okay," Pat said. "I gotta get to my lecture. You'll take care of the tab, won't you?"

"Sure, sure," Bender said. "What do you think?"

"Okay. *Ciao*, baby."

The property clerk's office, where most of the evidence collected in Manhattan was held pending trial was on the second floor in the Police Headquarters Annex on Broome Street, practically around the corner from Luna's. There was a series of counters, and dozens of cops, detectives and plainclothesmen were waiting at the small, narrow windows to pick up bits of evidence for upcoming court cases or to return evidence that they'd taken out. A sign over the window read, "All hand guns and narcotics before 10:00 A.M., next window."

Another sign read, "New property will be invoiced before 9:30 a.m."

But upper-rank cops and detectives didn't pay attention to those signs, and the clerks, some of them on the rubber-gun squad—cops who'd had their pistols taken away for various emotional problems—were not about to buck a gold-shield.

The evidence was jammed into a 50 x 100-foot room that looked like somebody's attic—manila evidence envelopes stuffed into metal bins in rows of floor to ceiling shelves. Toward the back of the room, a 30 x 30-foot area was enclosed with heavy cyclone wire. The only items stored in that enclosure were narcotics, cash and pornography.

Pat wore a battered brown fedora, pulled low, and an old raincoat he'd picked up in somebody's apartment following a burglary. The clerk, barely looking up, shoved the sign-out book at him and he signed Detective First Grade Regan Doyle with the Badge No. 3764. In the rush of activities, the clerks barely looked at the men as they withdrew the property. It was assumed that anybody who knew how to act like a cop and sign the right name and figures must have been kosher. Even then, the clerk gave him a sharp look as he handed over the seventy-five-pound bulging, fiberboard suitcase.

Pat had spent the morning shopping in various supermarkets and discount houses. He'd bought a couple of plastic mixing bowls, a flour sifter, twenty-five five-pound bags of confectioner's sugar and seventy-five plastic half-kilo bags in different places in order not to attract too much attention.

By noon, Pat was locked into the dressing room of one of Sam Massey's construction trailers near the Major Deegan Thruway in the East Bronx. Carefully, he measured one pound of sugar into the mixing bowl and then a heaping teaspoon of the crystalline white powder on top of it. This he mixed vigorously together then sifted through the flour sifter and poured carefully into the new plastic bags. The tablespoon of heroin in the half kilo of sugar was just enough to pass the standard Police Department Marquis Reagent Test for the presence of heroin.

In addition to the mixing bowls, Pat had bought a pair of long, rubber kitchen gloves so that he would leave no prints on the inside of the plastic bags when he was filling them, and wore a gauze mask over his nose and mouth so that he wouldn't get stoned himself before he was finished doing the mixing.

Over his natty houndstooth sports jacket and whipcord pants, he put a pair of construction coveralls that were hanging on a hook in the locker room. Later he threw them into the hamper with the rest of the clothes headed for the linen service, to be picked up in the morning.

Though it was Bender's idea, he was surprised he hadn't thought of it before himself. It was almost perfect, because once the material was used as evidence in the trial, it would be destroyed. Since the test would show that there was indeed heroin in the bags, nobody would ever be questioned about it. Even if somebody should discover that the bags were filled largely with sugar, there would be no way of establishing that this was not what was in them in the first place, when they were seized as evidence.

Carefully, Pat packed the bags of sugar-and-heroin mixture back into the shabby, fiberglass suitcase and buckled it. He packed the bags with the real heroin into four TWA flight bags he'd bought in a discount shop that afternoon.

Just before closing time, he stopped by Broome Street again and checked the fiberboard suitcase back into the property clerk's office. It had been gone less than eight hours.

The hundred and fifty half-kilo bags of real heroin lay nestled comfortably in the back of the white Capri.

CHAPTER 29

There were some things about the arrangement that didn't appeal to Pat very much. He didn't like the idea of sitting there on the street, unprotected, with a million dollars' worth of white powder in his trunk waiting for the pickup. The temptation was too great. He decided to bring another man in on the deal to be safe. Tommy, Sam's chauffeur, seemed the right man for the job. He called him that afternoon and told him he had a chauffeuring job for him and would pay $200 for the night's work. Tommy was glad to pick up an extra buck moonlighting.

Sam, who was in on the action, okayed the employment of his chauffeur. At 1:30 A.M., with Tommy behind the wheel of the Capri, Pat circled the park. At the end of the park was the giant archway reminiscent of Paris's Arc de Triomphe and beyond it, the Brooklyn Museum.

The Grand Army Plaza was nearly empty at this time—only an occasional bartender returning home or some late partyers. Most of the lights in the swank apartments around the plaza were out. Brooklyn was sleeping. As they circled the block, they saw nobody except a few dog walkers. Pat looked each of them over carefully and decided that they were not likely to be connected to the pickup.

Tommy, of course, had no idea what the caper was about. He was strictly there to drive. It was not his habit to ask questions. After circling the block twice, Pat had

Tommy drive back two blocks behind the plaza and slowly advance up Flatbush Avenue as he checked each of the parked cars at the curb, shining a flashlight inside to see if there were anybody concealed there. At the same time, he shined the flashlight into the doorways of the stores along the street.

When he was sure that all was clear, he had Tommy park the Capri under the street light, just before the traffic signal leading into the Grand Army Plaza. Then, he went around to the trunk where the flight bags of white powder were cached and checked them out once more.

Lying on top of the bags was a handmade Parker shotgun, a present from Sam, and one he used frequently on his hunting trips to Ancramdale. There was a shell in each chamber loaded with heavy deer shot. Pat took the shotgun out of the trunk and pocketed a half-dozen additional shells. A .38 was a good weapon, but at that distance Pat preferred the shotgun.

He stationed himself behind the iron fence, near the gate, concealed by overhanging forsythia bushes. It was still fifteen minutes before time. Pat squatted on his heels behind the fence, waiting.

Tommy sat listening to WABC until Pat signaled him to turn the radio down so they could hear any approaching sounds.

At precisely 2:00 A.M., a black Buick sedan came cruising up the long, empty stretch of Flatbush Avenue. Without hesitation, it steered slowly and smoothly to the curb behind the white Capri. The lights flashed three times and Tommy, following instructions, opened the door and got out of the car, standing next to the Capri. At the same time, the doors of the Buick opened and a man got out on each side. The one on the right was small and wiry, the other, tall and lithe but with bulky shoulders. Both wore fedoras and dark business suits. Both had pistols in their hands.

The little man who had gotten out on the passenger side spoke.

"Who are you? You're not Conte!"

"I'm *with* Conte," Tommy said.

"Where's Conte?"

"Right here," Pat said, and stepped out from behind the fence with the shotgun leveled.

They turned in surprise. Pat noticed that both were wearing silk-stocking masks. As the men turned toward Pat, Tommy reached into the waistband of his trousers and pulled out a big Army .45 automatic. But before he could level it, the big man whirled and dropped the bulky, crew-cut chauffeur with one shot in the left eye.

Tommy fell beside the Capri without a sound. Before the big man could get his balance, Pat tore half his throat and one side of his head away with a blast from the Parker and swung the barrel over to cover the smaller man who was cringing next to the open car door.

"Okay, throw the gun out," Pat said.

Already he could hear windows raising on the plaza opposite. There was sure to be a police call any minute. He wondered why they had not chosen a more isolated place for the meeting.

"Come around here behind the car," Pat said, pointing to the back of the Capri's trunk.

"Take it easy, Conte," the man said. "Take it easy. Everything can be arranged." His voice was muffled by the pressure of the silk stocking on his lips, but the voice sounded familiar.

Pat moved quickly around past the man to the side of the car.

"Okay," he said. "Now face me."

The man turned around, standing behind the white Capri now and next to the trunk. As he turned, there was another roar as the second shell from the Parker shotgun left a hole in the small man's chest as big as a grapefruit. He fell over backwards, reeling into the shiny grill of the parked black Buick.

Pat ran to the other car and took a fast look at the interior. There was a black, chromium-trimmed attaché case on the seat where the driver had been. Pat reached in and grabbed the case. It was not locked. When he opened it, he saw several bundles of bills topped with hundred-dollar bills. He pulled one out of the suitcase and riffled through it. It was a Chicago roll. Everything was newspaper, except for the bills on top.

There were twelve bundles on the top. Pat smiled grimly. What a stupid con. The case could not have held a million dollars anyway. He never would have been fooled.

At this point, Pat could only hope that nobody had been watching the proceedings from a window. The building immediately facing the park was largely offices and the cars were protected from the apartment house on the far side of the park by the foliage of the tall trees. Still, there might have been witnesses. There was nothing much Pat could do about that.

Moving quickly, he opened the trunk of the Capri and took out the flight bags. He swung around to the front of the car. The top was down. He lifted the rear seat and into the space under it quickly threw as many bags of the white powder as he could fit.

There were still twenty bags left. The ten kilos were worth a fortune. They had a street value of a half million dollars, but there was nothing to be done but sacrifice them.

Pat distributed the remaining plastic bags in the flight bags. He quickly ran over and threw all of these bags, empty and partly full, into the back of the Buick. Already he could hear the whine of approaching sirens and he knew there would be no way to get away without taking a big risk of running into a patrol car.

From the far side of the plaza, he could see two cars racing toward the corner and another one could be heard coming up Flatbush Avenue.

Within five minutes the entire broad stretch of the Avenue was clogged with patrol cars. Pat stood there and held his gold shield where the light could hit it.

"Lieutenant Conte here on the job," he said to the sergeant that first approached him.

Pat had been thinking furiously the whole time the cars approached him as to what he would say. Subconsciously, even during the battle, he had been laying the ground for an alibi and he had it down fairly well.

"I was following up on some work I was doing for the CIB," Pat said, "and I had a meet with an informant on this corner at 2:00 A.M., but before I could meet the informant, this Buick pulled up behind me, two men got out, shot my driver, and ordered me to climb into the trunk. Fortunately, I still was carrying the shotgun—it's over there in the trunk now—that I use for hunting and I was able to whirl and shoot both of the men before they were able to get me."

The policemen whistled in admiration. "Pretty lucky, I would say."

"You said it," Pat said.

"And *some* shooting!"

"Well, when you're up against it, there's not much choice, is there?"

"Say, you're Conte, the hero cop. Isn't that what they call you?"

"That's right," Pat said, smiling.

"Boy, this one ought to get a pretty big play."

"I hope not," Pat said. "I've had enough publicity already."

"No way you're going to avoid it," the sergeant said. "We'd better call the detectives."

"That's right," Pat said. "Call Brooklyn North. I'll wait here. You can let some of those cars go."

"Okay, lieutenant," the sergeant said and went to pass on Pat's instructions.

"Hey, how many stiffs you got here?" he said.

"You got three DOA's," Pat said, "my driver and the two hoods."

"Do you know who they are?"

"Not yet," Pat said. "They still got masks on."

"What do you think they were after?"

Pat shrugged. "Who knows with these guys? Maybe they wanted to get even with me for something I've done to them, some collar I planned, or maybe they didn't even know who I was and just spotted the car and figured I was good for a hit."

"It's really weird," the sergeant said. "It's really weird."

CHAPTER 30

Pat engaged in a brief discussion with the sergeant.

"I think we better leave everything the way it is," he said, "until the detectives get here. This case is going to raise a lot of hell. We've got three DOA's here and Christ knows who those hoods were, but they were pros."

"Who was the guy with you?" the sergeant asked.

"He was a friend of my father-in-law's just helping out," Pat said.

Within fifteen minutes, detectives were on the scene, along with a couple of men from D. A. Aaron Koota's office. A gunfight with three dead men was not an everyday occurrence, even in Brooklyn. In the background, Pat could see a black Plymouth pulling up and parking on the far side of Flatbush Avenue. Two men in raincoats and snap-brim hats got out and showed some credentials to the cop screening people from the scene of the crime.

As the men moved under the yellow glare of the street light, Pat could see that the taller of the two was Doyle. He was still busy assembling the story he would tell the detectives in his head, making sure that there was nothing to trip him up. But what was Doyle doing here? There didn't seem to be any federal rap involved.

After some discussion, the cop on duty let the two FBI men through the cordon.

Doyle headed straight for Pat.

"What's up, Pat, my boy?"

Pat shrugged.

"Beats me. Just one of those weird unexpected beefs."

"You get into a lot of those, don't you?"

"What's that supposed to mean? Don't break my balls, Doyle. This has been a tough night."

"I thought you were with the CIB. What are you doing over here this time of night?"

"Are you interrogating me? You got no business on this case, Doyle. Go back to your earphones."

"Don't get mad, Pat. Just asking, one friend to another, right?" Doyle flashed a broad smile of complete innocence.

"What are *you* doing here, is more the question?" Pat said.

"We been doing a lot of checking on organized crime, Pat. You know that. Duncan here is from the federal narcotics team. We sort of work together. Heard there might be a dope angle on this."

"Are you trying to jerk me around, or something?" Pat said suspiciously.

Doyle looked surprised. But he was overacting it, Pat thought.

"Christ no, Pat! Just trying to keep in touch. You'll fill me in on any details I need later, I suppose. Don't forget you owe me a couple now."

Pat said nothing for a moment.

"I'll get to you soon, Doyle. Meanwhile I'm busy."

By this time at least a dozen marked and unmarked cars were blocking the streets. The last to arrive was an unmarked Ford coupe. A stubby moon-faced figure got out of the car with a detective's badge pinned to the outside of his jacket.

Pat left the two feds and sauntered over to where the Ford had parked. The moon-faced detective and another man who had been riding with him headed straight for the Capri and Buick around which the three corpses were scattered. The shorter man's waddling gait and the pale, perspiring face behind the steel-rimmed glasses stirred Pat's memory. It was Harry Hoffman, his old duty sergeant from Elizabeth Street. Pat waved as Hoffman approached.

"Harry, you old son-of-a-bitch. What are you doing here? You in Detectives now?"

"That's right," Harry said. "Captain, Brooklyn North."

"What's up? This official?" Pat asked.

"Well, not yet. Just trying to get the picture. Looks like you're in for another medal, huh? You fuck!" Hoffman laughed, mirthlessly.

Pat now remembered that Hoffman was something of a gung-ho, straight-arrow type. It was probable that he'd come up fast because of the succession of Steve Kennedy to the Police Commissioner's post.

"I haven't got the picture straight in my own head yet," Pat said, speaking slowly and carefully. "I had a meet with an informant here by the park. They told me to wait near this traffic light and that I would get some information for a good collar."

"How come you didn't turn it over to Brooklyn?" Hoffman said, matter-of-factly.

Pat laughed. "Listen, would you? I got this from an informant that I developed myself. I'm not turning him over to anybody. Besides, I figured it might have some connection with some of the stuff I've been doing with CIB."

"I thought you were detached from active duty there doing public relations stuff," Hoffman said.

Pat grinned. "Once a cop, always a cop. You don't think that I'm just going to go around making speeches for the rest of my life? That's just temporary duty."

"Ah-huh," Hoffman grunted, taking out his

notebook. "Well, let's get a rough idea of what the picture is. How many DOA's you got here, anyway? I heard on the radio there were three."

"That's right," Pat said. "My driver and these two apes over by the Buick."

"Your driver on the job?" Hoffman asked.

"No. He works for my father-in-law. This was something I was chasing down on my own."

Hoffman's pale eyes, the color of faded denim, surveyed him coolly from behind the steel-rimmed glasses.

"This whole thing's a little bit irregular, isn't it?" he asked.

"A good cop's got to make some street decisions, doesn't he?" Pat said.

"Okay. Just give me the rough outline of the story for the moment. We'll have the lab people go over everything and we'll take a full statement down at headquarters."

"Sure," Pat said. "Well, I pulled up and I was waiting for this informant when the black Buick pulled up behind me. I got out and Tommy, the driver, got out to see who it was, and these two guys got out and threw down on us. Tommy went for his gun—he had a licensed pistol—he runs payrolls for my father-in-law sometimes. I mean he *used* to. And the big guy guns him down.

"It happened so fast, I didn't even have a chance to go for my own piece, so they frisked me and they made me open the trunk of my car and I don't know whether they were going to knock me off and stuff me in the trunk or just stuff me in the trunk and take me for a ride. But I had this 12-gauge Parker in there that I use for deer up at my country place."

"Deer season is next month," Hoffman said.

"Yeah, but you can hunt deer on your own land," Pat said, "and sometimes I get after them when they start bothering my apple trees up there in Columbia County."

"Yeah, so what happened?" Hoffman said. His voice didn't sound like that of an old friend from early police rookie days. It sounded more like a cop dealing with a perpetrator.

"Listen," Pat said, "don't lean on me. I nearly got fucking killed!"

"Right," Hoffman said, "but this is a serious case. There's going to be a lot of heat on. Three stiffs. You don't find that every day."

"Okay. So I turned around and I couldn't see inside the trunk. It's dark there. So I grabbed the shotgun and let go as fast as I could and that was it."

"Wait a minute," Hoffman said. "Let me get this straight. The shotgun was loaded, with shells in it?"

Pat hesitated. He knew that was a tough one, but there was no other way he could explain it.

"Yeah, I carry it around that way sometimes. Frankly, on a job like this, you never know what's going to come up, and if it ain't loaded, it's not much use."

"You mean you weren't carrying it just for deer?"

Pat smiled and shrugged.

"And you whipped around and hit these two guys who were holding guns on you before they could squeeze off a shot?"

"The Parker has a hair trigger," Pat said, "and I had heavy shot in there. It shoots a pretty big pattern. Those guys had just frisked me and they weren't expecting anything. Anyway, how do I know? I don't even know the guys. Maybe they were doped up or something."

The other detective, the one that had been driving Hoffman, had been prowling around, looking over the scene of the crime. Using a handkerchief carefully to avoid smudging any possible prints, he had opened the rear door of the Buick. As he unzipped the first of the TWA flight bags, he gave an involuntary shout.

"Holy shit! Hey, captain, come here. Look at this!"

Hoffman and Pat both strode rapidly over to the

Buick. The detective, a short, dark, native Brooklynite by his accent, held out the open bag with the half-kilo plastic sacks of white powder inside of it.

"Get a load of this! If that isn't shit, I never saw it, and what a load!"

Hoffman stuck his head inside the car, casing the other bags.

"I'm taking possession of this stuff," he said, carrying it over to his car. "I don't want to leave it lying around here. This is turning into some case!"

"You're not kidding," the dark detective said. He had just opened the attaché case, still on the front seat of the Buick.

"Dig this!" He shined his flashlight on the open case.

Hoffman whistled in surprise. "Bring that out here but handle it carefully," he said, "and remember where it was."

The dark detective brought the case out and laid it on the hood of the Buick. He took out one of the packs of bills and riffled it.

"Phony," he said with disgust.

"What do you mean?" Hoffman asked. "Counterfeit?"

"No, no. But there's only one bill on the top and the rest is just paper."

"This thing gets weirder and weirder," Hoffman said.

"It sure does," Pat agreed.

Hoffman turned to him. "Now why would these guys with a car full of shit want to hit you and what are they carrying that bag full of funny money around for?"

Pat shrugged. "Don't ask me. I was just a target, but I figure somebody set me up to get hit. There's a lot of guys who hate my guts, you know."

Hoffman looked at him speculatively. "I guess there are."

"Maybe this informant double-crossed me. Maybe he tipped these guys off that I was going to hijack them.

Maybe they didn't even know I was a cop."

"Or maybe they *did* know and still thought you were going to hijack them," Hoffman said.

"Yeah, well, that could happen too."

A station wagon pulled up at this point with the crime lab equipment from Brooklyn North and a team of four men scattered all over the area, outlining the dead bodies in chalk, dusting the cars for prints, photographing the bodies for position.

Hoffman scratched his short, grizzled hair.

"This thing's weirder than a Coney Island sideshow," Hoffman said. "Look, it's late. Why don't we wait till the detectives get all this lab stuff together and you come over to Brooklyn tomorrow. We'll get the full statement on this. Of course, you know we'll have to book you on manslaughter charges till we get this straightened out."

"Yeah, I been through it a few times," Pat said.

"Well, with the publicity you'll get out of this one, you could be running for mayor by next year," Hoffman said, and Pat thought there was some bitterness in his voice.

"I could do without it," Pat said.

CHAPTER 31

Lieutenant Arthur Marseri thought Pat could go all the way with the Brooklyn shoot-out—the Medal of Honor, highest award in the department.

Pat's commanding officer, Deputy Chief Inspector John Brady of the CIB agreed, and had Pat write up the incident and submit it for consideration to the Honors Committee.

"They're a tough bunch, but we'll use whatever suction we've got. Generally speaking, if you pass the screening committee, you don't get much static on the top level," Arthur said. They were sipping iced tea on the rear terrace of Pat's house in Riverdale.

"Who's on the committee?" Pat asked.

Arthur counted them on his fingers.

"*Uno*, the First Deputy Commissioner. That's George Colby. He's a political appointee and will go any way the wind blows. *Due*, Johnny Behan is Chief of Detectives now. He's a friend of ours. You met him at Father Raimundo's wingding years ago. In fact, it was the night you met Connie. You can count on his vote. *Tre*, Chief of the Organized Crime Division, Ben Mann. He's in our pocket too. I gave him every big case he ever cracked. It was one of the ways we kept Sam Massey's name clean all these years. The Chief of Field Services, that's Seamus Doyle—Regan's uncle. You'd know better than me which way he'd go."

"Funny thing is that I *don't*. In the beginning, Doyle was friendly as a puppy, but lately he's been acting very

438

suspicious. I think he's after us. This family specifically. I'd say no on that one."

"Haven't you got anything you can use on him?"

Pat mulled the idea.

"He's such a fucking straight arrow. I don't think you could nail him for stealing pencils from the front desk, but I'll think about it. What's so hot about me getting this one anyway? I got enough medals now to sink a fucking barge. I can't make captain for at least a couple of years. . . ."

"I've been checking. Do you realize that if you get this one, you'll be the most decorated man in the department?"

Pat looked pleased.

"No kidding?"

Arthur was serious.

"You know, you got the law degree now. That's something I never had. The family has been bugging me for a while that it's time we got you working at something better, more substantial . . ."

"Like what?"

"You're already one of the best-known cops in the city. This one will make you a hero. In a little while maybe we could start thinking about some kind of job in government, maybe even an elective office."

"Shooting high, aren't you?"

Arthur threw him a cynical glance.

"Don't kid me, Pat. I've known you too long. You've been hinting at that for years. And I think you're right. You're made for it. Those speeches and TV spots you did for the department, they were good stuff. You got a good record, you can hold a crowd, you're active in the Columbia Society and the Italian-American Defense League. You make a good appearance. You're a family man—and most important, when you make your move you will have a strong organization and a limitless campaign fund behind you. Can you lose with cards like that?"

Pat looked thoughtful.

"In all due modesty," he said, "I have to admit you're right—and that the thought has crossed my mind in the past. What's the next move?"

"First, let's get the medal. Then we wait and see where's the best spot to get your feet wet."

But the problem was more complex than Arthur imagined. The Honors Committee had delegated a committee under Detective Captain Harry Hoffman to investigate the request of Pat's commanding officer that Pat Conte be given the Medal of Honor.

Hoffman had been working on the case for more than a month, and he had the feeling that there were many loose unexplained ends. In his mind, the problem wasn't whether Pat should get the medal. It was whether Pat should be indicted for murder one.

Also on the committee were Captain Donald McQuade of the Traffic Division, and Captain Edward Weber of Emergency Services.

Three weeks after Pat's application for the Medal of Honor went in, he was summoned to a meeting with the Honors Screening Committee at headquarters on Centre Street.

Pat realized that before he met with the group, he would have to do a lot of homework. He went over his story (which had been reduced to a written report) with meticulous precision, closing all possible gaps of logic or evidence. It still came out with a lot of tough questions to answer, and Pat was sure that Harry Hoffman would ask them. It was time to do some research in the little library of black notebooks in which over the years Pat had been jotting valuable information about fellow members of the force.

The night before the meeting, Pat pulled aside the rug

and lifted the bit of parquet covering his concrete floor safe.

At four in the morning, he was still poring over the scrawled notations. He was pretty sure he had the right handle for Captain Harry Hoffman, and McQuade would be duck soup, but what could he get on Weber?

At 4:15 Connie wandered in, still half asleep.

"What are you doing, banging around down here at this hour?" she asked drowsily.

Pat closed the notebook he was working on and made a halfhearted effort to throw some papers over the others.

"Don't worry yourself. It's just some research for my hearing tomorrow."

"Why do you need so much research? It isn't a court trial. What are all those little books?"

"They're my notebooks. Now go to sleep," Pat said, impatiently.

"I don't see why you need all that material just for a little hearing. I never even saw those little books before."

"For Christ's sake!" Pat snapped. "Will you go to sleep and stop bugging me?"

"I'll go," Connie said, serenely, "but I know one thing. Whatever you're doing down here has nothing to do with medals for heroism."

She turned and left. After another twenty minutes, Pat, exhausted, copied the essential material he needed, returned the books to their repository, and went up to his room, still stuck on the problem of Captain Weber. He had almost fallen asleep, the problem still tumbling about in his lower consciousness, when it came to him. Weber was Tom Berkholder's rabbi! He was also Tom's uncle! Throwing the covers aside, Pat trotted downstairs, threw open the trapdoor, and searched for his earliest notebooks, the ones dating back to his patrol

days with Tom. With excitement, he scribbled several
pages of notes, replaced the book, and went upstairs to
catch a few hours of sleep before the sun came up.

The next day, he made it a point to arrive at headquarters an hour before his ten o'clock appointment. He
hoped he would be able to get to one or two of the committee members before the hearing, but they all apparently arranged to arrive at the last moment.

The meeting was held in a large conference room on
the third floor, generally used for upper-level
departmental hearings.

The four police officers sat around a yellow oak table
with manila folders in front of them containing Pat's
written statement on the shootout in Brooklyn, plus his
commanding officer's recommendations concerning the
medal. The three captains apparently had reports based
on interrogation of various witnesses. There were also
detective reports on various other points investigated.
Hoffman led the questioning. The other two just listened
and took notes.

```
HOFFMAN: We are all impressed with
your decorations and credits,
Lieutenant Conte, and wish to give
full attention to this here
application for the Medal of Honor,
but we got a few questions regarding
the incident. First: What in hell
were you doing at Grand Army Plaza
at 1:00 a.m.?
CONTE: I told you, I was meeting
an informant.
HOFFMAN: There is no record of
your being involved in any current
investigation.
CONTE: I had no idea what the
informant wanted to tell me, but I
```

felt it was worthwhile to hear him.

HOFFMAN: Why did you have a civilian driver on your personal payroll at the wheel?

CONTE: I explained in my application, I believe, that I did not want to involve the department officially unless I knew what the case was all about.

HOFFMAN: I see . . . Now about the Lincoln. Was it yours?

CONTE: It is the property of Mr. Al Santini, a businessman.

HOFFMAN: How come you were using it?

CONTE: He is a friend of the family. He often loans it to me if I need a vehicle.

HOFFMAN: Isn't it true that this is actually your own car?

CONTE: No. It's just that Mr. Santini is a generous and kind friend.

HOFFMAN: How do you explain the dope and the money in the other car?

CONTE: I have no idea what that stuff was doing there, sir. Maybe my informant was setting somebody up for a collar.

HOFFMAN: Frankly, Conte, and off the record, this whole thing stinks and so does your story. I think you knocked those guys off and . . .

CONTE: Wait a minute, captain. If you have any charges, you better make them. This is a hearing on my medal, remember. What would I want to knock those guys off for, anyway?

The dope was still in the car,
wasn't it, and the money? Ten kilos,
I believe.
HOFFMAN: <u>Five</u> kilos, I should know.
My man took it out of the car and
we weighed it together.
CONTE: Oh?

The interrogation went around like this for more than
an hour, with neither side scoring any major points.
Hoffman finally adjourned the hearings, pending further
investigation. As the superior officers filed from the
room, Hoffman took Pat aside confidentially.

"Conte, I'm gonna get your ass on this. If you think I
buy that line of bullshit, you're crazy. You've been
working with the mob ever since you've been on the
force. I was wise to you on that first job in the Sixth in
the luncheonette. But this time we're gonna get you
good. I'm gonna nail you on murder one on this one."

Pat remained impassive.

"I tell you what, captain. If you're determined to
follow that line, let's step back into the hearing room,
and I'll give you some material that might help with
your decision."

Puzzled, the stocky officer followed Pat back to the
table, where Pat again opened his folder. With reference
to notes, letters and documents, he clearly explained to
Hoffman that first it would be a very bad mark on
Hoffman's record: if it became public that Norman
Hoffman, Meyer Lansky's man in Havana, was Hoffman's brother. Furthermore, Hoffman had taken at
least three paid-for vacations at the Hotel Nacional, and
had been seen gambling at the $500 table in Sans Souci,
once during the time he was supposedly taking a special
training course with the FBI in Washington.

And finally, there were *ten* kilos, not five, in the

Buick in Brooklyn. Hoffman's assistant, Sergeant Archie Bonner, had bought a new house in Valley Stream for cash two weeks after the incident, and a Mercedes sedan. If heat were applied to Sergeant Bonner, it is possible that he might crack and tell the source of his sudden wealth.

"In view of this new evidence, Hoffman," Pat said, closing his folder, "I think you better rethink your whole approach. And believe me, there is more where this came from."

Pat left the room without waiting for Hoffman's answer.

Leaving headquarters, he stopped in at the B & G Coffee Shop on Broome Street. Captain Edward Weber of Emergency Services was having an order of waffles and bacon. Pat slipped into the booth opposite him. Weber looked up with annoyance.

"Yes?"

"I just wanted to ask you about my old pal, Tom. I used to ride with him, you know. Understand he's a sergeant now in Manhattan South."

Weber grunted, slicing the waffles into precise squares.

"We had some terrific times there in the fifties riding the car in the Sixth. I wonder if Tom still has those same habits. I mean, there was a lot about the special Village life that he liked, if you know what I mean."

Weber looked up angrily.

"What are you trying to pull, Conte?"

"Your nephew's a fag, and I can prove it."

Weber nearly strangled on his breakfast.

"Aaarg! You filthy sonovabitch!"

"Take it easy, captain. That isn't the worst part. I got a list of payoffs and contracts he was involved in that would pop blood vessels at the Internal Affairs Division. But the worst part I was saving. Tom Berkholder could go up on murder one for beating one of his fag friends to death and throwing him off a roof. Ask him. Of course, we might not prove the case, but it would definitely be in the papers. I can guarantee that. Enjoy your breakfast. And about that Medal of Honor hearing, I'm sure all of your questions will be straightened out."

Pat had one more member of the screening committee to see. He met Captain McQuade in the lobby of the New York Athletic Club, where he had been keeping in shape with a few sets of squash.

"You realize that it is very unethical for you to see me separately like this. It would look as though you were trying to influence me."

"Don't be silly, captain. It's just that I ran across some records in my files concerning your nephew—what's his name—you know, the actor in the Village? You might just want to look them over. Of course, these are just stats from the official files . . ."

Pat handed over five pages of citations concerning police calls to various apartments occupied by young McQuade, including notations from the investigating officers' notebooks concerning narcotics, orgies, homosexuality and excessive noise.

"Just a little light reading for your off hours, captain," Pat said evenly. "Of course, I regard this information as confidential—for the present."

The captain sat red-faced looking through the dozens of listings complete with dates, times and names of investigating officers.

"Well," Pat said, "I got to be going. You're in great shape, captain. I understand that squash is a terrific conditioner."

There was still one hurdle before getting an okay for the award, and that was the Honors Committee. In general, the committee would accept the recommendations of the screening committee. But Chief Seamus Doyle was a question mark.

Pat tried for several days to see him in some personal or informal fashion. But the chief was a man of rigid formality. Finally Pat simply went up to his office on Centre Street and announced that he was outside with some important information. After a pause and some discussion with the sergeant acting as secretary, Pat was shown into the spacious office on the third floor of Headquarters building.

Doyle was cool. He sat behind his desk in his dark gray flannel civilian suit with the Emerald Society tie, a pencil in his hand and a legal pad before him.

"What can I do for you, lieutenant? I don't have a hell of a lot of time."

"You know who I am?"

"I read the papers."

"You know that I am also a first cousin to your nephew, Regan?"

"What's that got to do with the price of potatoes?"

"In my opinion, your nephew is out to get my ass. I would rather talk about this someplace else, but if you want it here, that's okay with me."

"So what if he is? Is your ass holy or something? You're in the mob up to your neck. You think we don't know that? If it takes the feds to nail you, that's okay too. Jesus, and they got *you* of all people up for the Medal of Honor! I'll tell you this, Conte, there's not a chance as long as I'm on that committee."

"Exactly what do you want from me, Doyle—*Chief* Doyle?"

"I want you out of this department—dishonorably, if possible. I want your ass on a murder one indictment or whatever we can get. You are a filthy stain on this department's honor."

Pat allowed a small, chilly grin to play over his face.

"Commissioner, you haven't got the luck of the Irish going for you on this one. You, in fact, have nothing.

The screening committee is going to recommend the medal. They are not going to find a single thing on me. I'm clean. But I'll make you a deal."

"I don't make deals with . . ."

"I'll swap Regan's career and rep for the medal plus an honorable discharge as this department's most decorated policeman, plus an A-1 reference and character rating."

"You're crazy!"

Pat reached into his flat calfskin portfolio and extracted a set of photostated notes.

"Regan Doyle on a certain date, which I have here, assaulted a police officer, impersonated a New York City detective, used his credentials for personal reasons, and spent that same evening with an unmarried woman, one Katie Mullaley, in an apartment on Eleventh Street. I can prove all of that with witnesses and documents. Not too terrible, you might say. But you and I know that is enough to get him dismissal with prejudice from the FBI, with no chance at another job in law enforcement or security. That would hurt him a lot."

"You'd do that to your own cousin, and to . . . that girl, a girl that has been your friend for years?"

Pat laughed. "Don't give me that cousin crap. You guys did everything but drain Regan's blood to try to get rid of the Italian corpuscles in his veins. And Regan—he's been making a career out of trying to nail my ass and the rest of my family's too. That's hardly cousinly.

"Anyway, that's the deal. Take it or leave it. I'll know when I get the medal that everything's okay. But don't forget, it's a good deal for you. You get me off the force anyway, and there's no way you can make any of that other shit stick. If you *could* you would have shoved it up and broken it off long ago.

"Good afternoon, chief," Pat said, saluting sharply. "Thanks for your time."

CHAPTER 32

Sam usually ate dinner with Pat and Connie on Fridays. On these nights, Constanza would take over the cooking chores from Esperanza, and, away from the need for status seeking and big impressions, they would enjoy a simple Italian meal, usually spinach and bacon salad, followed by *linguine* with white clam sauce and *veal alla piccata,* one of Sam's favorites. For dessert, Constanza would whip up marsala and eggs into a frothy *zabaglione.*

For this occasion, the Friday after the presentation of the Medal of Honor, Sam had brought a bottle of Asti Spumante.

The conversation, as always when Connie was present, tended to be fitful and lurching, overshadowed always by Connie's martyrdom to her son, Sebastian, and to the image of him sitting in his box upstairs, grinning, drooling and endlessly batting a spinning wooden toy that hung over his crib.

Connie had long since stopped asking Sam to come up and look at his grandson. His attempts at interest and sympathy were too transparently clumsy to be anything but painful. Occasionally, Sam would ask questions like, "Is there anything I can do? Money is no object if we can help the boy." But Pat had explained time and again that with Down's Syndrome there was no hope.

Nevertheless, Connie spent endless hours on research and as a volunteer at the National Association for Retarded Children. Unfortunately, most of the work of that organization was devoted to what they called "educable" retarded, and Sebastian was not in that exalted rank.

"Still," Sam said to his daughter, "that's wonderful work that you do. Father Donato was telling me the other day that they valued you very much in that organization and at the church, too."

"Sure, Pa," Connie said. "Finish your veal. I'll bring ou the *zabaglione*."

When she went to the kitchen, Sam turned apologetically to Pat.

"I really came to celebrate your medal and to talk over your future, but I suppose this kid thing is her whole life these days."

"That's right," Pat said. "She keeps asking questions and calling in specialists and hoping somehow that what she knows is true can be changed. There's no hope for the kid. We should have put him in an institution long ago, but she says as long as we have the money to keep him at home, he's happier here. I don't know what she means *happier*. The kid barely recognizes me."

"Well, well," Sam said. "She's a mother. You know what mothers are."

They chewed on the fine, white veal thoughtfully and listened to the slapping sound of the beater from the kitchen whipping up the *zabaglione*.

"So what's the deal? Arthur tells me you're leaving the force."

"Well," Pat said, "We kind of agreed on that, but I got a couple of months to decide on what my move will be. I was thinking of maybe starting to practice law. It's about time, but then Arthur said there's a good job for me up in Albany. The commissioner and all the deputy commissioners will recommend me for it. I know that."

"Well," Sam said, "we still have some influence of our own in Albany, not so much through the city here but through Maggadino up in Buffalo. They're all Republicans up there, you know. What's the job?"

"Well, it would be special counsel to the governor on crime in the streets. With my background, I'd be a logical man for the job and I could show how the state programs are helping to cut down on violent crime."

"Good, good," Sam said. "It's getting so a person isn't safe even in his own home. There's entirely too much of this raping and mugging and holdups. It's criminal what's happening now. You could do a lot of good in a job like that. It's about time they started concentrating on what the real crime is and not interfering with a person's legitimate business. But is there any future in this sort of thing? Wouldn't you be better off going into practice right away? You know, we could use you in the organization. I have enough business interests that need the services of a good lawyer. We have connections with some top law firms."

Pat sliced into the tender meat thoughtfully.

"I tell you, Ba. I'd like to get together with you and Don Antonio, Father Ray. I have some ideas. With Kennedy stirring things up in Washington and all the new laws that apply to a lot of our work, I think it's time we had somebody in Washington, somebody we could depend on."

Sam looked up with interest.

"The Democrats wouldn't put me up at present, not with Wagner in charge and DeSapio out of power, and, of course, we've had our trouble with DeSapio anyway, but I think with the publicity I've gotten and the publicity I can get in this job, we can create an independent candidacy and run me for Congress next election."

"You think so?" Sam said, doubtfully.

"We can get help from all around the state. Maggadino has friends in the upstate region. Here in New York, we can count on other friends. Lucchese has a lot of political power. Costello wouldn't help us, but he can give good advice still. The Italian vote we know we'll get, and I've been working with the Italian groups anyway for a couple of years now. The Jews are getting worried about all the nigger crimes and they're beginning to turn. They used to be all civil rights and live-and-let-live, but now that their own schools and neighborhoods are threatened, they're getting worried. They'll go for a law-and-order candidate like me."

"It would take money," Sam said.

"I've got a pretty good kitty myself. That last deal was a very good profit, you know."

"Yes, yes," Sam said.

"And I thought we could get a little help elsewhere. After all, everybody wants a friend in Washington."

"Oh, yes, you could get help, a lot of help," Sam said. "I don't think you'll have to go down into your pocket."

Connie came in with the tray and the three steaming *zabagliones*. Sam pulled the Spumante from the silver cooler and opened it with a resounding pop, pouring the bubbling clear wine into the Waterford stemware with a flourish.

"And, now," Sam said, holding up his glass, "we drink to the hero, heh? *A salute*."

Pat smiled modestly and picked up his glass. Connie held her glass up a few inches in a halfhearted gesture. Sam looked at her with disapproval.

"What's the matter? You're not proud of your husband?"

Connie ventured a weak smile. "Sure, I'm proud of my whole family," and they drank the bittersweet white bubbling wine in unison.

Pat knew, of course, that the decision he reported to Sam would ultimately have to be approved by the commission, by Vito in Atlanta and by Meyer in Miami and by Charlie Lucky in Naples. According to Pat's information, the organization already had two or three "friends" in Congress, including one from Southern

California and one from New Jersey. But in recent years, there had been nobody reliable from New York, and nobody who was a "made" member.

Work had to be started well in advance of the election if he was to run as an independent candidate. It would mean getting petitions signed in every one of the fifty districts of the state. It was a situation in which the organization's connections would prove invaluable. Without a statewide organization, it would take a fortune to get on the ballot. The new job would give him a chance to travel all over, hitting some of the smaller cities of the state and stressing ultimately what would be his campaign note—the war on crime in the streets.

Pat felt that he had made good connections with the Maggadino family on his previous trips, but his strength was somewhat weakened by his brief friendship with Al Agueci because Agueci had been shooting his mouth off around Buffalo. He and his brothers had been involved in the big narcotics bust which had sent Valachi, Vinnie Mauro, Don Vitone and the others to the federal pen.

Now, Al was out and complaining that the organization wasn't doing enough to help his brothers. Valachi had tried to warn him that badmouthing the boss was not a good policy. Stefano Maggadino was old and irritable and had little use for young upstarts.

Just after Thanksgiving 1961, Pat saw a small notice in the newspaper. The burned and mutilated body of a man named Albert C. Agueci of Scarborough, Canada, was found in a field near Rochester, New York. Pat used his contacts to get a police report out of Buffalo on the killing. The Buffalo cops described the state of Al Agueci this way:

> His hands were bound behind his back and his ankles were tied with long cord and he was strangled. His jaw was broken, half his teeth had been

kicked or knocked out. Substantial
portions of meaty tissues were
removed from the calves of his legs.
His body was doused with gasoline
and ignited. His body was mutilated
beyond recognition. This was not
only to cause his death, of course,
but this was to send a message to
anyone else who had the temerity or
the gall to try to resort to
vengeance against one of the dons
of the empire.

The report came from the office of the Assistant
Chief of Detectives, Michael Amico, who was in charge
of the Criminal Intelligence Division of the Buffalo
Police Department. Amico was one of the most
knowledgeable men in the state about the organization,
and he willingly filled Pat in about the details of
Agueci's murder. After all, Pat was lined up in the
statewide war on crime.

In the family, 1961 had ended very badly and 1962
wasn't starting very well. The federal narcs were still
trying to tie Lucky to the big dope deal that Tony Bender had launched so disastrously.

At the urging of the Federal Bureau of Narcotics, the
Italian police began to grill Charlie Lucky late in January 1962. They sat back, smiling patiently, as Lucky
went over his often-repeated story that he was just a
legitimate businessman trying to make an honest living
and had nothing to do with the world of crime. But he
seemed nervous and upset.

Finally he pleaded for a break in the questioning,
pointing out that he had to go to the airport to meet an
important motion picture producer named Martin Gosch
who wanted to film the story of Lucky's life before it
was too late.

The cops let Lucky go in the company of an English-speaking Italian detective named Cesare Resta. Resta and Charlie Lucky waited for the arrival of Gosch's plane from Rome. Lucky fidgeted nervously and kept running to the water cooler for paper cups of ice water.

When Gosch arrived, Luciano introduced Resta to him by name, but not by rank. The three men started to walk out of the air terminal, Charlie still sipping at his cup of ice water. But they'd only gone a few steps when Luciano turned deadly pale, broke into a cold sweat and began to stumble, grabbing for the portly producer's arm, mumbling, "Martin, Martin, Martin."

Ten seconds later, he was dead from a heart attack.

Don Vitone had mixed feelings when he got the news. He was distressed to lose an old friend, but glad to hear that the case against Luciano wouldn't go to court because, in fact, Charlie Lucky *did* have something to do with that dope shipment. On the other hand, Don Vitone realized that he would now have to consolidate his hold as number-one man in the States. One of the priority jobs was attending to Bender.

Don Vitone began to look for a man who knew Bender well, that Bender trusted, who could be counted on to take care of the job efficiently.

CHAPTER 33

Pat Conte's new assignment out of Albany suited everyone. While the ostensible purpose of the assignment as Special Counsel on Crime in the Streets seemed to indicate a role in law enforcement, Pat's job was actually 90 percent ceremonial and public relations.

In the cities there was a big tide of protest against violations of civil rights and police brutality, but in the small towns of New York State there was more *fear* of civil rights demonstrators, black nationalism and general anarchy than there was of the police themselves.

Pat designed a uniform for traveling upstate. It consisted of a double-breasted blue blazer with gold buttons, a blue shirt and a modest-striped tie and gray pants. The blazer with the gold buttons suggested a police uniform, but Pat's appearance in the Ivy Leaguish outfit did much to dispel the popular stereotype of the cop as a dirty, brutal figure and much to abet the concept of him as an earnest supporter of society, law and morality.

Since New York City papers circulated widely throughout the state, Pat was already known in most communities he visited. In any case, he would send a press release ahead, signed by a public relations man in the governor's office which would summarize his achievements as a hero cop.

There were few towns in which he visited where he didn't get at least a two-column head and a photo in the local paper. The state supplied him with a stack of eighty-by-ten glossies for press purposes, and mats giving a gleaming portrayal of Pat's police work were available to weekly papers that wanted to save money on typesetting.

When in Albany, Pat would pay a courtesy call from time to time on Sergeant Crosswell, the nemesis of Apalachin, and discuss the progress of his war on organized crime, but he spent more time with Jerry Foley, a former New York newsman attached to Governor Rockefeller's public relations office, learning the ins and outs of building a public image.

Foley, a red-haired former West Side street kid, had considerable political savvy, and was an expert in handling audiences and developing local volunteer leaders. Jerry's recommendations were sound and practical.

"In the first place, Pat, you're speaking *too* well. Don't try to sound like a college graduate or a lawyer. Stick to your image as a hero cop. Be natural and easy.

"Get a haircut. They don't like long sideburns in Oneonta and places like that. Makes you look too much like a guinea greaser. Usually I suggest that a candidate get a good tooth-cap job, but you're fine in that department.

"It's okay to romance the women volunteers but don't fuck them unless you have to. Just keep them thinking that if you weren't a happily married man, you'd really *love* to give them a roll in the hay, but don't *do* it. You got too much to lose. A jealous woman or a paternity suit could ruin the whole thing before it even got started.

"Try not to take too many *goombahs* on your local committees. Get a balance. The Jews are good workers and usually a pretty soft touch for campaign funds. The Irish are the big power in the bigger upstate cities. You could have a tough time with them, but you're an independent so you can go around the machines. Every one of these small-town political machines has got a few

disgruntled would-be office holders who'd gladly jump
the party and spill the beans on their old cronies for the
promise of a good state no-show job. Promise 'em anything, and make good wherever possible. When the time
comes, you can always stall with more promises, if you
can't deliver. . . ."

Talking to Jerry Foley was like taking a back-alley
lectures series in practical poli sci. Nothing he was saying had been taught in any of Pat's college courses.

As he had done all his life, Pat kept a careful
notebook on the names and proclivities of the people he
met in his travels to Rochester, Buffalo, Amsterdam,
Binghamton, Poughkeepsie, Rome, Saratoga Springs,
Schenectady, Troy, Syracuse, White Plains and
Yonkers. In each town, he made a point of meeting
the Democratic and Republican leaders, determining the
strength of the party in each place, finding out who the
insurgents or potential insurgents were, checking out
any third-party movements, particularly of a conservative nature and finding out who were friends of the
family, or "friends of friends."

He found that with his ready-made reputation and the
florid introductions he got from the chairman (often the
local chief of police or the district attorney) he had a
head start in holding an audience. Also, to his surprise,
he found that he *enjoyed* talking. He began to learn,
with the help of Foley, the rhythms of speechmaking,
the inflected pauses, and, of course, all the various shib-
boleths and keynotes which would guarantee applause.

Basically, his theme was shock at the loss of family
authority, and the increased laxness and liberalities in
the schools, the wildness of youth, and the threatening
growth of slum areas, which everybody took to mean
black ghettos.

Generally, Pat spoke at high schools, before the
Chambers of Commerce, Rotary Clubs, American

Legion and Veterans of Foreign Wars and women's groups.

Rockefeller's office was delighted with his performance. He was more than earning the $24,000 salary which had been set for the job, and the equal amount he was allowed for expenses. (This was known in Albany as a "lulu," an allowance in lieu of expenses to save him the trouble of making out itemized accounts.) But Pat's expenses weren't too bad on the road. Usually he didn't spend more than three or four days at the most away from the city.

He drove a modest Plymouth sedan, which had been allotted to him out of the state motor pool with the seal of the Crime Commission on the side of the car. He carried an honorary shield from the state police in place of his New York City tin, and out of habit and a certain sense of continuity, carried his off-duty Smith & Wesson and the holdout ankle holster, too, where it seemed advisable.

On the days when he was not traveling the outer ranges of his beat, Pat operated in New York with an office the State provided him in the State Supreme Court Building in Foley Square. It was convenient to his old haunts on Mulberry Street so that it was seldom more than a week that he was out of touch with family doings, either through meetings with Sam or trips to Luna's or Teddy's or Ferrara's Pastry Shop, or one of the other haunts where he might run into his old friends, plus, of course, the Alto Knights, the Mulberry Street SAC among other valuable listening points.

He was heavily booked on speeches in the city, also, especially in Queens, Brooklyn and the Bronx, where the mania for protection against violence had become endemic. Pat noted in his speeches, with humorous irony, that as the walls of the prison were being broken down to make it a comfortable and more pleasant place for the criminals, the people in the city were surrounding themselves with iron bars and gates so that it was the *population* that was in the prison cells and the criminals that were loose.

Once every quarter, Pat would make a short stop at the Columbia Society (where his sponsor was always Captain Arthur Marseri), the Patrolmen's Benevolent Association and the Lieutenants' Association. The thing about Pat's speeches that made them so effective was that they were sincere. Pat *really* hated street hoodlums. He hated people that raped innocent women. He hated spades who ripped off people's pocketbooks and mugged people in alleys. He hated drunk-rollers and fags, and fag-rollers, too. He hated the Murphy Game and the B-girls and the cowboys who stuck up gas stations and bars and little tin-box banks. He hated black leather motorcycle gangs, and vandals who broke down park drinking fountains and concrete benches and scribbled on walls, and he hated burglars, shoplifters, sneak thieves, dips, cannons, yeggs, drifters, gypsy switchers, peepers, flashers, sady-mays and other sex creeps, insurance floppers, hotel prowlers, muggers, joy riders, pimps and hooples.

He usually got the audience's attention right away with a dramatic opening. One of his favorites was lifted from some West Coast Ph.D's thesis on law enforcement.

"How do you think of your average police officer?" Pat would say, standing before that eager audience in his dark blazer with the shining buttons, his hero's record firmly engraved in their minds, his hair crisp, curly and gleaming with Alberto VO-5, his teeth shiny and white as a television sink.

"A big paunchy giant of a man, uncouth and uneducated. You think of him as a man who becomes violent when someone violates one of the laws of his territory. He's been portrayed as a combination of a

physical Samson, an intellectual midget and an emotional cripple. Is it any wonder then that this negative stereotype has confirmed in the average citizen's mind the belief that a policeman is someone to be either tolerated, disregarded or even avoided, that a policeman occupies a social position somewhere between the law-abiding and the criminal elements of society? It is just this image, fostered by hostile press elements and near-sighted do-gooders that has caused the enormous rise in crime in this society, a rise, even now, six times that of our population growth."

That usually caused a whispered gasp of shock. Then he backed up his statement with heavier authority. Quoting Walter Arm, New York City's Deputy Police Commissioner (Pat didn't mention that he was in charge of public relations), he said: "Commissioner Arm has pointed out that never has police stock been at a lower point. Never before have police been under such constant—and largely undeserved—criticism. Never before have public expressions of confidence in police been so meager." This always brought a spontaneous burst of applause.

"The blame is not to be laid at the station house door. A very small part of it is caused by the actions of a few policemen. A much larger part of it is what appears to be an organized campaign aimed at weakening law enforcement and respect for law and order."

If the group was a patriotic one, Pat usually closed with a quote from William H. Parker, Police Commissioner of Los Angeles: "A dangerous custom has arisen in America wherein the hapless police officer is a defenseless target for ridicule and abuse from every quarter. It is a dangerous custom, because our society is destroying its ability to protect itself by discouraging those qualified from taking up police service as a career and creating such an uncertainty in the mind of the police officer as to what is appropriate action that inaction may become the order of the day. This is a situation long sought by the masters in the Kremlin. The bloody revolution, long the dream of the Comintern, cannot be accomplished in the face of a resolute police."

Pat knew he could count on this to produce long, sustained applause, whistles, stamps, cheers and frequently a standing ovation. His speeches were almost invariably quoted, not only in the news pages of the local papers, but on their editorial pages the next day.

Pat hired Burrill's clipping service and started on the third volume of his scrapbook, already fat with hero citations.

At the end of March 1962, Pat Conte parked his Plymouth under Sam Massey's familiar porte cochere in Riverdale. Sam was waiting for him in the den, the fire lit, the brandy poured. He was wearing a cream-colored, Irish knit cardigan over a yellow viyella shirt. His black horn-rimmed reading glasses were low on his nose and Pat saw lines of age in his face which seemed to have grown overnight, cut into the leathery tan of the horseman and golfer. Sam rumpled his well-groomed mass of iron-gray hair carelessly, leaving it hanging over his eyes in a Will Rogers cowlick.

"I really hate to bother you, kid. You know you're like a son to me."

"What is it, Ba? Is there anything I can do?"

"It's something *only* you can do. I've been in touch with Atlanta this week."

"Don Vitone?"

Sam nodded.

"How is he?"

"How is he?" Sam snorted. "How can a man be in stir with his business all going to pot, with all sorts of people trying to move in on him and stab him in the back from every direction? He's upset. That's how he is. These kids in Brooklyn, then Profaci, now Gambino is on his back to make some kind of peace and the biggest troublemaker is in his own back yard."

"Bender?"

Sam nodded. "To tell the truth," he said, "even before Lucky died, they had a meeting. Don Vitone sent word over and he got the okay. Now, somebody's got to reach him, but we don't want the word out all over town. It's got to be a very cozy kind of job. If the word gets out that he's hit, all hell will break loose. We don't need any more violence and trouble. Don Vitone is afraid that he'll crack wide open if the feds get him on this drug rap."

There was a long silence as Pat waited for his father-in-law to get to the point.

"I hate to ask this, son, but can you handle it?"

Pat smiled, remembering the Grand Army Plaza.

"I can handle it," he said.

Sam put his hand on Pat's knee. "You know you're more than a son to me. I don't want you to get in any trouble and I don't want you to be in any danger. You're doing a great job out there in the sticks, and I think that we're really going to be able to put you up for the Washington thing, so we don't want any scandal, but who can you trust these days except your own family? Don Vitone particularly said that he didn't want Gerry Catena or Jimmy "Blue Eyes" or any of those guys to even know about this."

"I'll need a couple of guys to get him out of the house—guys he likes and trusts."

"All right," Sam said. "We'll find those guys, but I don't want even them to know where he winds up. I think a very suitable place might be up in Columbia County. You know, that limestone up there, it's like marble. It's like a monument. Like a monument in a cemetery."

"Yeah," Pat said. "I know what you mean. As a matter of fact, I have to be up there in a few weeks. I have to blast out a little stone for a new fence and patio."

"That's a good idea. You should keep the place fixed up."

CHAPTER 34

The obvious choice to decoy Bender out of his comfortable stucco house on Palisades Avenue in Fort Lee was Tommy Ryan Eboli. Pat was not surprised at the choice. He knew that Ryan, though a boss, was tough enough to do jobs on his own. It was Ryan, with Johnny Dee, who had personally worked over a couple of brothers who offended Bender in the early Village days. Ryan and Johnny Dee hit the two men with ball bats on every part of their bodies as people walked by on the street, unconcerned. The two brothers spent six months in the hospital.

Ryan told Pat that he got the okay to take care of Bender directly from Mike Genovese, who'd been visiting his brother in Atlanta the week before.

Pat felt flattered to have been chosen to take part in the deal, which was obviously being done at a top level. Like most of the other capos, Ryan had none of the look of a killer. He was a good five inches shorter than Pat, with graying hair balding at the top, a sad mouth and a long Roman nose.

Early on Sunday of April 8, a chilly spring morning, Tony Bender got a call that Tommy Ryan wanted him to sit down with Pat Conte and straighten out the problem of the attempted dope hijack in the Grand Army Plaza. Bender had claimed all along that it was not his doing, that word had gotten out about the seventy-five kilos of heroin and that the ambush had been a freelance venture. Pat wondered if Bender really could believe that he would buy that story. But with Ryan,

Bender's old pal, acting as intermediary, there was no way that Bender could refuse the meeting.

At precisely 10:00 A.M., Bender looked at his imported French gold watch, kissed his aging, red-haired wife, Edna, told her he was going out to buy some cigarettes and would be "back in a little while."

"Anthony," Edna said, "put on your coat. It's still cold out there. You know you're not so young anymore."

"That's all right," Bender said, smiling his little scholar's smile. "I got on that thermal underwear you gave me, and besides, I'll be right back."

It is doubtful that Edna believed the cigarette story, but she was not used to asking questions. She peered through the window and saw that there was a black 1961 Cadillac waiting with what appeared to be a couple in the back seat and a third man driving. She let the curtains drop and went back to finish her *panettone* and coffee.

Earlier, the Cadillac had slowed down at 238th Street and Riverdale Avenue to pick up Pat Conte, a few blocks away from his home. He had simply told Connie he was going out "to meet some people" and would be away until evening.

Pat was surprised as he got into the car to see a small, dark woman in a fake-fur coat and a broad-brimmed black felt hat sitting in the rear seat.

"Who's this?" he asked Ryan, who was sitting at the wheel.

Ryan laughed, uproariously. "It's Chalutz. You know, Charlie Gagliodotto."

"Oh, yeah," Pat said. "I think I'll sit in the back," and he got in the back of the Cadillac, next to the tiny figure.

"How's it going, Chalutz?"

The little man in the fake fur coat extended his manicured fingers. *"Mezza-mezza."*

Pat had only met Gagliodotto once before, at the Copacabana, but he'd been wearing men's clothes at the time. Word in the organization was that Gagliodotto had pulled off at least thirty hits. Generally speaking, the people in the family called him their "fag hit man," but not to his face. As far as Pat was concerned, it would have been foolhardy to sit in the front seat with Chalutz Gagliodotto behind him. Pat, in fact, sat with his arms folded and his hands comfortably close to the Smith & Wesson in a shoulder holster.

Ryan was still chuckling. "Everybody thought it would be better to have Chalutz do the job. Christ, I know Tony too well. I really wouldn't want to do it and you've done so much, we really hated to ask you. The best thing is to leave it to Chalutz."

The little man in the felt hat smiled and patted his big black leather purse. Ryan drove smoothly, guiding the big black machine over the bridge and humming to himself. If he was disturbed by his mission, it didn't show. Chalutz sat tensely on the edge of his seat, his tiny feet in their sensible low heels pressed solidly to the floor. He kept nervously snapping and unsnapping the clasp of the black handbag.

Ryan honked twice lightly on the horn as the car swung around in front of Bender's comfortable stucco home. Moments later, the dapper little man came running out wearing a dark, mohair suit, his professorial glasses glinting in the early spring sun. He nodded to Ryan and Pat as he slid into the red upholstery of the Cadillac.

"Who's the dame?" he asked Ryan.

Chalutz was sitting well back in the deep seat now, the hat throwing a shadow over his face and the black wig covering his ears.

"It's okay," Ryan said. "It's Conte's girlfriend."

He put the car in gear and started smoothly up Palisades Avenue, heading north toward the bridge.

"I don't think we should talk in front of her," Bender

said, cautiously. He had thrown his skinny arm over the back of the red Cadillac seat. Pat could see the pinky ring he wore—a small star sapphire, surrounded by diamonds, the huge gold cufflinks and the gold wristwatch. His left arm, alone, must be worth $25,000, Pat thought.

Bender seemed unhappy at the added presence in the party, but he said nothing for a while. He joked with Ryan as Ryan drove.

"You're not putting on any hair, Tommy."

"Neither are you," Ryan joked.

"What do you hear from Don Vitone?"

"*Tutti de bene.* You know, he's okay. I saw Mike the other day. He was down there. The only problem they got with him is he plays such lousy *bocce* that the other guys have to stand on their heads to lose the games."

Bender giggled nervously. "That's Vito all right. You know, I remember him from his wedding. We stood up together."

"I know, I know," Ryan said. "He thinks well of you."

"Sure, sure," Bender said. He turned his head back to Pat sitting in the left rear seat. "I know that was a terrible misunderstanding. I feel terrible sorry about Tommy getting it, but I swear on my mother's grave, I had nothing to do with it."

"We can talk later," Pat said, quietly.

Chalutz's constant snapping and unsnapping of the handbag was driving Pat out of his mind. Ryan drove past the bridge and up toward Palisades Parkway. Bender looked out the window.

"Remember the Riviera?" he said. "That was some spot. We pulled a lot of money out of that. It's a shame it had to go."

He watched as the car pulled onto the Palisades Interstate Parkway.

"Listen, where're we going? I told my wife we'd be

right back. I don't want to be gone too long. We could settle this in a few minutes. I just thought we ought to have a face-to-face sit-down."

Bender seemed to have forgotten that it was not his idea to have the meeting in the first place.

"We'll just go here by the river."

The car pulled off at the first Palisades scenic overlook, a large, paved parking area with a view of Yonkers across the river. Spring was on the way, but it was still a raw day, and fortunately there were no sightseers in the area.

Tommy Ryan parked the car at the overlook. "Beautiful view, ain't it?"

"It's gorgeous," Bender said.

"Listen," Ryan said, "I just want to talk to Pat for a minute and get his slant on it. Then we'll come back and get rid of the dame and we can talk over there where there's no taps or bugs or anything. You know what I mean?"

Bender smiled with appreciation of the cleverness of this idea.

Pat and Ryan got out of the car and strolled over to the grove of fir trees, rimming the steep drop to the river.

Chalutz must have been waiting. Only a few seconds elapsed before there was the sound of four flat blasts from a revolver. Ryan sighed, for a moment seeming to show a sign of regret.

"I guess that's it. You know, he had it coming. If it wasn't for him, Vito wouldn't be in stir now, and neither would Mauro. . . ."

"You don't have to convince me," Pat said. "I had my own beef."

"Yeah, that's right. The son-of-a-bitch nearly got you killed, didn't he?"

"*Sangue lave sangue,*" Pat said. "Blood washes blood."

"Hey, that's good," Ryan laughed. "I didn't know you could speak Italian."

"Only a few words."

Chalutz claimed that he might break his fingernails if he helped to shift the slight body of Bender who was crumpled on the red floor of the Cadillac, so they sent him up to watch the entranceway while Ryan and Pat transferred the limp form to the trunk.

"This car's going to be a mess. There's a lot of blood there," Pat said.

Ryan laughed. "Don't worry. It'll be on its way to the steel mills in Gary by morning."

Pat slammed the trunk lid down and got back into the rear of the car. He didn't want to sit in front with Ryan since there were bits of blood and brain still scattered on the dashboard and the floor, though Gagliodotto had done his best to wipe off the spots.

They said little on the two-hour drive to Ancramdale. Ryan and Pat exchanged views on sports and boxing. Ryan was positive that Sonny Liston would soon take the heavyweight title from Patterson.

"That Patterson has no balls," he said. "Liston will murder him."

"Listen," Pat said, "I think Archie Moore could take him if he was a little younger. He can almost make the weight, too."

"You're right, you're right," Ryan said.

Near the redwood bench, where Pat had sat with Sam, philosophizing, were piles of heavy link chain and three or four concrete blocks. Ryan and Pat wrapped the chain several times around the well-shod feet and narrow shoulders of the limp figure.

"It's a good thing he don't weigh much," Ryan said, "or we'd never be able to lift him up and throw him in."

"I'll put one of these blocks on his feet," Pat said. "That ought to be enough."

"Wait a minute," Chalutz said. "That's no good." He fumbled in the pocketbook again and took out a pearl-handled folding stiletto with a six-inch blade. Quickly, he kneeled beside the crumpled body, pulled out the monogrammed shirt and unbuckled the silver belt buckle with the jeweled initials, AS, then deftly he plunged the long shining blade into the fish-belly-white stomach and began to saw it, energetically across the waistline.

"What are you doing? Are you crazy?" Pat said.

"If you don't cut their bellies," Chalutz said, "they always float up, even with chains on them. It traps the gas."

Pat turned away while Chalutz finished the job, then he and Ryan took the prone form by the feet and shoulders.

"Wait a minute," Chalutz said, and grabbed Bender's trailing right arm, still bright with jewelry.

"Leave that stuff alone," Ryan said. "Are you crazy? Don't you have any respect?" and the two men, counting to three in unison, strained and heaved the encumbered body over the sheer wall of the quarry into the black water.

"The contractors are coming tomorrow," Pat said, "to blast some more stone off the side of the quarry here. A lot of it will settle down to the bottom."

"Good," Ryan said. "Well, I'll see you," and he and the strange black-hatted womanish figure got into the Cadillac and drove off.

Pat stretched and walked in the sun. He was pleased to notice that the crocuses were beginning to emerge in the flower beds around the brick building and buds were already forming on the fruit trees. Sighing, he climbed into the state Plymouth. He had driven it up the day before, and left it there, returning to the city with Sam.

As he drove the familiar hilly curves of the Taconic back to the city, Pat felt no sense of release or remorse.

He only wished that this would be the last of these jobs that he would be called on to witness. There had to be a stopping place for these things. And yet, Ryan was a *capo* and *he* was still taking part. Pat supposed that it was all a matter of taste.

CHAPTER 35

When Pat got back to the house that night, Connie was waiting for him in the kitchen in her negligee. The table was piled high with books and reports in manila folders—work she was doing for a definitive report on the educability of children suffering from Down's Syndrome.

"You didn't have to wait up, Connie."

"I know, but I have work to do anyway. Do you want something to eat?"

"I'll just have a glass of milk," Pat said. "Got anything in the icebox?"

"Just some meat loaf and some cold spaghetti."

"That'll be okay."

"I'll heat it for you."

"No, no, that's okay. I'll eat it cold."

He went to the refrigerator and brought the two platters out, juggling them along with a bottle of milk. Connie, sighing, got up from the table and brought him a plate, napkin and silverware.

"You didn't tell me you were going to the country today," she said.

"What makes you think I went to the country?"

"Well, you've got that limestone dust all over your shoes and the cuffs of your pants."

"Oh, yeah," Pat said. "I had to go and pick up the car. I left it there last time I was up and drove back with Sam."

"You mean when you drove up with him yesterday?"

"Did I mention that?"

"No, you didn't, but I knew."

"Yeah, well Sam wanted to advise me on some construction work so we went up and I felt too tired to drive back, so I drove back with Sam."

"How did you go up today?"

"Oh, I had one of the boys drive me up. . . ."

"None of what you said makes sense."

"Oh, for Christ's sake. Just do your fucking reports and stop messing into what I'm doing."

Pat propped up the early edition of the *Times* which he had picked up at the newsstand on Broadway. He now felt that he had to read *all* of the New York dailies to keep up on what was going on, and that was a job in itself.

"Do you want to say hello to the baby? You haven't seen him in a couple of days."

"Yeah, well I'll look in on him later. I want to finish the paper now," Pat said, absently.

There was nothing in the *News* or the *Times* about the disappearance of Bender, but then, it was quite early. Pat wondered whether there would be any report at all, or whether Bender would be allowed to pass quietly from the scene, not noticed for weeks or months.

Three days after her husband drove off, Edna Bender appeared in a leather jacket and toreador pants at the Fort Lee police station to complain that Bender hadn't been seen since he stepped out for a "little while" on Sunday.

"Do you have any idea what happened to him?" the captain asked.

"I'm not the kind of a wife that goes through her husband's pockets," Edna said. "For thirty years he gave me my household money and anything I needed. Last weekend, he cleaned up the swimming pool and prepared the garden for spring. I've been sitting by my little radio for three days hoping for some news flash, but I have no idea why he went away."

Later the reporters questioned her.

"I tell you, I don't know what happened to him," she said. "Maybe he took sick and didn't want to bother me with a phone call, or he might have run into trouble. There've been a lot of stickups in our section by youngsters. If they held him up and then noticed who he was, they might have become frightened and killed him and left him somewhere in the woods. Nobody who knew Tony would want to hurt a hair on his head."

Bergen County Prosecutor, Guy W. Calissi, said he wasn't going to spend the taxpayers' money looking for Tony Bender. The police chief at Fort Lee, Theodore Grieco, said he had no plans to look for the missing *capo*.

"He's lived here for sixteen years and has always been a good citizen and was never any trouble," the chief said. But he finally sent out a Missing Persons alarm anyway.

The alarm described Bender and specified not only what he was wearing, but the jewelry he had on when he disappeared.

"It was a good thing," Pat thought, "that we didn't let that nutty fag grab any of it."

For weeks New York reporters worried at the story, but didn't seem to be able to pull out any threads. Bobby Kennedy identified Bender as one of the top ten Mafiosi in the United States. Federal Narcotics Commissioner Harry J. Anslinger listed him as one of the most important narcotics smugglers in the world. Tony's enemies in the organization were listed and mulled over. Note was made of the fact that he was the last one to see Little Augie Pisano before he was bumped off.

Bender was discussed as a rival of Albert Anastasia and a possible plotter in his assassination. Inspector Raymond J. Martin of Brooklyn South told reporters: "It is quite possible that Tony Bender has been taken care of by his underworld enemies."

Much to Pat's surprise, the FBI quickly got in on the act. Several agents, including Regan Doyle, converged on Edna in the Strollo home.

"I don't see how anything could have happened to him," Edna said, "since you fellows have been doing such a good job of watching him all these years."

Pat met with Regan Doyle the next day and asked him if he had anything on the Bender case.

"I was out there," Doyle said. "That's some crazy lady he has."

"How come it's a federal rap?"

"Well, he operated in New York and he lived in Jersey, and besides, there was a federal narcotics investigation going on at the time of his disappearance, so it seemed logical. Frankly, I made the push for us to get involved."

"Did you have something on him?" Pat asked.

"Plenty," Doyle said, "but not much that would stand up in court."

He looked at Pat speculatively. "You knew him pretty well, didn't you?"

"Sure," Pat said. "I worked in the Sixth long enough."

"Didn't I see you with him a couple of times at the Copa?"

"Sure. When I was with CIB. I had to check out with everybody. That's how I developed my informants. You talked to him, too, didn't you?"

"No," Doyle said. "I never talked to him personally, but I have talked to some of the others. I'm going to talk to a lot more of them in the next few days."

"Listen, he's probably scratching his balls in some tropical island. That guy was too tough to get nailed. He'll turn up like a bad penny."

"You really think so?" Doyle asked.

"Sure. What makes you think anything else? You got anything to go on?"

"Why would he just walk out of the house and tell his wife that he was going to be right back?"

Pat grinned. "You met her, didn't you? Maybe it wasn't such a sudden decision. Maybe he *didn't* tell her he'd be right back. Maybe she just told that to the cops."

Regan changed the subject.

"Incidentally, congratulations on the medal and the new job."

"You wouldn't have heard any of the details from your Uncle Seamus, for instance?" Pat asked. He wondered if the old captain had squealed on him, but if he had, he doubted that Regan could have acted so cool.

Things had reached the stage of a cat and mouse game between the two cousins. Regan wouldn't admit that he was gunning for Pat, and Pat wouldn't admit he *knew* just what Regan was up to.

Three months later, Joe Profaci died of cancer in the South Side Hospital on Long Island. The only one he'd seen in those final months was his brother-in-law, "The Fat Man," Joe Magliocco. Pat stayed away from the funeral, as did anybody of any importance in the organization. Everybody knew that the place would be swarming with FBI men and New York detectives.

Pat began to feel that you could count on your fingers the remaining stars of the organization. Places at the top were opening as the bosses grew older, but, of course, there were people coming up from the bottom, too, like the Gallos, whose position was considerably strengthened by the death of Profaci.

But the Gallos were broke and things were quiet in Brooklyn for a while.

About two weeks after Profaci died, at 7:30 A.M. at the U.S. Penitentiary in Atlanta, Georgia, Prisoner No. 82811—Joseph Michael Valachi—grabbed a two-foot length of iron pipe from a construction job in the jailyard and brained an aging mail robber named John Joseph Saupp, whose only crime was that he bore a remarkable resemblance to Joseph (Joe Beck) DiPalermo, the man Valachi was certain had been picked by Genovese to kill him.

Since the incident took place in a federal pen, it immediately fell under the jurisdiction of the U.S. attorney. Valachi was flown to the Westchester County Jail, just north of New York City under the cover name of Joseph Demarco and held in the hospital wing apart from other prisoners. At that point, nobody but the feds knew that Valachi had decided to spill his guts. The case, at first under the control of the Federal Bureau of Narcotics, which had made the original pinch, was quickly taken over by the FBI.

It wasn't until the end of September that Pat got a clue as to what was going on. Actually, he, pieced it together from some information Regan Doyle leaked about a crack FBI agent named Bob Towers who had been working out of the Westchester County Jail with what Doyle said was a terrific informant.

It happened that Pat, in the course of his upstate tours, frequently stopped into penal facilities. That fall, Pat visited the warden of the Westchester County Jail, doing research for a speech on the "increasingly permissive" aspects of penology. Over a cup of coffee, Pat learned from an informant that the FBI was talking to a mob VIP in the hospital wing.

"I don't know who the guy is. Some character they booked under the name of Demarco. I hear that's not his real name. Just a name the feds gave him so that the mob couldn't get at him. I know one thing. He's a killer. He brained some guy down in Atlanta."

Pat had heard through Mike Genovese and Tommy Ryan about Valachi's weird act in the federal pen, and now everything fell together in his mind. Valachi was spilling his guts to the FBI.

CHAPTER 36

With the FBI suddenly waking up to the problem of the organization and Valachi singing like a canary in the Westchester County Jail, it appeared at first that the whole organization, countrywide, was in trouble, and above all Genovese, because it was Don Vitone who was Valachi's principal target. Many of the people who still didn't believe that there *was* such a thing as the Mafia, became ardent believers. The gravel-voiced, gray-haired hood told his story for a solid week before a nationwide TV audience. Going through a rogue's gallery of known criminals presented to him, he identified 289 family members and gave their associations, but, at the same time, he tried to protect certain friends by refusing to connect them to any specific crimes.

There were cautious and hastily called councils in the family. Phones were distrusted more than ever and so were any locations that might be bugged. Even private cars and bedrooms were suspect. Pat found increasingly on his upstate tours that he was questioned about the organization. The family policy was to completely deny the existence of the outfit that Valachi called Cosa Nostra and to minimize Valachi's own character and importance.

During question sessions and especially in informal gab fests, Pat would point out that Valachi's nickname in the mob was "Cago," which was the Italian word for excrement. Pat pointed out that he was a low-ranking hood trying to gain prominence by identifying himself with more important people.

"If Valachi is telling the truth," Pat said to a group questioning him in Buffalo, "then how come the FBI hasn't yet had a single indictment out of his testimony? Because it's all a grandstand play. This is all an attempt to discredit every Italian-American in the country. It is part of an attempt to imply that all of the foreign-born are more likely to be involved in crime than the native Yankees. But, while they're going after the gamblers and the prostitutes, who, after all, are only giving people what they ask for, who is protecting us from the muggers and the rapists that attack us in the streets and in our homes?"

As Chairman of the Committee on Crime for the Italian-American Defense League, Pat sent out many letters accusing Valachi, the FBI and the Federal Government of attempting to discredit anybody who had an Italian name. Valachi, on the witness stand, was asked by Senator McClellan to tell why he was cooperating with the Federal Government at the risk of his life.

VALACHI: The answer to that is very simple. Number one, it is to destroy them.

McCLELLAN: To what?

VALACHI: To destroy them.

McCLELLAN: Destroy who?

VALACHI: The Cosa Nostra leaders or the bosses, the whole—how would you explain it—that exists.

McCLELLAN: You want to destroy the whole syndicate or the whole Organization?

VALACHI: That is right. Yes, sir.

McCLELLAN: Why do you feel it should be destroyed?

VALACHI: Well, through the years, first of all I was concerned and second, they have been very bad to the soldiers and they have been thinking for themselves all through the years. It is all put together and I put together so many things that it all comes to that. To destroy them.

Valachi's testimony *didn't* destroy the family, though it disturbed it considerably. One of the most irritating things was the total security under which Valachi was kept. It tended to weaken the authority of the organization that they could not put a cork in the mouth of his squealer.

Regan Doyle, in his insulated room on 69th Street, was listening to conversations picked up through various electronic devices and now with the keys Valachi furnished was beginning to fit it all into a mosaic. There was one typical conversation Doyle listened to in which "Petey Pumps" was complaining to Mike Scandifia about the increasing knowledgeability of the F.B.I. teams.

PETE: Well, the son-of-a-bitch. He hands me Carlo's picture. Carlo Gambino's. 'You know him?' he asks me. I say, sure I know him. How long you know him? I know him twenty, thirty years.

MIKE: They didn't expect you to say nothing.

PETE: Can you tell us anything about him? The only thing I could tell you about him is that he is a businessman, been in business all his life, brought up four kids. They had a good education. They're all in business. They all went to college and married a profession. I said, what else could you ask for? He's got a very nice family. See, over there, what they do? They want to get a message through, I mean, get a message through someplace. There's no question about it.

(BOTH TALKING AT ONCE)

MIKE: They want to put the heat on you, me.

PETE: Yeah.

MIKE: Because here is the proof of it. They've gone to every captain.

PETE: Yeah.

MIKE: And they called them captains. One guy said foreman. The other guy said *caporegime*. I mean, they're going right to each head, to the head of everybody they're going to. But for them to say this, and when he told me this I said: Jimmy, I think he already saw them.

PETE: Yeah.

MIKE: I think he already saw them, I said. Now, to put the heat on him to go get his daughter, I said, that don't make no sense to me. I said where the fuck does this come into the picture? Now they don't want to embarrass you. They don't want to go to the convent to see your daughter.

PETE: What are they going to embarrass me for? What can they do, go up there?

MIKE: Well, God forbid, they can't . . . they can't throw her out.

PETE: No.

MIKE: They couldn't throw out Al Anastasia's brother. How they going to throw her out?

PETE: Nah, they can't throw her out.

MIKE: Embarrassment that your daughter is a nun. I mean, Jesus Christ, it's supposed to be an honor!

PETE: They can't do nothing. They won't do nothing.

MIKE: Dirty cocksuckers. Now they bring out everything, Pete. The Cosa Nostra is a wide-open thing.

PETE: Yeah.

MIKE: It's an open book.

PETE: It's an open book.

MIKE: Pete, you know as well as I do, familiarity with anything whatsoever breeds contempt. We've had nothing but familiarity with our Cosa Nostra.

Then, in another part of the tape, Doyle heard this.

MIKE: I said it two years ago. You got to go deep in the fucking holes and make new tunnels. That's what we gotta do.

PETE: Underground.

MIKE: Underground. Underground and reorganize and come up and leave a couple of fucking bodies on every fucking corner and every fucking stool pigeon we got a line on. There hasn't been any of that. I don't want to be vicious. I don't want to be bloodthirsty, but Pete, you talk to people and they're not afraid no more. They're looking to defy you.

PETE: Yeah.

MIKE: They're actually looking to defy you, so you don't want to say Jesus Christ you don't want to be known as a bloodthirsty guy. Where is all this going to get us now? Guys walk in, they want to spit in your face. I mean every . . . not every third guy . .

but every guy that walks into the station house or the FBI office is given an opportunity to be a rat. So he's got a house. So he's got a business. He's got a few dollars. He's facing twenty years.

LARRY: We got a lot of no-good cocksuckers there. There's even a fucking guy, one friend over there that we think . . . I know. I know all about it. This cocksucker. Nice fellow.

LARRY: This is ours. This cocksucker. I got to take this cocksucker . . . this dirty motherfucker . . .

MIKE: You know where you got to put him? You know what I told Pete. You got to pick a lamp post. He's got to put the . . . hang 'em on the lamp post. You understand. You gotta cut his prick off. You gotta put it in his pocket and you gotta give him a nice slash and leave him up there. That's what you gotta do. That will serve notice to every fucking rat stool pigeon what's going to happen when and if he finks.

Fortunately for Pat Conte, Doyle and his organization didn't have ears everywhere. They didn't hear this conversation between Pat and his father-in-law, Sam Massey:

PAT: There's only one thing we gotta do, Ba. We gotta keep very cool and lay low. There's going to be a lot of blood spilled over . . .

SAM: Right. We gotta work on the political angle.

PAT: Nobody can say we didn't do our share, but I'm making a lot of ground now politically. Maybe I can do us some good that way because the shit's really going to hit the fan.

SAM: That's right, Pat. It's time for us now to be more the foxes and less the lions, as your friend Machiavelli says.

CHAPTER 37

The attack on the Cosa Nostra gave Pat a stronger hand with the Italian-American organizations, which deeply resented the implication that all crime was run by the Italians. In speaking before mixed groups, Pat tried to indicate that an attack on *any* minority was bigotry of a sort that in the end was harmful to all.

In Pat's mind, a constituency was forming. It consisted of blue-collar minorities, who mostly voted Democratic, but were now put off by liberal Democratic policies in regard to civil rights and liberalized crime control laws. To this, Pat hoped to add the natural conservative votes and many of the upstate Republicans for whom the policies of Rockefeller and Javits were jarring.

It was gratifying to Pat that his liberal and radical friends from college days at NYU and Baruch seemed to be changing with the times. Art Winburg, after having his apartment ripped off twice and having had his wife mugged in the subway by a black high school student, suddenly had modified many of his attitudes about slum locations and school integration. He now had two kids in PS 41 on Greenwich Avenue. It was a good school where *de facto* segregation was maintained by a division into so-called bright classes and less advanced classes. The way it worked out, the bright classes were all white and the others all black. If a kid had trouble making the grade, he was given help in one form or another to move into the all-white group.

Winburg shrugged philosophically. "I think Negroes deserve all the rights they can get, equal pay, votes and so on, but I don't want my kid going to a class where he's going to be shaken down for his milk money or have

484

his bicycle taken away from him at knifepoint."

"That's not the way you used to talk."

"Well, I haven't changed my ideas, but I'm worried that maybe we're moving too fast. Either we've got to get some of this violence under control or I'll have to leave the city."

"What would you think," Pat said, "of forming a group, a group that would study this problem of violence in the streets, find out who is responsible and how to bring about the necessary changes? A non-political group, but a group with political pressure."

"Yeah," Winburg said, thoughtfully. "A group like that may be able to accomplish something, but can you get the right people together?"

"I'm going to try," Pat said. "I've done a lot of work on this and I've now got quite a name in the crime prevention area."

"That's true," Winburg said. "But listen, this isn't going to turn into some kind of fascist organization, is it?"

Pat laughed. "I don't think it's fascist to protect your home and your children, do you?"

"I guess not," Winburg said. "Let me know if you get the thing going."

"Do you think Ellie or any of the other people, Jim Bailey, for instance, would be interested?"

"Well, it's a little tough for Jim Bailey to take your side. After all, he's black."

"Yeah," Pat said. "I keep forgetting that. But he lives in the West Village and sends his kid to the Bank Street School of Education. He's just as likely to be a victim of crime as anybody else."

"Well, you can try him."

"What about Ellie?"

Winburg shook his head. "I doubt it very much. The last I heard she was going around with some Black Muslim maumau, a big son-of-a-bitch with a beard."

Pat kept a straight face but winced inwardly. It griped his gut to think of those hungry lips surrounding some big black joint. But to Winburg he only said, "I'll call her soon and see if she's interested and I'll be in touch with you again."

"Okay," Winburg said. "Good luck."

Affairs of New York State had kept Pat out of the Village for months. The Monday following his discussion with Winburg, he called Ellie from Rochester and arranged to see her that Friday.

"I got a date, Pat," she said. "Can we make it some other time?"

"No. That's when I'll be in town. Break the date. This is important."

"Of course, baby," she said. "It's always important when I see you."

"That's not what I hear around campus," Pat said, and hung up before she could question him more.

Pat parked the Capri in a lot on Hudson Street and walked over to Ellie's house on Bank Street. Even in the few years since he had been coming there the hall showed signs of deterioration. Three or four of the mailboxes were bent up at their brass corners and a steel plate had been put on the door lock. Textured green paint had been applied to the halls, to cover graffiti, much of it gouged deep into the plaster. Despite the thickly spackled paint, Pat could make out the words, "Nigger Lover," crudely dug into the plaster of the wall. There were several horizontal lines running through the words as though someone had tried to gouge them out again.

Near the mail boxes, someone had written in a neat hand, "For a good blow job, call 634-8295." The doorbell plaque also had been obviously the target of local vandals, with many of the nameplates scratched or removed. Pat pushed the button opposite 4B. It was one of those on which the name had been removed. He waited for the crackling, brittle voice on the building intercom, but there was no answer. For a moment, Pat wondered whether he had been mistaken as to the time and the date. He looked into his notebook and it was clearly indicated for Friday, 4:00 P.M. Probably the bell didn't work.

Pat went downstairs and walked down to Bank Street and Greenwich Avenue to Jack Barry's bar from which he called Ellie's number. There was no answer. Pat knew that Ellie was given to experimenting with drugs. Aside from the grass she had given him, she had tried several times to expand his horizons with LSD, cocaine and amyl nitrate. He decided that he'd better make a personal check on the situation, and returned to Bank Street.

He punched the button on Apartment 1A which was located so that the owner could see through the glass of the hall door without opening the inside door. There was no answer and Pat tried 1B. The door opened a crack and Pat flashed his New York State police badge through the window. A languid young man with an enormous bush of gingery hair sprouting in all directions from his head like a dandelion in seed, slouched to the door and stood peering through the window at the gold badge. Finally he shrugged and opened the door.

"It's all right," Pat said. "I'm just checking one of the apartments."

"Hang loose," the pale young man said and retreated.

Pat mounted the four flights of creaky stairs, past the trash bags and plastic garbage pails to the top landing, still bright with the sun shining through the skylight.

He rang the bell of Ellie's apartment and heard the two-toned chime responding to his pressure, but he listened vainly for the sound of footsteps. There was only silence. Angrily he pounded on the red enameled door. At the second blow from his fist, the door moved a good inch. Obviously, it was closed, but not locked. Pat shoved the door open wide and stopped transfixed.

All of the carefully nurtured plants in the wide, skylighted windows had been slashed and the curtains pulled down, leaving a bare expanse open to the sky. The pots behind the couch also were smashed, with dirt scattered all over the table and floor.

The modern prints and reproductions and posters had all been torn violently from the white walls, leaving pale oblongs in their place. Across one wall in letters almost two feet high were the letters, "BLAC." There was a line indicating that another letter had been planned and had trailed off. The lettering was in pale, brownish red, the color of dried blood.

On the wide comfortable couch where he had first come to know Ellie intimately was a jumble of raw-edged limbs and parts of what could only by mental reconstruction be assumed to be a human form. A bare leg lay stiff and pointed up toward the ceiling, ending in a raw, red stump on which clumsy handfuls of white powder had been thrown, absorbing the blood and turning it to a bright brown mud color. The other leg lay stretched out full length in front of the couch, apparently still attached to the torso. Where the legs had joined the body, there was only a bloody hole. A sharp instrument had excised the entire pubic area. A dismembered arm lay draped, as though still belonging to a carelessly lounging houri, over the back arm of the couch. Shreds of ligament and tendon hung from its stump, mercifully turned toward the fabric.

The torso itself was nude and dappled with a rash of small vertical lines. A Sabatier knife projecting sidewise from the ribcage indicated that they were stab marks. Strewn over the couch and parts of the body were the stalks of Ellie's carefully nurtured plants with their eerie, hairy blossoms hanging limp. Where the face might have been expected to appear, a batik pillow perched as though to blot out the horror of the sight.

From behind it streamed unmistakable straight skeins of
strawlike blonde hair—Ellie Vogel's hair.

Pat retreated from the scene. His forehead broke out in
a damp sweat and he ran to the corner of the areaway,
where the ladder led to the roof and some empty garbage cans had been clustered. Leaning against the
plaster wall, he retched into one of the cans. The door
to the only other apartment on the area opened in
response to the sound of Pat's vomiting. A man's voice
called out.

"Anything wrong out there?"

"Yes," Pat said. "Call the police. Tell them there's
been a homicide. Tell them to get here right away."

Ellie's neighbor, a tall, gangly man with well-cut
brown, wavy hair, blushed. His face went red, then pale.

"In there? In that apartment? In Ellie—in Miss
Vogel's apartment?" the man said.

"That's right. Call the fucking police!" Pat said, "and
stop standing there. Hurry up!"

"Yes, sir," the man said, and jumped back into the
apartment, closing the door behind him.

Pat leaned both hands on the banister, staring down
the four flights of stairwell and tried to get his breath
back. He wiped the strings of mucus and vomit from his
chin and scrubbed out the spot on his tie which had
dipped into the stream gushing from his mouth.

Pat desperately wished for a glass of water, or beer,
or mouthwash, or *anything* to clear the taste of death
from his tongue. But he knew better than to go into the
apartment or disturb anything. Instead, he stood wondering how he'd explain his presence to the cops. But
that wasn't difficult. After all, he'd established with
Winburg that he was planning to form a citizens' group
against violence and that he was going to consult Ellie
on the subject. Since Ellie was active in local politics, it
was a perfectly logical situation, and the time of day was
not suspicious.

CHAPTER 38

The gruesome murder of Ellie Vogel stirred rage in Pat Conte that was the strongest and most genuine emotion he had felt in years. It was, perhaps, the very sincerity of his statements on the subject that made such good copy for the press. Reporters jumped on the fact that he had been calling on Miss Vogel in order to enlist her services in a citizens' organization.

It was Winburg who thought of the acronym which dramatized the situation of civilians in a state of siege against the crimes of violence—AGONY—The Anti-Crime Group of New York. The aptness of the acronym and the chilling timeliness of Pat's announcement brought a flood of letters, offers of funding and public statements of support from police officials, politicians, prosecutors and newspaper, radio and television editorialists. Most gave unqualified support to the vaguely expressed aims of Pat's group.

"We feel it is time that the citizens of this state showed that they are vitally interested in the business of stopping crime. This is not to say we are interested in vigilantism, but rather that the law enforcement agencies of the state only derive their power from the consent of the people and, to some extent, we will get only what we deserve and truly desire from them. In my years of experience as a police officer, I have seen the public image of the police and its morale go down every year. This is bound to reflect itself in the energy used in the fight against crime. I call for all interested citizens to support your local police, not only with words, but with actions, and to build up a system of communication between the citizens and the police department rather than the barrier that has been growing in recent years."

Pat had letterheads made up, using his New York and Albany offices as mailing addresses. It was important to him that the group did not appear to be strictly New York based. While AGONY was a private organization, propagandizing for it fit in very well with the lecture tours and activities that Pat indulged in in his job as Special Counsel on Crime in the Streets.

AGONY also served as a handy channel for fund raising. Contributions poured in from individuals, clubs and foundations. Even Governor Rockefeller sent a personal check for $1,000. The family, of course, through various fronts, gave—heavily.

Some of the newspapers reacted to Pat's campaign with caution, particularly *The New York Times* and the *New York Post,* but all of the upstate papers enthusiastically endorsed the hero cop and his plan to halt violent crime. The *Post* cautioned that AGONY, while expressing admirable goals, might become a tool in the hands of racists and political reactionaries. The *Times* perceptively questioned the possibility of political opportunism on the part of Pat Conte.

This suggestion didn't bother Pat at all, since the discussion of his political future would simply stir up helpful speculation.

Evidence gathered during the investigation into Ellie's death failed to pinpoint the murderer. Witnesses in the building said that she had been seen with a series of tall, striking-looking bearded black men, some of whom she entertained in her apartment overnight.

Mrs. Gordon of apartment 1A, who noticed most of the comings and goings of the building through her front window said: "Maybe they were all the same man. I don't know. They all look alike to me." Her remark was not reported in the newspapers, but a composite photo based vaguely on the descriptions of two or three neighbors was published in several newspapers. As Mrs. Gordon said, it looked like anyone of five thousand black militants.

It was the letters in blood on the wall which convinced the police that if they found the black visitor, they would find the murderer.

"I assume," Lieutenant Anderson, Manhattan West Homicide, said, "that he was about to write 'black power' or words to that effect, but was interrupted. This is the crime of a diseased mind, but it is a crime of political violence. The attack on this woman was essentially an attack on what the murderer saw as a hostile white society."

Pat visited Manhattan West Homicide Squad two or three times a week. Although he was no longer on the force, he was given full courtesy, not only as an ex-cop, but as a state official. The apartment had been dusted for prints and three or four strange sets had been found, but none seemed to be on record at the FBI. The knife handle, however, had been wiped clean, and none of the prints could be definitely linked to the murder.

Several smudges indicated that the murderer had used surgical rubber gloves.

CHAPTER 39

Most of the newspapers accepted the theory that the murderer was a black and that the murder, itself, was a product of the city's racial tension. Certainly, that tension seemed aggravated by the incident. In one week, a television actor, strolling on MacDougal Street with his white girlfriend, was beaten up. The shop of a black homosexual dress designer on Madison Avenue was vandalized by a street gang and the parents' group of a school in South Brooklyn pulled their children out of class in protest against the busing of blacks into the area.

In a radio interview on the Barry Gray show, Pat reiterated his interest in settling the race problem in the city, and in the country in general.

"But," he added, "these steps must be taken with care and attention to the explosive possibilities. Accelerated integration of schools and housing are bound to produce friction which can lead to violence. There is still a tremendous gap between slum-bred children of Harlem and Bedford-Stuyvesant and those of the middle-class areas. Certainly, it is understandable that parents do not wish to see the educational, cultural or safety level of their local school lowered by the forced integration of less culturally privileged elements."

"Then you're against integrating blacks into our public schools?" Gray asked.

"I am in favor of it," Pat said, "but I'm not in favor of *artificial* integration. I think that the schools should follow the population pattern. I think that removing children from their natural environment and sending them to school miles from home only aggravates the tension involved."

Pat met with Jerry Foley in Albany and suggested that he would be glad to pay a thousand a month for Foley's services as speech writer and political communications expert. Foley had no objections. The fact that these were unreported cash earnings meant that they almost doubled his salary.

Shortly after Foley went to work for Pat, items began to appear in gossip columns and political commentaries hinting that Pat Conte was the type of man the country needed in public office. Several went so far as to suggest his candidacy for various posts—assemblyman, City Council, and even for governor. Pat paid a bonus of twenty-five dollars for each item that appeared.

At first, Pat gave some thought to running with one of the regular parties, but it soon became clear that they had their long-standing lines of communication to candidates and endless, complex networks of mutual obligations. Besides that, Pat did not like the idea of being under the orders of some Democratic committeeman or local chairman.

The AGONY group, while it was not large, furnished an excellent publicity platform for Conte, as did the Italian-American Defense League. It would only be a matter of time before someone thought of the idea of allying these and other splinter groups into a valid, political arm—and eventually a political party.

Winburg was a valuable acquisition. The years had turned him from a liberal, racial integrationist into a doctrinaire opponent of interracial schools and housing. Winburg owned a remodeled brownstone, in the East Twenties, just beyond the Gramercy Park area and had organized a block association whose main, unexpressed goal was to keep blacks and Puerto Ricans from moving into the rapidly improving block and debasing real estate values.

At first, Pat had hoped to win over Bailey. It would have been good for the organization to have at least a token black on its board, but Bailey wasn't buying.

"No matter how you slice it, Pat, the thrust of this group of yours is bound to militate against blacks. I may live in an integrated neighborhood and send my kid to private schools, but that doesn't make me white. Just because I don't choose to suffer some of the disadvantages of my black brothers, doesn't mean that I'm abandoning them. Your group is standing in the way of the tide of history and it's going to wash right over you."

"I'm sorry you feel that way, Jim," Pat said. "I don't think you understand the aim of the group. Blacks are just as much the victims of crime in the streets as whites are, in fact, more so. The figures show that blacks are the *principal* victims of street violence. Why aren't you interested in helping them?"

"I *am* interested," Jim said. "I'm interested in having more black men on the police department. I'm interested in cleaning up corruption that keeps the black man down. I'm interested in the white racketeers that run the numbers and gambling and vice in Harlem and dope. If we got rid of them, we might have less of a problem in the black areas."

"Don't make me laugh," Pat said. "In the first place, the blacks are moving in in all of those areas and you know it, and in the second place, where you're dealing with dope and prostitution, you're going to have violence no matter who's running it."

"Let's just say," Bailey said, reasonably, "that you see things in your way, and I see them in mine, and there's no way that I'm going to join your group. I only hope for the sake of our friendship that I'm not assigned to do any stories on it."

"I only ask one thing of you, Jim. If you do a story, come to me first, and don't listen to my enemies without giving me a chance to answer."

"Okay. That I'll promise," Bailey said. "What about Ellie's murderer? Any clues?"

"Nothing much," Pat said. "They've questioned maybe eight or ten guys that were known to have been seen with Ellie. Most of them had alibis or at least were clean enough that they couldn't be held."

"Did they ever think they might be looking for the wrong man?" Bailey said. "I mean, just because she's been seen dating black men doesn't mean it's a black man that murdered her."

"What about the writing on the wall?"

"How do you know how it would have finished?" Bailey asked. "Maybe it would have said, 'blacks must die,' or 'black motherfuckers.' Who knows what it would have said?"

"Maybe," Pat said. "Maybe it could have been some other person, but right now that's what they're looking for—a tall, black, bearded activist."

"Don't they have a file on sexual deviants and potential sex criminals? I have a feeling this is more of a sex crime than a political one," Bailey said. "You have access to those records. Why don't you check into that?"

"I just might do that," Pat said, as they shook hands and parted. But as Pat climbed back into his car, he thought to himself, "I hope to Christ the murderer isn't some white loony. That wouldn't do me any good at all. It's *got* to be a black."

Investigation of the murder of Ellie Vogel moved slowly. Unfortunately, beards and fuzzy hair were very much the style that year among upwardly mobile blacks. The result was a rash of beatings of blacks who vaguely answered the description concocted by the police of the major suspect in Ellie's murder. Given special attention and rousting were those who were seen walking in streets of Greenwich Village with white girls. But the questioning produced no results and Pat felt his AGONY group had to broaden its base of attack.

Just seven weeks after Joe Valachi took the stand in Washington, on November 22, 1963, the nation was shocked by the assassination of John F. Kennedy. The keening of mourners was heard across the nation, and around the world. After the reaction of stunned grief came an outcry against violence in the streets. Barry Goldwater, on a law-and-order ticket, was nominated for president by the Republicans to run against Lyndon Johnson.

In Pat Conte's world, the assassination had several repercussions. For one thing, Attorney General Robert Kennedy, numb with shock and grief, ceased to pay as much attention to his barely launched war on crime. Lyndon Johnson, anxious to maintain his friendship with J. Edgar Hoover, did not press in this area. Valachi's testimony was overwhelmed by the current of world events. Pat Conte, in the eyes of his constituents, emerged as a prophetic leader who had seen the handwriting on the wall.

Pat preferred to see the assassination, not as the politically motivated act of a demented maverick killer, but as another symbol of the lack of adequate control of the criminal in the streets.

Late one night that winter, Pat sat with Art Winburg in Ratner's, eating onion rolls and cream cheese and talking politics.

"Did you notice anything in the streets around you coming here?" Winburg said, reaching into the basket of fragrant baked goods.

"Yeah. I noticed dirt. I noticed Puerto Ricans. I noticed hippies."

"Right," Winburg said. "Look around you here. We're in an old-time Jewish restaurant, right? This kind of place used to be the heart and soul of this neighborhood. They used to have the old Jewish theater down on Second Avenue. They had Rappaport's, Orchard Street and Hester Street and Delancey Street.

They were all Jewish. But if you draw a line from Fourteenth Street across Manhattan, what you have to the south now are Puerto Ricans, Italians, mainly, in some sections, Chinese, and then Russians and Poles and then over in Staten Island, you have the same mixture, with maybe even more Italians, and throughout this area every night there are muggings, burglaries, rip-offs, sex crimes, holdups and so forth, right?"

Pat looked puzzled.

"What I'm getting at," Winburg said, "is that the area I just described happens to be the Seventeenth Congressional District. It's a weird district which takes in everything left over in the ass-end of Manhattan plus a good part of Staten Island. Remember, we've been talking about the possibility that you might someday run for Congress.

"On my timetable, that was still a good two years off. But things are different now. If Bobby Kennedy can run for Senate in New York State with this little preparation, then you can make a try for Congress. DeSapio no longer controls the Democrats, the Republicans are confused, the Conservatives are just beginning to get a toehold. All it takes to get on the ballot is three thousand signatures. Christ, you could round that up just among your relatives, your own family."

Pat looked at him for a minute. "What do you mean? I have no family. I'm an orphan."

Winburg smiled. "I mean your *goombahs*. You know—all those guinea pals of yours. I'll tell you something else," Winburg said. "That area hasn't gone Democratic for a long time. There's no really solid party loyalty, and those minorities are scared by the blacks moving in. So far, there is no substantial black group in the area, but it's coming. People down there don't want to see their area turned into a Bed-Stuy or a Harlem or even, for Christ's sake, a Corona."

"Keep talking," Pat said. "You interest me."

"Look, if we run you as an independent on the law-and-order ticket, what's the worst that can happen? You can lose, right? But your name will be flashed all over the area, you'll get a lot of newspaper and television coverage and the number of votes you'd get can be used as leverage next time, either for an official party nomination or for some kind of patronage job."

"I'm not looking for a job," Pat said, "but the congressional deal interests me."

Pat caught the eyes of his friend in a long, intense stare. Winburg saw a diamond-hard light that he had never seen in those hard black eyes.

"It's not only Congress I'm aiming for either," Pat said.

"Okay. One thing at a time. Don't forget, all this is going to cost money," Winburg pointed out.

"We've got the money. Besides that, these congressional campaigns don't cost that much. You got a small area to work in. If you've got a good organization and a lot of volunteers, you can perform miracles. You don't really need TV or even citywide papers."

"True, true," Winburg said. "God knows, we've got the volunteers these days."

"Okay," Pat said. "I'm going to talk to some of my money people. I think we can raise a pretty good kitty. Meanwhile, I want a report from you. I want to know everybody we can count on I want to know about the local Democratic and Republican clubs and how strong they are, who they're planning to run, and I want to know any hot local issues that we can focus on. Never mind about Johnson, Goldwater and Kennedy. We'll stick with the local issues. If we're running as independents, they're going to have to push down a separate lever for us anyway. Check out crime control, of course. That'll be one of our main pitches. Check out the schools. Don't forget the local storekeepers. They're really important, and there's a lot of little shops down that way."

"There's one possible drawback," Winburg said.

"What's that?"

"You live in Riverdale."

Pat smiled. "You know where I was born and raised? Right in this district with my good friend, Father Raimundo Marseri, who somehow, I think, is going to do us a lot of good. Come to think of it, I spend more time in that district than probably any other anyway. I'm down there all the time. The Mulberry Street vote we got."

"It's a start," Winburg said.

CHAPTER 40

While the planning for Pat's political future was going on, Giuseppe "Bad Eyes" Magliocco was perfecting a plan of his own. Joe Bonanno, the last of the original five commissioners appointed after the Castellammarese War, had come to feel that the post of senior *capo* was rightly his. He was fifty-eight and had developed a deep scorn for the commissioners of the day, some of whom had been only petty thieves when he was already a member of the council. He made a habit of staking out for himself any open area declared by the commission, such as Canada and the Southwest. But in Canada, he ran right into Magaddino's territory and friction developed between Bonanno and the other members of the commission.

Bonanno felt that by making an alliance with Magliocco, who had taken over the Profaci family, he might be able to take over the whole organization—provided three men were out of the way—Magaddino, Lucchese and Gambino.

Bonanno gave the job to the Fat Man—Magliocco, and Magliocco, in turn, farmed out the contracts to a pushy young hood named Joe Colombo. Colombo was a man with more ambition than balls. He saw a greater profit to himself in going to the commission and tipping them off to Bonnano's coup.

Magliocco and Bonanno were both summoned before the board to face charges. The Fat Man panicked and made a full confession. He was banished from the Cosa Nostra, fined fifty thousand dollars and sent home. His family and his seat on the commission were given to the stool pigeon, Colombo. Bonanno never showed up for the commission meeting. He disappeared somewhere on the West Coast, not to turn up for a year, but Magliocco was not to get off that easily.

Sam conferred with Pat about the means by which he could be eliminated without provoking a war from the Profacis or indicating any disrespect.

"Sam, I'll tell you one thing. I'm not going to be involved in these things any more. I can't do the job that I'm doing and still go around 'finding' people for the organization. You can understand that."

"Sure, sure," Sam said. "I was just asking your advice. You've got a good head for these things."

"When are you meeting Tommy Ryan?"

"I'm meeting him tomorrow at Alto Knights."

"Okay. I'll be there. I have an idea."

The two *capos* met with Pat early in the evening when there were few people in the bar. Pat again brought his table radio. He was convinced that by now the FBI had a bug in every organization hangout in the city, not to mention private apartments and even in the flats of mistresses and business associates. The three men ordered a giant antipasto and a bottle of Riserva Ducale.

"Pat," Ryan said, "you're the champ!"

"Che se dice?"

"Bene, bene," Tommy Ryan answered.

"Well, we eat, eh?" he said, pouring oil and vinegar over the salami, tuna fish, pimentos, hard-boiled eggs, olives and mushrooms on the huge plate before them.

"Listen, Tommy and Sam," Pat said, "I don't want to stay too long. In the first place, there's lots of business to take care of. In the second place, I think I gotta cool a lot of these associations. There's a lot of people watching these days. You know what I mean?"

"You're right, you're right," Sam said. "We all gotta lay low."

"Sam said you had an idea," Eboli said.

"I have," Pat said, reaching in his jacket pocket.

He pulled out a long aluminum tube about the size of a Havana cigar.

"This is it."

"What the fuck is that?"

"It's something I picked up when I was over in Europe. The Russians like to use this. It's called a cyanide gun. Inside is about five drops of hydrocyanic acid. When you fire it, a spring breaks the glass, the acid vaporizes in the face of whoever it's pointed at. That person dies instantaneously—and this is the part that's important. They almost always diagnose it as a heart attack case. You know, that Fat Man has not had a good heart for a long time. You take it, Tommy. I'm not on this job."

Eboli took the tube gingerly and put it in his breast pocket.

"How much?" he said.

"Come on," Pat grimaced with disgust. "This is for the family, right? I'd do it myself. I just can't be directly involved anymore. You know what I mean."

Pat buttoned his jacket and got up to leave. The other two started to follow him.

"No. *Mangia, mangia.* You guys stay. I gotta go."

A couple of days after Christmas, the three-hundred-pound Fat Man collapsed into a plate of snails he was eating in the kitchen of his estate in East Islip, Long Island. Nobody noticed the dark figure leaving by the back door and driving off in a black Cadillac. The guard lounging at the front gate gave a friendly wave to one of Magliocco's regular associates as he drove out between the stone pillars. It was an hour and a half before the body was found. Everybody thought it was very sad, but inevitable.

"That man would never stop eating. He just got fatter and fatter," Gambino said when he heard the news.

In Sam Massey's den a toast was drunk between Sam and his son-in-law.

"To our late friend," Sam said, holding the amber fluid up to the light, "and to our future congressman."

"I'll drink to that," Pat said, laughing.

Winburg proved to be a good prophet. The timing was perfect for an independent to run. The Democrats were split between the reform element and the regular party. DeSapio's rule was in a shambles. Costello was all but retired, and even had he been interested in helping Pat's election, he would probably not have much energy to give to it. Lucchese, on the other hand, was a valuable ally and still had plenty of underground political clout.

Barry Goldwater was not popular in New York City, but then, neither was Lyndon Johnson, and Goldwater's ongoing attack on crime and violence in the streets served to keep the electorate tuned in to the problem which Pat had decided to make his only issue.

The newly born Conservative party was growing in strength in Pat's chosen district, but had no candidate to run, so that Pat could count on the Conservative vote in Staten Island, where a large part of his electorate lay.

Art Winburg estimated that Pat would get 75 percent of the vote in Staten Island. The Democrats had chosen Jim Bryan, a hulking, old-line Liberal labor man and an Irish Catholic, but the labor vote was increasingly shifting to the right those days and more likely to vote Conservative than Democratic. Of the 450,000 votes in the district, 300,000 were in Staten Island.

By far, the largest national minority in the district was the Italians who comprised 12 percent of the population. Only 6 percent of the area was black, but 6 percent was Chinese and 7 percent was Spanish. The Poles, the Irish, the Russians and the Germans and a sprinkling of

English-descended voters accounted for 2 percent each of the electorate.

The Republicans, anxious to keep the liberal Manhattan segment of their party which had spelled the difference in the seesaw rivalry of the area, ran Al Carter, a friend and associate of John Lindsay, who was finishing his own successful term in the Eighteenth District to the north. But Lindsay's magic was not likely to work in the southern tip of Manhattan and Richmond.

Between Pat's personal financial support, family money and "voluntary" contributions organized by various unions owned by the family in that area, Pat had access to a fat campaign pot.

Pat coined a name for his independent party—the Citizens' Protection party. Winburg protested that the initials CP might be confused with the Communist party, but Pat laughed that off.

"You must be joking! These people down here never heard of the CP. *Commies* they heard of, not the *CP*. Besides, Communists haven't been on the ballot in years."

"I suppose you're right," Winburg said.

Pat used Winburg's political acumen as a guide, but he had a firm hand in running the campaign himself and had a sure instinct for the people of "his" district. Since only about 180,000 of the people in the district voted, if Pat could get a good turnout from the people who were his natural support bloc—the Italians in Richmond and Little Italy, the frightened old Jews in the housing developments, the resentful Puerto Rican shopkeepers, who were waging a constant battle with the blacks, and the Middle-European minorities—he had a more than even chance against his divided opponents.

Early in the year, Pat launched a newspaper, financed by AGONY. The paper was called *The Citizen,* and concentrated almost entirely on crimes of violence in the area, taking a righteous stand on police corruption, municipal neglect, mob rule—particularly by the blacks—and the city's neglect of the Seventeenth District in general.

Pat brought Jerry Foley down from Albany to edit the paper and help in speechwriting. Foley hated living in New York, but the money was good and the future seemed bright. In any event, he only took a leave of absence from his state job, though he was reasonably certain that Rockefeller, if he ever found out what the work was that Foley was doing, would tie a can to him in short order.

Through the unions and the family, Pat quickly enrolled a corps of voluntary paper boys who spread 100,000 copies through the district every week. Included in the paper in addition to crime news were certain self-help boilerplate items—knitting formulas, recipes and even (for the Staten Islanders) a column on gardening.

Pauley Federici was recruited to run the public relations aspect of the campaign and prepared a strong statement against the growing violence of crime in the streets for Pat's opening speech, which was carried on local television news by three stations.

Federici was extremely valuable also in organizing pressure group support, particularly of the Italian-American Defense League, which became a virtual wing of Pat's candidacy.

It was he also who suggested using Connie to organize church groups, particularly women.

"You'll have to convince my wife on that one. She's devoting most of her time to prayer and retarded children these days."

A vice-president of public relations for Ruder and Finn, Federici had through the years maintained a youthful and dynamic outlook. His marriage to a Jewish girl he had met as an undergraduate at LIU had ended in a friendly divorce three years earlier, when it was

discovered that Paul and Sharon had different ideas
about the new sexual freedom, with Sharon being the
freer in attitude.

What had attracted Paul to Pat's campaign, aside
from their boyhood friendship, was his deep concern with
the safety of his three children, who lived with their
mother on 103rd and West End Avenue, designated by
The New York Times as one of the "most dangerous
blocks" in the city. Federici's youngest child, then
seven, suffered from a rare retardation syndrome called
phenylketonuria, a metabolic disorder which left young
Kevin with a half-developed intellect. It had been Constanza who had called to Federici's attention the work
being done on diet control for such children by Sister
Mary Theodore at the St. Colletta School.

Unfortunately, the advice was too late, but Federici
was grateful for the information that *might* have saved
his child from the disorder had he known of it a year or
so earlier.

Paul knew he would be able to win Constanza over to
taking an active part in the campaign. Their long meetings on the problems of retardation, and Paul's ex-
officio advice to Constanza through the years on fund
raising and PR for her various activities had welded a
bond of sympathy between them. "If I ever had a sister,
I'd like her to be like you," Paul once had told Constanza.

Constanza at first resisted.

"I'm not political, Paul," she demurred, "and to tell
you the truth, I prefer to have as little as possible to do
with Pat's affairs."

"You could do a lot of good, Constanza," Federici
said, taking her hand. "Two of the planks in Pat's platform involve federal financing for parochial schools,
and a federal grant for research in retardation. No matter what is happening between you two—and I'd rather

not know about that—you must think of the good you could do."

They were sitting in the Conte kitchen drinking coffee, Paul's hand clutched Constanza's in mute appeal. Under the table their knees were in warm contact. If there was a steamy quality to the air in that sunny room, neither recognized it on a conscious level.

Constanza agreed to help organize the women if she could have Paul's consultation and advice on the project.

"Done!" Paul said, kissing her on the cheek. "And now, I have got to get downtown again. Fridays are my visitation day."

He pulled a present he had bought for Kevin from the shopping bag he was carrying. It was one of those games where kids learn to hammer square shapes into square holes and round ones into the appropriate opening.

"Yes," Constanza said, "it would be worth trying that. Distinguishing squares and circles can be a good exercise. And triangles, too." She fluttered her dark lashes at him in mock flirtation.

"Triangles of course," Federici said.

As Election Day approached, the polls showed Pat running inches ahead of his two opponents, short of a majority by far, but reasonably assured of a plurality.

In October Vincent X. Rooney, a former associate of DeSapio's, but now closely tied to the mayor's office, approached Pat and suggested a dinner at Whyte's, a posh, financial district steakhouse. But Pat refused and insisted that Rooney come down and discuss his business at Pat's storefront office on Grand Street in Little Italy. Reluctantly Rooney agreed, and late in September, the pair met on a rainy fall afternoon.

Pat cleared the miscellany of eager young workers, old friends and hardened pros out of the rear "private" office and invited Rooney to sit down. From a battered, secondhand refrigerator in the corner of the office, he produced a couple of Pepsi-Colas.

"Have a drink, commissioner?" he said. "We're operating on a shoestring down here, you know, so I don't have anything better to offer you."

Rooney looked at the frosted bottle with distaste.

"Fine. That will be fine."

"Now, commissioner, what did you want to talk to me about?" Pat said, seating himself behind the scarred oak desk.

"This is quite a show you're putting on," Rooney said. Pat opened his eyes wide.

"What do you mean?"

"I mean all this poor-mouth humbleness. You got more money in your tin box than your two opponents combined."

"Do I?" Pat said. "Maybe you know more than I do. But you're not here to discuss my finances I don't suppose, or are you about to offer a contribution?"

"You know, your opponent Bryan is making a very good show. He's been spending a lot of time with your guinea friends over there on Staten Island, and they're not as solid for you as you think."

"Is that right?"

Rooney pulled a folded, letter-sized piece of paper out of his inner jacket pocket.

"I thought you'd like to take a look at this survey we ran. As you can see, your recognition factor is only 60 percent, compared to 80 percent for Bryan, and according to the figures here, Bryan should slide in with at least a 5 percent plurality."

Pat looked at the paper without expression.

"Well," he said, "according to this, I oughta just quit. Right?"

Rooney smiled for the first time. "That's the idea."

"I don't see how quitting would do me any good at all."

"It might."

"How is that?"

"Well, you know, the mayor hasn't been too happy with the police department for a long time."

"I sure know *that*," Pat said.

"What we really need is a man that knows how to control crime and still has some kind of contact with the cop on the beat. We need a career man in that job. We've always had politicians."

"That sounds like a good idea," Pat said. "I've always been in favor of that."

"The police commissioner is a very powerful man in New York City and the job is a citywide one. It covers all parts of the city, not just one small district. The police commissioner has his name in the papers at least once a week."

"Sounds like a terrific job."

"The mayor thinks that you would be an ideal man for that job."

"I'm flattered," Pat said. "I would like to say that if I lose this election, I certainly would like to consider the mayor's offer."

"The mayor's offer is good only if you don't run," Rooney said. "By the time the election is over, he will, of course, have had to make his choice."

"I see," Pat said. "Well, let me think it over."

He took a sip of the Pepsi-Cola.

"Well, I thought it over, and you can tell the mayor to go fuck himself."

"You're making a mistake. The mayor still has plenty of clout. If he decides to lean on you, he can see to it that you're buried."

"He wouldn't want to do that," Pat said. "He might even want to help me. After all, he probably wouldn't want to see the tape of this conversation, which I just made, published. It would look an awful lot like he was trying to bribe me, wouldn't it? Good-bye, commissioner."

For a beginner, Pat had a firm control of the principles of political give and take.

At 11:30 the night before election, Pat got a call up in Riverdale from Homicide West. It was Tom Berkholder, now Detective Sergeant.

"Listen, Pat, I don't know if you care, but I think we got the guy that pulled that Vogel job down in the Village. And listen, he's not a *black* guy like we were looking for. He's a *white* guy! Some creep. He lived in the same house with her."

There was a silence as Pat digested this information.

"Skinny kid lived on the same landing?"

"Yeah, that's right. He's the one that called the job in to the Sixth."

"You haven't said anything to anybody yet, to the newspapers or anything?"

"Christ, no! We just got the guy. Caught him bothering some girls in the playground and we brought him in here. We talked to him a little. You know what I mean?"

"Yeah."

"The next thing you know, he's screaming that he done it, the Vogel job."

"When did this happen?"

"It just happened. I knew you were interested so I thought I'd give you a ring. I owe you a couple anyway."

"You got the district attorney's office in on it yet?"

"No."

"Okay then. Just hold it. Don't do anything. Do me a favor and hold it for a half hour. I'll call you."

"Sure. He ain't going nowhere, the shape he's in."

"Okay. I'll call back."

He pulled out the drawer in the night table next to his bed and fumbled in it for the little black notebook he kept with him at all times. Finally, he found the number he wanted. A sleepy voice answered.

"Hello. Arnold?"

"Yeah?"

"This is Pat. Pat Conte."

The voice brightened up. "Oh, yeah, Pat. What can I do for you?"

"You know that all-night coffee shop that we meet in sometimes?"

"Yeah."

"I want you to go down there and wait. I'll call you in just a half hour."

"Cheeze. Give me a chance to get my pants on, will ya?"

"Be there in a half hour. This is important."

A half hour later, Pat dialed a number from a phone booth on upper Broadway.

"Arnie?"

"Right."

"Listen. Homicide West has a kid who just confessed the Vogel job."

"No kidding!"

"I don't know if he did it or not, but I don't think this thing should be given any publicity at this time. From what I hear about the confession and what I saw of the murder, the kid is obviously a nut. I think we should have him put away up in Rockland for mental observation for a long time. We can close out the case, but I don't think we should announce anything about it for at least a month or so—not till *after* the election, that's for sure."

"What do you want me to do?"

"I want you to get an ADA down there with the right kind of instructions. Do you know what I mean? I don't want any indictment on this. I want him held for mental observation and I don't want any publicity either."

"Gotcha. But what's the idea?"

"Let's say I just think that breaking this news right now would have very unfavorable repercussions."

"Okay. I guess you know what you're doing," the voice answered.

"And, Arnie. This won't do you any harm. I'm gonna win, you know."

"I know, I know."

"Okay. Keep it in mind."

There was a click and the conversation was over.

On Election Day, all the numbers runners in the entire district offered a free play to those who would turn out and vote. It was a patriotic gesture, but, of course, the offer was made only in solid Conte districts. By 1:00 A.M. on the first Tuesday in November, it was clear that Pat and the Citizens' Protection party had won by more than 35,000 votes, a substantial margin for that district, which went for Goldwater by 25,000 votes.

Pat stood, smiling happily, in the crepe and bunting-hung storefront on Grand Street, shaking hands, drinking wine and kissing, his arm comfortably around the rigid waist of his wife, Connie.

"I would like to thank all of you here," Pat said, "for the fantastic job you've done on this campaign, on my own behalf and that of my lovely wife, Connie, who's been such a help through this whole difficult race by taking time away from her important work for retarded children to help with the campaign. Again, I thank you all and I pledge to do my best to make our streets safe for ourselves and our children and to give you all a voice in Washington."

Constanza smiled automatically and acknowledged the burst of applause, and then turned to her husband and whispered what seemed to be a wifely murmur of affection and approval.

"You son of a bitch! You didn't say anything about your own child, did you?" she said, her eyes bright with suppressed tears.

"You're right."

He held up his hand for silence.

"I would like also to say thanks to you in the name of my poor, unfortunate, handicapped child, Sebastian, of whom you may have heard. Though he can't be with us in body, he sends his blessing to us through his mother and my loving wife, Constanza."

Several of the women bystanders reached for handkerchiefs to wipe away a sudden spurt of tears.

Constanza turned and walked from the room out through the back door to the street.

Everyone noticed that she was deeply moved.

BOOK III

CHAPTER 1

Following the plan agreed on in the family council two years earlier, Pat played a very cool hand during those early years in Congress. He followed congressional etiquette by saying nothing on the floor of the House of Representatives during his first year and very little during his second. It had been agreed that he would do only the absolutely essential chores in regard to family business during those early years. More important was establishing his position in terms of patronage and committee assignments.

It took a good part of his first term to convince the New York Democratic Committee that they should run him as their candidate in the Seventeenth District the following term, but the success of other spoilers, John Lindsay's successful run for mayor on a fusion ticket, and the growing strength of the Conservative party convinced the conflict-ridden Democrats that Conte, as a winner, was more important than their own chosen candidate as a loser.

In his old campaign headquarters on Grand Street Pat set up a law office and handled chosen cases of his constituency for little or no fee. He also joined the prestigious Wall Street law firm of Maroney, Goldburg and Schweikert, which handled Sam Massey's construction firms, and many of his other interests, too.

Pat showed up at the offices on Pine Street no more than three or four times a year. It was not necessary for him even to refer any of his Washington contacts to his law firm. It was enough for Maroney, Goldburg and

Schweikert to mention that their new junior partner was
a congressman for them to show a 50 percent increase
in their law business.

Pat was also given a partnership by Guido Paterno in
the Paterno Insurance Company. Here again, Paterno
had only to mention Pat's connection with the firm to in-
sure a substantial gain in business. After all, a man had
to have insurance, so why not give it to someone who
could possibly help him someday with a problem in
Washington?

A careful check of Pat's life style would probably
have revealed that it was on a scale well above that
which a junior representative could afford. But then,
that wasn't unusual for congressmen. He rented a neat
duplex in Georgetown in which he spent three to four
nights a week during the congressional sessions,
sometimes less.

He learned through the family grapevine who the
other congressmen were who could be counted on as
"friends of friends." Sam Giancana had his man.
DeSimone had a man from the West Coast. There were
representatives from Maryland and Florida, Texas and
Arizona and Nevada and California who could be
counted on, and there were family contacts that reached
the very highest level of the House of Representatives,
but obviously, these were to be used cautiously.

Although most of the men in Congress who were
"friends of friends" knew who the others were, they
never met as a group. Usually, it was not necessary to
call on the Honorable Colleagues in order to tell them
which way the vote had to go. If a friend introduced a
bill, then naturally his other friends would vote for it,
unless this action would get him in trouble with his own
constituency.

Pat left some of the more obvious bills to colleagues
with more security and seniority—bills for special par-
dons which would enable citizens about to be deported

to remain in the country, special immigration bills which, if questioned, might be embarrassing. He did introduce a bill for the legalization of Detrino, a cancer drug developed by a Canadian medical firm in which Sam was interested, but the drug lobby—in Washington equally as powerful as the family lobby—managed to defeat this bill.

One of his most important bits of legislation in his first term was the passage of Title Three status for a housing project in Father Ray's parish. The project would replace several falling-down warehouses south of the police headquarters, and remodel the tenements of which the old people were so proud, despite their broken-down, slumlike appearance. In some way, people in Pat's district loved their crowded, rat-ridden hovels.

Pat earned a lot of votes by fighting against a federally funded expressway which was to cut across Manhattan south of Broome Street and would have meant the loss of many of these tenement houses. His most ardent supporters were lower-middle-class and therefore were not particularly interested in low-income projects as such, since they would not be eligible. As for aid to parochial schools, and federal subsidies for retardation research, Pat promised Federici and Constanza that he would propose them when the time was right.

Gambino, Catena and some others on the commission were anxious for Pat to do as much for them as possible while he had the power. But Pat kept his own counsel. He was playing the waiting game and was interested in more than immediate gains. Sam Giancana's man, Roland Libonata, had been exposed to an unfavorable spotlight for his family connections, and Cornelius Gallagher of New Jersey had been attacked in a series of muckraking articles in *Life* magazine. Pat was not anxious for that sort of publicity.

He liked the attention that he had been getting as a

congressman. He had become used to adulation in his travels as New York's hero cop, but now, for the first time, he was treated as a prince and began to enjoy doing the work which could earn the gratitude of his "subjects."

Although plans had been made much earlier, Pat managed to acquire by osmosis a great deal of the credit when the Verrazano Bridge was built and named for an Italian. Of course, the fact that it immediately jumped land values in Richmond added luster to this gem in his crown.

In the beginning, most of his patronage was based on deals he was able to make with city officials and friends in Albany. He was able to get Art Winburg a no-show job as an assistant commissioner in the Highway Department.

Paul Federici was added to Pat's permanent staff as legislative assistant. Federici was earnest, honest, energetic, clean-cut and had not the vaguest idea of Pat's connection with the organization. In his job as Pat's administrative alter ego, Paul often had to run errands between Riverdale and Washington. Sometimes, for weeks on end, he was Pat's only connection to news from his own home.

Paul and Constanza finally drew up a bill on mental retardation which passed on a straight vote along liberal lines.

Pat brought Constanza to Washington on the day the bill was passed and had pictures taken holding her around the waist proudly and kissing her on the cheek. He was generous enough and shrewd enough to give all the credit for the bill to Constanza.

After the ceremonial signing of the bill, and the publicity pictures, Paul Federici drove Constanza back to New York.

To break the trip, they stopped at Danny's on North

Charles Street in Baltimore for Chesapeake Bay seafood.

"This is my treat to you, Constanza," Paul said. "No expense account on this. That would be out of Pat's pocket. This is personal.

"This bill we put through together is the most significant thing in my life. Who knows? Maybe some of this research will make it possible to prevent tragedies such as were inflicted on my Kevin and your Sebastian."

They drank a toast in white wine, and plunged into the soft-shelled crabs. Later as they were getting back into the car, aglow from after-dinner brandies, Constanza took Paul by the shoulders and looked into his eyes.

"This has been one of the most wonderful days in my life, Paul."

They were in the parking lot, standing very close. Paul could feel her warm grapey breath on his cheek. He leaned toward her and suddenly they were clutched together, breast to breast and hip to hip in a grinding, probing kiss that was definitely not in the sister-brother category.

Paul broke apart first, redfaced and breathless.

"Let's not do that again, shall we?" he said. "I don't think I can take much of that sort of thing, and neither can you."

Constanza looked back at him with an amused half-smile and said nothing. They finished the rest of the drive in relative silence. The crackling car radio filled the pregnant air with pleas for cigarettes, used cars and consolidated loans, but the noise wasn't loud enough to drown out the unspoken thoughts in both their minds.

Three weeks after the passage of the bill, Pat had a private conference at the "Powerhouse" on Fifth Avenue, and six months later Constanza Conte, in honor of her work for retarded children, was installed as a Lady of the Order of the Holy Sepulcher by Pope John XXIII in a ceremony at St. Patrick's Cathedral.

Pat tried to choose his associates with discretion, but it was still necessary to deal with some of the mob's recognized fixers. The most distasteful one was Georgie Scalise. Usually, Pat tried to meet Scalise in New York. If in Washington, he would meet him at one of the out-of-the-way clubs.

Not that Scalise was seedy-looking, but he definitely looked like the George Raft type of hood. His graying hair, moustache and eyebrows were dyed a perfect brown and his skin was tanned by a sun lamp to match that shade.

Generally, he also wore large coordinated sunglasses in a similar brown tint. His clothes always matched perfectly from head to toe.

Early in his stay in Washington, Pat was asked to take part in an organization sit-down concerning the fate of Joe Bonanno, but he politely refused. A contract was put out on the ambitious don, but Bonanno disappeared into the hinterlands before the contract could be executed. A little later that year, he was kidnaped from in front of a New York steakhouse and held for six weeks at Don Antonio's estate in Columbia County. But Bonanno was a shrewd old negotiator. During the time he was there he managed to talk the commission out of killing him by pointing out that if he died there would be a nationwide gang war and that his son would see to it that word got out that he was executed and hadn't just disappeared.

On the other hand, if he were let go, he promised to turn over his family and all of his rackets and retire. The mob, still under pressure as a result of the Valachi hearings and the newly active FBI, decided that peace was the better course, and besides, Bonanno's interests were worth millions, even when they were split up among the remaining five families.

Pat's reelection in the off-year of 1966, with the endorsement of the Democratic party, went smoothly. But his victory was clouded by the fact that during his annual Christmas visit to Don Antonio's estate in the company of Arthur Marseri, Father Ray and Sam, the old gentleman, unable to cope with a large piece of veal which he'd tried desperately to crush between his toothless gums, choked on the meat and pitched forward on the brocaded dinner table just after the pasta course. Pat leapt to his feet and bent Don Antony's head back, trying to extract the piece of meat, but it was too late. The old man's frail physique gave up the ghost in a choking, phlegmy gargle.

Magaddino sent a special hearse from Buffalo with a crew to handle the funeral. The old man was buried in the garden among his statues. Nobody outside of the immediate family was invited. But later, Sam called for a special memorial dinner at Paolucci's on Mulberry Street. It was like a royal command performance. Giancana came from Chicago and DeSimone and Cerrito and Licata from California. DeCavalcante was there from New Jersey, Patriarca from Rhode Island, Trafficante from Florida, Marcello from Louisiana, Gambino, of course, and Catena and the rest from New York, including the new *caporegime*, Joe Colombo. Missing, of course, were Joe Bonanno and Meyer Lansky, who sent regrets from Israel.

Seated across the street, cramped into a paneled television repair truck was an uninvited observer, or rather, three uninvited observers—Regan Doyle and two photographic technicians, recording by infrared light the faces of every mourning guest.

CHAPTER 2

In the beginning, Pat, without party backing, got only the most insignificant of committee assignments, but even as the lowest ranking member of the Judiciary Committee, he was able to get on the subcommittees for immigration, citizenship, and international law, and the subcommittee for criminal justice. As a member of these subcommittees in the lowest minority, he had little power, but it gave him access to valuable information.

During his second term, he remained on the committees and gained seniority. But by then he was a member of the Democratic majority, which gave him considerably more influence and access to the chairman.

It didn't take long to learn where the real power lay in Washington, and Pat wasn't surprised to find that the lobbyists were a hell of a lot more powerful than the cities' elected representatives.

Through Scalise and his own family connections, he quickly found his way to favor in the office of the Speaker of the House, John McCormack and was amazed at the amount of traffic between McCormack's office and New York. The Speaker, himself, was often absent but Pat found that favors could be handled by the Speaker's genial and powerful assistant, Nathan Voloshen.

Even *Pat's* background hadn't prepared him for what money could do in the nation's capital. He learned that payment of the right amount in the right place could grease the way for almost any favor, from the fixing of a judge to the granting of a federal pardon.

Money funneled from Sam Massey's various organizations through the Speaker's office resulted in lucrative contracts. At the same time, Pat himself adamantly refused to become involved in any of the shady doings, even to the point of flatly refusing to act as a courier for payoff cash. Pat had bigger plans.

What impressed Pat more than anything else about Washington was the mediocre caliber of most of the men he met, particularly in the House. He gave it a lot of serious thought. He had always been under the impression that the nation's best men were elected to Congress, but he soon found that the number of burning idealists in Washington was roughly equivalent to the percentage of dedicated "good" cops in the New York Police Department, and this was a long way from a majority. Even the straightest lawmaker would usually sit still for a little back scratching. It was more or less necessary to get his own pet projects passed.

Pat, with friends and "friends of friends" all over the country through the organization, was able to do favors for a lot of Washington's "temporary residents" and despite his junior ranking, by the end of his second term he was highly regarded in the "club" as a man of influence, a good man to know.

Also, by the end of his second term, he knew where a lot of very important bodies were buried. He was pleased to find when he checked his record book that he had useful and revealing dossiers on more than half of his fellow House members. That, and the fact that he was owed a lot of uncollected favors, led him to figure the odds at about three to two that with the aid of a little heat in the right places, he could get damned near any bill he wanted passed by his colleagues—provided it wasn't too raw, and didn't step on too many toes.

It was good to know. It gave him a sense of power

he'd only known before when he had a gun in his hand.

In his first year, Father Ray urged him to sit back and be quiet, take a traditional role and not make any enemies. If he was to make any enemies, let him wait long enough to choose the ones he made and the friends he might also make by the same process.

Although many of the wiser congressmen, particularly those from the big cities, sensed that Pat had more connections than an ordinary "hero cop" could have made, very few—even of those who were members of the organization one way or another themselves—could be certain of Pat's standing.

Pat would have to be regarded a wealthy man, if all of his financial affairs had been made public, but it was doubtful that they would or could be. Most of his assets were concealed in his private safe, safe deposit boxes, or Swiss and Bahamian banks. Certainly, he now had enough money to satisfy almost any whim. But, in many ways, his life remained on a fairly simple level.

For the eyes of his constituents, he maintained a comfortable but not luxurious flat on Grand Street. His real home still was the house in Riverdale, whose value he managed to increase considerably by buying adjacent lots in all directions. It was not hard to bury fifty or even a hundred thousand in home improvements, especially when the work was done by friends who could supply minimized invoices on the work.

But the heated swimming pool, electronic burglar alarms, cellar-to-attic air conditioning and heating system, heated garage and lavish landscaping, all absorbed substantial amounts of money. Another small fortune had gone into garnishing Pat's upstate property to which he has able to add a hundred acres inherited from Don Antony. He had already gained prestige in Columbia County from his hero cop lectures and service with the state government. But now that he was a member of Congress, he was truly a citizen of the highest repute in that Republican, upstate community.

But beyond a certain point, Pat began to realize, his money bought only power. Now that he *had* money, many of the things he formerly had to pay for were free. Congressional junkets gave him considerable travel with expenses paid with the attendant fringe benefits that usually only the super-rich could afford.

With Genovese in jail and Gambino maintaining a weak control over a debilitated commission in New York, there was no longer any clear, strong *capo di tutti capi*. The number-one power in the organization now was unquestionably Meyer "The Bug" Lansky. Through Jimmy "Blue Eyes" Alo, Meyer's ambassador in New York, Pat managed to make discreet connection with the resilient little Jew who had survived them all—Lepke, Luciano, Costello, Genovese. There were even some who believed that it was Meyer "The Bug" who actually fingered the Apalachin meeting as a means of consolidating his power and preventing the organization from becoming too strong. Everybody knew about Meyer, but nobody did anything about him.

What little activity the FBI involved itself in concerning organized crime, now centered on the Italians. The Mafia was far easier to understand and more popular as an opponent than the coterie of political and financial operators that insulated Lansky from the dirty work of the mob.

It was probably the death of Don Antony that caused Pat to begin counting on his fingers the number of family heads with national power left. Sam Massey was respected and influential, but Sam had no ambitions to become *capo di tutti capi*. It fitted neither his ambitions nor his needs.

"Listen, Pat," he said. "I wouldn't lift a finger. All along I've been legit. Why change? You get up there and everybody's gunning for you. I got what I want. I got my own family," he laughed. "I got a son-in-law I can be proud of, I live here like a prince and I'm not young anymore. Do I need those headaches? Does Carlo look happy to you? Does he look like a happy man? Look at that face. It's like a prune. The man is drying up inside. He never has any pleasure from life. I don't need that."

They were stretched out beside the pool of the Fontainebleau Hotel in Miami. The bill was being picked up by Meyer Lansky. Pat was lying on his stomach to hide an erection which grew more painful by the minute, because he couldn't take his eyes off of the brown form of Katie Mulalley as she knifed into the chlorinated green waters of the pool. Katie was the featured singer in the hotel's Plantation Room.

On the grass, a hundred yards away, Constanza sat reading and occasionally twirling a brightly colored wooden toy that engaged the attention of her immobile but sun-bronzed son and heir. Even she had now realized that Sebastian would never learn to walk or talk and could barely focus his attention on anything more than five feet away from him. His constant need for attention and his inability to return anything but the most basic sort of affection had necessitated the hiring of an endless string of maids, sitters and nurses.

But, in the end, it was only the continuity of Connie's love and attention that made for any warmth in the dim life of Sebastian, who sat happily smiling, batting the wooden toy and gargling the incomprehensible sounds that Connie constantly hoped would verge on speech.

Pat rolled quickly into the pool, hoping the cool water would solve his problem. When he emerged, he called for a deck of cards and dealt out a hand of gin to his father-in-law.

"You know, Ba. In New York a couple of years ago, I spoke to a couple of pretty big-deal Democrats. They asked me if I wanted to run for governor."

Sam looked up with interest. "Democrats? You never told me that."

Pat carefully arranged his cards into melds. "It wasn't worth talking about. They were just feeling me out. It was a meaningless gesture at the time anyway, because they knew there was no way I could beat out Rockefeller. But it's an important job. I haven't given up the idea."

Katie climbed out of the pool and shook out her long, tawny hair after pulling off the red bathing cap. Her figure was still perfect and now with the even bronzing of the Florida sun she looked as tasty as a cinnamon bun. She walked over and said a few words to Constanza, kissed little Sebastian on the top of his downy head, and stopped behind Pat for a moment to watch his play of the hand. Her fingers rested lightly on Pat's bare shoulder. Even that fleeting touch made him want to throw over the cards, the drink and the playing board and rush her into the nearest cabana.

"I'm going upstairs to take a nap," Kate said. "Gotta get in shape for the show tonight."

"If you were in any better shape than you are right now, you'd bust," Sam said, smiling.

"See you. And tonight, I want some applause—real loud!"

Pat followed her sensuous walk with his eyes. Even only a few yards away, she still looked like a twenty-year-old. Sam called back his attention by knocking with nine points, and Pat was stuck still holding two queens and an ace.

"Get rid of the pictures," Sam said. "How many times I have to tell you that?"

"I was thinking."

"So thinking makes you lose?"

"Well, I was thinking about something else. Rocky's got to go for the presidency in '76. It's his last chance. He'll be sixty-eight by then. He can't possibly run again for governor in '74. It would look too bad to quit in the middle of the term. If he quit . . ."

Sam assembled the cards and squared them neatly on the playing board, passing the deck to Pat to cut.

"You've got big eyes, Pat," Sam said, "but then, maybe you're the man that can do it."

Pat played absentmindedly, his eyes fixed on some palms in the mid distance.

"This is a waste of time," Sam said in disgust. "Your mind ain't on the game. What are you thinking about, son?"

"Nothing," Pat said. "And everything."

Even to Sam, he would have been embarrassed to admit his thoughts. Everyone knew that the governorship of New York was one of the most important stepping stones to the top job. If an Irish Catholic could become president, why not someday an *Italian* Catholic? With the family in a state of disorganization, Pat Conte suddenly realized that he was within smelling distance of becoming the most powerful man in the whole fucking world! He chuckled in delight at the thought.

"What are you laughing at, you crazy kid?"

"Nothing," Pat said again. "And everything . . ."

A Cuban boy in a white jacket came over bringing him a phone on a long extension.

"It's for you, Senor."

Pat took the phone and listened for a moment. The voice which was a soft, low contralto said only two words.

"Anytime, tiger."

"Right," Pat said, and hung up.

He gathered his sunglasses, the ever-present transistor radio and his cigars.

"Gotta go up to the room, Ba," he said. "I got some business to attend to," and with a wave at Constanza and Sebastian, he strolled off toward the main building.

CHAPTER 3

It was not exactly news to political insiders that Pat Conte had ambitions for the State House. The thought began to germinate in many minds that he might not be a bad candidate at that. With Rockefeller out of the running and Nixon headed for impeachment, the Democrats had their best shot at Albany since Rockefeller took office in 1958.

There were a number of good potential candidates in the field, but none of them spelled political magic. All three leaned toward the liberal side, but Pat Conte, with four terms as a Democratic legislator, had swung quite a bit to the left, himself. He supported federal funding for public transportation, particularly subways, federally supported middle-income housing, liberalized loan policies to small businessmen and mortgagors, Teddy Kennedy's public health bill, and increased Social Security benefits. These were all rifle shots aimed at specific elements of his constituency.

He dragged his feet on civil rights, but modified his truculence so that he was no longer identified as a racist candidate. He had minimized his support from the Conservative party and preferred to be thought of now as a latter-day Fiorello La Guardia.

Mainly, it was his constant appearance on the newspaper pages and on television in connection with congressional crime investigations, plus his ten years of stumping the upstate hinterlands, that gave Pat a formidable identification with the statewide electorate that transcended his urban origins. The practical reality was that Pat now had a bigger and better more solidly financed organization than all of the other candidates put together. There was, in fact, no way of stopping him. And there didn't seem to be too many people who *wanted* to stop him, except, maybe, the reform element of the Democratic party.

The public found it hard to distinguish between the sort of crime Pat had consistently fought and organized crime. Besides, Pat had actually taken part in many moves against organized crime (when it was to the interest of his own family).

Just as he had moved to the left in his political spectrum, he had moved theoretically into an ecumenical position on the mob scene, sliding over from the strictly Sicilian-oriented association of his childhood to a sort of a co-prosperity sphere in conjunction with Meyer Lansky and his ambassador. Jimmy "Blue Eyes" Alo.

Through Lansky, Pat was able to get support from many Jewish liberals in New York not otherwise accessible to him. Money was fed into hundreds of business and private outlets from Pat's family and private sources and leaked back again as legitimate campaign contributions. If he needed it, Pat could tap campaign war chests as big as Rockefeller's, but for the coming election, it didn't look as though he would need it.

Rockefeller, sliding out of office to prepare the way for his last presidential try in '76 had left the Republicans saddled with a colorless and unimaginative incumbent. Yet the Republicans had no choice but to run him.

It wasn't long before a Citizens' Committee for Conte appeared, headed by Art Winburg, with Guido Paterno supplying support from the business side and Father Ray ably holding up the spiritual wing. Katie Mullaley was a great asset in organizing the showbiz segment for Conte, and Pat's longtime interest in theater and show business stood him in good favor here. One of his platform planks was a promise of state-funded and federally-aided New York State theater to bring the wonders of Broadway to the hinterlands.

Ultimately, Pat was even able to win over Jim Bailey, now a influential public relations executive. Jim had mellowed, too, and was now less militant about black rights and more interested in getting his children into good colleges that were not permissive, or for that matter overrun with blacks. To provide a completely balanced ticket in his organization, Pat had Irish Jerry Foley in charge of public relations.

Early in 1973, Pat took the traditional "Three-I" tour—a requisite for New York candidates—Ireland, Israel and Italy. Constanza went with him reluctantly, since Pat pointed out that it would simply be too difficult and dangerous for Sebastian's health for him to go along, and yet it would look strange if Constanza didn't go.

Sebastian had been through several sieges of upper respiratory ailments. Most medical experts doubted that he would live more than another five years, but for the moment his health was good. Constanza installed two full-time registered nurses with special training in the care of retarded children and had Dr. Pileggi promise to check by phone several times a week before she finally consented to go on the trip.

"It could be sort of a second honeymoon for us, honey," Pat said, and was sorry as soon as he had said it.

Constanza looked at him with a cool, level gaze.

"Do you think, Pat, that I don't know that you're using me, and Sebastian, too?"

"Look," Pat said, "let's not start any trouble at this point. Get some nice clothes and enjoy yourself. We'll stop in Rome and I'll arrange for you to have an audience with the pope. Okay?"

"Fine," Constanza said, but she didn't smile.

CHAPTER 4

If anyone was deeply disturbed by Pat's candidacy, it was Regan Doyle. After a blazing start with the New York office, bolstered by support from Bobby Kennedy as attorney general, Doyle's star began to fizzle in 1963 after the assassination. It was all but extinguished following the second Kennedy assassination in 1968.

The FBI activities against organized crime continued, but on a diminished basis. A lot of the newer agents, who spent their time investigating black militant plots, kidnaping and bank robberies, saw Doyle as an aging but colorful remnant of the old gangbusters days.

Pat Conte had been forced to walk a tightrope concerning Colombo's Italian-American Civil Rights League. Basically, he damned it with faint praise. Gambino and the Genovese family, including Tommy Ryan, were completely opposed to Colombo's line.

"For Christ's sake," Pat said once. "Gambino doesn't even think of himself as an Italian-American. He thinks of himself as an Italian-*Italian*."

Everybody in the family picketed Joe Colombo's second big Italian Unity Day rally in Columbus Circle on June 28, 1971. Pat Conte made sure he didn't attend. He didn't need to walk around carrying signs saying, "Kiss me, I'm Italian," or "Italian Power" to assure himself of the Italian vote. His name, his constituency, his continued support of Italian-American causes and Father Ray by his side were enough.

But Colombo went ahead with his grandstand play,

beaming in the New York summer sun in his shirt sleeves, surrounded by red, white and green decorations, hot dog vendors, ice cream wagons and dozens of cameramen. There were even a few blacks in the crowd. Colombo waved and smiled at a fat black woman standing a few yards away. He also waved back and posed for a black movie photographer standing nearby.

But as he turned to move toward the platform, the movie photographer raced up behind Colombo and pumped three 7.65 caliber bullets from a German automatic into him at close range. Colombo fell to the ground, bleeding from the head and neck. Almost simultaneously, another burst of shots rang out and Jerome Johnson, the black movie photographer, died with a half dozen shots in his midsection.

It was assumed Colombo would die any minute, but in the end he lived on a vegetable, even less capable of communication than Sebastian Conte. Everybody said that Joey Gallo and his mob had done it, and the Gallos did little to disillusion the public of this idea. In fact, Crazy Joey began to attract almost as much attention as Colombo. By March 1972, everybody in town knew there was an open contract out on Joey Gallo. It was just a question of finding him at the right moment.

On April 6 they found Joey Gallo in Umberto's Clam House on Mulberry Street. He was buried on April 10 in a five-thousand-dollar bronze coffin, dressed in a black pinstripe suit, a blue shirt and a black polkadot tie. There was nobody from the organization at his wake. Nobody knew that better than Regan Doyle, who was watching through binoculars and the viewfinder of a two hundred millimeter Nikon from a flat across the way on President Street.

It wasn't long before a frightened hood named Joe Luparelli, well known to Doyle from his years of mob surveillance, sneaked into New York, turned himself over to the FBI, and talked and talked and talked. Doyle wasn't assigned to the Gallo murder. Most of that work was left to the New York police under Inspector Al Seedman, but everything that Luparelli said about the mob went into Regan's extensive files. Three weeks after the Gallo killing, Doyle led a raid on Carmine "The Snake" Persico's farm in Saugerties, New York. The feds had obtained a warrant to search the farm, which was reported to be a hideout and an arsenal for the Colombo organization.

The tip was a good one. Doyle and his men found a dozen rifles, shotguns and pistols in the rambling main house and another batch almost as big in the barn. According to Doyle's information, at least five more members of the Gallo mob were slated to be rubbed out in order to bring a finish to the Gallo-Colombo war.

Between Colombo's hit in June 1971 and the following year, there were eighteen killings, all connected to the Gallo-Colombo war. After that, there were still more victims. A New Jersey laundryman was mowed down in a Manhattan parking lot. A young burglar and drug dealer was knocked off ten blocks from Ciprio's Restaurant. Another Gallo pal was bumped off outside a Manhattan hospital and another associate murdered in a car near Prospect Park. A Queens man was left in an auto in the Bushwick section of Brooklyn with six bullet wounds in his head and neck. A second cousin of the Gallos, Alfred Bianco, was shot as he was drinking an early-morning cup of coffee.

The next month, the Gallos made an abortive try at taking young Anthony Colombo, but Anthony's bodyguards were intercepted and there was an eighteen-shot barrage loosed at the fleeing, failed assassins. Just over a month later, Tommy Ryan Eboli, acting boss of the Genovese family said good-bye to a woman friend and walked to his chauffeured Cadillac. He was cut down by a gunman in a passing truck, taking five bullets in the head. Eboli's chauffeur took off for Jersey, leaving his boss in the street.

Doyle found himself working on as many as a dozen federally connected homicides at once.

Suddenly the mob began to be aware of the growing pressure from the FBI. They realized the seriousness of the repercussions when the FBI probe got as far as Jimmy "Blue Eyes" Alo, who denied he'd ever visited the Nyack hideout in which the Gallo killers had been lurking. But Doyle and two other agents, acting on information from Luparelli, had kept the apartment under surveillance and it was the testimony of the FBI men that finally nailed Meyer Lansky's bag man and ambassador.

According to Pat Conte's Byzantine strategy, there was a bright side to all of this. With Gambino weakened and even Lansky's family operating short, Pat's power was greater than ever. The betting of the mob was that he would win the election, making his position even stronger. But there was bad news, too. Bit by bit and thread by thread, Doyle was beginning to realize that for more than ten years he'd been sharing drinks and coffee with the man who now seemed to be on top of the organized criminal world.

In May 1974, Regan Doyle was contacted by one Paul Terli. Terli was the head of a concrete-mixing firm which was a subsidiary of the Massey construction empire. When the ceiling of one of Massey's slum rehabilitation projects in the Seventeenth CD collapsed, killing three Puerto Rican children and their unmarried mother, Terli had become the fall guy and was charged with criminal negligence for deliberately supplying substandard concrete. But Terli was not a man anxious to face investigation. There were too many things in his past. Without consulting anybody in the organization, he had dropped from sight, and now the word all up and down Mulberry Street was that there was an open contract on Paul "The Hook" Terli.

On April 22, one of Doyle's informants in a Howard Johnson's bar in Tarrytown called him and said that Terli was willing to meet Doyle for a talk.

"Okay." Doyle said. "I'll meet you, but no deals in advance. You know that. You can take my word I'll play square."

There was a pause on the end of the line, and Doyle knew it was an even chance the next sound would be the click of a hung-up phone. But after a minute, the voice which sounded desperate, said, "Okay." They set up a meet in the parking lot of Howard Johnson's in Tarrytown. It was like a hundred other rendezvous that Doyle had set up in his career, most of them pointless and profitless efforts by some hood to get off the hook, some of them deliberate fakes. Half the time, nobody at all would show up, with the informant getting cold feet. But only by checking them all out, or at least all that seemed likely, could he develop a proper team of informants, and without informants, there were no cases.

In this case, what intrigued Doyle was the fact that Terli's name rang a bell. He looked him up in the enormous file on the organization he'd built up over the years, and found only a brief notation. Terli, more than ten years ago, had been the man who identified the body of one Stanley Stanrilowicz, who had been found hanging from meat hooks in a Royal Meat Company truck.

Only a few weeks later, Royal Meat was taken over by one Al Santini, believed to be a member of the Marseri and Genovese families of the organization.

Before closing the file drawer, Regan followed another hunch and pulled the sheet on Al Santini. Santini had a record of arrests for embezzlement, tax evasion, a couple of very early raps for violation of the Sullivan Act, one rape charge and one extortion charge. No convictions. In the file was a small Xeroxed clipping with Santini's name circled toward the bottom. It was a clipping from an early edition of the *News* which carried the story of Pat's shoot-out in Brooklyn, the one in which he had won the Medal of Honor. Al Santini's name appeared in the story because the car, the white Capri that Pat had been driving that night, was registered to him.

CHAPTER 5

Because of the relatively late decision to run for governor, Pat's "Three-I" tour had come after the start of the campaign, but Winburg judged it as extremely important.

"The Italian part of the trip isn't too necessary," he explained, "since you've been there a number of times, but this election is going to be won by the votes that Rockefeller formerly pulled in the metropolitan areas and these include a lot of Irish and Jews. Rockefeller had a good hold on the Jewish vote. Now, with the war tension, the Yom Kippur war, the oil embargo and all that sort of thing, it's absolutely essential that you make the Israel trip, and to some extent, the same thing applies to Ireland. The trouble with the North, the bombings and so on, have created a highly emotional state, and a visit to Ireland, and a direct report from you to the electorate could count for a great deal."

Constanza was sullen and unresponsive as a traveling companion, but brightened up a bit at seeing the holy sights in Israel and was almost radiant over her reception by the pope and her visit to the Vatican. It was on the third day of their stay at the Shelburne Hotel in Dublin that Pat got the call from Dr. Pileggi, or at least that is when the phone message was delivered. It took another three hours to get the transatlantic call through.

The doctor's voice was thick with sleep when he answered.

"Hello, Pat. It's three in the morning here. Sorry if I don't sound very wide awake."

"What's the trouble?" Pat said. "It's the kid, isn't it?"

There was a pause. "Pat, he's pretty sick. You know he's had all these respiratory troubles. Now he seems to have developed bronchiectasis and he's running a high fever. I took the liberty of putting him into Montefiore Hospital yesterday afternoon. I've been trying to call, but I haven't been able to reach you."

"This bronchiectasis, is it serious?"

"Pat, *anything's* serious in a kid like that if it takes place in the lungs. He's been coughing up pus and blood and he's developed quite a bit of fluid in the chest cavity. I've got a drain on, and I'm giving him antibiotics."

"Do you think we better get right back?"

There was a pause. "Well, he's a mighty sick kid."

"Okay, well, we'll get on the next plane. Ah, that is, we've got a reception with Dermot Ryan, the archbishop. It could be very important to me in the election, but it's only a matter of hours then we'll get a plane out tomorrow night."

Constanza came out of the bathroom as Pat was completing the call. Her face was rosy with the heat of the shower, and her short, dark hair curled appealingly in damp ringlets about her face. In her long, clinging negligee she looked much like the girl who had accompanied Pat to Switzerland so long ago, when Sebastian's poor mangled chromosomes had first been mixed into a vital brew. Connie was rubbing the dampness out of her hair with the big, white hotel bath towel.

"Is there trouble?"

"Nothing serious," Pat said, "but we'll go home a few days ahead of time. I'll book a plane for tomorrow night if there is one."

"It's okay with me," Connie said, sitting at the vanity table to comb out the short curls. "I'm anxious to get home and see Sebastian again. It's the longest I've ever been away from him."

"I'll get us home as soon as I can."

Pat got an enthusiastic reception at the big lunch that Archbishop Ryan's staff had arranged for him. The Irish felt a certain affection for anybody who was a New York cop and a Catholic at that—so many of them had relatives on the force. A press release, giving his credentials as a hero had gone before him, as well as the fact that Pat had been in recent communication with the pope.

As he had done at each of the previous stops, Pat had a local movie cameraman take films of him walking about the city, and particularly chatting with the archbishop in front of St. Patrick's Cathedral. All of this would be spliced into a campaign film to be used on television and at various meetings.

It was not until they were bundled into the chauffeured limousine on the way to the airport that Pat told Connie the real reason for cutting their trip short.

"I didn't want to worry you, Connie, and maybe there isn't that much to worry about. I spoke with Dr. Pileggi last night on the telephone."

Connie gave a little gasp. "It's Sebastian! Something's wrong with Sebastian!"

"Now take it easy," Pat said. "He's got some kind of lung trouble but Pileggi's in charge and he's giving him antibiotics and doing everything that can be done. There's nothing you could do if you were there."

"I knew I shouldn't have left him! I shouldn't have listened to you. What is this all for anyway? Your goddamn stupid campaign. And I left that child alone for two weeks. This is God's punishment."

"Look," Pat said, "the kid was under the full-time care of nurses. Anything that happened to him would have happened anyway."

"I should have been there."

"It's probably nothing," Pat said. "You know he's

had these illnesses before. They get those sort of things."

Constanza's eyes drilled into him with a look of sheer hate.

"I'm holding you responsible."

For the rest of the trip, Constanza barely spoke. She spent her time nibbling at her cuticles, looking out the window, fingering her rosary. She even refused to get off the plane during the half-hour stop at Shannon until forced to do so, and then she simply sat in the waiting room without looking at any of the shops.

Pat tried to call New York from Shannon, but was unable to get through before the flight was called again. When the plane landed at Kennedy, an Aer Lingus hostess boarded the plane as soon as the ramp was down. She escorted the Contes from the plane into a small anteroom in the reception are t. Father Ray, Sam Massey and Art Winburg were waiting. Their looks were grim.

Contanza seemed to sense the situation at once. Before any of them could say anything, she let out a soul-shattering gasp.

"Mother of God!" she said. "He's dead! Sebastian is dead! He's dead! Daddy, for Christ's sake, tell me!"

Sam said nothing, but approached and took Connie in his arms. Connie laid her head on his thick, tweedy shoulder and sobbed. The sound came out in long, hard, dry croaks.

"My baby, my baby," she said. "It's God's punishment."

Sam looked uncomfortable. He patted her back awkwardly and said, "Take it easy, darling. Take it easy."

Pat asked Father Ray, "What happened?"

Father Ray sighed. "The boy died early this morning. He more or less drowned in his own fluid. There was nothing we could do. The antibiotics just wouldn't take hold. The infection had gone too far. He wasn't strong you know, and his lungs were very susceptible. Dr. Pileggi said that children like him seldom last even this long. It was a miracle that he lived as long as he did."

Constanza looked up from Sam's shoulder. Her face was blotched with red as though she'd suddenly contracted some strange skin disease. Her lashes were matted from tears and her eyes were staring. Each of the men watched her in silence as she took several deep breaths, trying to get control of her voice. She looked at Pat.

"Pat, I want you to drop out of the campaign. I want you to quit. This is a punishment from God and you know very well what for."

"We'll talk about it later, honey," Pat said, gently.

"We'll talk about it now, *now,* you son-of-a-bitch! God forgive me. I don't know what I'm saying. You'll quit! Do you hear me? I say you'll *quit!*"

Father Ray signaled unobtrusively, and a nurse who had been waiting in the corner of the room came up with a glass of water and some pills. Sam took the plastic cup and the pills from her.

"Here, take these, darling. We'll talk later. You're very upset, and God knows, you're entitled to be."

Pat approached and tried to take her in his arms.

"Stay away from me, you bastard!" she screamed. "Stay away. I'll kill you I swear if you come near. I'll kill you!"

Winburg looked around nervously to see if anybody was around to hear this, but there was only the nurse and the hostess. He took them aside and explained the situation, that Constanza was hysterical and temporarily deranged by the death of her son. Both nodded understandingly. Distracted, hardly seeming to know what she was doing, Connie swallowed the pills. She turned to Father Ray.

"It's a punishment from God. Isn't it? You should know."

Father Ray patted her shoulder gently. "It's not a punishment. You're the best woman in the world and Pat is a wonderful man. God moves in his own ways. For this child, maybe it was the best. I'm sure he's happier where he is now."

Constanza's eyes, glazed already from the effects of the Valium, gazed coldly at Father Ray.

"You would say that, wouldn't you? Yes, you'd say that. You're one of *them*. You don't work for God. You work for *them*."

But Father Ray acted as though he hadn't heard her.

"All right, child. All right. God is with us. He will look after us. I gave the boy the last rites myself, and I know he's in heaven with Him."

Connie's eyes were already beginning to go dull and her shoulders drooped with shock and fatigue and the effects of the drug. Winburg had made arrangements and a young man from Irish International-Airlines led them down a side passage and out a back door, avoiding the waiting reporters in customs.

"Have no fear, sir," he said. "We'll collect your luggage and have it sent on to you at home. There's no need to be going through all of these formalities with you, in your time of trouble."

Sam's limousine was waiting outside of the terminal with Tommy's younger brother at the wheel. He had been driving for Sam ever since Tommy's death.

Constanza fell back, limp, nearly unconscious, on the deep upholstery. Pat sat beside her and tried to take her hand, but even in her semicomatose state, she pushed him away, so he moved over and let Sam sit beside her and hold her hand.

The heavy car glided quietly off toward Riverdale. Winburg was sitting in the jumpseat opposite Pat. Watching from the corner of his eye to make sure Connie was really sleeping, Pat whispered, "How is all this going to affect things—the election?"

Winburg shrugged. "To tell you the truth, it couldn't hurt you. There'll be a lot of sympathy. Who can put a knock on somebody who's gone through what you have?"

"Well," Pat said, sighing, "to quote Father Ray. God moves in mysterious ways."

CHAPTER 6

As the campaign months drew to a close in the fall, Pat concentrated his efforts on the cities. He was in essence a city candidate, but not only from New York City. There were great clusters of minorities—Italians and Poles and Jews and Irish—in upstate metropolises like Buffalo, Syracuse, Troy, Albany and Rochester. Increasingly, they, too, were having problems of crime and crowding.

The rural and farm vote was much smaller than people supposed—less than 15 percent of the electorate, and they were votes that were expensive and hard to line up. Pat decided to settle for whatever his normal quota would bring him there, and for the converts he could make through his extensive television appearances. He carried a plentiful supply of Pepto-Bismol and did the obligatory, international gustatory scene. He ate *pirogen* in Yorktown, *cuchifritos* in Spanish Harlem, *zeppoli* and *calzone* on Staten Island and bagels and lox in Bay Ridge.

He paid concerned visits to vandalized and burned-out synagogues on the Lower East Side and promised to see that state laws were imposed against this sort of brutalization and that state funds were supplied for reconstruction.

His shift to the Democrats had been a fortunate one since there was a tremendous wave of voting against the Republicans in the wake of the Watergate scandals that year. In New Jersey, the gubernatorial race had shown a record Democratic majority. While Pat's opponent carefully avoided open support of Nixon, he was not in a position to repudiate the president and was furthermore inextricably tangled in the coattails of Rockefeller, with whom he had served as elected lieutenant governor for four terms. Without Rockefeller's more forceful personality and polished platform manner, his record stood easily vulnerable to attack.

Pat pointed out that the governor's vaunted narcotics programs had cost the state more than a billion dollars and had not made any serious dent in the problem. More people were dying in his methadone program than had been dying from heroin, and the drug traffic was greater than ever.

During Rockefeller's regime, the state budget had more than quadrupled to 8.75 billion dollars. Taxes had quintupled. Many of them were regressive against the poor and middle class such as Rockefeller's 4 percent sales tax, the rise in the state cigarette tax from three cents to fifteen cents, the rise in the gasoline tax from four cents to eight cents.

In poor areas, Pat mocked the governor's ineffective campaign against "welfare cheats." In counterattacking, he stressed his own integrity and experience, but Pat chose to interpret the former lieutenant governor's remarks on integrity as an attack on his Italian background. This tended to backfire on the Republican. To counter his years of experience in the state house, Pat had only to point out the Republican record in Albany.

"It is no problem for a poor incompetent to get elected if he's riding the coattail of a *rich* incompetent who can spend six and seven million dollars on each campaign. Despite his enormous war chest, the governor has had to bolster his position by passing out two million dollars a year to state officeholders who never showed up in their offices.

"It's the Republican contention that you can't get a decent man to hold a job in this state without paying him as much as forty thousand dollars a year to do nothing!"

Pat was even able to venture into the brittle area of mob domination when he pointed out that one of the honored members of the Governor's Club, an exclusive group of contributors that had raised more than two million dollars for the Republican campaigns, was Antonio Magliocco, brother of the late, dead "Fat Man" Magliocco and reputed to be a member of the Joe Colombo family.

As for the governor's campaign against "Organized Crime," Pat said, "Let me point out that in the same Governor's Club with the alleged mob member are such sterling crime fighters as former United States Attorney, Whitney North Seymour, Jr., John W. Ryan, Jr., a member of the State Commission of Investigation, Robert J. Gallati, Director of the State Identification and Intelligence System, and Archibald R. Murray, Administrator of the State Division of Criminal Justice. Can you picture what a jolly party that must have been on the lawn in Pocantico Hills on the governor's lush estate? All those people paling it up, downing martinis with Joe Magliocco?"

Pat's attack on Magliocco was a two-pronged barb. It hit the governor's integrity, and through him, the Republican candidate and at the same time weakened the Gambino family.

Galloping inflation was a big problem that year.

"What have the Republicans done about the inflation in this state, about the growing prices of food, gasoline and rent? They've done their best to get rid of rent control, they've supported rising gasoline prices and food prices, but they have promised to appoint a commission, paid out of *your* pocket, voters, to *investigate* the problems caused by inflation. That promise was made a year and a half ago! We're still waiting for their action!

"That's what the Republicans have done for you, voters, during the four terms of millionaire rule. And what are they leaving behind? A billion-dollar boondoggle in Albany, The Mall! Some people call it instant Stonehenge, Rocky's erector set, Nelson's Folly or Rockefeller Center North. These supposedly hotshot business minds managed to smuggle through a project estimated at a vague two hundred and fifty million. It will now cost the taxpayers of New York a *billion and a half* by the time it's finished, and show a benefit to nobody except the private financial interests backed by the Rockefellers and their banks. And the Republicans say that this 'urgent' project will be a benefit to the people of Albany. That's a laugh. They tore down housing for three thousand families to build the Mall, made plans to resettle nine hundred families and then abandoned those. This gives you an idea of Republican concern for the common man. Nowhere has Rockefeller's yes man spoken out about this shocking situation."

The receptions Pat got were heartening. He had a strong campaign. He was riding the crest of a Democratic turnabout and he had charm and charisma that made his opponent look like a mud fence. Repeatedly, he challenged his opponent to face-to-face debates on television, hoping for an encounter like the famous Kennedy-Nixon debate of 1960, but the Republicans were too shrewd for that.

Art Winburg selected a Glenfiddich malt whiskey from Pat's well-filled and well-concealed liquor closet in the back room of his storefront headquarters on Grand Street.

"I hate to jinx us, Pat, my boy," Winburg said, "but I don't see any way they can pass us at this point. The polls, the *Daily News* straw vote, the *Post* editorial, everything's going right according to plan."

"L'chaim," Pat said, toasting his campaign manager.

"Next year in Albany," Winburg said. "About the only thing that could hurt you now," he added, wiping his lips with a red, white and blue paper napkin, printed with the American flag and the words, "New York for Conte," "is having somebody come up with some fantastic skeleton in your closet, a skeleton bigger than Watergate."

Pat answered with a tight smile. "We know there's no chance of that," he said.

But Regan Doyle had other ideas.

CHAPTER 7

From the start of the campaign, Doyle had redoubled his efforts against organized crime, trying to zero in on Pat's connection to it. He had an impressive portfolio linking Pat to most of the mob leaders. He also had photos of Pat with mobsters like Genovese, Bender and Tommy Ryan Eboli. But he had nothing *specific* to pin on Pat. Pat had enemies in various parts of the mob and many that would have been willing to see him nailed to a cross, but those that Doyle was able to dig up were either too terrified to talk or simply didn't know enough.

Doyle had lengthy tapes on conversations involving almost all of the top mob men, but many of these came from bootleg or suicide taps—worthless in court. For at least five years, Pat had said nothing in any of the places observed by the FBI which could be picked up by their microphones. The few times when he did meet with any important mob chiefs, he had that damned transistor radio going full blast, blotting out all of the conversation or occasionally only letting through a fascinating tidbit.

As time ran out, Doyle, still without a case against Pat, desperately tried leaking teasers to reporters and columnists, but Pat disparaged all attempts to link him to organized crime as the product of anti-Italian television and newspaper campaigns.

"This popularization of the so-called Mafia idea," Pat said in a speech, "is an insult to America's twenty-two million law-abiding Italo-Americans," and went on into a recitation, not only of the great Italian contributors to American culture, such as Enrico Fermi, A.P. Giannini, the banker, Frank Sinatra and Philadelphia's mayor, Frank Rizzo, but of the many Italo-Americans importantly involved in the war against crime such as former Police Sergeant Ralph Salerno, and Charles Siragusa of the Federal Narcotics Bureau.

"For every 'bad guy' that these slanderers can point out with an Italian name, I can point out twenty solid, industrious, God-fearing, crime-fighting Americans of Italian descent. The innuendos that have been circulating concerning me and my Italian background should be brought out into the open. They are vicious, racist attacks that are almost beneath my contempt."

So, Pat was even able to turn Doyle's whispering campaign into a political asset. Doyle found that complaining to Katie did no good, either. Of course, he was not able to tell her all of the confidential information available to him. But over the years, he had constantly harped on Pat's mob associations. It wasn't that Katie didn't believe them. It was that she underestimated their importance.

"Look, Regan, all I know is that Pat has been decent to me—oh, once in a while, he's roughed me up—but he's also helped me. He's used a lot of influence to get me jobs, not only in New York, but in Miami, Chicago, Vegas, Los Angeles. I know that he's helped raise money for a couple of my shows that went on the rocks and he's gotten the landlords to extend the leases at some theaters where we were going to be put on the street. He's been a real friend. If he's involved in some kind of business between these different Italian mobs, I don't want to know about it. It's something between them."

They were having a late-night hamburger at P.J. Clarke's on Third Avenue.

"You think it's just a game of cops and robbers, just like the movies, don't you?" Doyle answered angrily. "A genial bunch of godfathers avenging justice with some kind of noble Sicilian flair. Okay, let me show you something."

He pulled a sheaf of transcripts in manila folders from

his battered briefcase and put them on the checkered table cloth.

"Here," he said, "read this paragraph. This is a tape we made of a conversation between a hood named Ray DiCarlo and a gun named Tony Boy Boiardo, whose father's estate has a crematory where they burn some of these high-class victims—and they're not all Italians. Listen, read this paragraph."

He showed her a half page of transcript.

> TONY BOY: How bout the time we hit the litle Jew . . .
> RAY: As little as they are, they struggle.
> TONY BOY: The Boot hit him with a hammer. The guy goes down and comes up so I got a crowbar this big, Ray. Eight shots in the head. What do you think he finally did to me? He spit at me and said, "you guinea fuck!''

Kate read the passage silently.

"You know who your lover-boy pal works for?" Doyle said. "He works for his father-in-law, Sam Massey and Sam Massey is the head of a sub-family that belongs to Vito Genovese. You've heard of him."

Kate nodded. "Who hasn't?"

Doyle turned a page or two and showed her another section of the same transcript.

"Okay, read this. This is between the same guy, Ray and Anthony "Little Pussy" Russo, who is the chauffeur, or used to be, for Vito Genovese."

> RUSSO: Ray, I seen too many. You know how many guys we hit that way up there?

RAY: What about the big furnace he's
got back there?
RUSSO: That's what I'm trying to
tell you before you go up there.
RAY: The big iron grate.
RUSSO: He used to put them on there
and burn them.

"And I'll tell you something else," Doyle said. "That guy didn't just burn the people he knocked off. He burned the bodies of any victims the mob had to get rid of. Fun, huh? Here, I'll show you something that we picked up from Tommy, you remember, the nice chauffeur for Sam Massey that got killed in Pat's shootout in Brooklyn? I'd just like you to look at this transcript we made a couple of years ago on him."

TOMMY: That no-good Mick Sullivan.
He was six months behind on his
interest payments, then he threatens
to go to the cops. You know what I
did to him? I took him out to the
dump in Flushing and I got this real
thin piano wire and I twisted it
around his neck. I turned it real
slow so he'd know what was happening
to him and then I left him there on
the dump so everybody would know
he was garbage.
UNKNOWN VOICE: It's the only thing
to do. If you let them, they walk
all over you. I remember a job I
did for Patriarca up in Providence.
This guy Marfeo is eating some pizza
in a joint called The Korner Kitchen
Restaurant. Miceli fingered him for
me. I'd never seen the guy before.

So I walk in, I pull out my piece
and I make everybody lay on the
floor and I push Marfeo into the
phone booth and I close the door and
I let him have four slugs, right in
the head and the chest. It was broad
daylight. I walk right out. Nobody
said nothing, nobody saw nothing.
Providence is in good control. They
know what's good for them there.

TOMMY: What did the guy do?

UNKNOWN VOICE: How the fuck do I
know? They just asked me to come
up there.

TOMMY (LAUGHING): Yeah, it's that
way sometime. One time Sam sent me
to do a job. I didn't even know the
guy. He crossed Sam up on some deal
in the basketball thing. He was like
a college guy or something, you
know? So I didn't even take a piece.
I just took this ball bat. I go up
to his house, way up in the East
Bronx near White Plains Road, you
know?

UNKNOWN VOICE: Yeah, I know that
section. My uncle got a farm there.

TOMMY: So I just figure out the
right angle and I push the bell. I
see the kid's car. It's out in front
so I know he's home.

UNKNOWN VOICE: Yeah, so what
happened?

TOMMY: So the kid opened. I don't
say a word. I just let him have one
big smash, right in the face with
the bat. Crashes his head right in.

The kid goes down. He don't know a
thing. I wrap the bat in newspaper.
I drive away, and later I throw the
bat in the furnace in the cellar
of my house. It was perfect. You
know what I mean? No weapon, no
ballistics tests, nothing.
UNKNOWN VOICE: You get paid?
TOMMY: Sure. I got a five-C bonus.
You know I was already on the
payroll, so it wasn't like I was
an outside man.
UNKNOWN VOICE: Yeah, that's right.
In the family it's different.

Regan replaced the transcript in his folder.

"Nice people, eh?" he said to Katie who was turning pale.

"That's enough, Regan," she said. "You don't have to overdo it."

"No, no," Doyle said. "I'm not sure you got the picture yet. And none of these guys we're talking about, none of these victims, are members of the family, right? These are *victims*. I'd like you to look at one more thing. I got this when I was in Chicago. It was the first thing that made me realize what this mob was up to, but there's something now that might tie up to it.

"These guys are talking about a fellow named William Jackson, who was a big, three-hundred-and-fifty-pound slugger for the outfit. Somewhere along the line, he crossed up Sam Giancana. Sam is a big buddy of Genovese, you know, and of Sam Massey."

Kate tried to interrupt. Her face looked pinched and white.

"Regan, why . . . ?"

"No, wait," Regan said. "I want you to read this. Now, these are two informants named James Torello and another hood named Fiore Buccire. They're talking to a guy named Jackie Cerone, and they're telling him how they got rid of this fat William Jackson.

> TORELLO: Jackson was hung up on that
> meat hook. He was so fucking heavy,
> he bent it! He was on that thing for
> three days before he croaked.
> BUCCIRE(LAUGHING): Jackie, you
> should have seen the guy! Like an
> elephant he was, and when Jimmy
> hit him in the balls with that
> electric prod . . .
> TORELLO: He was flopping around on
> that hook, Jackie. We tossed water
> on him to give the prod a better
> charge and he's screaming . . .

Katie's face went white and beads of perspiration formed on her upper lip.

"If you're trying to shock me . . ."

"No, wait," Doyle said. "I just want you to read one other little bit by this guy Torello. Here, it's on this page. Here, read this."

Screening the confidential areas, he held a page of transcripts in front of her.

> TORELLO: The stretcher is best. Put
> a guy on it with chains and you can
> stretch him till his joints pop
> . . . Remember the guy who sweat so
> much he dried out? He was always
> whining, 'water, water, water . . .'
> I think he died of thirst.

Katie threw the paper across the table to Doyle.

"Regan, I'm not reading anymore. What are you trying to do to me?"

The FBI man reached over and took Katie's hand in his.

"I'm not trying to do anything to you, Katie. I'm just trying to get you to see *what* it is you're working for and *who* it is. It's not Marlon Brando and the Warner Bros. stock players on some back lot. These people are heartless and bloodthirsty and they don't only kill their own. They kill *anybody* that gets in their way, and they *like* doing it! Don't you understand? It's not just business. It's business and pleasure to those guys, and that includes your friend, lover-boy Pat Conte."

Katie took a sip from her scotch and soda and the color began to return to her face.

"Look, Regan. I've known the man for twenty years, and so have you. Sure, he may get rough once in a while, but he's not one of those monsters that you just showed me tapes of. I know that. Pat would not kill, and he's done a lot of good. He's helped set up a law for retarded children. He's helped a lot of people get into this country, not only from Italy either. For God's sake, I've even heard him speak *against* the mob. Sure, I know about Connie's father. I knew that a long time ago, but I don't think he's really in that business, not for years. For God's sake, he held me on his knee when I was a kid. I think I would know a killer if I saw one."

Doyle sighed in frustration. "You don't think Pat Conte could do anything like that? You think he's too kind?"

"Not exactly kind . . ." Katie started to answer, but Doyle interrupted.

"No, no, I know what you mean. 'He's just not that sort of person!' You got a lot to learn, Katie and I hope to Christ you learn it before . . . before it's too late! If it isn't already . . . !"

"What the hell do you mean by that?"

"I can't tell you yet," Regan said. "But I sure hope I'll be able to expose the truth about that bastard soon. Soon enough to keep him from getting elected."

CHAPTER 8

Regan Doyle's informant, Terli, was a hard man to locate. He failed to show up for the first meeting in Tarrytown. They made another rendezvous in Diamond Jim's Inn in Spring Valley, only to have Terli call again and transfer the meeting to the bar in the Motel on the Mountain in Suffern.

Before Doyle actually met with Terli, he spent a lot of time checking out the GIIF which had summaries of information on mob leaders. and he checked the file on Terli. Terli, it seemed, had contacted the agency twice during the past year and offered to swap information on the Mafia for tips on anybody in the organization that was out to get him.

In his own personal file, Regan found a memo that he had tucked away on a hunch.

```
TO: SAC, NEW YORK //CI //SI //R
                                (Prob)
FROM: SA JOHN LYNCH //PCI //PSI //R
                                GHETTO

SUBJECT: PAUL TERLI
DATES OF CONTACT 1/22, 26 and 27/73
PURPOSE AND RESULTS OF CONTACT
//NEGATIVE
//POSITIVE
//STATISTIC
Informant called on 1/22/73, offered
to supply information on "Cosa
```

Nostra" in return for information
from bureau re hostile members of
said oganization. SA Lynch met with
informant 1/26 at Blarney Stone Bar,
44th Street and Third Avenue, New
York. Informant has record for
several arrests, including
narcotics, rape, assault and car
theft. No convictions. A/K/A Paul
Turley and Thomas Pauley. Believed
to be soldier in family of Sam
Massey of Genovese family. Subject
admitted to being informant to
NYPD, CIB. Ralph Salerno of CIB
confirms. Informant claims inside
knowledge of Massey and Genovese
operations, including illegal
contracting and construction methods
in Hunts Point Houses in Bronx and
also in slum clearance project in
Mulberry Street area. Claims he
can prove criminal fraud resulting
in accident fatal to four tenants
in Mulberry Street housing area.
Suspect says that he is falsely
suspected of being informant by own
family and has been threatened with
execution. He is five foot seven,
dark complexion, slightly pockmarked, long thin nose, black eyes,
wears tinted black horn-rimmed
glasses. Informant was neat and well
dressed with tweed sports jacket and
open neck sports shirt. Unable to
observe hairline because of felt hat
which he wore at all times. Photos
unavailable from CIB at present

time. SA Lynch expressed interest
in information offered by informant,
but subject was apparently
frightened by someone or something
he saw in bar. He excused himself to
go to men's room and slipped out
rear door on 44th Street side.
Before SA could follow, he had
eluded pursuit by passing through
parking garage, north side 44th
Street and taking taxi on 45th
Street side. This informant
apparently had valid information
according to later conversation
with Sergeant Salerno.

There were more bits of paper. A copy of Terli's
yellow sheet and photos had finally been gotten from the
police department. Terli was thirty-nine and had attended Erasmus High School and Brooklyn College for
two years. As far as Doyle could make out, he was one
of the younger executive-type hoods.

Terli had been a bookeeper for the Royal Meat Company, through a good part of the fifties. Elsewhere in the
records, Doyle had the notation that Royal belonged to
Al Santini, and Santini was the owner of the car that Pat
had been a passenger in on the day of his great, dramatic
shootout, the one that won him the Medal of Honor and
got him discharged from the department. There *had* to
be a connection.

Later, Doyle noticed, Terli had been employed by a
series of corporations in the construction and building
supply business, all of them connected in one way or
another to Sam Massey. Early in January, Terli had
been arrested along with Anthony "Fat Tony" Salerno,
Joseph "Joe Fay" Moretti, James "Uncle Jimmy" Pan-
dolfo, Charles "Ruby" Stein and several others in con-

nection with a massive eighty-million-dollar loan shark ring. This case had been prepared by Chief Assistant District Attorney Alfred J. Scotti of the Rackets Bureau.

Terli had been released on twenty-five thousand dollars surety bond, pending a hearing. There wasn't much in Doyle's file on this case, since it was at present strictly a New York City case, but there was a notation of a conversation with Salerno in which he commented that he believed that Terli had gone into hiding and that he had not been seen in the city since.

Sure enough, that July, when the hearings came up, Terli had skipped bail and the bond was forfeited. Putting this all together, Doyle reasoned that Terli *did* have something to worry about. If Scotti had the goods on him in the loan-sharking thing, he may have spilled his guts about anything he knew. The fact that he was the first one of the group released on bail indicated that he may have cooperated with the cops, or maybe the cops wanted the others to *think* that he had cooperated. Then, jumping a twenty-five thousand bond that had been put up by "Fat Tony" Salerno was not a good idea either.

Doyle reasoned that Terli did have some basis for fearing that the mob wanted to rub him out. When he finally drove the winding approach to the Japanese-style Motel on the Mountain overlooking a morass of underpasses and overpasses of Route 17 and the New York Thruway, he understood why Terli had finally settled on this spot. The access road could be watched from above very easily, even through the window of the bar. The approach to the bar through a landscaped path of Japanese plants and stones was also visible.

There was a rear entrance which led down to the wooded hillside on which the motel was perched. A man could scramble out the rear door, down into the woods, and come out somewhere on the road below and it might take some people who were after him a long time to find him. Doyle wondered if Terli had a car parked down there somewhere.

The meeting was called for four in the afternoon and the bar was nearly deserted. Earlier in the day, Regan's partner, Lynch, had taken a room in the motel only a hundred yards from the cocktail lounge and was there operating a receiver for the tiny transmitter Doyle was carrying, wired to a mike in his tie.

Terli must have had very few clothes, Doyle thought, because he was wearing an outfit almost the same as the one described in Lynch's memo—a tweed jacket, an open-collar sports shirt and a green, shaggy felt hat with a pheasant's feather in it. His pockmarked face was a yellowish tan. He was sitting at a booth near the huge picture window of the bar and spotted Doyle as soon as he came in.

Regan hated that. He knew he had the look of "the man" and never had been able to get rid of it.

"Siddown," the nervous little man said. "What are you drinking?"

"You buying?" Regan asked.

"What for? You guys got an expense account, don't you?"

"Sure. In that case, what will *you* have?"

"I'll have a Virgin Mary," Terli said. "I can't afford to go around drinking these days. I mean, I can *afford* to, but I can't take any chances on getting drunk. You know what I mean?"

"Yeah," Regan said. "You got something for us?"

"Yeah, but I don't want to talk here."

"*You* set the meeting."

Terli glanced around him nervously. "Yeah, I guess you're right. I guess this place is okay."

"Listen, you don't have to give me the whole ball of wax right now. Just enough so we know what we're dealing with."

"It's this guy that's running for governor."

Regan kept a poker face, but there was a heightening of his color and a roaring in his ears as adrenalin started to pump into his veins.

"You're talking about Pat Conte."

"That's right. Old Pat Conte. I knew him when he was a kid. I knew him back in the old neighborhood on Mulberry Street. I was even in his club."

"Well, if he gets elected, you ought to get a great job in Albany."

Terli looked disgusted. "Come on. Quit kidding. I ain't got all day."

"Okay, then. Spill it."

Terli bit his lip nervously and took a sip of the spicy tomato juice laced with Tabasco and Worcestershire.

"If I talk, I gotta get protection, right?"

Regan smiled. "Sure, if you've got anything to say. I haven't heard anything yet."

"Listen, those cocksuckers are going to make me die a slow death if they ever get their hands on me."

"Okay. Talk."

"I don't know how to tell you this. You probably wouldn't believe it in a million years. Conte has been a *hit man* for the Genovese family for maybe twenty years!"

Regan said nothing.

"You're not surprised?"

"I'm listening," Regan said. "You got any evidence, hard evidence?"

"I was with him on one job. The one where this truck driver got knocked off in the Royal Meat truck down on West Street."

"Then you're an accessory on the job. How're you going to get around that?"

"Listen. I'd rather stay alive. I'd rather be in prison. You guys did a good job protecting Valachi and Vinnie Teresa. Just protect me. I don't want to die!"

"Okay. What happened?"

"Well, we were just going to hijack the load, but the guy gave us a lot of trouble and we hadda knock him off . . . we hung him up on the hooks in the truck."

"What do you mean 'we'? Did Conte help you? Did he actually help you put the guy on the hooks?"

"Sure. Sure he did! It was all his idea."

"I see. That's a pretty old case. You got any evidence on that besides your word?"

Terli reached into his pocket and pulled out an envelope. He opened it part way to show a thin silver cigarette case. Doyle reached for it, but Terli pulled it back.

"Don't touch it, for Christ's sake! That's the whole evidence."

"What do you mean?"

"Well, when we hung this guy up, you see, this here cigarette case fell out of his pocket. Usually we don't take anything. I mean, you're not supposed to rip off the body or nothing like that if you do a job. Just leave it. But I figured I could take this case, so I picked it up and Pat grabbed it away from me. He said we should leave it with the stiff and he put it back in the pocket. But when he got out of the truck, I took it back again and I put it in my pocket. Later on, when I got home, I got to figuring that silver takes a hell of a fingerprint, and here I had the case with my prints, Stanrilowicz's and Pat Conte's. I figured that could come in handy sometime, so I took it out real careful and I put it in this here envelope and I put the whole thing in a safe deposit box and I had it there ever since. Now, you tie that to the fact that he had no alibi for that time, and the fact I been connected with his father-in-law's businesses for twenty years, and what do you have? Maybe enough for an indictment. Maybe enough for a conviction. Murder one. The statute don't run on that one, you know."

"I know," Doyle said.

"Besides that, I got a stack of papers and pictures,

too. Connects Conte all up and down the line to the Massey family and to the Genovese family, about how Santini gave him a car every year, but kept it in his own name. About how the whole thing is financed by Guido Paterno and Conte is a member of Paterno's bank, pulls down ten thousand a year for doing fuck-all. I got plenty of stuff."

"When can I see it?"

"It'll take me a couple of days to get it. I got it hidden away."

"What about that cigarette case? You gonna let me have that now?"

Terli looked doubtful.

"You give me the cigarette case, I'll give you the protection. Right?"

"Deal," Terli said, "but you gotta hide me good."

"I got an extra car outside with a man in it. We'll put you right in the car and we'll move you up to a safe house in Massachusetts."

"Shit. I ain't any safer with that son-of-a-bitch Patriarca up there than I am with the guys around here. They're all together."

Regan sighed. "We're not going to tell Patriarca, dummy. You got a car parked near here somewhere?"

"Yeah. It's down on the road below."

"Okay. We'll have it put away somewhere in a couple of days. Anybody's watching the car, they won't have any idea where you are and nobody will know but me and my man. We won't even tell anybody else in the bureau. Okay?"

Terli sighed. "Yeah. I guess it's okay, but I think I'd rather be in the pen right now."

"You will be. Don't worry," Doyle said, "but it will take time to set up the right kind of protection. I don't want to move you till I'm sure I'm covered. These guys got ears all over the place."

"You can say that again," Terli said, wiping the tomato juice from his upper lip. "I feel like they're watching me right now. Let's get out of here."

The next morning, Doyle sat down with the SAC on East 69th Street and laid out what he had.

"This is dynamite," the SAC said. "No question about that. But you have to be very careful on stuff like that. We're dealing with a man who may be the next governor of New York. Looks like he will be, too. It's a pretty touchy business."

"The man," Doyle said, "is a *murderer*. What's the difference what the fuck he's getting elected to? I'm sorry, I didn't mean to use that language, but the man is a vicious criminal. He's not just a petty embezzler or a loan shark. He's probably pulled fifteen or twenty jobs in his life."

The SAC hesitated. "Yeah. You may be right. But so far we just have this one case of murder plus maybe a lot of stuff—if this guy's stuff is good—linking him to the mob. If we spring this before the election and it's only a few days away, we could be accused of trying to influence politics in New York State."

"And if we *don't* spring it before the election," Doyle said, "we're going to have to deal with a man who's a governor."

The SAC rumpled his thinning, blondish hair.

"Listen, I think we have to get to Washington on this. I'll send an AirTel. I'll be back to you very soon, very very soon, and for Christ's sake, don't tell anybody about this, even the other agents."

"Right," Doyle said.

CHAPTER 9

The FBI has an impressive network of agents, but not nearly as good as the one that organization has. The bartender at the Motel on the Mountain was a member of Sam DeCavalcante's family in North Jersey. He recognized Terli the first time he came in to case the bar and thought it might be a good idea to tell old Sam about it.

By the time the message filtered through DeCavalcante to the commission and finally to Sam Massey, Terli was gone. When he showed up the next time, Gino Bertoni, the bartender, made his call directly to Massey.

"This is Bertoni at the Motel on the Mountain," he said.

"Yeah," Sam said, cautiously.

"You know that guy we were talking about the other day? The guy that was in here?"

"Yeah, yeah," Sam said.

"Well, he's here right now talking to some big guy that looks like the feebees to me."

"Right," Sam said. "Call me if he leaves. Get the number of any car he leaves in."

Sam called Pat right away. Pat absorbed the information with only a few monosyllabic responses and hung up. He called Bertoni back at the motel and told him to get information from the toll booths as to which direction the car with Terli in it was headed.

Ten minutes later, Bertoni called to say that the car with the two feds and Terli was headed north on the New York Thruway.

This left a lot of territory to cover, but it gave Pat a direction to work in.

He called the Thruway police, identified himself, and told them that he had confidential reasons for checking the activities of a Plymouth sedan with license plates numbered 4G1847.

He requested that all booths be alerted and that information be relayed to him instantly when the car checked out of the Thruway.

Two and a half hours later, Thruway Police Headquarters called with the information that the Plymouth had turned off the Thruway onto Route 90, the connecting link to the Massachusetts Turnpike. Pat asked the New York authorities to request courtesy surveillance on the Massachusetts highway. He was positive that the FBI would not have requested special clearance from the highway authorities, since the G-men had no idea they were being watched. Two and a half hours later, the trail went cold when the Plymouth was reported leaving the turnpike at Exit 14, headed north on Route 128 toward Waltham.

Pat, after getting the last report collected a pocket full of dimes from the newsstand in the Commodore, went through the underground tunnel, and started making calls from a booth in Grand Central.

The first call was to Henry Tamaleo, Ray Patriarca's number-one man in the Boston area, where the family was known as "The Office."

He asked Tamaleo to put a check on as many exits as possible of the limited access Route 128, which circled the Boston area like a constrictor.

"If they've headed that way, Pat, you don't need any highway watch. Those feds got to be headed for Gloucester. They're taking the fucking stoolie to Howard's joint. You'll never lay a hand on him there."

"What do you mean?"

"It's a big estate in Dolliver's Neck, a very classy part

of Gloucester owned by some Warbucks named John Babcock Howard. It's way in the woods, and they got guards, patrol dogs and the whole bit. It's a fucking fortress."

"How do you know this?"

"Because that's where the feds took Joe Barboza when he turned squealer. We sent Pro Lerner in to try to nail the guy. He's a top man, but the fucking feebees had him in there tighter than a gnat's asshole."

There was a pause while Pat assessed the situation.

"You still there?" Tamaleo asked nervously.

"Yeah, yeah. Keep your pants on, I'm thinking. It sounds like we got to nail the sonovabitch *before* he gets to the Howard place. You got any idea where they get off the highway?"

"Well, 128 ends right in Gloucester. To get to the Howard joint they got to go on 127a."

"Okay. You get a couple of cars there, and try to head the Plymouth off and grab Terli before they get him salted away."

"Listen Pat. We'll do this. But this is a big one. You know what I mean? Feds and all?"

"Don't shit me, Henry. You guys tried it before, you can try it now. How many men has The Office got in Dannemora, Attica and Elmira? You don't think a friendly word in Albany could be helpful?"

"Okay. You got a deal. What do we do when we get him?"

"Just hold him. I'll be there in a couple of hours, maybe three. I'll call The Office in Providence for a message where to contact you."

Sam had reached Pat at the new central headquarters of the campaign in the Commodore Hotel. Pat's staff had taken over three complete floors in the hotel and on the floor above, Pat had a private suite consisting of an office and a bedroom with a view of Grand Central Station and the Chrysler Building. It was nine before he got the final report on Terli. He poured three fingers of Grant's and a splash of soda, took some ice from the small fridge in the kitchenette and sat watching the brilliant light-play of office windows against the purple sky.

He had no way of telling what Terli had actually spilled. By now, his channels to the federals were pretty well closed off by Doyle. The CIB tended to be tightmouthed and Salerno was well known as a straight arrow. Even fully trusting Pat, it was doubtful that he would leak anything so confidential, and, of course, if Terli had said anything *involving* Pat, then asking would only attract unfavorable attention.

But, there was a lot at stake. Terli knew about the whole deal with Royal Meat. He knew all about the secondhand plumbing inside the walls of the newly renovated slums in Little Italy for which the city had been charged the price of new plumbing and the secondhand, rusted beams which had given way in the disaster on Mulberry Street. He also knew an awful lot about the financial structures of Sam Massey and Pat Conte and how they interlocked.

Even if no convictions were gotten, if Terli talked, it would cast a shadow on Pat's candidacy that might be enough to defeat him, just as rumors of corruption had been enough to eliminate Mario Biaggi from the mayoralty race the year before. The whole massive, impressive structure that Pat had spent his life building was in serious danger from Paul Terli. Terli had to be blown away.

Pat had long ago become disgusted with the endless brutality that was so much a part of the system that he lived under. In the beginning, there had been an electric charge of excitement in every job, in every hit, but later it had just seemed stupid and boring and dangerous. It was age, maybe, or just good sense taking over. But this was one last job he'd have to take care of himself.

From his attaché case, he took the unregistered police .38 special which he'd gotten from a shipment stolen from the docks years ago. He put it into his regular clip-on holster in place of his usual pistol. He called Constanza in Riverdale and told her that he was staying at the Commodore overnight and didn't want to be disturbed, to leave a message if she wanted to call. He called the switchboard and told them that he was taking no calls. He slipped into his blue cashmere overcoat, hung a "Do Not Disturb" sign on the outside of the door, slipped downstairs, took a Jamaica subway to Jackson Heights, 74th Street and Roosevelt Avenue, got out there, and took a cab to La Guardia where he caught the shuttle for Boston.

He knew that at some point he might leave a trail behind, but he wanted it to be as slight as possible. In the cab he had slumped down, said nothing to the cab driver and left an adequate but unremarkable tip. On the plane, he debated what sort of transportation he would use in Boston. A rented car would be good but he would have to show his license and he had no false identification with him. But then he thought of a gambit that might work. It was late and the girl at the National Car Rental desk at Logan Airport was dozing. He called her aside quietly, flashed his badge and explained that he needed the use of a car for a few hours, that it was on official business, that he would pay cash.

The girl looked confused, but Pat had sized her up. In fact, he'd looked over the crew of all three desks before he'd chosen this one. There was something sharp and hungry in her look.

"Of course," he pointed out, "you don't have to turn in this cash. There'll be nothing on paper. Believe me, it makes no difference to me. It's just that we have to operate very confidentially on this one, if you know what I mean."

He winked conspiratorially at the girl.

"Here," he said, slipping a fifty into her hand. "Buy yourself a fur coat."

From a phone booth at Logan, Pat phoned Ray Patriarca's office in Providence.

"That car you wanted us to get for you is ready," the raspy voice on the line from Rhode Island said. "If you want to pick it up, the salesman can be reached for the next half hour at GLoucester 3-4876."

It was the number of a booth on 127.

One of Tamaleo's boys answered the phone.

"This is the customer for the Plymouth," Pat said. "Any trouble?"

"Naah! We got your merchandise at the stop sign coming off the highway. Just blocked the road. Your guy like to shit a brick."

"Any shooting?"

"Naah. We cuffed the feds and left them laying on the floor of the car down by Halibut Point. I guess somebody'll find 'em tomorrow. Want us to take care of the fink before he shits all over the car?"

"No. Start toward Logan Airport. Call The Office in an hour and give them a number where I can reach you. I'll tell you where to drop the package."

An hour later, Pat called Tamaleo's man at a booth in the South Boston Market Terminal. Pat had been doing some reconnoitering in the meantime.

"Just make the delivery behind the bushes at the entrance to the Franklin Park Zoo. I'll be around watching. When you see me blink the lights, leave the package and just take off. I'll be in a red Impala."

The zoo was only a few minutes from the airport. If there were no hangups, Pat could have the job done, and be back in the hotel in two and a half hours. He pulled the .38 from the holster and checked that there were shells in all chambers. Later, the unregistered pistol could be deposited in the Charles River off the Storrow Memorial Highway, en route to the airport. No witness would be able to connect Pat to the job. Even if Tamaleo talked there would be no way of proving Pat's connection. Besides, as far as anybody knew, Pat was enjoying the sleep of the dead at the Commodore Hotel in New York at that very moment.

There was an AirTel waiting for Regan Doyle that morning when he got to the office at 69th Street. It told him to proceed directly to bureau headquarters in Washington for a conference with Clarence Kelly, the chief who had succeeded Pat Gray, who had succeeded J. Edgar Hoover.

It was Monday, November 4, the day before the election. Doyle pocketed the AirTel with a tight smile of satisfaction. He jumped into the bureau car and raced out to La Guardia where he caught the shuttle. He was in the bureau before eleven o'clock that morning. The chief was waiting for him. The new chief was a man after his own heart, an ex-cop, a pro, an ex-SA. He would understand in a way that J. Edgar never could have.

After a short wait in the anteroom, still cluttered with the Dillinger decorations he remembered from his training days, he was ushered into the huge office of The Director. There were a few new touches, photos, a slightly more informal look, but there had not been time to make any serious changes. The chief directed Doyle to sit down opposite him across the broad, mahogany desk, still decorated with the American flags.

"That report you sent in. It's dynamite."

"I know," Doyle said. "I've been working on it one way or another for nearly twenty years."

"You deserve a lot of credit," the chief said, "but you have to have one hell of a case before you move on something like this. This would be a national scandal. It would look very bad for our government."

There was a vaguely familiar ring to the argument that Doyle recognized.

"But I've got a witness, an eyewitness."

The chief reached into his drawer and threw a telegram across the desk.

"This is confirmation of something I got on the phone early this morning. They found Terli in the bird house of the Franklin Park Zoo in Boston this morning. He had been shot five times in the head by a .38. They cut off his pecker and stuffed it in his mouth. He was just laying there, half covered with bird turds."

Doyle slumped into the leather arm-chair.

"We've still got a case. We've got Terli's confession on tape. We got a witness to the tape. We got that cigarette case."

"You know better than that. Without Terli, we've got nothing. They'd laugh us out of court.

"What about the cigarette case with the fingerprints on it?"

"We haven't even dusted it yet."

"But suppose the three sets of prints *are* on it?"

"You think we can prove in court that they were made on the murder site, with the witness dead now? Maybe somebody robbed the thing and sold it to Terli. Maybe Terli let Pat take a cigarette out of it. There could be a lot of maybes that don't make it into a murder case. You know the rules of evidence. The U.S. attorney would laugh us out of his office, let alone a jury."

"Well, we can bring charges against Conte on fraud. We can check out his income. We could put the IRS on it. It'll knock him out of the governor's race for sure."

The chief turned in his swivel chair away from Doyle, toward the wall, toward the big flags hanging behind him. He seemed to be speaking into the wall.

"I don't think I'm getting through to you, Doyle. This is not just my opinion. It's what I've been told by the attorney general's office."

The Director sighed, unhappily.

"And between you and me, the AG got the word from

higher up too. Would you believe that we've got to drop this case for reasons of national security?"

"Jesus!" Regan said, softly. "Where does it all end?"

"Stick with it, Doyle," the chief said, "but don't push it. It'll all add up some day. Jobs change, offices change. Look at me. Did anybody ever think I'd be in this seat?" He extended his hand to Doyle. "You've done a terrific job. At least you and I know that, and I won't forget it."

Doyle shuffled out wearily through the double doors, down the marble corridor, down the brass-doored elevator to the street. As he stood by the curb, waiting for a cab to take him to the airport, he looked up at the dull gray sky and whispered.

"God, whose side are you on anyway?"

CHAPTER 10

That week everybody was feeling the pressure of the approaching deadline. Not that there was any real tension in Pat Conte's headquarters. The polls, the opinions of the pros, Roper, Harris, all gave it to Pat by a good plurality. It was the Democrats' year, and there was even a good chance that Pat would sweep in enough delegates to overturn the Republican majority in the state legislature for the first time in more than twenty years.

On Monday night, November 4th, Pat went home to Riverdale for the first time in days to get a good night's sleep, undisturbed by traffic noise, telephones or eager, young aides. Despite the brisk weather, he felt hot and sticky. His armpits seemed to be sending out acrid steam. His chin was blue and scratchy and his hands grubby from hours of shuffling papers, shaking hands and scratching backs.

Except for the nightlight in the vestibule, the house was dark.

Pat trudged wearily up the stairs, threw his clothes in an untidy heap on the Bergere chair, grabbed his heavy terrycloth robe, went into the bathroom and turned the strong spray of the shower on full blast as hot as he could stand it. The steaming jets of water turned his bones to a soft jelly. He stepped out of the shower, feeling clean and relaxed and decided to shave that night to save time in the morning. He'd need another shave by nightfall, anyway. It would probably be midnight or later before his opponent would concede, even with early heavy returns from the city. They always held out hope for those outlying districts "not yet reported." But he already sensed what the outcome would be.

Pat had seen him in his last television address that night, and beneath the forced optimism and cheer, Pat had detected sagging muscles and lines of defeat in his opponent's face that even television pancake couldn't hide.

Before retiring, Pat ran downstairs in his slippered feet and mixed a stiff nightcap of Scotch and soda which he took up and put on his night table to sip as he glanced through the household mail that he'd picked up from the hall table.

There was a soft, shuffling sound behind him. Pat turned around to see Connie, dressed in that long, sheer negligee, the steam from the connecting bathroom rising around her, like the clouds in one of those movie scenes that takes place in heaven. There was an ethereal yet sexy quality about her. Her face seemed composed and serene, as though all her decisions had been made. The grief lines that had striped it since the death of Sebastian seemed to have softened and blended into that remarkable, rosy, childlike skin. It was the first time Pat could remember her entering his room at night in more than ten years. He wondered if there was something about the stimulation of the campaign, all the adrenalin that it sent charging into one's system, that perhaps had in some freak way turned her sexuality on.

"What is it, Constanza?" he said, softly. "Come in. Sit down."

He patted a place beside him on the bed. Constanza came in and began to hang up the clothes that were strewn across the Bergere chair.

"I'd like to talk to you, Pat."

"I know. We haven't had much chance to talk together, have we? It's been a grueling six months."

She carefully draped his blazer and gray pants across

the walnut valet stand, took off the clip holster and put it with the pistol on the night table.

"I'd like to talk to you about tomorrow, about the election," she said.

"Sure. Shoot."

"I want you to withdraw."

Pat looked puzzled. "I don't think I understand."

"I want you to resign from the campaign tomorrow morning."

Constanza had been high-strung and hysterical for years. Pat wondered whether she had finally scored a breakthrough over the steady regime of tranquilizers and gone completely off the deep end.

"I don't think I heard you right."

"You heard me right. I want you to quit tomorrow."

"I see," Pat said. "Well, we'll talk about it in the morning."

He saw no point in arguing with a crazy woman.

"No," Connie said. "We'll talk about it *now*. Because if you *don't* resign, I'll see to it that you never breathe a free breath in your life again, and I can do that."

"Okay, Okay. We'll talk about it in the morning."

"No, listen to me, Pat. You never listen to me, but I want you to listen to me now. I know you've had a safe deposit box all these years where you've put all your rotten loot, but *I've* had one, too. And you know what's in it?"

"What?"

"Xeroxes of almost every check you ever wrote, photocopies of letters and contracts, notations of visitors and the times they came and the times they left, telephone company records, who you called and when and what time, written summaries of any conversations I could hear from in the closet or through the keyhole or anyplace else. I've even had a little suction-cup gadget for the last four or five years that I could stick onto the phone and pick up conversations on any extension in the house.

"I've got it, Pat. I've got it all. I've got everything on you from embezzlement, extortion, loan sharking and bribery, clear up to murder. I've even got copies of those notebooks where you keep your blackmail information.

"I also analyzed a lot of those things. I took book-keeping, you know, in that dumb girls' finishing school, and I could show Sam and Lucchese and other top men how you have been skimming 20 percent off their share for years.

"I may seem a little dim-witted and crazy to you, Pat, but I'm not. At least not in that department. I can think very well. It's not because you're responsible for the death of Sebastian, though in my mind you are. It's because you're an evil man. You are a creature of the devil. I don't think anybody can stop you now but me, and that's what I intend to do."

Pat listened in silence, thinking. *Could* she have that material? Could it be as damning as she said? She seemed to read his thoughts.

"Don't think I just have inconsequential stuff, Pat. It took a few years, but I found the combination to your safe taped under the drawer of your desk where any simpleton burglar might have found it. How could a cop like you be so stupid? I even found the little concrete box under the floorboard, and I noted down the amounts and even the serial numbers of any money I found there from time to time. That adds up to quite a sum, a lot that Sam and Don Vitone and the other big *capos* never knew anything about. You see, it's not just the law that will stop you, Pat. It's the *family*!"

There was a tight, rueful smile on Pat's face.

"So, you see, if you don't retire gracefully tomorrow for reasons of health—your wife's health, your health —whatever you want to say, I'll take all of this stuff to the police, to Sam, to the commission, and it will be over for you."

Pat stared at Connie for a long time. It was amazing how desirable she still looked. As she spoke, sitting in the Bergere chair, his gaze kept straying to those beautifully perfect, pink-skinned legs, to the mysterious shadows above.

Her eyes, now bright with tears of emotion, had diamond highlights reflected from the bedside lamp, and her skin from the deep V of the nightgown to her neck and shoulders was a deep, flushed pink. Pat recognized that color. It was the flush on the skin of a woman who's just been satisfied by her lover. He said nothing but thought for a while. Then, a low, choked laugh seemed to rumble up involuntarily from his stomach.

"You big son-of-a-bitch!" Connie said. "You don't think I'll do it, do you? Well, I *will*! I'll do it right now!"

Pat laughed tolerantly. "No, no, honey. Don't pick up the phone. I'll take care of everything tomorrow. Don't worry. I'll take care of it all."

She looked at him in disbelief.

"I hope you don't think you're kidding me," she said, "because I'm going through with this. I have lived without self-respect for twenty years, just an incidental rag around the house, someone to be paraded out on occasions where a wife had to be displayed and a blood contact to your new godfather, Sam. And don't think you'll be able to do anything to me because you know that Sam wouldn't allow it."

Pat smiled again, almost benevolently. "You've got the wrong end of this handle, Constanza. Sam and I are in the same family, and it's a different family from the one you're in. You know, we actually take an oath, those of us who are old-timers, and the oath is that our loyalty to the family *we* have together is greater than it is to any *other* family, to any *blood* family you might say. Now, when you talk like this, it isn't *you* that has to go to the commission. It's *me*. I have to go and explain what you're threatening to do. I have to explain that you might bring the whole house down on us, and then . . ."

"I don't believe it. I don't believe that Sam would . . ."

Pat laughed, those marvelous even, white teeth flashing luminescently in the semidarkness of the bedroom.

"Sam wouldn't? You don't know your father as well as you think you do. Sometime, look it up. Look up what happened to your mother and why she died so early, so long ago. You might see a fantastic parallel to what's happening now."

Pat put down the drink and took Constanza by the wrist.

"You have been a candy-assed bitch since I married you. I wonder how many men would take that Christly bullshit you've been laying down for twenty years? How many guys would let those beautiful tits and ass alone, just because their wives were hysterical priest-ridden bitches? Or does Father Maroni let you play with his cock behind the confessional?"

Connie gasped in shock.

"You're inhuman!"

Pat tightened his hold on the frail wrist. He reached over and grabbed the neckline of the sheer peignor and ripped it to the waist, exposing the two heaving breasts, still taut and perfect in shape. With his free hand he reached out and squeezed the right breast, pinching the nipple painfully between his fingers.

"Such beautiful tits, such a wasted ass." He reached around and squeezed her buttocks brutally. His eyes, bright with anger and suppressed passion caught hers in a hard, fixed stare.

"So you're going to the cops. You're going to the commission? You snotnosed bitch! I ought to stick it up your ass and break it off, you stupid worthless cunt. Fucking's too good for you!"

His eyes now had a glazed half-mad brightness. His penis under the cotton pajamas was visibly erect.

"I know what's good for you!" His eyes searched around the room and lit on the jar of Alberto VO-5 that he used to dress his hair.

"That's the stuff!" he said, dragging her by the wrist as he flipped the top off the jar and jammed two fingers into it, coming up with a small mound of the clear yellowish grease.

"This is gonna be great! I've been waiting for this!"

"Pat, you're acting crazy!" Connie screamed.

"No. I'm acting *sane*. This is the way I should have handled you long ago. Maybe I *would* have if I wasn't getting plenty of good cunt from your little pal, Katie. Didn't know about that one, did you?"

But Pat didn't wait for an answer. With a violent thrust, he twisted Constanza's arm behind her, forcing her to lean forward in a vain effort to escape the pain. Holding her by the twisted wrist, he led her to the bed and threw her face down on the mattress.

Reaching under the torn negligee, Pat groped savagely between Constanza's exposed buttocks and smeared the VO-5 around the wrinkled pink anus, shoving his fingers forcefully into the opening up to the knuckle.

"Pat, you can't!" Constanza screamed. "Pat, please! Please!"

But Pat was already lifting Constanza's protesting body by the waist, elevating the grease-smeared crack to the height of his now-turgid penis, and minutes later he was sunk deep inside her, gasping and grunting in an almost instantaneous animal-like orgasm.

When he had finished, he pulled his penis out as quickly as he had shoved it in, wiped the stains from it on Constanza's peignoir, drained the rest of his drink and crawled between the covers.

"Well, good night, Constanza, my darling. That's the

best time I've had with you since we cooked up that freak kid of yours. Or do you want to crawl in here with me? Maybe that little number is what you needed to turn you on."

Constanza, sobbing in great, croaking gasps, said nothing. With broken movements, she pulled the torn peignoir about her bruised body and walked from the room, her lips set tightly, tears running down her cheeks.

As she passed through the lighted bathroom, Pat watched her and thought, "What a beautiful ass! What a loss!"

CHAPTER 11

Pat was up early on Election Day checking with his district captains by phone, listening to radio accounts of the turnout. The weather was good, which Pat counted as a point on his side. Good weather and a big turnout usually favored the Democrats. In addition to the old pros and the family backing, Pat had acquired a considerable following of younger people —volunteers.

There was nothing in his opponent's candidacy to attract the young. Pat, on the other hand, represented drama, excitement, glamour.

Pat and Connie shared the breakfast table in silence, Pat buried in the newspapers and mail, Connie, staring across the table at him with a dull but persistent stare as though a sharp edge of hatred was trying to push itself through a blanket of tranquilizing drugs.

Pat told her what to do, where to go, what to wear, and she responded as an automaton. With breakfast, Pat handed her four Valiums.

"Here," he said. "Take these with your juice. It's going to be a tough day and I know your nerves are very much on edge."

Like an obedient child, Constanza took the pills and swallowed them, one at a time with a little birdlike motion of her throat.

By the time they arrived at headquarters in the Commodore, it was after lunch and enough early returns were in to set a mood of cheer and optimism. The walls of the big main hall of the headquarters were hung with banners, "Conte for Governor," "A Hero for Governor," "Conte for Safety in the Streets," "Conte Will Clean Up New York," "Conte, Man of the People."

Hundreds of eager young men and pretty volunteers

in straw boaters with tricolor bunting, with the motto, "Conte's the One," in gold, were bustling around carrying messages, early reports, trays of coffee and donuts. Long tables were set up at one end of the room with huge tally sheets for recording the votes in the districts as they came in, and huge blackboards lined the rear platform of the headquarters for posting new votes.

Of course, the earliest complete returns wouldn't be in until nine or ten in the evening, but there was a mood of almost mystical joy that could only grow out of a certainty of victory.

Pat, holding Connie closely by the arm, circulated through the big room, smiling, shaking hands, embracing, accepting enthusiastic juvenile kisses on the cheek from the girl volunteers and earnest shoulder clasps and handshakes from the young boys. Winburg had done a terrific job in whipping up enthusiasm in the younger group, and Katie had recruited a fantastic number of young actors and actresses who added a youthful beauty and vitality to the scene.

Some of the male volunteers didn't look too virile. That was okay. Lindsay had picked up a couple of hundred thousand fag votes during his mayoral campaign by easing the pressure on the queer bars. Pat, too, had made a few moves that showed a tolerant attitude in that regard. He had to. After all, most of the queer bars were owned by the family.

On the second floor was an executive suite for the VIP guests and top level campaign managers. Winburg was up there with Guido Paterno, Father Raimundo, Santo Ganci of the Italian-American League and Paul Federici, as well as Kate Mullaley. Pat passed among them with back pats, *abrazos,* hugs and a quick, hearty kiss for Katie, with a surreptitious squeeze on her bottom.

Pat picked out an earnest girl volunteer to watch Connie, keep her supplied with tea, coffee, sandwiches and whatever else she wanted.

"I want you to look after my wife and don't let her out of your sight. She's very nervous and excited and I want to know immediately if she goes anywhere. Meanwhile, you can both watch TV here in the corner, keep an eye on the returns, make notes on any comments that you think I ought to know about. It's an important job I'm giving you. Do you understand, Nancy?"

The bright-eyed girl with long, dark hair he'd chosen for the job looked at him very earnestly and nodded her head up and down. Her eyes shone and her cheeks were flushed with the excitement of the moment and the proximity to the great man. She wore a black skirt and sweater with a white collar that gave her something of the look of an oversexed nun. Pat made a mental note to keep an eye on her for future times.

"I'll look after her, Mr. Conte. Don't worry," she said, "and good luck."

"Thanks, Nancy." He had spent months on a Bruno Furst memory course learning to associate names with faces and had developed one of the most important politicians' assets—an ability to remember the name and connection of almost everybody he had met, even once.

Father Raimundo was in conference with Paterno and Winburg. Paterno reached into his pocket and pulled out a thick manila envelope which he handed over to Winburg. Winburg went into a corner, counted it silently, and then delivered it to Paul Federici.

Pat went into his private office, adjoining the executive suite. He took with him a tall, iced glass of Diet Pepsi. It was going to be a long day, and he didn't want to start in on the booze too early. He didn't want any sign of that quavering, emotional tone or suspiciously shaky posture that so many candidates evinced when they made their acceptance speeches.

He started going through the sheaf of reports,

estimates, summaries and memos that Winburg had handed him when he came in. There was a four-page memo from Winburg himself that summarized the whole affair. Even Winburg, traditionally cautious and pessimistic, found it hard to keep a tone of smugness out of his memo.

After vacillating on the fence, the *Daily News* had finally come out with an editorial, only the day before, for Conte, (the first Democrat they had supported for governor in more than twenty years). Winburg had drawn a big circle around the editorial in red Magic Marker with several exclamation points. Written across the grayish typeface of the page with the Magic Marker were the words: "If *this* doesn't sell them, nothing will!!!!"

Pat was reading it and smiling when there was a knock at the door connecting to the executive suite.

"Yeah, what is it?" Pat said.

Federici looked in.

"Sorry to bother you, Pat, but there's an old friend of yours here to see you. Regan Doyle."

Through the open door, Pat could see that Doyle was standing right behind his campaign manager.

"Okay," he said, "let him come in. Close the door."

Regan walked into the room. He looked more massive than ever. He was wearing a dark, off-the-rack, blue double-knit suit, bulging slightly at the lapels, and one of those ever-present FBI hats, which he took off as he entered. His face had aged more than Pat's over the years, and there was a droop of jowl under each side of his square-cut jaws. Doyle's nose, Pat noticed, was beginning to show little purple road maps of veins, and his face had lost its habitual, ruddy color.

"Hello, cousin," Pat said. "Sit down. What can I do for you?"

Doyle sat on the edge of the leather upholstered rented Itkin chair and put his battered and bulky briefcase down beside him.

"I suppose there may be a recorder in that," Pat said, pointing to the briefcase, "but then we won't say anything we don't want on the record. Will we? What will you have to drink? Scotch? Martini? Diet Pepsi? Let's see. You drink bourbon, don't you?" he said, reaching, swiveling in his chair to the small walnut paneled refrigerator behind him.

He plucked a couple of cubes from a bucket inside and went over to the bar in the corner and poured a generous Harper's and water for Doyle.

"I'm sticking with the diet drink for a while," Pat said. He patted himself on the waist. "Getting a little flabby here around the middle and I want to stay in shape for the rest of the day. Anyway, *slainthe*. May the best man win."

Pat thought for a minute that Doyle was going to refuse the drink, but he took it, stared into it for a minute, and said: "Right. May the best man win," and took a sip from the drink without raising it to Pat.

"Something on your mind?"

"Nothing I can do anything about right now," Regan said. "I just came in to see what the great man looked like on the eve of his victory."

"You should be happy to see an old friend succeed. What are you torturing yourself about?"

Regan's voice roared, out of control, like steam bursting from an overloaded safety valve.

"You know fucking well what I'm unhappy about! I'm telling you one thing, Pat. If you win this election, I'm going to break you. I'm going to break you wide open!"

"Come on, Doyle. Settle down," Pat said. "What are you so pissed off about?"

"Terli, for one thing."

Pat looked puzzled. "Terli? Terli? Oh, yeah. That's some guy that's connected with Sam, I think, in the construction thing. Right?"

"Yeah."

"I used to know him years ago. Years ago I knew him in the meat business. Say, he had some kind of a bad break, didn't he? Seems like I read about him."

"Yeah. You read about him," Doyle said. "You know goddamn well what happened to him."

"Well, he was probably mixed up in some kind of shady business. You know, those guys, they take care of their own. You know what I mean? He was probably mixing with some very dangerous people."

"Who do you think you're shitting?" Doyle said. "You're with them up to here."

"That's a strong statement, Agent Doyle."

Doyle unbuckled his torn leather briefcase and poured the contents out on Pat's desk.

"You think I can't back it up? Just take a look at these things. Take a look at some of these pictures?"

There was a sheaf of at least fifty eight-by-ten glossy photoprints, many of them blown up into an oatmeallike graininess. In each of them, the unmistakable lines of Pat's sharply cut features could be seen in conversation with another man, or sometimes several. The faces were familiar. Some of the photos seemed to have been taken as much as fifteen years ago. There were pictures with Don Vitone before he was put away, with Vinnie Mauro, with Jimmy "Blue Eyes" Alo. Amazingly, there was even a shot taken during Pat's honeymoon with Roughhouse Hoffman in Havana.

"Hey, where'd you get this one?" Pat said. "This must be from the Narcotics Bureau. You guys weren't following me around in those days, were you?"

"We get cooperation sometimes."

"So, what have you got here? A family album?"

Regan Doyle smiled without humor.

"Yeah, you might say it's just that. Every one of those guys in the photos with you is a top family man, identified either in the McClellan hearings, at Apalachin, by the Kefauver Committee or in a court of law."

Pat shuffled through the pictures with idle curiosity, as though he were making selections for a wedding album.

"So what have you got here? You think this proves something, whatever you're trying to prove?"

"It proves that you've been an intimate associate of mobsters, practically from the beginning of your career, and as time went on, the men you saw were closer and closer to the top."

"Of course," Pat said. "I was a cop, wasn't I? I was in Criminal Intelligence. Later I was with the governor's anticrime staff, and as a legislator, I was a member of the anticrime subcommittee of the Judicial Committee. It's natural that I would see these men and try to find out what they were up to, assuming that they are what you say they are. I don't think these photos prove anything, except that I'm a very diligent crime investigator."

"I've got tapes, too, and film that match up with a lot of these pictures."

"Now who's bullshitting?" Pat said. "If you had any tapes that gave you anything solid on me, you would have acted long ago. I'll tell you something. I'm not admitting any of this crap that you're trying to lay on me, but I've been around too long to say anything that you're likely to pick up on your suicide taps.

"Fortunately, I believe the U.S. Attorney's office is a little more temperate and let's say less *prejudiced* than you are. You got some kind of an axe to grind, don't you Doyle? Do you really think I'm any different from the other candidates? You think the Rockefeller boys and their pals don't have their tie-ins with big business and maybe with some pretty shady people, too? I'll tell you something, Doyle. It's time that you grew up a little. I think you think you're working for the Eagle Scout pack."

He leaned on the desk and bored a hard look into Doyle's hostile eyes.

"This is the big apple. This is politics. This is what it's all about. You think that every man in politics doesn't have somebody he's got to answer to, right up to the top, as you're beginning to find out?"

"Not the same people *you* answer to," Doyle said bitterly.

Pat laughed. "You'd be surprised. You think the other side has *clean* crooks, like in Washington, D.C. You think Irish and Wasp crooks are nicer. They're more moral, less greasy than Italians? You know the first place that I met your president? It was on Paradise Island and he was in a joint owned by his buddy and that joint was in hock up to here to the mob, and he knew it. You're wasting your time, Doyle. Why don't you just take your retirement pension and open up some nice industrial security outfit and get rich like the rest of your ex-G-men pals?"

Doyle gathered the photos and reports silently and replaced them in the briefcase. He put the drink, still untouched, except for the first sip, down on the polished mahogany top of Pat's desk.

"Pat, you were crooked from the start, back when you were a patrolman. I don't know why it took me so long to tumble to your act."

"Because you were *stupid* from the start. Unfortunately that one-half guinea blood wasn't enough to smarten you up. There must have been a mistake somewhere. You couldn't be a cousin of mine!"

Doyle's eyes flared with rage.

"I'd be glad to give back every drop of that blood right now if I could put a stop to your insane ambitions.

"You've had so much easy success, so much power, I

think you think that you're the annointed one of God or something. You've even got Katie blinded . . ."

"And that's not all, Regan. You don't like that. You know that all I have to do is *look* at her and she goes all hot in the crotch?"

Doyle clutched compulsively at the desk top. For a moment it looked as though he was going to vault over it and leap at Pat's throat. Visibly he took three or four deep breaths, trying to bring his emotions under control.

"I'm not going to jump you now, Conte. I'm gonna damage you so it really hurts. I'm gonna cut your balls off. I'm gonna get you so good that even Katie will see what a vicious prick you are. I'm the monkey on your back, Conte. You're never going to be rid of me, until you're behind bars or dead.

"I couldn't stop you this time, but I'm putting you on notice. If you ever get into the state house, you'll stay there over my dead body."

Pat stood there, his eyes narrowed, both hands leaning on the desk as though he were studying a particularly difficult problem. He waited until Doyle looked up from fastening the brass clasp of his battered briefcase.

"Over your dead body, you say? Okay, I'll keep that in mind. Was there anything else?"

His voice was low and flat and cold—very cold—like a lump of dry ice. Doyle picked up his hat and headed for the door.

"I'll be seeing you, Conte."

Then, in a flash, Conte had his politician's mask back on as the door opened. There was a broad grin on his face.

"Sure, sure, Regan. Stick around. Have a few drinks. Enjoy yourself. Watch the returns. Stick around for the victory party."

Doyle started to slam the door behind him, then apparently thought better of it and pulled it quietly, but firmly closed, as he left.

CHAPTER 12

Pat sat down at his desk again, staring at the door. Would the killing ever end, he wondered?

First Constanza, and now Doyle. If he wasn't taken care of in some way, he would be a dagger poised at Pat's back for the rest of his life. Doyle didn't have it all together, but the evidence he had now would lead to more. Terli's mouth was closed, but there would be other informers.

Pat still had a remnant of respect and affection for Doyle. But the Irishman was pressing hard.

"That thick Mick!" Pat sighed to himself. "Doesn't look as if he'll ever learn—until it's too late!"

There was a soft rap at the door again and it opened a crack without his responding. It was Katie.

"Wasn't that Regan I just saw going out of here? He really looked burned about something."

"Yeah, that was Regan. Come in, Katie."

Pat got up and met her at the door. He took her by the arm and walked her over to the leather couch in the far corner of the room.

"Let me get you a drink. I got to relax a little, too," Pat said, and abandoning the Diet Pepsi, he mixed a pair of tall scotch and sodas which he brought over and placed on the coffee table in front of Kate.

"Take off that silly straw hat," he said, lifting the plastic-decorated boater from her head and sailing it across the room.

"You look like the intermission entertainment in Your Father's Moustache."

Katie stirred the drink with her forefinger, a habit she'd picked up from Pat, and Pat picked up his drink, held it up and toasted her.

"To my best and most beautiful volunteer."

Katie smiled.

"Thank you, kind sir, and to victory," she said, holding up her glass.

Pat put his drink down on the table and sat beside her, taking her hand in his.

"Katie, I meant that. You don't know what it's meant to me to have you as a friend, and more than that all these years. I don't think I knew how much it meant to me until that time down in Miami. I don't think I could make it, Katie, if you weren't around."

Katie's eyes avoided his.

"Don't say that, Pat. You needed me for certain things, and maybe I needed you, too. You weren't getting what you needed at home, and I couldn't stand the idea of tying myself down to one man and giving up my work. So we used one another."

"Is that all it was to you, Katie?"

She shook her head. "No. No, I know it was more than that. It would be silly to say that it wasn't."

Katie clutched at her drink with emotion that was almost desperate and drained it with three or four determined gulps.

"Pat, I think I should be getting back to my work. There'll be a million calls, and people will want to know what to do."

Pat stood up, walked to the door and turned the key in the lock.

"Relax, Katie," he said. "Relax. There's nothing we're going to do today that's going to change anything. It's over and we've won. Now, come over here."

He held out his arms to her and she walked stiffly toward him. He took her in his arms and kissed her very tenderly, very gently. Her lips were warm but unresponsive. He kissed her eyes and nibbled at her ear and began running his hand up and down her back. He took her by the hand and led her to the couch and sat her down. Then, he began to kiss her more passionately, biting at her neck. His hand came up and started fumbling at the buttons on her white satin blouse. She pushed him away.

"What are you doing, Pat?"

"What do you *think* I'm doing? I'm making love to you!"

"For God's sake, Pat! Have some sense of time and place. They're all out there, right in the next room. They know I'm in here. People will notice."

"What do I care?" Pat said. "What are they going to do? Fire me? Quit? *They're* not the bosses. *I* am. I don't do things to please *them*. They do things to please *me*."

"And I do things to please you. Right?"

"Right," Pat said. "Now, stop fucking around. Come on. I want you. I want you right now. God, I really want you," and he began clawing again at the buttons. She pushed him away again, this time with some violence.

"Pat, stop it! I don't want you to do that. Stop it *now!*"

Pat's face flushed with suppressed violence.

"Stop it? Stop it? What do you mean, *stop* it? Who the fuck are you to tell me to stop it? I don't take orders from you."

He reached over and grabbed the tied-back skein of taffy-colored hair in his big fist, pulled her head back and kissed her savagely and brutally. Katie turned her head from side to side, trying to escape his pursuing lips and finally, in a flash of anger her sharp teeth came down on the tongue that he was thrusting into her mouth. Pat winced and reacted by reflex. His right hand swung in a short, open-handed arc, caught her between the jaw and the cheekbone with a sharp, splatting sound. The force of the blow sent Katie reeling backward and she stumbled over the coffee table and onto the floor.

"What the fuck do you think you're doing?" Pat said, furiously. "You almost bit my tongue off!"

Katie sat where she had fallen for a moment, shaking her head with shock, then she looked up at Pat and laughed out loud.

"You can't believe it, you son-of-a-bitch, can you? You really can't believe it. You can't believe that *anybody* could turn down your irresistible charms."

Pat half turned away from her then extended a hand and helped her to her feet. He took a deep breath, trying to regain control of his temper, then he breathed a short but deep sigh.

"Okay. What's the big idea? Why did you do that anyway?"

"Because it's over, Pat. I'm through. I can't seem to get that across to you, but it's over right now for good. It isn't just because of the election. It's because of a lot of things I learned during the election."

"Doyle's been talking to you, right?"

"That's only part of it."

"It can't be over, Katie. It will never be over. You know that."

Katie sighed, pushing back the loose strands of hair that had fallen across her face as she took the force of Pat's blow. Carefully, she tucked back the tail of the satin blouse that Pat had pulled out. Her voice was controlled. Pat wondered if it was the Stanislavsky method she was using or the Strasberg School of Acting.

"This is the end of the line, Pat. There's no place to go. There's just no future for us."

Pat half sat on the edge of his desk.

"It's funny you said that, Katie, because I had made a big decision last night concerning you."

She cocked her head to one side and looked at him oddly, like a talking bird that's trying to understand human language.

"About me? What decision did you make about me?"

"When the returns are in and it's all definite, I planned to ask you to marry me."

Katie couldn't believe what she was hearing.

"You must be out of your mind!"

"You're thinking about Constanza?"

"Of course, Constanza. Constanza. Everything. The whole thing."

"Katie, Constanza is in a lot of trouble. She's not all there. You know that? She's not really all *there* psychologically, and then, nobody lives forever, do they?"

Katie's eyes widened into an almost hypnotic stare.

"My God. What are you saying?" But she *knew* what he was saying.

"I can't believe this," she said. "I can't believe this."

She darted to the door, turned the key and began to run from the room. Pat grabbed for her and caught one shoulder, tearing loose two top buttons of her blouse and ripping the fabric at the buttonhole.

"Let go, Pat! Let me out of here. If you don't, I'm going to scream right into that room."

Grimly Pat released his grip and Katie ran through the crowded room, her eyes tearing, oblivious to the curious looks of those who caught the flashing path of her exit.

CHAPTER 13

But at least one person in that bustling, crowded room had noticed Katie's tearful exit. As she stumbled from the room into the hotel corridor, a woman's low voice arrested her flight.

"Katie, wait. What happened?"

Constanza was standing in the doorway, Nancy, her nunlike appointed bodyguard close behind her. Constanza rushed into the hall and seized the sobbing woman by her shoulders. The whole left side of Katie Mullaley's cheek was still red and swollen from Pat Conte's blow. Her face was splotched and puffy from tears. She clutched nervously at the dangling, pearl button and torn fabric at her bosom. Constanza's placid face seemed to take on resolution as she stared at her disheveled friend. She turned to Nancy, her volunteer keeper.

"Is there anyplace we can go?"

"Mr. Conte said to watch you, to stay with you all the time."

"It's all right. I'll be with Miss Mullaley."

"Well, I guess one of these rooms here isn't being used."

She opened the door to one of the hotel bedrooms which had been temporarily converted into a storage place for mimeographed press releases and campaign literature. In one corner were piles of cardboard boxes with extra straw boaters. On the dressing table were heaps of red, white and blue arm bands with the words, "Conte for Governor," printed on them.

"We'll talk in here," Constanza said, clearing off a space on the bed and on one of the chairs.

"Well," the girl said, doubtfully, "I guess it'll be all right."

"Don't worry. We'll be right here!" Constanza said.

When the door closed, Constanza stood for a minute, holding her friend by the shoulders of her torn blouse and staring into her shattered eyes.

"So. You, too, Katie. My God! That man is unbelievable. Let me straighten you out."

Katie, wordlessly, allowed herself to be led to the bathroom where Constanza dampened a towel with cold water and dabbed at Katie's flushed and swollen face. Turning away from her friend for a moment, she opened her black leather purse.

Holding it carefully, so that her friend could not see the rest of the contents, she extracted a pin from the bag with which she made what repairs she could to the blouse.

"That should hold it until we can find a needle and thread," she said. "Was it very bad?"

Katie looked at her friend curiously.

"You *know* about us, don't you—about Pat and me?"

Constanza nodded.

"I've known for a long time, but it still hurt when he told me about it last night . . ."

"I didn't want to hurt you . . . Whatever it was, it's over now. I'm sure of that. I should have listened to Regan Doyle years ago."

Constanza stroked her friend's shoulder—a tentative gesture of affection.

"I really didn't mind about you, or even the others. It was the other things he did that I couldn't live with." She fished in her purse and came up with a Valium.

"Take one of these. It's all that kept me going all these years. But I don't think I'm going to need them now."

She ran the water in the bathroom sink, and filled the toothbrush glass with cold water. Wordlessly, Katie accepted the pill. Constanza turned away again, and took out eight Valiums which she flushed down the toilet.

"He's been trying to keep me doped up the whole day, but I want my mind clear today. I want it to be *very* clear."

The two women stood, staring into each other's faces, silently for a full minute after Katie had swallowed the pill. Slowly, Katie's startling, electric-blue eyes began to glisten and fill with tears. Looking at that familiar face with that crisp cap of curly black hair, its eyes like two jet beads and that startling, baby-pink complexion, she realized that she was looking at a dead woman. The very feel of Constanza's soft hands on her shoulder seemed to burn her skin and Katie thought: "I'm responsible for this. I'm as responsible as if I'd turned a gun on her and pulled the trigger."

"Do you want to talk, Katie?" Constanza said, softly.

Her face now seemed to have a saintlike glow. The drug-induced dullness had gone, but had left a dark, serene surface. The face looked big-eyed and saintlike like those early paintings of the Christian martyrs.

"Do you want to talk?" Constanza said, leading her back into the bedroom.

Gently, she pushed Katie down into the upholstered hotel bedroom chair and sat down on the bed facing her, very close, their knees touching. She took her friend's limp hand in hers and Katie looked back at her with pained eyes like splintered glass.

"I suppose I really knew all along," Constanza said. "I just wouldn't accept the reality of it. I think maybe I even preferred it. I preferred to think of him with you than with a totally strange person, and I suppose there was something right about it."

Slowly Katie began to speak, her voice coming out flat and toneless, low and without inflection, like someone reciting signs in a confessional.

"It wasn't right, Constanza, but it was something I

couldn't help. It was like some evil thing in me, some bad thing. I think I saw a reflection of the bad side of me in Pat, and it was what drew me to him. He had some kind of hold on me, almost from the beginning, and I couldn't fight it. It ruined everything for me. Every time I thought I might have another life, be in love, care about someone, he was there like a black shadow over everything. I know Regan would be good for me, and we would be good together, but in some way, Pat made all that impossible."

She clutched compulsively at Constanza's hand.

"You must believe me, Constanza. You know we've loved one another since school. If I'd thought that you and Pat were together . . . complete . . . I don't think I would have done it. It was wrong, I know, but it seemed *less* wrong."

"What do you want from me, Katie?" Constanza asked gently. "Forgiveness? You know you have that. Absolution? I can't give you that, Katie. I'm not your priest. Peace? I suppose that's what you want. Perhaps I can give you peace in my own way."

Katie squeezed Constanza's hand, but she couldn't look into her eyes again. Staring down at the hotel carpet, she said, "I'll come back to you later, Constanza. I'm going now. I'm going to find Regan. I'm beginning to understand what he's been trying to tell me."

The door opened and Nancy, the volunteer, looked in.

"They're going downstairs now, Mrs. Conte. Mr. Conte said he'd like for me to bring you down. Are you all right?"

"I'm all right," Constanza said.

"I'll see you later, Constanza, I hope. Darling Constanza," Katie said and ran from the room.

Constanza followed Nancy down the hallway to the elevator which would take them to the big ballroom.

CHAPTER 14

The ballroom downstairs was pandemonium. The floor was covered with streamers of crepe paper and campaign literature. A Dixieland band was playing "The Battle Hymn of the Republic" in jive rhythm. From time to time, a sweaty shirtsleeved volunteer would stumble to the microphone with late returns which were greeted with whistles, roars, applause and laughter.

Paul Federici was hanging onto the microphone, his face shiny with sweat and glowing with satisfaction.

"I would like to announce," he said, his voice echoing in the multiple speakers scattered around the room. "I would like to announce that the CBS computer has just conceded the election to Conte!"

There was a roar that threatened to lift the carved plaster ceiling from its gilded columns. Nancy, the volunteer, held Constanza by the arm for a moment till the roar subsided, then led her to a place at the table in the center of the platform. Federici beamed.

"And here is now, folks! The future first lady of New York State!"

There was another booming roar of cheers and whistles and the band swung into the strains of "The Most Beautiful Girl in the World." Connie's face remained placid and unmoved and it seemed to the crowd suitably dignified for the wife of the future governor.

As she was led to her chair, the only sign of tension was her tendency to fumble nervously at the clasp of her purse. The crowd began to chant wildly, exultantly:

"CONTE FOR GOVERNOR! CONTE FOR GOVERNOR!"

Constanza's dark eyes, the tranquilizing film almost gone from them, rolled over the sea of faces, straw hats and colorful campaign parasols.

From her position above the crowd, she could make out few individuals, but in a corner she could pick out the bulky form of Regan Doyle, leaning against a plaster pillar, his arms folded, his face watchful and resigned. Weaving through the crowd, she could see the unmistakable cascade of caramel-colored blonde hair that could only be Katie. She had changed from the torn blouse to a black and white polka-dotted western shirt, and she pushed her way through the boisterous crowd, obviously looking for a friend, looking for someone, looking for Regan Doyle, Constanza was sure.

Katie Mullaley's searching eyes finally caught the blurred impression of Regan Doyle's face at the edge of the crowd. Impatiently, she pushed her way through the closely packed surging cheering bodies to the outer rim where Doyle stood waiting. Free of the mob finally, she ran sobbing his name.

"Regan! Regan!"

She threw her arms savagely around his neck, pressing her face into his collar.

"Oh, God! How right you were Regan! I knew it all the time, but I just wouldn't admit it!"

Doyle held her shoulders comfortably, his eyes still sweeping the crowd.

"Regan! We've got to *do* something. He's going to kill her. I know it sounds crazy, but he *is*. You must have some way to stop him!"

"Believe me, I'm thinking of every way I can. And I'll do it, even if I have to go over the head of the bureau. Anyway, he won't try it now. It's got to be some time after the election. I promise I will work out something . . .

some *way* to stop him. This is a man I've *got* to stop!"

"Come!" Katie said, pulling him by the hand. "I want to get up there. I want to be near Constanza in case anything happens."

Regan hesitated for a moment.

"Nothing will happen now. It's the wrong time."

"Please. I want to be there anyway."

Slowly, they began to push their way through the crowd. On the platform, Connie was still sitting with a composed maddonalike smile on her face, her hands folded over her purse.

Paul Federici came over and stood in front of her.

His face was radiant with a sense of joy and achievement. Impulsively, he took Constanza's face between his hands and pressed his lips to her hot, dry forehead.

"You're a saint!" Federici said. "An absolute, goddamn saint!"

Constanza said nothing, but returned a gentle smile. Federici looked up, caught a signal from the wings. He rushed to the microphone.

"I've just got the word, folks! He's coming! He's coming now! Our hero, Pat Conte, the future governor of the State of New York!

Pat emerged from the wings, his oiled hair haloed in backlighting, his strong teeth gleaming in that dazzling charismatic smile. He held his hands over his head and clasped them together in a boxer's gesture of victory. The crowd roared its approval in a single deadening wave of sound. Then somebody started a clapping chant.

"CON *TEE* VIC TO *REE*! CON *TEE* VIC TO *REE*! CON *TEE* VIC TO *REE*!"

The future governor smiled and blew kisses at the crowd with both hands.

Constanza Conte sat sedately in the First Lady's seat, watching and smiling that shadowed smile. She watched her husband almost with affection. In some ways he was such a beautiful man. So graceful, so sure, so pure in his evil.

And Constanza knew then, more certainly than ever that there was a God who watched every sparrow and hawk. Otherwise why was she there at this precise moment?

The band struck up "The Sidewalks of New York."

The roar of the crowd was deafening.

Constanza looked toward her husband, who was making his way slowly through the forest of hands reaching out to touch, stroke or hold him in that moment of triumph.

Without shifting her gaze, Constanza opened the clasp of the black leather purse she had been carrying. Her hand reached in and clutched the warm walnut grip of the Police Positive Special. The band launched into the strains of "For He's a Jolly Good Fellow," and Constanza waited, patiently smiling, for her husband to come and take his place beside her.